THE HARVESTER SERIES   BOOK ONE

DORMANT
DIVERSION

WE DO NOT COME IN PEACE...

SARAH LAUER NAKAWATASE
& DIANE LAUER

Black Rose Writing | Texas

The author grants the final approval for this literary material.

First printing

This is a work of fiction. Names, characters, businesses, places, events, and incidents are either the products of the author's imagination or used in a fictitious manner. Any resemblance to actual persons, living or dead, or actual events is purely coincidental.

ISBN: 978-1-68513-143-2
PUBLISHED BY BLACK ROSE WRITING
www.blackrosewriting.com

Printed in the United States of America
Suggested Retail Price (SRP) $22.95

Dormant Diversion is printed in Gentium Book Basic

*As a planet-friendly publisher, Black Rose Writing does its best to eliminate unnecessary waste to reduce paper usage and energy costs, while never compromising the reading experience. As a result, the final word count vs. page count may not meet common expectations.

For our friends who are also family,
and for our family who are also friends.

DORMANT DIVERSION

CHAPTER 1

MOLLY
Kitty Hawk, North Carolina

Molly itched. For weeks, it had kept her awake at night and consumed her days. In her mind, this burning itch was jagged and orange, curved like a fishhook and digging, always digging into her.

To keep from drawing blood, Molly had cut and filed her fingernails into unsightly stumps weeks ago. *Would this ever stop?* she agonized.

Her gaze swept over the assortment of tubes, bottles, tubs, and powders covering every square inch of the kitchen tabletop, all supposed remedies. *Not worth the effort*, Molly thought, considering them without confidence.

Although changing clothes aggravated her discomfort, the pool was calling. She ran upstairs, pulled on her suit, and made her way outside into the scorching heat.

Sweat collected everywhere as she stared at the crystal blue oval reflecting flashes of light. Since the government had cleared the lot next door and put up a relay harvester, Molly no longer needed to skim leaves from the pool before swimming. She jumped into the deep end, and chilly water enveloped her skin. Every muscle in her body unclenched.

"Oh my God." Relief. Tears formed in her eyes as she surfaced. The several seconds it took for her body to register the water's temperature gave a momentary pause to her agony. It wasn't enough, but it was better than nothing.

"Damn it." Her fingers once again moved automatically to the original area on her right thigh where this had all started.

As Molly gently tread water, the ring on her right hand, a gift from her mother, brushed against her left arm. She thought nothing of it until noticing her left arm was no longer itchy. Molly looked down toward the spot where the ring had touched her wet skin and saw a tiny perforation forming. From this minor irritation, the skin was opening outward. Pressure from within her body created ever expanding fissures on the skin, snaking across her limbs like tiny rivulets of lava. What was happening to her? The pressure grew as the fissures deepened at an alarming rate. She continued to tread water as eruptions from these gashes expelled snowstorms of skin, swirling around with each of Molly's movements. Some snowflakes were microscopic, others were the size of snowballs as they peeled away.

Horrified, Molly raised her hands above the pool's clouded surface to rub her eyes. Maybe she was experiencing some weird floaters. Both hands slipped from her eyes, and in her palms were two small discs. She had rubbed off her own eyelids! Molly flailed in panic, trying to get to the side of the pool. Mounds of sloughed skin churned in her wake.

She reached out and touched the pool's decking. *Breathe*, she thought as she caught herself holding both her breath and a soft, spongy piece of skin. She knew she was dying. Her stomach heaved but brought up nothing, and then it happened. Molly wasn't itching anymore, or burning, or inwardly screaming to be let out of her own body. She felt perfectly normal for the first time in weeks.

She ceased to care about the awkward piles of rejected skin peppering the pool's surface. Instead, she climbed out and gently toweled off while inspecting this new body full of perfectly unblemished skin. It was smooth and flawless, but then it wasn't.

As Molly's skin dried more thoroughly in the sun, a new texture pushed up from beneath the surface. The color changed, and a pattern emerged. She wasn't stroking skin anymore. Molly's hands moved slickly over quickly forming scales. Her mouth opened to scream, but produced no sound—still no itching. Nothing festered under the surface. No more unbearable sensation threatened her sanity, only scales.

CHAPTER 2

We are all living upon a frog's back, and someday the frog will jump.
—Japanese Folk Proverb

Washington, D.C.

Waiting anxiously in his formally appointed office, Ed Marker was the man in charge. Sometimes, he felt like the man, period. Stick-straight black hair that held its shape enhanced his strong features, and a clean-cut suit wrapped his broad shoulders. He wasn't necessarily a handsome man, but imposing. His dark, probing eyes had a way of cutting through bullshit.

"Shane," he buzzed out to his administrative assistant.

"Yes, Secretary Marker." The impeccably dressed, efficient young man answered the Secretary of Energy immediately.

"When was Patrick Hagen due for his meeting?" Ed knew very well that it had been a full thirty minutes ago!

"He's thirty minutes late, Secretary Marker. Would you like me to try contacting him?"

"No thanks, but would you mind buzzing me at two-thirty? I may get caught up and forget my meeting with Barry Davis and the reporter."

"Yes, sir."

Calm down, Ed told himself. Everything was finally in place. Why let the only rotten apple in the barrel ruin a day like this? After all, he was living his dream as head of the most ambitious power initiative in the world, the Harvester Project.

Pollution-free, unlimited energy, at last, thought Ed happily. The cynics had scoffed for years while pushing coal, oil, hydroelectric dams, and nuclear reactors. Fortunately, they'd been wrong, and Ed was reaping the rewards of their misguided efforts. He massaged his hands, unconsciously thinking about his years as an environmental activist. He'd always been the one holding a sign, hoping to catch the interest of those who'd rather not be involved.

Seven years ago, the concept of change from within had begun to burn inside Ed, and he'd honed in on a government position. *Now, look at him! Just like cream*, he thought proudly of his smooth and continual rise up the Department of Energy ladder. He was one of the youngest to hold his position at the DOE, if almost forty could be considered young. Secretary of Energy—you had to be on the inside if you wanted to bring about any type of genuine change.

Qualifications? Absolutely. Ed leaned back in his large leather chair and surveyed the many and varied tastefully framed diplomas hanging on the wall. He'd probably known more about their projects than they had, and still did. A physics degree from MIT had clinched his high entry-level position, but Ed Marker could honestly say that he'd never caved.

Clean and efficient were the only two adjectives he'd ever wanted to see prefacing an energy proposal. Granted, Ed admitted sadly, he'd revised his definition of both clean and efficient. The decimal points in his DOE figures were never in the ideal columns, but they were a hell of a lot better than when he'd begun. Those figures would soon be obsolete, Ed reminded himself.

"Secretary Marker? Secretary Marker? Excuse me, sir."

It was Shane, and God bless him. He was effortlessly punctual, as always, trying to pry Ed out of his thoughts. The young man earned his salary, Ed admitted.

"It's almost two-thirty, sir. If you leave now, you'll have plenty of time to make your meeting."

"Thanks, Shane. I'm on my way. I'll have my phone on in case you need to get in touch with me." Sliding his laptop into his shoulder bag and grabbing his jacket, Ed rushed out the door past his assistant's desk. "Oh, and if Patrick Hagen shows up, tell him that the plane leaves tomorrow at eight-thirty sharp, and we won't be waiting for anyone."

It was probably better this way, Ed admitted to himself easily. He didn't want anyone ruining what they had worked so hard to create, and that was just about all Patrick Hagen knew how to do anymore. Pushing the elevator button for the eighth floor, Ed couldn't help but hope that Patrick would miss the plane tomorrow, as well.

Two floors away, the elevator doors opened silently and Ed strolled briskly down the hallway toward a pair of impressively paneled doors. Without bothering to knock, he turned the ornate brass handle and walked in.

"That time already?"

Ed noted the surprised look on Barry's face, as if this meeting hadn't been planned for days. He had found out through his position at the DOE that scientists were a different lot. Ed could tell that time passed either too quickly or too slowly for Barry, and probably always had.

"Sorry, Ed. I knew you were coming. I just got bogged down in details. Have a seat."

As he moved farther into the office, Ed could feel his tension draining away. Barry's workspace was all the things he wished his could be. Not that it was any larger or more prestigious, because it wasn't. Unfortunately, Ed had appearances to consider. "You're lucky that the only image you have to project around here is science genius," Ed said good-naturedly. "This place is like some huge walk-in closet that needs to be cleaned out, Barry."

"Hey, watch it!" Barry laughingly took exception to his boss's complaint.

"Maybe we should move the interview to another location," Ed said, glancing around the office. Tiny dust particles swirled in the strong rays of summer light coming through the window. "I thought you were going to straighten things up for the meeting today."

Barry's office was messy, yet comfortable. On the walls were posters and pictures of everything from whales to windmills. Barry had baskets of plants that he, not his assistant, watered; and geodes filled with sparkling points sat on tabletops beside Slinkys and empty yogurt containers.

The offbeat inventor of the harvester was perched like a banty rooster at the only free desk in the room. Both of the other desks were overflowing with stacks of reports and his beloved junk. Against the wall farthest from the door was a cabinet topped by an exquisitely detailed scale model of a harvester. Its delicate branches flowed from the top like a mature dandelion or a weeping willow, giving the harvester a very natural appearance for a man-made object—flexible yet strong. Ed walked over to turn on the recessed lighting directly above it.

"Do you mind?" Ed asked.

"Knock yourself out. The lights always seem like overkill when I'm the only one in the room." Barry wandered over to join Ed beside the cabinet. "It is beautiful though, isn't it?"

"Sure is," Ed agreed, "not to mention the fact that it's real and it works! I don't want to change the subject, but our plane leaves first thing in the morning, eight-thirty, got it? Never mind." Ed waved away any worries. "I'll text you just before I leave the house," he offered, fully aware of Barry's questionable track record for punctuality.

"Good plan, boss. Wouldn't want someone else to christen my ship." Barry said with a smile.

"You know I wouldn't let that happen, but we've got to keep watching our backs. Patrick Hagen missed another meeting with me today. Hopefully, he's not out gathering more ammunition to throw at us tomorrow."

Ed was growing annoyed just thinking about Patrick again. He deliberately spoke in a measured tone, but his tension was slowly seeping into Barry's office like a poison cloud. "There's not another person who could get away with ignoring my request for a conference. He's done this too many times now."

"Don't get too excited." Barry blew a thin coating of dust from the miniature harvester as he issued the advice. "Give Patrick enough rope, and he'll eventually hang himself." He looked at Ed matter-of-factly. "People like him usually do."

Ed didn't respond. Instead, he stood there, considering Barry's perspective on Patrick Hagen. Ed didn't think it would be that easy. He knew Patrick too well to believe that he would stop trying to sabotage the project. People with nothing to lose were dangerous.

"He'll take himself down, Ed; just give him a chance." Barry admired the Allium-shaped harvester model with the backlighting one last time and walked back towards his desk.

"I'd pay good money to see it." Ed moved an armful of boxes off a wooden chair across from Barry's desk and took a seat. "But he's not going to take the project down with him. Once we get the system in motion, Patrick Hagen won't matter anymore. He and all the other prophets of doom will have nothing more to write on their protest signs."

"It works, Ed," Barry attempted to soothe his frustrated companion. "It worked in the lab, in the trials, and it'll work tomorrow. There's a physical principle involved. This isn't astrology. It's science."

"I know," Ed concentrated on unclenching his teeth. "But sometimes it all still seems too good to be true. Some days, I just know I'm going to wake up from the dream."

"Listen, Ed, it's too late for Patrick to stop anything. He's a pain in the ass, but tomorrow we'll be getting ready to throw the switch, anyway. Think of it, tomorrow we finally go national."

Ed's cell phone vibrated. "Yes, Shane?" As he listened to the voice at the other end of the line, the vein in Ed's temple began to throb.

"I'll be there shortly." Ed put his phone back in his pocket with calculated restraint, as though he were afraid of smashing the thing to pieces.

He looked at Barry. "Patrick Hagen just showed up for his meeting two hours late, and he had the balls to ask Shane to let me know that he'd be waiting in my office."

"You have to admit, the guy's got an interesting approach." Barry's attempt at humor fell flat. "Look, you go ahead. Don't let him get to you and don't worry about the interview. I can handle it on my own. I've talked to so many news reporters I can't imagine this one would have questions I haven't already answered dozens of times."

Ed would let Barry field this interview on his own. He was right. They had gone through so many of them already. Ed didn't need to micromanage Barry's responses any longer.

The further Ed got from Barry's office, the calmer he became. Odd, he thought, until realizing that the frustration had just been displaced by disappointment, but disappointment in whom? Was it with himself for putting such faith and effort into an ungrateful protégé, or Patrick for such outright betrayal? It really didn't matter. If Ed was totally honest with himself, he was more hurt than agitated.

Ed was in this position thanks to his own stupidity, and he knew it. Patrick had been his closest friend in college, and Ed had helped him along professionally. They'd always been predictably like-minded until the harvester, and now Patrick was snapping at his heels like a rabid dog. Ed didn't expect gratitude, but Patrick's vicious attacks against the harvester were visceral. This project was finally giving meaning to all Ed's years of "fighting the good fight," and he'd be damned if Patrick would take it all away.

CHAPTER 3

The heart is the first to see defeat, but the last to admit it.

The perpetually disheveled Barry went over some last-minute figures as he waited for the reporter. With his burnt orange hair in constant disarray and a slack tie hanging from his neck, he was indeed the academic type, minus the glasses. Barry's eyesight was as perfect as his mind was scientifically brilliant. While social niceties might escape him, an incorrectly calculated equation would never do the same. He set about collecting the detailed papers he'd be taking with him tomorrow, carelessly stuffing them into an already overloaded bag.

"Come on in," he called loudly enough to be heard.

"Mr. Davis?" The reporter opened the door herself and stepped into the cluttered office.

"Make yourself at home. Sorry, but I'm a little preoccupied. Tomorrow, we go nationwide, you know."

"I certainly do." She approached Barry with her hand extended and introduced herself. Her sleeveless summer dress set off her toned arms. "Janet Bloom, from the *Washington Post*, Mr. Davis. I was hoping to get a story about your feelings on the eve of such staggering personal success."

"Well, I don't have much more than about fifteen minutes to spare, but I'll be happy to do what I can."

"That's fine. I appreciate your taking the time to meet with me." She took out a small device. "Is it okay if I record our conversation? I'm trying to capture the real Barry Davis."

"I don't mind," he said. "You're just doing your job. Where would you like me to start?"

"How about the beginning? Tell me about how you came up with the idea in the first place," she said.

"Okay. Well, as you know, the law of conservation of energy states that energy can neither be created nor destroyed." He had answered this question dozens of times before.

Ms. Bloom nodded in agreement.

"It can, however, be converted, but we've been doing that for years. Solar and wind energy are examples of energy conversion. These methods of conversion were steps in the right direction, but it was the concept of harvesting energy that brought us to where we are today."

Barry continued spouting his energy ideals until she interrupted his long string of principles and equations. "Now tell me, Mr. Davis, all about the difficulties you encountered in your efforts to build the prototype."

"Believe it or not, I built the very first harvester in my mother's garage. I was able to get all the materials for the project online or from the university."

"You ordered your parts from Amazon?" She waited for more.

"Absolutely. You can get anything online, though I didn't just use Amazon," he laughed, then continued. "There was no need for nuclear material or anything hazardous. Remember, we're in the business of clean energy now," he explained.

"This sounds like a great deal of time and dedication at such a young age," Janet interjected.

"There was nothing else I would have rather been doing."

"You've come a long way, Mr. Davis."

Barry looked over at the harvester model. "You know, the current model isn't that different from the prototype. Funny story, I used the prototype to power my parent's house with only a small fraction of its output. Of course, it wasn't perfect back then. I almost scared my mother to death after I turned it on. She screamed, and I ran inside to find her crouched under the kitchen table surrounded by shattered glass. All the light bulbs had exploded."

Janet's eyes widened. "Is your mother going to brave the ceremony tomorrow?"

Barry laughed. "She'll be there. Luckily, I finally succeeded in regulating the frequencies to within reasonable modulation, and then converted the house permanently with no more broken glass." Barry checked the clock. "Sorry, Ms. Bloom, I've got to be going now."

"But Mr. Davis, we haven't even covered..."

"Again, I apologize, but I'm out of time for today. I've got an early flight tomorrow and I still have to pack."

"Of course," Janet was deeply disappointed. "Maybe after you get back, we can continue our interview."

"Maybe," he let her down gently. "Thanks for coming by." He opened the door to show her the way out.

After she had gone, he hoisted up his documents for tomorrow and walked to the coffee cart that was parked outside the entrance to the DOE. They had a little of everything—from pastries to sandwiches, from sushi to salads. This was always Barry's first and last stop of the workday.

• • •

Ed walked back into his office to find his ex-college friend and current coworker, Patrick Hagen, standing in his office. Patrick was tall, lanky, and classically good-looking with loose curly hair that never looked out of place. At one time in their lives, they had been close. Ed had known Patrick very well, but no longer recognized the man standing before him.

"Finally," said Patrick, watching Ed as he set his bag down on his desk.

"Really?" Ed responded. "You're over two hours late. I don't know who you think you are, but I think you're a Project Analyst for the Department of Energy, and you're way out of line."

"The facts are there, Ed. Why can't you see them?"

"What are you trying to do here? This is what we've always wanted. This could change everything." Ed sat down behind his desk. "It's a solution to our air pollution and energy production crisis, all in one."

"You've settled for the quick fix," Patrick shot back. "It's still not too late, Ed. Open your eyes. I know it's deceiving. On the surface, it looks like the perfect solution. Who could oppose it, right? Just read the files and you'll see why we can't move forward with this."

"What can't I see?!" Ed was the Secretary of Energy. He'd had a hand in this project from its inception and would not tolerate any more accusations, even from an old friend.

"They're dangerous," Patrick said with a sense of burning urgency. "I was late because of another call I'd received from Ray."

"What did Ray have to say this time?" asked Ed. He was not sure how this Ray had passed a security clearance. His resume for the past thirty years consisted of mostly private investigator work supplemented by nighttime security jobs.

"Spontaneous combustion, Ed."

"Come again?" What did that mean?

"Some old woman back in the hills lights up like a firefly, but it doesn't burn her. Ray saw her do it. He said it's like she burns inside and it makes her whole body glow. Ray talked to her, and she said it all began on June fourteenth."

"And?"

"That was the start-up date for the relay harvester built on the field adjacent to this woman's property."

"How did Ray find her?" asked Ed skeptically.

"She figured it was weird enough to be worth her first trip to the town doctor. It was the doctor who called it in on the 800 number we have on our website. Ed, she was in a field with the harvester when it happened. Ray said she couldn't have been more than fifty feet from the thing."

"So you didn't personally witness any of this." Ed had little faith in Ray, not purely based on his general lack of qualifications, but also because of his surly disposition.

"There wasn't any time for that," Patrick replied. "The switch party is tomorrow at the Governor's mansion in Raleigh."

"I know. We're supposed to be on the same flight, Patrick, but if you're not feeling up to it, I understand."

"You can't shake me, Ed."

Ed looked at Patrick, wishing he would just go away. Even if there was anything in his files worth reading, Patrick was right about one thing—it was too late now. The switch party was tomorrow and there was no turning back. They'd invested trillions in the construction of harvesters all across the country, largely paid for by the acquisition of this same technology by any country that could afford it across the globe. There couldn't be any problems. If the rollout of this project was unsuccessful, it would mean economic devastation.

"Please. I have so many files, but I've selected just a few. Please, before tomorrow, just take a look at them, just these." Patrick set a small stack of files on Ed's desk next to his bag.

"Damn your files. Every crackpot in the country is calling in weird, unexplained events. They're calling from all fifty states, Patrick, not just North Carolina." Ed had to keep from rolling his eyes. "Do you seriously think I haven't been briefed on this?"

"Then you should already know what's in the files."

"These callers are having personal revelations, bizarre physical ailments, and eight-toed babies. You name it and John Q. Public is experiencing it. They're blaming it all on the harvesters, but they're only being tested in North Carolina. Explain all the other states' files to me, would you?"

"If you'd read the files carefully, you'd see the difference yourself, Ed. Most of the reports from North Carolina differ from the rest. The investigators can't explain them away to drunks or psychotics. They're just plain, normal people with families and jobs. Not one has a background in environmental activism or claims to be a psychic medium. There's a real fundamental difference in those documented, unexplainable cases."

"Come on, Patrick. You know that from the moment we announced we'd be randomly testing harvesters, the DOE has been expecting exactly what you've found. Every scumbag and lowlife in America has crawled out from under their rock, hoping to file a claim against the harvesters. They all have their hands out and dollar signs in their eyes."

"You can't seriously believe that, Ed!"

"Oh, can't I? Tomorrow, we go nationwide, and nothing in any of those folders of yours will stop it."

"Did you know we've had trouble with the turnover rate of the investigators?" Patrick turned the conversation.

"I don't have much faith in PIs."

"You know better than that, Ed. Most of them are FBI. Not Ray, of course, but most everyone else. The DOE wanted nothing but reliable information. God only knows why, since you won't read any of it."

"Information is only as good as its source, no matter who collects it." Ed insisted.

"Do you want to know why they're quitting?" A beat. "No, of course not, but I'll tell you, anyway. They're scared. They're scared so badly that they're sending their careers up in little puffs of smoke, just like me, Ed."

Ed looked momentarily startled. "So you do know what you're doing."

"I'm not stupid, just scared like all the other people who've been paying attention to North Carolina for the past month. Ed, did you know there's an entire field next to a harvester that's growing like Jack's beanstalk? The crops are so tall they can be seen in the next county."

"There could be any number of factors responsible for that."

"Or just one." Patrick trained his eyes on Ed.

"Look, Patrick, even I'm willing to admit the harvesters might have something to do with a few isolated incidents. I'd be a fool or worse if I wasn't, but you can't lay every problem in North Carolina at the feet of the harvesters. That farmer probably just got some fertilizer mixed improperly at the factory, which led to these super crops."

"Ed, I have five cases here in the folders. If you'll read them, I'll stop bothering you. I'm still going after the harvesters. They're not safe. In fact, they're so dangerous I can't sleep at night, but if you'll read these five cases, I'll stop trying to get you involved."

"I've read enough reports, Patrick."

"You haven't seen these," Patrick calmly continued. "Take it or leave it. Read them and I pull my thorn from your side and walk away."

"Okay," Ed agreed, equally subdued. He knew he wouldn't be able to get Patrick out of his office any other way. "Leave the folders and go. The plane leaves at eight-thirty tomorrow morning, and we won't be waiting for anyone."

Patrick said nothing more and left the office, passing Shane without acknowledgment.

. . .

The immense, docked ship was loaded and ready for release. Its soft, burnished sheen was reminiscent of an antique piece of silver. Inscriptions darkened the fresh, unmarred hull. Tracking and communications equipment had been checked, then re-checked and calibrated to perfection.

As always, the ever-present investors looked on. Theirs was no small accomplishment. In a hedonistic society such as theirs, the return on this unusual choice of investment would be well worth such staggering start-up costs. Today, their project would begin, as the ship was launched carrying its innovative and expensive cargo.

Amusements were harder to come by as each phase period passed. Naturally, in a two-layered society made up of those who did and others who were done for, there was a high priority placed on amusement.

The most heavily committed of the investors lovingly rubbed the magnificent hull, tracing imperceptible indentations marking the doorway. Unexpectedly, he was slightly injured by an overlooked jagged imperfection at the seam. He watched the slow purple trickle of precious inner fluids seep slowly into the metal crevice of the door frame. His fury knew no bounds. He was in pain, and it was inexcusable. The orders were given without hesitation, and the sentence carried out immediately.

The lag time between this launch and the actual opening day of their new toy could be off by as much as multiple phase shifts, but the uncertainty of the date would only add to both the excitement and the value.

This probe being made ready for launch was to be the beginning of a new world of entertainment. A world genetically engineered by the best their subclass had to offer. Its stated purpose would be to provide new experiences and sensory stimuli for those willing to pay the price, and it would be a high price indeed! These were definitely not to be cheap thrills.

The probe had a programmed set of parameters. First, it would only take an interest in planets reflecting the necessary amount of light. That in itself narrowed the range considerably. Upon closer investigation, there were to be certain temperature, atmospheric, and elementally based specifications within which it could operate properly. The only absolute restriction was the directive not to involve any planet already containing life forms.

Unfortunately, several guidance and delivery systems were unable to endure centuries upon centuries spent hopscotching across the galaxy in search of the perfect planet. Because of these unanticipated difficulties, the ship came much too close to an unsuitable planet, one already supporting simple life forms. It came so close, in fact, that it could not escape the planet's gravitational pull.

CHAPTER 4

MABEL CLAIRE

Franklin, North Carolina, June Fourteenth

Ya'll drive careful, now." Mabel Claire hollered after the car, progressing slowly down the dirt road. The thunderstorm that had blown through before supper had drenched the ground, so there were no swirling clouds of dust blowing at her from behind the car. Instead, she could hear the squish of tires as they dipped into full potholes.

"Bye, Memaw." Little Sarah's voice drifted from the open back window.

Aged and bent, Mabel Claire raised her hand and waved until the car disappeared around the bend. "Lord love 'em, they sure can tire a body out." Even her voice was tired, not loud enough to scare the dust off a spider web.

Slowly, she turned from the fence and walked over to sit on the porch steps. This was her favorite part of the day, eventide, when the day gave way to the night. Times when she had more energy, Mabel Claire would gather the herbs she needed 'round about this time of day, when they gave off such a purely potent scent. Of course, they'd be too wet tonight after the storm.

She loved her children, she surely did, but it was always a relief when their visits were over and she could get back to her world.

Then, it began. There it was, the first one, over across the field near the thicket—a small neon flash like the quick wink of an eye. The month of June had always been her favorite. She loved the fireflies. Why, as a girl, she'd prayed and prayed for her backside to light up just like them flyin' June bugs up in that field. It was a certain truth that God, in all of his wisdom, knew which prayers to answer, and her scrawny, tired old backside was proof of that.

They were twinkling away just like sparks off a hundred Fourth of July sparklers. Mabel Claire couldn't rightly remember when she'd seen 'em so thick like this. It seemed like they must've come from miles.

"Gettin' chilly." Her comment fell softly into the darkening air, which was moistening with the encroaching night. Mabel Claire stood and straightened out her stiff, dampened joints, ready to call it a night; but as she massaged her back, the night changed. She could feel it first. Then, not believing her own eyes, she saw it happen.

All the bugs got dark at the same time and the air felt strange. The hair on her arms stood straight up on end, and her whole spirit sort of arched up inside of her.

Lord, Lord, what was happenin'? Her tired old joints cracked and dried as she stood there, but they surely felt stronger, and she wasn't tired. Just as she felt that her body couldn't take any more, she eased on into the flow.

It was like a big, deep, warm river in August, currents slowly circling her body with a growing strength, carrying her along. The hairs on her arm went suddenly flat, as the high field lit up again with the fireflies, only this time they didn't twinkle. There must have been tens of thousands of them, all lit up at once and calling to her.

"MABEL CLAIRE, COME DANCE WITH US. THE EGG IS HATCHING!"

At first, she walked, but then she found herself running up the hill to the field. The dirt was still fresh where they'd been digging to install that energy harvester thing. It was all right, though; the honeysuckle would grow right back over the ugly thing in no time.

Up there it was even louder, and the words built up into a terrible pressure inside her head. Mabel Claire had to put her hands to her temples to hold everything in place, but it wasn't working. Her head was getting larger beneath her hands, and her skull was making funny crackling noises. Oh Lord, this was bad, and she prepared for the end, but then the pressure changed. Her head felt hot to the touch, and she had to pull her hands away. It was a nasty feeling at first, until it spread throughout her body.

It wasn't natural, but Mabel Claire didn't mind. The June bugs wanted her to dance with them. She felt six years old again, and it was a sweet gift. The egg was hatching, and she would be a part of it. Now, at her most joyous moment, she began to glow, but not just her backside. Mabel Claire lit up from head to toe and danced until morning beside the ugly machine in her beautiful field.

CHAPTER 5

The luck of the draw only works for gamblers.

They had a full contingent at the airport. The DOE had chartered a commercial flight from Washington to Raleigh on this muggy July morning, and every seat was filled.

"Barry, your seat is next to mine," said Ed. "I want to hear about any last-minute adjustments you're going to suggest beforehand."

"Don't worry. As far as I know, there won't be any." Barry assured him.

Barry and Ed took their places in line and shuffled through the boarding gate. Security was tight because there were a lot of other big-shot elected officials going along for the show. Like all good politicians, they'd waited to see which way the wind would blow before choosing sides.

None of that mattered now though, because the science and trials had spoken for themselves. Safely strapped in and experiencing lift-off, Ed's stomach wasn't doing very well, but he was holding up.

There had been a vocal group of protesters at the airport, but he'd been spared dealing with them because of all the political security.

Barry looked over at his seatmate. "Snap out of it." A double-take. "Hey, are you okay?"

As happy as Ed was about their invulnerability, on another level, it rankled the activist he'd been for so many years. "It's just that I was on the other side of those signs for so long. As much as I don't want to hear them, they still deserve the opportunity to be heard." Before he had a chance to dwell on this, Ed looked across the aisle into the face of Patrick Hagen, who saluted smartly.

Who needs the discontented hordes, anyway? I'm lucky enough to have my own personal malcontent to deal with, Ed thought.

"Ignore him," Barry told Ed as he was putting the final touches on his speech.

It wasn't terrible advice and Ed settled deeply into his seat, successfully putting on the mental blinders he'd developed so quickly at the DOE. Choosing to ignore Patrick for now, Ed focused instead on the unsettling case files he'd read. He'd finally taken the time to look at them. Ed knew he should be much lighter-hearted today, but Patrick had been right. Those reports had been disturbing.

Today, they were taking the first real step towards a world fit for a future population. Why did he keep thinking about a cornfield from hell? After all, there were dangers inherent to anything new. What about the standard list of sprawling side effects documented in the FDA's testing of every new drug? Ed attempted to convince himself. The small percentages of the population they affected didn't keep the drugs off the pharmacy shelves, did they?

Ed could hear Barry's speech rehearsal begin softly in the seat beside him. The excited inventor was muttering unforgettable words of wisdom under his breath, trying to keep any grand and sweeping arm gestures at a minimum so as not to disturb his closely seated neighbors.

Adjusting his seat to a more comfortable position, Ed recalled the speeches he and Barry had given in the Senate hearings. Ed's stomach churned thinking of how close they'd come to losing the battle. The harvester had been a death bell, tolling for the oil and utility companies, and they'd reacted extravagantly in their final efforts at self-preservation. Luckily, Ed had been in charge of the opposition. Talk about the ultimate protest—shades of the old days. He leaned his head back and enjoyed the memories.

Thanks to the DOE's beautifully understated defense, which Ed and his committee had presented, the public had easily weighed the pros and cons. *Inspirational, truly inspirational*, thought Ed as he opened his eyes and came out of his brief trip down memory lane.

Barry turned to look at his neighbor. "You're not asleep." He had finished rehearsing. "What's first on the agenda once we land?"

"The whole day is tight." Ed rattled off the itinerary, which he'd memorized. "They'll take our bags over to the hotel rooms for us. Our first stop is a pre-ribbon cutting luncheon with the newly elected Governor of North Carolina. You'll throw the actual switch around three o'clock. After that, there will be a celebratory reception and photo opportunity. The press will be at the reception too, so we can't let down until we get back to the hotel afterward."

"Okay by me. Guess I'll just limber up." Happily, Barry curled and extended his index finger again and again. "Could be a tight switch," he winked.

"Right." Ed cringed at Barry's attempt at humor. Too much time alone in a lab. He leaned over to look out the window beside him. "Ugh, I thought looking out windows was supposed to curb motion sickness."

"Yeah, but in a car, not a plane," said Barry.

"Don't worry, I'll be all right. I probably should have eaten breakfast." Either that, Ed thought uneasily, or maybe it was the fact that his eyes were really scanning the ground beneath them for a giant cornfield.

Oh well, queasy or not, there was always plenty of work to do with the DOE. Not everything had to do with the harvester project. Ed pulled out his laptop and set to work. Thanks to his intense concentration on one subject after another, the rest of the flight passed quickly, and a contented murmur eased them into an uneventful landing. The Governor's luncheon, despite politics, steadied Ed's stomach a good bit, which boosted his morale noticeably. There were four long banquet tables and the fuller Ed's stomach got, the more optimistic he became. By the time Barry was asked to pull out his limber digit, the case files were the furthest thing from his mind.

Even the face of Patrick Hagen scowling from across the room couldn't dampen his mood. The files were just that, Ed insisted firmly to himself. Files—a collection of words which could be, and had been, manipulated to over-exaggerate.

Ed had no doubt that today would be assigned holiday status somewhere down the line. He looked on proudly as across the room, a very dapper Barry Davis flipped the all-important switch, bathed in the blinding light from hundreds of camera flashes. In reality, he entered a passcode and pressed *enter* on a tablet at the podium. Simple, over and done. A roar went up, and the applause went on and on. Ed was struck again by the simplicity of it all as he looked through the picture window beyond Barry to gaze lovingly at the huge harvester, silhouetted against the North Carolina sky.

There it stood, looking more like a living thing than a machine, and Ed's heart beat faster because of it. Ed shifted his weight from side to side. He'd been standing far too long, and magnificent though the ceremony was, he scanned the perimeter of the room for vacant seats. No such luck, he realized quickly.

At the other end of the room, Barry was riding high, making certain that his voice carried loudly over the silent room. "The harvester is both extremely flexible and durable," he extolled. "With standardized, easily replaceable parts, a strong wind will never topple an extended harvester. Instead, it is designed to bend like a willow in the wind." Yup, he had them eating out of his hand.

Though it all sounded too good to be true, Ed knew that all of Barry's claims *were* true. After all, Ed had been in charge of setting up the initial testing and trials, and he'd done his job.

"Designed for maximum absorption potential," Barry continued, "it is patterned to behave like a living creature. The harvester's roots are designed for something akin to osmosis. They are long conductive cable tendrils which, when activated at the time of installation, bore downward and outward into the surrounding area." Barry paused dramatically for a drink of water.

What a ham. Ed smiled and shook his head as Barry continued.

"Its trunk is a practically indestructible telescoping tube from the top of which extends what looks like a giant iridescent dandelion, ready to burst into seed at any moment. There are two types of filaments used in the head of each harvester. One gathers and the other disperses the acceptably transformed and modulated energy patterns. They do this simultaneously, twenty-four hours a day, rain or shine."

Ed wanted to turn around and stick it to Patrick Hagen. He could feel the man's gaze burning into the back of his head, but there were too many cameras around, and what did it matter? Barry had just literally turned on the United States of America. It was too late for Patrick Hagen to do anything about it, or at least Ed hoped so.

Reaching the end of his speech, Barry explained in conclusion, "Once the cycle is begun, it's self-perpetuating. You start it or you stop it. It's as simple as that!"

The crowd roared up again. Barry waited for the applause to die down and said a few additional words to all those assembled. God, he looked happy, and why not, thought Ed generously, he deserved it.

While Ed was deep in thought beside the canapés, the ground shook momentarily as though a train might have come through on nearby tracks, but no one in the crowded room seemed to notice. Honestly, it was barely noticeable. Champagne slide ever so slightly from side to side in the glasses on the skirted tables where they'd been carefully arranged. This was the only visible sign of the unimpressive event. Even if anyone had noticed, an earthquake would have been a hard sell. After all, quakes were traditionally a

West Coast event, and North Carolina was about as East Coast as you could get.

Ed spied Patrick anxiously checking his watch. Patrick then turned and walked miserably over, extending his hand. It was hello, thank you, goodbye, and eat my dust all rolled into one firmly given shake.

"I've already given you fair notice," said Patrick. "Hopefully, the damage that's been done is reversible. Anyway," he shrugged, "see you around."

Ed watched Patrick leave with an overwhelming sinking sensation. God only knew what reports he'd find on his desk tomorrow. He thought about that slight tremor he had felt and the thought crossed his mind that it could have been related to the harvesters. No. He was being paranoid. It was a good thing that Patrick was leaving. He was a constant reminder to Ed of all the warning signs he had ignored.

The following morning brought no news of the tremor that had actually registered fractionally on the Richter scale. Everything that had happened in the last twenty-four hours had been overshadowed by the launch of the harvesters, the clean energy of America's future.

CHAPTER 6

BOBBY FREEMAN

Four Corners, North Carolina, early July

Bobby knew that the spring rains had been good and the sun warm. He had to admit that the weather had been perfect, but not this perfect. Deeply tanned and etched with wrinkles, Bobby Freeman stood on the edge of his field staring hard at his crops. He'd been at it all morning.

If he'd known things were going to work out so well, he probably wouldn't have let those government people use his lower field to plant that new thing, the harvester. It was a weird-looking contraption. Bobby had to admit, though, that the government paid well, and upfront, too.

Farming being unpredictable like it was, he and Emily had decided that a bird in the hand was better than counting on a good season. The last two years had almost put them off the farm. Between the drought and the bugs, there hadn't been a whole hell of a lot to sell. Thing was, farming was all Bobby knew how to do. He had roots that went down into this land deeper than his crops, or at least deeper than they used to go. Still, hitching up his worn denims, he had to admit that it had all worked out just fine. The money from the government had been enough to get them out of hock, and it looked like this year's crop could put them in the running again.

Now, he stood, turning slowly in a circle, and knew something was not right. It might look right to someone else, but he knew better, and so did Emily. Soon the other farmers would talk. They'd want to know what fertilizer he was using. Neighbors would want his soil and water tested, and he wouldn't blame them.

Standing silently, he could hear it happening again. Bobby didn't want to hear it, but it didn't seem to make any difference. Covering his ears, the sound was just as loud. He could hear the roots going down into the loamy soil until they hit the clay beneath. Then they slowed as the nutrient-gathering tendrils bored their way through the earth until reaching solid rock.

Bobby's crops were anchored so tightly that he couldn't imagine how he was going to plow the fields under come fall. Maybe he wouldn't be able to. The thought of riding through the field made him sick to his stomach anyway, and he was ashamed of himself. Bobby was scared stiff to go into his own fields. Things weren't normal in there, and he didn't know what to do about it.

Thank goodness he could hear Emily calling him to lunch. He gratefully turned to go, but not before he saw it happen again. The corn was growing before his very eyes. Each of the green rows had been about a foot high when he'd set out to watch them this morning, but now they were much higher.

No one would have thought he'd ever be complaining about his fields growing, but it was only early July. The growing season had just begun, and Bobby didn't even want to think about what could be happening by August.

He hurried toward the house, but before he got far enough away, Bobby could have sworn he heard voices, something about hatching eggs. Shuddering, he ran.

• • •

By late July, things had changed considerably. Bobby had just finished walking to his mailbox. It was down by the fence, and this was the most exercise he got nowadays.

He'd been right to worry about the corn, if you could call it that. Around the edges of the field it still looked like corn, but the damn stuff was at least twenty feet high in places, and the stalks were looking more like tree trunks every day. At least he'd gotten the neighbors off his back and scared to hang around his place, thanks to Emily's idea.

"Tell 'em you accidentally got shipped some experimental radioactive corn, and that the people who came around later to investigate told you that's why it's so big. An' tell 'em it's not safe to be too near it," she had said.

Bobby stood scratching his head with a hand full of mail. At least they weren't overdue bills. With the corn being so strange, it was lucky he'd let the government use his land after all. At least he and Emily would still eat, thanks to those government checks coming in regular as clockwork.

Radioactive seeds—despite it all, he had to chuckle. It wasn't 'til after he'd already spread the story that Em had told him how she'd gotten the idea from an old episode of Gilligan's Island.

Getting ready to walk back up to the house, Bobby suddenly couldn't stand the thought of sitting on the porch swing, watching his corn crop grow for another afternoon. He had tried to explain it all away to Em. "What's the point in tending to the fields? They're growing fine without it. Guess I'll have me a lazy summer and enjoy it," but they both knew better, even if they didn't talk about it. What was there to talk about anyway, besides a grown man who was too scared, clear through to the bone, to do what he oughta be doin'.

Well, this was the end! Bobby put the mail back, cocked his hat over one eye for luck, said his prayers, and strolled into the rustling field past the radioactive sign they had put up themselves. Immediately, he felt better. Whether he was eaten, trampled, or just plain fainted from fright, at least he'd gotten his courage up enough to do something—anything.

This wasn't so bad, he admitted, moving further into the green. Outside of the corn, it was in the nineties and dead calm. Bobby still had the sweat dripping down into his collar to prove it. Here in the corn, it had to be fifteen to twenty degrees cooler, with a breeze blowing through. Bobby had never stopped to think about all the rustling and waving the stalks had done, even on stock-still days like this one, but he sure was thinkin' about it now.

His arms were cooling in the towering shade, and he tentatively wrinkled his nose at the pleasant smell, not like corn, but good just the same. Bobby felt comfortable, enjoying his meandering walk. It all seemed to be so *right*. Why had he waited so long?

Bobby Freeman knew that Raney County was farm country, and that meant flat, cultivated land as far as the eye could see. Sure, there were trees around the farmhouses and sometimes along the sides of fields as wind blocks, but there weren't any forests, or at least there hadn't been before.

As Bobby got deeper into the field, he saw the stalks had grown together, twisting and weaving themselves into mammoth tree trunks as they reached upwards. Here, deep in his cornfield, was a forest of giant corn stalks morphing into something else.

Bobby took off his hat and looked up at the trees that weren't trees, spreading a covering canopy that changed the light reaching the field floor to lavender. He saw holes in the sides of the "tree things" where branching extensions protruded from the main trunks. Then, he heard Emily's voice calling to him frantically from beyond the field. As her concern roused him from his stupor, Bobby knew he wasn't afraid anymore. Yes, it was all new, but it was also very old. He ran to get Em. She had to see it all. The egg was hatching, and he wanted to share it with her.

CHAPTER 7

PATRICK

Back at the DOE, Patrick sat in front of an ever-increasing mountain of paperwork holding yet another disturbing report. Before finishing the first three paragraphs, he heard Ray's unmistakable knock on his door, two longs and a short. That really was a sketchy knock. Patrick thought back to what Ed had said about Ray. How *had* he passed the background check?

"Come on in, Ray," Patrick invited wearily.

"How'd you know?" The grinning investigator stuck his head through the door.

"Have a seat, Ray." Patrick made the offer before realizing in dismay that there wasn't a vacant seat to be found. All the chairs in his office were stacked with reports waiting to be scanned on his computer. His office was looking a little like Barry's.

Ray whistled as he looked around the packed office. "You certainly have your work cut out for you."

"You should talk, considering the investigator turnover rate and all," Patrick reminded his friend.

"Believe it or not, the numbers have evened out over the past several weeks."

"Guess your guys are even smarter than I thought," Patrick said. "They must have figured out that it's better to be in the know than blind in this unpredictable and unprecedented situation."

Patrick walked to clear the chair in front of his desk. "Okay, so now have a seat."

"I repeat," Ray looked around the crowded office. "You need help. Won't they give you someone to scan all of this?"

"To be perfectly honest, since the request would have to go through Ed, I haven't even considered making it."

"I can see that." Ray sat perched on the edge of his seat, not planning to stay too long. "Listen, I've been thinking about the conversation we had yesterday, and I agree. Once you separate the real ones from the fakes, my caseload can be subdivided into the major and minor categories you suggested."

"Great." At least something Patrick suggested was being taken seriously. "I was hoping we'd be able to further define each of those categories, and then maybe implement some type of system to tag each case. It sure would make my job easier."

"Let's do it then. How about scary for the minor case labels and X-Files for the major ones?" Ray suggested sarcastically.

"Actually, I like it," Patrick surprised Ray. The fact was, before approaching these files, Patrick always took a deep breath. Sometimes, he even had to remind himself to let the air back out.

Ray glanced at his watch, but Patrick was determined to get in one more subject before his friend left for the day. "Almost quittin' time, Ray, but can I ask you one more thing?"

"Quittin' time," Ray laughed at the statement. "I've got two other cases to check out before heading home, but go ahead."

"Well," said Patrick. "I'm wondering whether you've noticed anything weird about your follow-up calls, because mine have taken on a strange similarity."

"Like what?" Ray was all ears. "Honestly, I don't do much following up. It takes all the time I have just to track them down, get the initial reports, and pass them on to you."

"Well, give me your take on it just the same." Patrick respected Ray's opinion on a variety of subjects. "So, these people are afraid when I first contact them. They pour out their fears to me by the hour, and beg for reassurances that I can't begin to give. But somewhere along the line, they've started to flip-flop on me, Ray. When I call for further updates, there's more that remains unsaid in the conversations. Something's just not right." Patrick closed the case file in front of him and folded his hands on top of the folder.

"Sounds like an interesting development, but who has the time to follow up on the unsaid when there are so many people clamoring to talk? I'll think about it though, and if I come up with any ideas, I'll get back in touch."

"Thanks," said Patrick. "How about I walk you to the elevator? If I stay here, I'll just be drawn into these damn files again and I need to get something to eat."

Patrick turned out the light in his office. They walked past the glass wall separating them from the 24-hour call center on their way to the elevator.

"Hi, Mr. Hagen." An older, gray-haired operator greeted him on his way back to the glass tank from his break.

"Hey..." started Patrick. He didn't know the man's name, gave a lame wave, and kept on walking with Ray.

"Come to think of it," Patrick mused, "we've gone through our fair share of operators, too. Hopefully, it'll even out with time. Oh shit!" Patrick glimpsed a determined coworker heading his way. "Look, Ray, I'm going to duck out on you. Here comes one of the office complainers. Get back to me with any ideas."

"Sure, talk to you later." Ray continued towards the elevators.

Oh great! Just what I need, thought Patrick, as he quickly headed back to the safety of his office. He turned the light back on. He was sure he could find a stale granola bar or something in his desk drawer. He had no time to deal with someone whose primary complaints revolved around missing toilet paper rolls and what they were eating for lunch. This type of minutiae bullshit was just a waste of time and brainpower. He locked his office door.

In the second drawer down, he found a half-eaten bag of honey-roasted peanuts. They would have to do. He opened his laptop back up and went through his e-mails. There was one from *Secretary Marker*—that still sounded weird. Patrick never would have predicted desk jobs in their futures the weekend he had turned twenty-one. That weekend, he and Ed had driven to Atlantic City on a whim. They'd lost a combined total of three hundred dollars, along with any memory of the cab ride back to their motel.

Patrick looked up and saw his reflection in the dark office windows. The summer sun had just set. *I look thin*, he noted, *and tired*, nothing like the solid, confident young man he had just recalled. The Harvester Project had taken its toll on him.

> *Mr. Patrick Hagen,*
>
> *You've completed your work as Project Analyst for the Harvester Project. Please see the attachments for details on your next three projects. They are all relatively minor, so I would expect that you could handle all three at once. Thank you for all the work you've done. We will continue to keep a minimally staffed harvester call line for any concerned citizens, but we plan to phase this out within the next three months.*
>
> *Secretary Ed Marker*

It wasn't anything Patrick hadn't expected. Honestly, he had been wondering why Ed had kept him on the project for so long. Maybe Ed just didn't want to throw up any red flags by switching staff. Whatever he was thinking, it had all worked. He had gotten what he wanted and America was now running on the harvesters.

Patrick was still at the DOE long after rush hour traffic had died down and decided to make another follow-up call. Maybe the flip-flops were all in his imagination. Maybe this job was taking its toll on his perception of events, he thought, dialing up Bobby Freeman. Was he still looking at things objectively?

"Mr. Freeman, this is Patrick Hagen from the DOE," he quickly reintroduced himself to the skittish farmer. "If you recall, we spoke several weeks ago about your cornfield, sir."

"Why sure, Mr. Hagen, I remember you fine. How are you doin'?"

How was *he* doing? Patrick was the one who was supposed to ask that question. "I'm very well, thank you, Mr. Freeman. How has your corn crop been doing since we spoke last? Is it still growing in such an unusual manner?"

"Why actually, I think it's slowed down a good bit. Ought to be tasselin' soon. Boy, these fields should give some case of hay fever, don't ya' think?" and farmer Freeman laughed.

What the hell had happened? This man had practically crawled through the phone lines when they'd spoken three weeks earlier. Yup, there was the confirming scribble in the margins of his notes. Patrick had been paging through them in case, by some weird chance, he'd been thinking of the wrong person. That wasn't the case. This pleasant farmer from Four Corners, North Carolina, had replaced a man on the edge of his sanity a mere twenty-one days ago.

"Yes, Mr. Freeman, hay fever could pose a problem." What else could he say? "Is everything all right?" Patrick gave him another chance to offer any additional information. "I know you were quite concerned the last time we spoke."

"Everything's fine. Big crops ain't such a bad thing after all. Emily and me can't wait to have us some of this fine corn on the cob." There he went again, laughing slowly and good-naturedly.

"Well, I'm very glad to hear the problem has resolved itself, Mr. Freeman. If there is anything else I can do for you in the future, please don't hesitate to call."

"Don't you give it another thought. We're fine, just fine, but thanks for callin'."

Click. The connection was broken. The man on the other end had used the word fine no fewer than five times, and Patrick knew because he'd counted. It was all wrong. Something had happened, but what?

Was Ed right after all? Was Patrick just a poor judge of the country's wackiest? No, he couldn't believe that. He was sympathetic, not stupid, and it had never been especially easy to put one over on him.

His assistant, Jenny, had been out for the day with a sick child, but was always available via text.

Could you make me plane reservations as soon as possible for as close to Four Corners, North Carolina as you can get, and put it on my personal VISA card? he texted.

Absolutely, she texted back with her napping child asleep on her lap. Her computer was open on the end table and she set to work.

Should I make return reservations also? her next text read.

He was probably raising her curiosity with this request. He was not a frequent flyer by any means, and she would definitely think it was odd that he was charging it to his own account rather than the DOE's. He trusted her to be discreet, though. They had worked together a long time, and he never begrudged her any time off when her kids needed her. He knew she always did her best to accommodate even on days like today when she called out, and he appreciated it.

No thanks, he responded. *I'm not sure how long this will take. Could you also have a small rental car waiting at the airport and book a hotel for the night?*

Absolutely—her trademark reply.

She was so efficient. Within ten minutes, he had a flight, a car, and a place to stay. Patrick knew he was speaking to thin air, but it felt great. "Okay, Mr. Bobby Freeman, let's just see how fine you really are."

Thankfully, Patrick thought, the quick plane ride was giving him a chance to plan his angle of attack. Reviewing only the most pressing cases, he still felt overwhelmed. "Could I please have a rum and coke?" Patrick requested of the flight attendant. He wasn't traditionally a drinker, but wanted a little something just to take the edge off.

He paged through the files he had crammed into his computer bag as he sipped his drink and ate the small bag of pretzels. Lulled by the hum of the jet engines, he drifted into a light sleep. Sleep had not come easily lately, and didn't last long this time when he was startled awake by the captain's announcement that they would make their descent into Charlotte. From there, he would have to drive to Four Corners. It would be a two-hour drive. Coffee. He needed a cup of coffee or two for that trip, he thought, still surprised that he had fallen asleep on the plane.

It was three cups of coffee later when he arrived at the Deer Creek Motel, a dump if there ever was one, he decided at first glance. He left his bags in the car and walked into the motel office smelling of cigarette-soaked drywall and Febreze. He patted the bell on the counter only once and the attendant came out from the back room.

"How can I help ya?" said the man without any inflection.

"I have a reservation. Patrick Hagen?"

"Sure, Mr. Hagen..." The clerk opened a reservation book and scrolled down the yellow-tinged pages with his finger—no computers in this place. "Here you are."

Patrick read the name on the clerk's tag: "Rodger."

"You're in room twelve," said Rodger, handing Patrick a metal key with a plastic key chain that had the number twelve handwritten in sharpie—no key cards here, either.

"Thanks," said Patrick. He was growing tired again and wanted to take advantage of the feeling before it passed and he found himself lying awake all night playing out all the worst-case scenarios in his mind, as had been his MO of late. Upon reaching his room, he dumped his bags on the floor, loosened his tie, laid down on the bed, and immediately fell asleep.

The morning sunlight seeped in through the musty curtains of the Deer Creek Motel and, despite breathing in a lungful of stale air, Patrick felt refreshed. He had been so tired he hadn't changed positions all night, still sprawled out on top of the comforter in his clothes. At least the place had hot water.

Well-rested and freshly showered, Patrick made his way to the motel office and found a young, gum-popping desk clerk who had taken Rodger's place. This was the perfect place to do things the old-fashioned way. He didn't want to turn on his phone. He didn't want to use any kind of GPS, because he didn't want to be tracked.

The morning clerk had set out a tray of complementary doughnuts that had visible dust stuck to the glaze. *Pass*, thought Patrick. He could find a drive-thru in town, but now he needed verbal directions to the Freeman Farm and a map. A wire carousel in the corner of the motel office boasted dozens of maps for the road-tripper from the 1990s. The edges of the maps curled over the wire racks, holding them in place.

"The Freeman Farm is about forty minutes away, sir."

"Thanks," said Patrick, holding out a map.

"Ah, that map is not accurate," she said, chewing her gum loudly, "but I can show you what's changed." She took the map from his hand and drew in the changes on the stiffened paper.

"As long as you're at it," Patrick had placed a twenty-dollar bill onto the counter, "could you find these for me, too?" After all, Bobby Freeman's wasn't the only case file Patrick had stuffed into his briefcase, and thanks to the pimply faced girl, Four Corners would not be the only town with a circle around it.

"Sure thing, sir, and I'll mark the patches of highway construction for you, too."

Jenny had rented him a nondescript four-door sedan, the type of car that never stood out. He pulled out of the Deer Creek Motel parking lot onto the main highway, which was only a two-lane road through the woods. He kept his eyes open for anywhere he could get something to eat. Bojangles—*I'll take it.*

He had eaten his way through three breakfast sandwiches by the time he had reached the final crossroad. Relieved to have finally arrived, Patrick laid the manhandled map aside. He turned off the main highway and onto a dirt road, the bumpiest road he'd seen yet. It could certainly use one of those highway construction crews. Maybe the ride was better in a tractor, he reasoned logically, because it sure wasn't much in a car. The Freeman Farm shouldn't be too far ahead now, he assured himself, reaching to roll up the window. Another car was coming towards him, kicking up a dust cloud behind it.

As the dust settled, the flat, waving green fields on the horizon were replaced by Bobby Freeman's fields, and even though Patrick had no farming experience, there was something very wrong. He loosened his tie and removed his suit coat. It was getting hotter by the minute, and he could barely breathe already.

Half afraid and half excited, he slowed the car to a crawl and approached ever so cautiously. Wanting to observe as anonymously as possible, Patrick pulled off the road as far as he could without going into the ditch, stopped, and turned off the car. In that first quiet moment, Patrick got a good look at the future. Yes, he decided, it was a good thing he'd come.

The Freeman cornfield was about three hundred yards from the road across another field to his right, but the scent of it was reaching him already. His nose tingled slightly, and the unusual aroma was making him hungry despite the breakfast biscuits sliding around in his greasy stomach.

It certainly wasn't your average cornfield, Patrick decided. It was no longer a cornfield at all. Taking out the binoculars he'd packed as an afterthought, he studied the field carefully and observed cornstalks the size of tree trunks in a well-established forest. It even looked like a great place to go camping, like some national park in the middle of nowhere.

From this vantage point, it was impossible to tell how large an area was involved. Patrick started the car and found the mailbox marking the Freeman drive, but was caught completely off guard by the crudely painted warning staked prominently next to the rusty postal box.

DANGER - RADIOACTIVE CROPS
KEEP OUT
FOR YOUR OWN SAFETY

What the? Patrick pulled past the sign. No one had ever mentioned radioactivity in any of the reports, and farmer Bobby himself hadn't said one word, either. Relying on a gut feeling, Patrick knew the warning didn't feel right. Even so, he wished he'd packed a Geiger counter rather than binoculars.

He pulled up in front of the house, where he quickly donned his sweat-stained jacket. The Freeman homestead could have used a coat of paint, but times were hard for farmers these days. Things seemed awfully quiet. Patrick noticed nervously that there wasn't any activity at all. Clotheslines were bare, and Patrick could see the equipment shed parked full. Shades were pulled low in the windows against the sun, and the garden needed weeding.

Patrick walked up the porch steps and rang the bell. No one answered. Guess they weren't going to respond, he decided, walking back down the front steps. The Freeman house was empty, nobody home in there.

It didn't matter for now, though. Patrick didn't have time to wait for the Freeman's return. Instead, he started towards the cornfield.

Still wishing he had that Geiger counter, Patrick couldn't help but wince as he approached the supposedly radioactive giant corn, despite his almost certainty that the warnings were all a sham.

"This is weird stuff," he noted quietly while standing on the edge of the corn, and tentatively reaching out to touch the closest stalks. They were at least six inches in diameter. That strange smell was overpoweringly strong now, and his nostrils tingled with more intensity. True to form, his investigative side gave one brief and fleeting thought to allergies. *What have I gotten myself into?* he asked. Every so often, a breeze from the field would carry even wilder scents out to him, although oddly enough, there was no wind today. It was so still, even the clouds weren't moving.

Well, he wasn't going to find out anything, just standing there. Whatever he'd come to see was in that field somewhere, and now was as good a time as any. The hair stood up all over his body, but he bravely placed one foot firmly ahead of the other as he stepped into the corn forest. Back in the day, he had always been the risk-taker. Even if Ed were here, he would probably be the one going first into the field.

Large black birds called loudly overhead, but only for a short while. About the time the corn became something else, he left all wildlife behind. There was no more scurrying on the ground as he passed by, no flapping and startled flight. There was also no more corn.

Patrick rubbed his eyes in disbelief. This was all so bizarre, but the tree things were beautiful, too. Their root systems snaked through the topsoil, anchoring the mystical giants. There were limbs—sort of—and holes evenly spaced all over the trunks. Adding to their wondrous appearance were vines that dropped in spirals from the higher limbs. They reminded him of the enormous banyan trees he'd seen in Florida on his last vacation.

This was nothing like what he had expected to find. There was probably much more to see, but he decided he had seen enough. Not wanting to get turned around, Patrick started in the direction from which he had entered the field, or the forest, or whatever this was now. After a few paces, it was apparent he had lost his sense of direction, and turned in circles, looking for something familiar to guide him out. This was precisely the problem. There was nothing familiar about any of this. Shit, which way should he go? He picked a direction, knowing that whichever direction he chose, the field would not go on forever. He could then follow the outskirts of the field back around to the farmhouse and his car.

Monitoring the ground directly ahead for roots and watching for low hanging limbs occupied his attention, when he spotted someone through the purple haze that blew through the trunks. Adrenaline flooded his circulatory system, and he stopped walking, peering through the shady mutated field.

"Oh my God." Patrick rolled his eyes at his ridiculous behavior and unwarranted fear. It was a scarecrow. A regular-sized scarecrow, the guardian of this field before it had grown beyond the need for protection.

He started walking again, and hadn't made it far, when he heard something move in a clearing beyond.

What was it this time? Patrick thought.

"Who's there?" snapped Bobby Freeman, stepping from behind an immense trunk, with Emily by his side. "Who is it?"

This was what he'd come for, wasn't it? Patrick reminded himself uneasily. Actually, it wasn't. This wasn't anything close to what he'd expected.

"It's me, Mr. Freeman. It's Patrick Hagen from the DOE. We spoke on the phone yesterday?"

"I remember, but what in the hell are you doin' here?"

"Just as soon as I figure out where here is, I'll be happy to answer that question."

"Welcome to our cornfield, Mr. Hagen," Emily spoke up shyly.

Patrick tried to keep his wits about him as he spoke. This entire scene had set his limbic system ablaze with caution. "Thank you, Mrs. Freeman, but could you tell me which direction to take to get back to my car? I parked it outside of the farmhouse."

"We can show you out, Mr. Hagen. But why would you ever want to leave?"

· · ·

Once the probe established an inescapable rotational orbit around the comparatively small world, the fact that this planet was completely unsuitable became irrelevant. The ship's computer had been programmed long ago, and now its dispersion sequence was initiated.

Valuable cargo was to be delivered just as if the ship was circling its intended destination. Now, from a small opening along the underbelly of the huge craft, small clouds of iridescent genetic materials were slowly ejected. They formed widening streams of flotsam behind the slowly descending ship, eventually hanging in the atmosphere and completely circling the planet in a thin layer as the ship crisscrossed the skies again and again, until finally landing softly on an exposed piece of ground.

Landing as soft and fine as talcum powder, the small seething bits of matter grabbed tenaciously with tiny barbed determination. Attaching to the very chemical compositions and crystalline structures of the planet's own creation, the unincorporated alien material was carried along for the ride. It waited only for the signal to begin its active invasion of the host material.

Unfortunately, this signal from the dispersal ship was jammed by the electrostatic noise of the planet's own creation and therefore went unrecognized. Finally, after a predetermined amount of time, the signal ceased to sound. No matter, the required material was in place and would remain so, waiting only for its signal. This signal would begin the planet's transformational process; it would be very unusual in its frequency signal modulations.

DORMANT DIVERSION

CHAPTER 8

SEAMAN SHULTZ
Off the Coast of Bermuda, 1962

Welcome, men," said Lieutenant Price, standing in front of a specially chosen group of enlisted men on a small naval craft five miles off the coast of Bermuda. "Take a good look at the men on this boat. You're an elite group, or at least you will be. You're the first soldiers in a new class of warriors." Lieutenant Price paced back and forth as he spoke. A natural sailor, perfectly balanced as the ship rose and fell with the choppy waves.

"You men will be the first Navy SEALS," the Lieutenant paused, all eyes were on him. "That stands for the United States Navy's Sea, Air, and Land Teams. President Kennedy has forecast the need for small units of highly skilled men to conduct direct action missions in any environment.

"So," Lieutenant Price pivoted slowly, surveying the entire line of men, "welcome to your first day of training, SEALS." A flicker of excitement played across his hard expression.

The twelve men continued to give the Lieutenant their full attention.

"Why Bermuda?" asked the Lieutenant. "It doesn't seem like the place to undergo grueling training, but I'll tell you now that these waters are unpredictable. The currents in the subaquatic caves can be strong. Your physical strength will be tested. Your nerves will also be tested in some of the tighter spaces." Lieutenant Price saw no hint of fear in the eyes of the men on board.

"You've all undergone psych evals and background checks. Know that if you're here, you passed." He continued to pace with his hands folded neatly behind his back. "Furthermore, the Bermuda Naval Facility was not constructed for oceanic research as commonly thought. It was built as an on-shore location for our Atlantic Sound Surveillance System. This is classified information. However, we are not here as part of the SOSUS project. We're here to train. Anything you see in association with SOSUS, you *didn't* see! Is that clear?"

"Yes, sir!" the men answered in unison. The formation of men kept their balance, knees bending in response to the rhythmic swells underfoot.

"As part of the SEALS program, you will be asked to enter dangerous situations. These will often be situations where your fellow soldiers have already failed. Our expectations are high, as will be the success rate of our missions!" Price paused for effect. "Today, though, we'll start with a simple dive. Under the seats, you'll find full face masks, double hose regulators, tanks, and suits. I want everyone ready to back roll in ten."

The trainees acknowledged the instructions, eager to put their skills to the test.

"Fall out."

In response to this command, the line of seamen stepped back, pivoted, and dispersed in synchrony—twelve men moving as one. A hum rose from the vessel as the trainees donned the dive equipment and readied themselves for their first exercise as members of this elite group.

"Sir, will you be diving with us?" the inquiry came from Seaman Shultz, fresh from rural Kentucky.

The Lieutenant squinted his eyes against the sun as he answered. "Yes, Shultz. I'll be leading you through today's caverns."

"Sir, yes, sir." Seaman Shultz responded, adjusting the bulky oxygen tank on his back.

After pulling on his own wetsuit, Lieutenant Price again addressed the new group. "Seaman Prescott will stay onboard, watching the weather and the mid-frequency active sonar."

The officer perched himself on the side of the boat, positioned for entry, and waited for the men to finish preparing. He looked up at the sky. Bright blue stretched all the way to the horizon, uninterrupted by a single cloud. The conditions were perfect for training.

"Once we're underwater, it's imperative that we stay together. This network of caves is sprawling. I don't want anyone breaking away and getting lost. A SEAL leaves no one behind." Another long pause. "Men, try not to kill your fellow soldiers. Do not be the one who causes anyone to run out of oxygen searching for your sorry, insubordinate ass."

With face masks and mouthpieces in place, the collection of trainees followed their commanding officer's lead, joining him on the wall of the ship, poised for submersion.

Lieutenant Price tightened his facemask and counted backward from three with his fingers. One by one, the divers dropped off the port side into the tropical waters. Under the surface, the Lieutenant led the young divers slowly down into the shadowy depths, leaving a trail of bubbles in his wake.

Shultz was the last in the descending line of SEALS. He followed those who would someday have his back in wartime situations, most likely in the South China Sea. Today, however, they were off the coast of Bermuda. He tapped Seaman McClain on the shoulder and pointed to a formidably sized barracuda coasting in the depths, sunlight playing off of its blue scales.

McClain looked in the barracuda's direction and turned back to the Lieutenant, gesturing for Shultz to do the same.

Focus, Shultz cautioned himself. This was his opportunity to put his dive skills to the test and see the world in the process. He kept his eyes forward but remained alert to his surroundings, watching for any encroaching predators.

A jagged opening in the ocean's floor admitted them into a system of caves serving as the day's training ground. Sand carpeted the entryway, dissipating as it gave way to cream-colored limestone from floor to ceiling. The procession of divers, lit only by the beams of their flashlights, snaked slowly through this natural hideaway.

Seaman Shultz kept pace on the dive, cutting through the water past the diverse sea life flourishing in this submerged tomb. Tiny translucent shrimp scampered along the rocks, pumping their tails in retreat as the divers passed through the craggy tunnels. The tight entry into the caverns eventually opened up into a massive sanctuary. Stalagmites jutting up from the cave floor met the stalactites hanging overhead, their presence indicating that this cave system had once been dry. Inside this colossal underwater theater, Shultz slowed. It was McClain again who gestured for him to follow more closely. The silent beauty and immensity of his surroundings had slowed Shultz, stalling his kicks. A few quick flicks of his flippers propelled him back to the group. It was a silent procession of sleek black creatures whose cascades of bubbles disturbed the quiet waters of this dark underworld.

Their final exercise on the dive had them squirming through a small fissure hidden behind a stalactite of generous girth. One by one, the divers squeezed themselves through the narrow space. Such close quarters would have been enough to send any claustrophobic into a full-on panic. Once all the trainees had made it through, the Lieutenant gave the signal to return to the boat.

Shultz wished they didn't have to surface just yet. The past thirty minutes had felt like only five, but he knew the Lieutenant had timed it right. They didn't want to cut the oxygen reserves in their tanks too close in case of any unforeseen circumstances preventing them from surfacing. He stopped momentarily to look back at the rock formations which had taken tens of thousands of years to form, fed by the steady drip of mineral-laden water when these had been dry caverns.

Wait. What was that? As Seaman Shultz prepared to follow the group to the surface, he saw something... a light? Could they have left someone behind? He counted all the trainees ahead of him and everyone was present. Then, he glanced back again, and the light was gone. It had been purple. He couldn't have been imagining this. This part of the dive was pitch black save for their flashlights, none of which shone purple. He knew better than to follow this curious light. The dangers of getting turned around in an unfamiliar environment and draining the oxygen tank were very real. He followed his comrades as they exited the caves.

Once onboard the training vessel, Shultz addressed his superior. "Sir."

"Yes, Shultz, what's your question?" Lieutenant Price faced the young man while removing his dive suit.

"What's beyond the large chamber? I mean, what's on the other side of the far wall down there?"

"You saw it then." Price's voice lowered slightly.

"Sir?"

"The Devil's Hole is on the other side of the cavern wall, Shultz. At some point, that area collapsed in on itself, leaving a deep blue hole. Beautiful really. It's full of jacks, eels, and sea turtles, but those are all closer to the surface. You wouldn't have been able to see anything from where we were."

"But, sir," Shultz began, "I thought I saw..."

The Lieutenant cut him off. "You saw *nothing*. We're only here for training exercises. Understood?"

"Sir, yes, sir." Shultz didn't push the conversation any further.

United States Naval Facility, Bermuda, Nineteen Years Later

"Vice-Admiral Price, sir." The soldier standing in front of the sonar screen removed his headphones and smartly saluted the newly promoted officer.

"Senior Chief Petty Officer McClain. It's been a long time." The Admiral dropped his salute.

"Yes, sir." McClain snapped his hand from a salute down to his side. "Since the Cuban Missile Crisis, sir."

"You're the only one of my first group of SEALS who's still enlisted, McClain." The Admiral removed his hat, revealing the gray that had taken up residence since their last meeting. "At ease."

"Yes, sir." McClain adjusted the headphones hanging around his neck and made one last notation in his surveillance log before changing the sonar range.

"So, tell me what's been going on here with SOSUS?" Price walked around the dimly lit surveillance room. "This place has had an upgrade." His footfalls echoed in the large space lined with state-of-the-art monitoring equipment.

"What's SOSUS?" McClain smiled. "The Bermuda base was built for oceanic research, sir."

Vice-Admiral Price recalled his long-ago lecture and returned the smile. "I hear that the behavior of some of our unwanted visitors has changed recently. Fill me in on the details." Price stopped pacing and looked McClain directly in the eyes. Their casual reunion had quickly given way to more serious questions.

"Sir, there've been too many Soviet submarines detected in the area," McClain reported. "They're coming closer to the Devil's Hole all the time. Our subs have kept them at an acceptable distance so far, but they're getting bolder and coming closer."

"That's exactly why I'm here," said the Admiral. "Secretary Brown is about to retire, but before he does, we have to move what we've been safeguarding in the Devil's Hole."

"I've been assigned here for five years and have never been given any indication of exactly what's down there. I'm only the sonar guy." The Petty Officer understood his assignment and responsibilities. "I don't have the required clearance for this conversation."

"Well, you've got clearance now." Price pressed his lips together and shook his head. "Even if you don't have questions, I have answers for you today," continued the Admiral. "Shultz knew what was down there. It's a shame what happened to him."

"You still remember Seaman Shultz?" McClain was surprised. He waited for more information as his superior officer placed his hat on top of the sonar screen.

"You men were my first SEALS. You always remember your first team." Price leaned against the cinderblock wall built to withstand the hurricane-force winds of the tropics and folded his arms across his chest. "From day one, Shultz was always the one with too many questions."

"I wouldn't think that the loss of an E-3 would be so well remembered." McClain thought back to the last time he had seen his fellow soldier before Shultz had gone out on that unauthorized dive.

"We let everyone believe Shultz got lost down there and ran out of air," said Price. "The waters around here have a way of washing away any trace of lost divers."

"What are you saying?" The thought that Shultz might still be alive had never occurred to McClain. As he processed this possibility, McClain led the visiting officer into a small break room. He took a bottled water from the refrigerator and handed it to the Admiral. "Have a seat, sir." The seaman gestured to a plastic chair with metal legs.

The two officers sat opposite each other at a laminate table made to look like wood. A wall unit pumped frigid air into the small room, making it a good ten degrees cooler than it was in the sonar room.

"Turn that thing off, McClain. It's freezing in here."

McClain switched off the unit, sat back down at the table, and waited for what his superior officer had to say.

"This is going to be a small mission. Ten men, small transport craft. No red flags. Nothing to raise interest."

McClain held up his hand. "Hold on. Before we get into the strategy for the extraction of whatever's down there, what happened to Shultz? I mean, we didn't work together that long, but like you said, you don't forget the men on your first team. Besides, he was a highly skilled diver."

"You're right," admitted the Admiral. "It wasn't a technical mistake, and it didn't cost him his life. He's still alive, in a way."

"In a way?" McClain's eyes drew up into small slits, confused.

"When Shultz disappeared, he was diving in the Devil's Hole. I guess his curiosity had overtaken his better judgment. Following orders was always a challenge for him," said Price. "We know he came into contact with what we refer to as Addie." The Admiral paused and took a sip of his water.

"Addie?" pressed McClain.

"Addie is a species which we have not been able to identify. We believe Addie to be extraterrestrial in origin, but not an adult. 'She' has been in what appears to be some kind of fetal or larval stage since her discovery in 1953."

"You have an alien baby in the Devil's Hole?" said McClain, looking at the Admiral and waiting for him to say he was joking.

"That's what we believe," confirmed the Admiral evenly. "We haven't tried to move Addie because we didn't want to risk altering the homeostatic environment sustaining her. Now that the Soviets are coming so close, we have no choice but to relocate her."

"So, what happened to Shultz?" The Admiral still hadn't answered the question.

"Shultz found Addie, McClain. He touched her, or her bubble, that is. From what I could see on the video footage, Shultz inadvertently pierced Addie's sac and came into contact with the liquid surrounding her. It looked like he was in a good bit of pain."

The Admiral touched his hand to his chin and exhaled slowly, trying to formulate what he would say next. "Of course, it was hard to tell because he was wearing his dive mask. Anyway, the scientists watching from the small observatory we'd built in the Hole extracted him from the water, but Shultz was unconscious. He was still breathing and had a pulse, but was completely unresponsive. He was airlifted directly to Walter Reed."

"So, he's okay? He's been back in the States this whole time?"

"I'm sorry to have to tell you this, but he's never woken up. We moved him to the medical facility at the Pentagon after he developed a weird anomaly on his forehead that came and went."

"Where is he? Can I see him?"

"We have bigger things to concentrate on now. I'm sorry, McClain," and he really was. "The Soviets simply cannot be allowed to find Addie. We've just finished building a facility that we feel can sustain her. This is where our SEAL team comes in."

"It's been a while since I've been out of this sonar room," reminded McClain. "Are you sure you want to start me back with a coma-inducing fetus? I've got a few grays now myself."

Price didn't find this amusing. "This is a matter of national security. It's going to require the kind of laser focus we had back when we pulled our guys from the POW camp in '72."

The combination of stagnant air and the intensity of the conversation suddenly made the room feel close. "Do you mind if I turn the air back on?" McClain asked.

"Sure, go ahead." The Admiral gave a wave of approval. He, too, had developed some beads of sweat on his forehead in the closet-sized room. "Listen, we'll need to extract Addie carefully and quietly. We have a ship that we'll use to carry her seven hundred miles to Norfolk, VA. Onboard, we have a tank and two biochemical engineers to regulate her container. From Norfolk, we'll take a small aircraft to Arizona."

"Arizona?"

"I can't tell you any more than that. We need you for the extraction, but that's where your clearance ends. You know the Soviets' patterns and the conditions of the waters."

"If I'm only needed for the extraction, why am I going to Arizona?"

The Admiral leaned in and folded his hands on the table. "We may need your diving expertise to adjust settings in the tank during transport."

"You mean I'll be traveling in the tank with this, Addie?" McClain furrowed his brow in opposition.

"You don't need to worry. We've installed appropriate safety measures. We just need to be ready for anything that might happen between here and Arizona."

"With all due respect, sir, I would think that this particular mission would have maximum funding and sufficient equipment for all contingencies. Why do you need me?"

Price looked at the concerned man. "Of course, what you say is true, but nothing is guaranteed. Despite our best efforts, there may be some jarring from point A to point B, and equipment can malfunction. What I need is a person with technical knowledge and dive skills I can trust, and that someone is you, McClain."

"What if she hatches or wakes up or something? What if I'm the next person with a questionable anomaly at the Pentagon?" All reasonable questions.

"These are your orders," the Admiral said flatly. His tone of voice left no opening for further questions. "Look, I know this is a lot to process, but it's very important. We need you all in. Are we clear on the assignment?"

McClain's only option was to confirm. "Yes, sir." Anything less would be career suicide, or worse. He knew too much now. There was no refusing this assignment. "All in, sir."

"Good," the Admiral finished the last of his water. Gooseflesh was forming on his neck. "Turn that damn unit off again, will you."

CHAPTER 9

First, the world was flat, then it was round, what next?

The stormy skies outside Ed's office windows on this late July afternoon matched his mood exactly. His nerves swirled inside his gut as the dark gray clouds churned outside. Patrick was missing, and Ed was worried. The man had put in for vacation and gone underground. There was no vacation; of that, Ed was sure. So where was he?

What was Patrick up to? The rain fell in sheets, hammering the question home again and again. Unfortunately, there was nothing in the DOE information loop to give any indication of his plans. He had also turned off his cell phone. Ed sipped a steaming mug of coffee to calm his nerves. Wherever Patrick was, he had better not be pursuing anything related to the harvesters, Ed thought. He had sent Patrick the project conclusion e-mail, and that was it. If he wanted to keep his job at the DOE, he would have to fall in line. There were plenty of people who would gladly take his position as project analyst. Their personal history could only carry Patrick so much further.

At the far end of his office, away from the window, he took a seat at his desk, placing the hot mug on a stack of files Patrick had given him. He tried Patrick one more time, and the call went right to voicemail. He needed another approach. Jenny. She was a bright woman, but no one could say no to a family emergency.

He dialed Patrick's office extension, and she picked up on the first ring. "Jenny, it's Secretary Marker. Listen, Patrick's sister called to say their father was going to need surgery. Do you know how I can get in touch with him?"

"No, Secretary Marker. He hasn't responded to any of my texts all day. I think he has his phone turned off."

This, Ed already knew.

"I thought it might have been a family emergency that called him away in the first place," she said.

"I don't believe so, but I think it would be nice if I could have him get in touch with his sister."

"Of course, Secretary Marker, but unless he's still in Four Corners, I have no way to reach him. I only made reservations at the motel there for one night. It's possible he stayed longer. Would you like me to find out?"

"No, thanks very much, Jenny. If you'll give me the name of the motel, I'll follow up on this myself. You've been a big help, and I'm sure Patrick will appreciate it."

It had been a sneaky thing to do, but necessary, very necessary, thought Ed as he dialed through to the Deer Creek Motel. Sounded like a dump, but no reimbursement, no luxury.

"Hello. Yes, I'm calling to see whether you still have a Mr. Patrick Hagen registered." As the clerk checked the log, Ed was almost sure he was too late. "Yes, I understand. Thank you so much, anyway."

Well, that was that, no Patrick, but the guy had been there for three nights.

Ed's cup of coffee turned cool as he stared silently out the window across the room. He supposed that Patrick could have gone anywhere to get away, but he'd gone to North Carolina, damn it! *The harvester state* they'd taken to calling themselves. No doubt, Ed thought snidely, they'd be coming out with new commemorative license plates in the next few months.

Patrick was like a moth to a flame. He had completely ignored Ed's change of assignments, and Ed was even further perturbed that Patrick's lack of compliance was eating up so much of his time. The Harvester Project was not the only thing he had on his plate as Secretary of Energy. Patrick hadn't taken any of this into account. Besides energy conservation, research, and waste disposal, also under Ed's direction were the nuclear weapons program and genomics research program.

If he wanted to focus, he would have to find Patrick. If he wanted to find Patrick, he just needed to track down the weak link in his old college friend's chain, and this was his obsession with the harvesters.

Ray would know where Patrick was, but if approached, he'd alert his friend. Shit, Ed ran his hand over his hair. Alerting Patrick would put him right back where he'd started. He was mad at himself. If anyone else were to have pulled something like this, Ed would have fired them right then. Patrick was almost out of chances. Ed decided to find Patrick himself. He needed to tie up this loose end to clear his mind and get back to all the other work that had been piling up. An avalanche of digital priorities had accumulated while they had been primarily focused on launching the harvester initiative.

"Shane?"

"Yes, Secretary Marker."

"Please make me plane reservations to Four Corners, North Carolina as soon as possible."

"Yes, sir. Would you like car and hotel reservations as well?"

"Please."

"Yes, sir, and Mr. Davis is here to see you."

"Come on in, Barry." Ed knew his voice could be heard all over the outer office from the intercom.

Barry admitted himself. "What is all that about? Where are you going?"

"On a wild goose chase."

"What's going on, Ed?" Barry could see that all was not well.

"Patrick Hagen has gone AWOL. He put in for vacation over a week ago and hasn't been heard from since. Most likely, he's gone underground to drum up some more opposition."

"Speaking of Patrick," Barry walked nervously to stare out the panoramic windows, "or if you'd rather not speak of him, have you noticed anything different in the trouble reports lately?"

"No, not really." What was Barry fishing for?

"Maybe I should have said, have you noticed anything the same in them?" Barry was sure he could not be the only one to notice the similarity.

"To be truthful, I haven't read that many of them, just a random sampling of the stack coming through weekly. I couldn't possibly read them all." *Liar*, Ed silently chastised himself. He certainly could have.

"I think you'd better," said Barry.

Ed attempted to silence the alarms going off in his head. "Please, just tell me what you have to say. I'm really behind."

Barry looked at him strangely. What *was* he about to say?

"I was waiting in a long line for coffee this morning in the plaza outside," Barry started. "There was only one girl working the cart. The older woman wasn't there."

Ed wasn't sure what would be so upsetting about a long wait for a latte. He gave Barry a look, indicating that he should get to the point.

Barry took a deep breath and continued. "When I finally got up to the register, I ordered my usual latte and blueberry scone. Anyway, I had some extra time since the Harvester Project was complete. So, I sat down to enjoy my latte on the brick wall next to the garden. Then I heard it..."

"Heard what?" said Ed, losing interest quickly.

"Someone or something," said Barry.

Could he be any more vague? "Barry, the whole plaza is full of someones and somethings."

"Just hear me out, Ed. Promise me you'll keep an open mind and won't think I'm crazy."

"Fine," said Ed, gesturing for Barry to continue with his story.

Barry pulled out his paper cup from this morning, but it wasn't a latte. "I dumped my coffee in the dirt and dug up this flower."

Ed looked at the flower sprouting out of the coffee cup. "And? I know you're not here to bring me flowers."

"This flower speaks, Ed." Barry held up his coffee cup filled with dirt and one singular flower stretching out of the soil. It looked like a cross between a daisy and a carnation.

"What?"

"Just listen," said Barry, bringing his find closer to Ed's desk. "It's saying *help me*. Actually, since I found it this morning, it has been speaking less and less, like it's getting too hard for it to continue. Now, it just says *heme*."

"Barry, I have actual work to do today, and I'm sure you do, too," said Ed, shaking his head. "I don't have time for this."

"Just listen!"

Ed was taken by surprise. He had never heard Barry raise his voice before. Stunned into a temporary silence, Ed listened, but nothing.

"Keep listening."

Still nothing. Then, no. Ed couldn't believe it. What had been a *heme* was now just *hee*. "What are you trying to do, Barry?"

"Look," Barry sat the cup on Ed's desk. He turned his phone off and laid it down on Ed's desk. He also took his jacket off, threw it on the chair, and turned his pockets inside out. "It's not a recording. Listen!"

Ed stayed silent and listened as directed. He heard it again and once more after that. Then nothing. How could this plant be producing that noise? There had to be an explanation for this.

"That's not all," said Barry. He pulled a small pin from his pocket. It was a pink breast cancer awareness ribbon. The one the older lady running the coffee cart had always worn. "I found this next to the flower this morning."

"So?" Ed checked the time on his laptop.

"Just hear me out. I know it sounds crazy, but," said Barry, "I'd read some of Patrick's case files and I called Ray. I asked him to find out where the coffee lady lived, if she was sick, or where she was."

"What did Ray find?" Ed played along, thinking this may speed things up a bit.

"It took him all morning, but listen to this. The coffee lady's name is Sherry—a sixty-three-year-old widow. She lives just outside of the city in a small apartment in Hyattsville, next to a vacant appliance repair building. She has a coffee cart on the University of Maryland campus too that she runs on the weekends. Her neighbors said that she didn't come home last night."

"Do you realize what we're entertaining here?" said Ed. "I believe in science, not magic."

"Ed, Ray found she lived only one block from a relay harvester and that she was not the first one on her street to go missing."

"So, tell me in so many words exactly what you're saying. Don't assume that I am drawing any conclusions," said Ed.

"Ed..." said Barry.

"Just say it!" Ed was losing patience.

"Look past the petals," Barry said, and waited.

Ed leaned in, still almost expecting some water to squirt out at him. That's what he was hoping for, at any rate. What he saw was truly unsettling. He had to back up and put his reading glasses on. He peeled back the petals again. Were those two seed beads? They couldn't be. It *couldn't* be. Not...*eyes*?

"I don't believe this," said Ed. "I don't believe what you're telling me. Really, I don't."

"You don't?"

"You must have lost your mind, Barry. Do you sincerely believe that this flower is the coffee cart lady?"

"But Ed, you're looking at her eyes," said Barry.

"I'm looking at *eyes*," Ed responded, "but I'm certain that Sherry has not mutated into a flower. It is much more likely that this flower has mutated. Either way, this is a scientific anomaly and very perplexing. It's bizarre enough to rival the news reports about the babies born with gills."

"So, what are we going to do now?"

Ed could ignore closed folders on his desk. He *had been* ignoring the closed folders on his desk, but this he could not ignore. In real life, in real-time, he was looking at a flower and the flower was looking back at him. He rubbed his eyes and replaced his reading glasses to have another look. He couldn't explain this away. There was no more room under the rug. He took off his glasses and pushed his hair back with both hands repeatedly as his heart raced and he panicked. This would not be a minor event. Ed could feel his hands begin to shake. It should have all been so perfect. The concept had been flawless. Skies would have cleared. Acid rain would have been a worry for past generations.

"So, what do we do now?" Barry persisted.

Ed steadied himself and rose from his desk. He walked over to the leather couch on the opposite side of the office and picked up a stack of file folders that Patrick had been piling up for him. He brought them over and dropped them loudly onto his desk. "Now, we play catch up. Start reading."

"Shane?" Ed called out to his assistant.

"Yes, Secretary Marker?" said Shane through the speaker.

"Please call Ray and have him locate Project Analyst Patrick Hagen." Ed did not wait for a response, released the intercom button, and started reading.

CHAPTER 10

Saguaro Rock, Arizona, 1990

Secretary of Defense George Bennett stood in the center of an elevator traveling down. There was no up. Dug into a natural escarpment in the Sonoran Desert lay the largest classified military base in the United States. Construction of the base had begun in the 1950s and the expansion was still taking place. The sedimentary, igneous, and metamorphic rocks comprising the Arizona terrain kept the prying eyes of satellites away from this facility. Saguaro Rock had the capacity to house entire military divisions underground, complete with terminals, research facilities, and a full arsenal, but he wasn't there for any of this. He was there for Addie.

Colonel Walker had contacted him a few days ago, reporting a change in Addie's condition. His report had been rather vague and the details non-specific. Bennett had been instructed to see it for himself.

"Secretary Bennett." Colonel Walker was there to greet him as the door to the elevator opened up to the negative thirty-second floor, or subterranean thirty-two.

"Colonel," Bennett responded, stepping out. "I'm looking forward to seeing what this is all about." The Secretary couldn't afford to waste time. He *was* very pleased to see the tight security and heightened military presence here on Addie's home floor. Precautions had been in place every step of the way since her discovery, getting more extensive and sophisticated over time.

"This way." Colonel Walker got into a motorized cart. "Please," he invited the Secretary to have a seat. "It's a small city down here now. This is the best way to get around."

"I can see that."

From the elevator, it was a straight shot to the lab. Their cart buzzed down the long corridor, passing offshoots to other sectors also bored into the rock. It was like a giant ant colony. The reddish-brown walls of the corridor were solid rock, forged from depositions of sediment over millions of years.

"This place goes on forever, Colonel." Bennett looked at his watch, noting the time.

"Hard to believe, I know. From appearances on the surface, you would never know any of this was down here."

"So, what's changed with Addie?" Secretary Bennett got right to the point. His principal focus was still on the Middle East. "I've got entire divisions of troops deployed in Saudi Arabia, but I've been called here. What's going on?"

"You'll have to see for yourself."

Walker turned the cart left down a narrow corridor humming with florescent lighting. He slowed to a stop and put the cart in park in front of an oversized metal door. "In here, Secretary."

Colonel Walker placed his hand on a scanning pad built into the wall and the door unlatched. Bennett followed the Colonel into the lab past soldiers posted with rifles on either side of the opening.

"Colonel Walker, Secretary Bennett," a spindly lab tech was perched on a stool recording something on his computer. He stood to greet the VIPs as they entered and offered to page Dr. Ross.

"Don't bother. I want to keep this visit as short as possible." The Secretary's eye didn't miss a thing as he strolled away from the other two men past rows of computer terminals displaying steady streams of lines and numbers on their monitors.

They gave the Secretary his space as he surveyed the lab. "What kind of mood is he in?" asked the tech in a hushed tone.

"He's in a hurry." The Colonel's face showed annoyance. "Where's Dr. Ross?"

"At lunch." A digital clock at the bottom of the computer screen showed the doctor had been gone for almost an hour. "He should be back any time now."

"Page him and let him know who's here."

"Will do." The technician dialed Dr. Ross and punched in a code used for unexpected visitors.

Bennett finished his circuit around the lab directly in front of the main terminal and pointed to the screen with its changing graphics. "What's this recording?"

"Do you see those spikes?" The tech nodded toward the screen.

Secretary Bennett looked at the name tag pinned to the young man's white coat: Josh Allen, Lab Tech. "I see them, but what do they mean?"

"Maybe you'd rather hear it from Dr. Ross," the nervous tech offered.

"No. I'd like to hear it now, please, Mr. Allen."

"Oh, okay. I mean, perfect." The tech hurriedly adjusted his screen toward the Secretary of Defense, who clearly outranked Dr. Ross.

"These spikes have been going on for years, but it wasn't until they transported Seaman Shultz to this lab facility that we could finally see any correlations between Addie and anything else."

"Go on," Bennett directed.

"They were doing some renovations at the Pentagon and wanted to relocate several long-term care patients to other facilities. It made sense that they would transfer Seaman Shultz to Saguaro

Rock. We have all the most advanced equipment, and from what I understand, it was contact with Addie that put him into his coma."

"It was. I've seen the report. It was back in the sixties, if I recall correctly," said Secretary Bennett, eyes locked on the terminal.

"That's right," agreed Josh, "but let's backtrack a little first. Seaman Shultz had been at the Dilorenzo Tricare Health Sector of the Pentagon for over twenty years. He was a fixture there. No family, really. He wasn't dead, still breathing on his own, heart beating, eating through a feeding tube. He's still like that."

"I know all of that already. What about the spikes, Mr. Allen?"

"Just hear me out," Josh continued, undeterred. "Or better yet, let's take a look at Shultz." Josh minimized the window with the spikes. He pulled up the video feed from Seaman Shultz's room and zoomed in on the man's face. "Does he look fifty years old to you?"

Not a wrinkle showed on the patient's face. He was in need of his daily shave, but the stubble was jet black, not a gray hair in the mix. No muscle tone, clearly, as his only exercise came from the physical therapist who stopped in twice a day to manipulate his body.

"He looks newly enlisted," said the Secretary, taking the mouse over from Josh and zooming in even further. "What does this have to do with the spikes?"

"After they had realized it was more than just good genes at Dilorenzo, they started testing to see what was keeping his cell reproduction from slowing down as happens in the normal aging process. This research was transferred to our facility, and we picked up where they had left off. We noticed the spikes as an incidental finding, and then the weird part started." Josh paused and took a breath. "Every time there was an increase in a certain frequency put out by Addie, the mark on Shultz's forehead would darken. The only physiological process that would cause this is a rush of blood to the vessels feeding this mark."

Secretary Bennett zoomed in even further to see the mark on Shultz's forehead. Without the rush of blood flow to the area, it was almost undetectable. He waited, and then, there it was. As blood rushed to the area, a blotchy shape stood out more clearly against Shultz's naturally ruddy complexion.

"Do I understand, Mr. Allen, that this forehead phenomenon began before moving Shultz here, without his being in proximity to Addie?"

"Yes, sir, but it has synchronized exactly with her rhythms since he arrived."

Josh took his mouse back, clicked, then dragged and dropped Addie's graph on top of the patient's. The timeline on the x-axis was a match and Secretary Bennett could see the overlapping spikes.

"See how these two graphs are a perfect match when the mark darkens?"

"They've been watching this for a while," admitted Colonel Walker, joining the other two crowded around the computer screen.

"Exactly how long have you been *watching* this?" Bennett asked Colonel Walker tersely.

"I don't know too much about any of this," Walker said. "I'm a weapons guy. With multiple battalions under my command here at Saguaro, I have little time for the lab. When this Addie thing is classified as a weapon, I'll make time."

"Just to make things abundantly clear," Secretary Bennett cleared his throat. "This project, testing, and learning from this *Addie thing,* is of great interest to the President. He wants to continue to be informed of her status on a regular and current basis."

Secretary Bennett turned and walked away from the screen and over to the second set of metal doors flanked by guards. "Is she in here?" It had been several years since he'd laid eyes on Addie.

"Yes, sir." The Colonel walked quickly past Secretary Bennett and once again placed his palm on a scanner, admitting them both to the inner lab where Addie had been housed for the past few years, ever since floor S32 had been completed.

There she was, suspended weightlessly in a massive tank, never changing, eternally peaceful, or at least seemingly so. She, or he, floated, wrapped in a translucent bubble that encapsulated a homogeneous fluid with a slightly purple cast. Addie was essentially just an amorphous shape with no discernable features.

Secretary Bennett stared at her until his eyes relaxed, and he was completely captivated. Her form had a beginning and an end, at least most of the time. She easily slipped from one density to another within her bubble, sometimes a solid, other times a wisp, but most times somewhere in between. As Secretary of Defense, it was his job to take nothing at face value, least of all Addie.

Since her discovery, it had been too easy to be slowly lulled into a state of non-expectation. At times, Bennett had wondered whether this was even an entire being. Had they been guarding a piece of cosmic dandruff or the equivalent of a pet rock? On the other more dangerous hand, could she be a swirling Trojan horse, a surveillance sentinel, or an undetonated bioweapon? Addie certainly wasn't telling. In nature, color equaled danger. The bright and beautiful would never be eaten. In Addie's world, where did she fall on this spectrum?

If only Shultz would wake up, maybe he would have some answers; but all efforts at revival had failed again and again. The newly discovered correlation between Addie and Shultz was the first documentation of an influence by the creature brought on by something other than physical touch, and Bennett didn't like it.

The click of the security lock brought Bennett out of this trance as the metal door opened, admitting Dr. Ross. "Secretary Bennett."

The two men shook hands. "Back from lunch?"

"Yes, sir." The novelty of Addie had never worn off for Dr. Ross. To him, she was not just a job or a research tool. She was his life.

Before engaging the Secretary with any further conversation, Dr. Ross inspected certain levels in the tank that registered in green on a digital screen. All the values were within range. Everything in the tank was monitored down to the lowest concentrations of ions measured in parts per billion. Only the infamous Dr. Ross could get away with completely ignoring the Secretary of Defense while he did this. Truthfully, there was no need for his personal touch as the computers ran these *checks* continuously, sending out warnings for any values approaching the outer limits of their ranges, but the doctor could not help himself. Addie was everything to him.

"I'd like to see Seaman Shultz." Bennett requested.

Ross stepped away from the tank, but not before he took one last look at Addie's levels. "I'll take you to him."

Seaman Shultz was housed in an adjoining room, looking just as he had thirty years ago. "Unbelievable." Bennett drew close to the patient.

"I agree." Ross also neared Shultz's bedside. "If we could only find out what's going on at a molecular level within his cells...what's sustaining this level of cellular reproduction. He's basically frozen in time. If we could come up with a way to generate this same anti-aging effect, we would be billionaires."

"What about this new correlation with the marking on this man's forehead, Doctor?"

"Josh has already filled you in?" asked Ross.

"Only that it happens. Let's go over the rest."

"Well, like Josh probably explained, it was an incidental finding. We monitor everything surrounding Addie; magnetic fields, frequencies, light, air pressure, ions and minerals in the water, everything."

"He said it had something to do with a frequency?"

"That's right, Secretary. It's an electromagnetic frequency. This we know, but it's unlike any other that has ever been documented. Right now, we have charged our team with developing a way to interpret the signature properly. We don't even have a means by which to measure it, and nothing falls within any measurable possibilities to date." Ross sighed and said, "we have an idea of what we're looking for but no instrument with which to measure it. We're working hard to create this advanced technology."

"So, is this visit about Addie or more R & D funding?" The Secretary raised his eyebrows. It always boiled down to money in Bennett's experience.

"Both. They're directly related."

"Well then, I'll see what the President wants to do," said Secretary Bennett, noting the time on his watch, again. "I'm glad to have seen everything with my own eyes, though. There are some things that can't be digested from reading a report."

"That there are." Dr. Ross conceded. "We're definitely making progress. With more funding..."

Bennett cut him off. "You know what to do. Have a report to me this week with the time frame, engineering outline, and projected costs. I'll be meeting with the President."

Before heading back to the surface with Colonel Walker, Bennett pulled Dr. Ross aside and handed him a business card. "My personal cell number is on the back. Do not go up the chain. Call me directly the next time Addie or Seaman Shultz exhibit anything unusual. Understood?"

"Understood, sir." Dr. Ross stood and watched as the two men drove off down the petrous corridor.

CHAPTER 11

The unknown is such a relative term.

The three finally caught up with each other at the Parkersville Knights Inn. Thanks to Ray, Ed and Barry would be waiting for Patrick when he returned to his home away from home. It had been a long time since Ed had done something like this on his own. As the Secretary of Energy, he always seemed to have people, but he wanted to keep this low profile. Patrick was also an old friend.

It hadn't been difficult to open the door to room twelve. Ed had managed using only his grocery store membership card. The security at small motels in the mountains of North Carolina was pretty much left up to the chain lock on the door once you were already inside.

"We don't want to scare him when he walks in," said Barry. "Should we wait in the bathroom?"

"He'll be startled either way, but I don't want to wait in a bathroom," Ed answered. "Who knows when he'll be back or where he went today."

The Secretary of Energy, lying in wait in a run-down motel in the middle of nowhere, Ed thought to himself. All thanks to his old college friend. The friend he had graciously brought into the department, the friend who couldn't leave well enough alone. Now, Ed knew too much to ignore it.

"He had to have gone somewhere documented in the files," Barry said matter-of-factly, taking out a pack of chips he bought at the airport. "You want some?"

"What kind?"

"Salt and vinegar." Barry crunched on the snack.

"No thanks," said Ed. "We should just wait here. All of his things are still here. He'll be back before he moves on."

"Want to watch something on TV?"

"Why not?" said Ed. He couldn't concentrate on anything, anyway. So, he left his laptop in his computer bag and turned toward the TV.

"What do you want to watch?"

"It doesn't matter, Barry. Watch whatever you want." Ed sat there staring blankly at the screen. Barry had turned to a local news station. They were still covering the harvesters and touting America's success in leading the world in the development of clean energy. *We'll see*, thought Ed.

Not far into the newscast, Ed heard the click of the lock, and the door opened. Patrick's eyes widened with surprise, seeing Ed and Barry camped out in his motel room. Ed wasn't sure if he was more shocked to find that his room was not empty, or shocked to see them in particular.

Before Patrick had a chance to close the door, Ed got up and walked toward him. "You were right. You were right the whole time, and I wouldn't listen. Ray not only told us where you were, he gave us a rundown on the cases you've been chasing. It was Barry who finally made me see it. Hell, he's the inventor and even he saw it before I would."

"It doesn't matter, Ed." Patrick sat down heavily in a threadbare chair. "It doesn't matter how or even why," Patrick continued. "Want to get some dinner?"

This wasn't what Ed had expected. They believed him. They were here to help. He didn't seem to care. Not even an *I told you so*, and how could he talk about dinner when there was so much that they needed to catch up on?

"They've got a Knights of the Roundtable dining room and the food isn't too bad," said Patrick.

"Did you hear what I said?" asked Ed. "We believe you."

"I heard you, Ed," Patrick said, with no hint of enthusiasm. "I'm sorry I didn't give you the type of reaction you were hoping for, but I'm exhausted. The leads, the strange happenings, the changes are never-ending. I just need food."

"Okay, then."

"To tell you the truth," said Patrick. "When I opened the door, I thought you had come to fire me."

"I could have done that with an e-mail," said Ed.

Patrick looked at Ed—his friend Ed, not the Secretary of Energy. "The difference between how you're feeling now and how I'm feeling is that I've been on the trail long enough to get used to all of this. You two still can't believe it's happening. So, what'll it be, his lordship's steak dinners or knight burgers?"

"Actually, I'm starved," Barry said, finishing the last of his chips. "A knight burger sounds okay to me."

"Me too, I guess." Ed thought about what Patrick had said about the information being new to him. It shouldn't have been. He should have listened to Patrick a long time ago. It had taken a flower sprouting eyes to convince him of what Patrick had been aware of this entire time. Ed couldn't believe it had taken him so long to see.

"We can call for room service," Patrick said. "But first, I'm going to take a shower. We'll talk after food. Why don't you guys start looking through some of the pictures I've taken. They're in the harvester file folder on the laptop." He grabbed clean clothes and headed into the bathroom.

While Ed and Barry clicked through the pictures on the computer, Patrick's shower ran on and on. By the time dinner arrived, Patrick appeared clean and much more relaxed, but Ed was wishing they'd waited until after dinner to go through the photos. They ate quickly in a relieved companionable silence, interrupted only occasionally by the crinkle of the paper wrapped around their burgers. As they moved through the cases, the reality of what they had done sank in deeper.

"It's not all your fault," Patrick assured him. "No one else would see it, either."

"It doesn't matter, Patrick. I've spent a lifetime trying to make people see unpleasant things that were staring them in the face. How could I have been the one to miss something this big?"

"You just did the wrong thing for the right reason. Stop beating yourself up," Barry broke in.

"No." Ed couldn't excuse himself that easily. "I did the wrong thing for the wrong reason. I wouldn't look, so I couldn't see. It didn't feel right even before we went nationwide, and I knew it somewhere on some level." Cracking his knuckles, he continued. "It felt wrong, but it *had* to be right." Ed's regret was written all over his face.

"Not true," Patrick disagreed with his friend. "I know you better than that. I'll give you stubborn, but not egotistical." His voice lowered with sincerity. "Ed, you don't know how good it is to be back on the same side again."

From an expansive upscale office at the DOE to the Knights Inn. Ed looked around at his two companions and the ugly green flowered decor. It reminded him of the late-night study sessions he and Patrick used to pull in college. They would spend all day supporting some cause on campus; save the whales, stop using pesticides, anything. Then, they would stay up all night to finish the school work they'd ignored all day. Pizza delivery and stale coffee had seen them through.

"Hey, I've got some good news," said Patrick, trying to lighten the mood. "I've narrowed it down further," he offered encouragingly. "All the reports I've been checking out have turned out to be near the larger relay harvesters. Apparently, it takes a lot of whatever the thing is putting out before it causes the changes I've been seeing. Unless there's also a cumulative effect, which would be the worst-case scenario."

"So, what are we talking about here, Patrick? Exactly what else have you seen?" Ed awaited his response, bracing himself for even more bad news.

"Only what's in the reports," said Patrick.

Ed let out the breath he had been holding in. The reports were bad enough.

"What about the cornfield?" asked Barry. "That would be a photosynthetic mutation—that is, if it were true. Was that report accurate?"

"Yes, and no." Patrick paused. "Yes, there *was* a giant cornfield in Four Corners, but no, it's not a giant cornfield anymore."

Looking at Patrick's face, Ed knew it meant trouble. "Did it die, or did they plow the thing under, or what?"

"No, it's still there, but just not a cornfield anymore. It's changed."

"Changed how?" asked Barry.

"It's not like anything you've ever seen before. The whole thing is a forest now, a forest out of some sci-fi movie. Here. Take a look."

Patrick scrolled through the file and enlarged a picture of a surreal lavender landscape. "This is Bobby Freeman's cornfield."

"I was afraid of that when we looked through them before," said Barry. "We need to find out what could be causing this, and why."

Barry leaned back on a pillow and his eyes lost focus as he retreated into thought. "I could possibly adjust the frequency output or modulation to stop whatever this is from happening. The process is affecting photosynthesis and mutational factors as well."

"What does that mean?" asked Patrick.

Barry didn't respond. It was as if he didn't hear the question at all. He began to sketch frequency bands and extrapolate calculations as the conversation continued around him.

Ed knew they had lost Barry. Maybe not for the whole night, but for the next few hours, at least. Barry's pen continued to fly as he generated page after page of formulas and equations.

"This coffee is about as bad as it was in college," said Patrick, walking over to the small complimentary coffee pot on the bathroom sink.

Ed nodded in agreement. "We'll find a solution. We have to." He looked over at Barry, still operating within his own mind.

By three a.m., Barry had filled half a journal with cryptic notes. "We've got no choice." Barry suddenly said aloud. "If they're causing so much trouble, they'll just have to be shut off."

Ed could see that Barry was upset by the possibility of his invention causing such anomalies. He was losing his objectivity. "Look, Barry," Ed started, "mathematical calculations on paper are one thing, but the ramifications of a shut-down are also unknown at this point."

Ed let this thought hang in the air. "What will happen to the chemical and biologic structures that have already begun to change if the harvesters are suddenly turned off? It could get worse."

"It's the only way," Barry continued blithely, "or maybe just shut off the large relays and replace them with the smaller ones that don't seem to be bothering anyone."

"Yet," said Patrick, "they don't seem to be bothering anyone *yet*. Maybe the smaller ones just take longer to affect things. We've already discussed the possible cumulative results. In that case, this whole thing could get a lot worse before it gets better. Maybe we should shut them all off."

"It sounds like a good idea, but we can't count on anything," said Ed. "And I'm not just trying to salvage this project. I've already put my career in jeopardy by being here. From a professional standpoint, I could be screwed, but I've been driven by causes before."

"We still have to know," Barry asserted. "It could be either the solution we hope for or the disaster we dread, but don't we have to know one way or the other? If it's not too late to turn off nationally and cut our losses, don't we have to try?"

"I think Barry is right," said Patrick. "We don't know what's going to happen to the compounds and molecules that have already been affected, but it may not be too late to save what hasn't been compromised yet."

"How do we know that anything has been untouched?" Ed asked. "In any of the output reports I've ever read, we have never isolated a certain distance that would render anything out of the path of a harvester's frequencies, even the smaller ones."

Ed knew he was right, but Barry was also right. The problem was that they all knew too much and not nearly enough. It was an impossible position. Still, Ed knew he would need to see firsthand the things that he had been told, the things he had been reading about in the reports. Somehow, he thought, seeing these things could bring the solution into sharper focus. Maybe then he would know what to do. But for now, it was getting too late to process anything else. His brain was overloaded and his eyes were red from fatigue.

"Guys," said Ed. "I can't do any more of this right now. I need some sleep."

"Fine," said Barry. "Are we all in agreement? We'll start with Mabel Claire tomorrow morning?"

"All right," Patrick said, shutting his laptop. He lay down on the bed. "So, did you guys get another room?"

"Yes," said Ed. "We have the two rooms on either side of yours. What do you say we all meet at eight-thirty?"

"I'll see you guys at eight-thirty in the parking lot," Barry confirmed, walking out the door.

Ed didn't know if he would be able to sleep even in his present state of exhaustion, but he had to try before their trip tomorrow. "Good night," he said, and shut the door to room twelve.

Their drive out to Mabel Claire Mabrey's took them through the Smoky Mountains—lush, green, and towering on all sides. They drove winding roads, following ridges and curves, eventually climbing through the pass.

"This would be breathtaking if we were here for any other reason," Patrick said, manipulating the car around curves in the road. "I'm glad to have you guys along."

"I can't say that I'm glad to be here," responded Ed. "I woke up this morning hoping it was all a bad dream. I knew it wasn't when I turned over and saw neon light flashing around the edges of the curtains."

Ed looked out of the passenger's side window at a scar running through the valley and up the opposite mountainside. Trees had been cleared to make way for now obsolete power lines strung like rows of stitches through an incision. What filled Ed's heart with lead was the huge harvester planted at the crest of the mountain, fully extended and doing exactly what it was meant to do. *What have we done?* He kept this question to himself, knowing that Barry had the same view from his window in back.

"I hate driving without GPS," said Patrick.

This jolted Ed back to the task at hand. He remembered that there would be no Google Maps issuing directions on where to turn. He vaguely remembered a time in his teens when GPS technology was not widely used, but that was decades past.

"Hey, Barry," Ed called to the back seat.

"Yeah?" said Barry. "What's up?"

"How's the navigating going?" asked Ed, looking into the side-view mirror, trying to make eye contact with the scientist.

Barry grabbed the map from the center seat and turned it right side up. "Where did you get these maps? They look outdated."

"Just take into account what's been marked in pen," said Patrick. "Not too much has changed on these roads since the nineties."

Barry held the map up with two hands. "We should be there soon," he said. "There's a turn coming up. It looks like a small road, though. We're looking for a dirt or gravel drive."

A solid hour had passed as all three men scanned the road's edges for a driveway that Ray had said would be marked by a mailbox with chipping white paint on the post.

"I think we missed it," said Barry.

"You think?" said Ed with a dash of anger in his voice.

"What if we turn around now and it's just around the next curve? We could drive back and forth all day," said Patrick, keeping his eyes on the mountain roads.

"Let me see the map." Ed turned around and extended his hand to the back seat. Barry handed it over. Ed could see that he was more than happy to relinquish his role as navigator. "Okay." Ed held up the map, reacquainting himself with this antiquated method of travel. "We just need to look ahead and see if we pass any of the big markers, like crossroads, before we turn around to search for the mailbox tucked into miles of trees."

They *had* missed it, by about ninety miles. "Look, there's route 32," said Ed. "We want to be back here somewhere." He turned to Patrick. "Turn around whenever you get a chance." *Damn, there was so little time as it was. At least they'd noticed their error before hitting the state line.*

"That cabin has to be hers," Patrick informed his travel companions with certainty. "The road dead ends, and there hasn't been another building since we left the main highway."

Ed was not pleased. It had taken them all day to get there. They didn't have that kind of time to waste, but they couldn't risk turning on their phones and being tracked. He knew he couldn't introduce any negativity into this already anxious group, so he took a few calming breaths while Patrick parked the car.

All three got out and Ed led the group up to the faded screen door, but after several minutes, there was still no response to his loud knocking.

"Either she's not home, or something's wrong, Ed." Patrick shifted restlessly beside the other two.

"Where would she go? There's nothing around for miles." Barry noted, as he turned away from the door and scanned the area in all directions.

"Besides, it's getting dark." Patrick agreed.

"Wait a minute, we're forgetting why we're here," Barry's voice was hushed, and his eyes were staring like they were going to fall out of his head. "Look!" He pointed to the lighted field far beyond the car. "There she is!"

Ed had read all about it, and had been preparing himself all day to see it, but still he couldn't believe his own eyes. There, in the neighboring field, surrounded by a cloud of flashing June bugs, floated the woman they had come to see. And if floating had not been enough, she was emitting light as if she were the queen June bug with her arms stretched out and her face turned toward the approaching night sky.

Slowly, they all walked through the high, wet grass toward the darkening field closest to the house. The meadow twinkled with the lights of a thousand fireflies, and there, in the middle of it all, was Mabel Claire. Next to her, was a huge relay harvester.

Ed looked up at Ms. Mabel. He had to shield his eyes as he introduced himself. "I'm Ed, and these are my co-workers. We're from the Department of Energy, ma'am." Ed paused, but Ms. Mabel paid him no mind. It was like she couldn't even hear him. He waited, looking up, still holding his hand above his eyes like a visor. Then she spoke.

"Sit a spell. Just let me finish this dance."

And that's exactly what she did. The woman floated down and allowed her feet to skim the earth. Then, glowing like a hundred-watt bulb, she hopped, skipped and danced for a solid fifteen more minutes before her light went out and she approached her three visitors.

This Mabel Claire sure didn't move like an eighty-year-old woman, Ed thought admirably. Just watching her made him feel tired, and he worked out three times a week.

"Thanks for waitin'. 'Bout the time you're eighty, it's hard to hurry through certain things, and young people lose patience so fast."

"You were doing some strenuous activity for someone who's eighty, Ms. Mabrey," said Barry, with his eyes fixed on the elderly woman, now standing next to the relay harvester.

"Call me Mabel Claire. It feels more comfortable."

"Certainly," Ed agreed, "but to be honest, I think we're all having a hard time believing what we've just seen."

"Does it hurt, Mabel Claire? Do you get hot to the touch? Can you control it?" Barry was blurting out questions, leaving no time for her to answer them.

"See for yourself."

Mabel Claire turned on her inner power. "In the beginning, I couldn't control it, but now I can. Just took some practice, but then I've got a lot o' time. Feel my arm, son." Mabel Claire held up a withered, softly glowing arm.

"It doesn't feel any different to me, ma'am," said Barry, "but how does it feel to you... on the inside?"

"Good question," and her eyes sparkled. Mabel Claire's arm had almost become too bright to look at without sunglasses. "Feel any different to you now?"

"No, ma'am, still feels the same. It only looks different."

"That first night I sat right down on a pile of old leaves to see if they'd catch fire, but they didn't. The next night I filled a bath and got right in, clothes and all, just to see what would happen, but I only got wet. Even took my temperature, and believe you me, I was some kind o' worried 'bout whether the thermometer was goin' to explode, but I was still 98.6, never changed one lil' bit."

Suddenly, she seemed more thoughtful. "I thought the Lord had big plans for me, but I suppose it's just this big ol' energy thing, or else you wouldn't be here now, would you?"

"No, ma'am, we wouldn't," Ed had to admit. He saw how disappointed she was that none of it had been a religious experience, after all.

"Sometimes I wished it never happened."

"Maybe if we shut off the harvester, you'd be the way you were before." The words tumbled out of Barry's mouth.

What had possessed him? Ed was angry and trying not to show it. After all, Barry was grasping at straws. They'd have to get him back to Washington. He'd be much better suited to lab work at this point.

"Or not." Patrick followed up quickly. "You might *not* be the way you were before."

Ed could have strangled Barry. They'd discussed it and come to a joint decision, but it certainly hadn't been to ask Mabel Claire Mabrey to be their guinea pig.

"Believe it or not, I've been thinkin' a lot about it myself," Mabel Claire admitted freely. "Somehow, I still want to think that God makes me glow, not this overgrown mechanical weed, but I can't be sure the way things are."

"It could be dangerous for you, ma'am. We can't lie to you." Patrick informed her.

"What d'you think has kept me from it, young man? I'm eighty, but I'm not a dumb woman, and I'd rather be eighty-one than dead."

"Yes, ma'am," the three men agreed with her. *Let her talk it out,* Ed thought. Then he motioned with his hands for the other two to keep quiet. There was no good choice here, but if it was something she'd already thought about...

"Guess this might just be as good a time as any. If I lost the gift, I surely would miss it. Forgot to tell you that even though the light doesn't make me hot to the touch, it does do something. It makes me feel forty years younger. When I glow, boys, I step higher and faster than I have in years, and my body doesn't pain me either. Yup, I'd miss it, but if this isn't a gift from my sweet Jesus, I'm not sure I want it, anyway. Guess I'd be just as proud to be plain ol' Mabel Claire again. You may as well turn it off, boys."

"Wait. Everybody wait," said Ed. "What are we talking about here? We need to be very clear.

"Ms. Mabel, you need to tell me in as many words that this is what you want, for us to turn off the harvester, that is." Ed reached out and took her hands in his. "You may go back to the way you were before, but we don't know what else could happen. What I'm saying is that the outcome *could* be anything, up to and including death."

"I may be from the country, Ed, is it? But I'm not stupid," she assured him. "I know this ain't normal. I don't know if it's science or the devil, but I lose myself near that machine. Getting on in years, I can't lose myself. I have to have clarity when I meet my sweet Jesus. If I'm lost in my lighted trance, I don't think I could pass on to the promised land. You boys hav'ta try."

"Are you sure this is what you want?" asked Ed, narrowing his eyes. This was an impossible situation. All human life had value, but just as Mabel Claire had said, she was at the end of her life and they needed to know what happens when a harvester is turned off. This relay harvester only seemed to be affecting one individual. In a way, they were sparing more lives by taking only the one, but she might not die when they flipped the switch. Death would be the very worst-case scenario. Shit. How did they find themselves in this situation? No. He couldn't go down that road again. Focus, he told himself. The only time that mattered was now. He could change none of his past actions. This brave woman deserved his full attention. She was the one risking everything.

"Barry, I don't see the switch," Patrick said. "Aren't there usually boxes on the sides of these things?" Patrick was walking in circles around the base of the harvester.

"The switch is inlaid and passcode protected for obvious reasons," Barry said. He walked up to the harvester and punched in his passcode. "Only a handful of people nationwide have a code, and every code is unique. So, if anyone is looking for us, this is going to give us away."

A small door slid open, revealing a second keypad. Barry looked up at the group. "I feel that turning the machine off is the right thing, but I want to be sure that you all are okay with this, especially you, Mabel Claire. Take as long as you like and let me know when you're ready." Barry had not yet touched the actual keypad.

"There's no need to drag this out, son. I've already said my prayers. I'm ready now."

Patrick had backed away from the harvester and stood alongside Ed, who was still holding onto Mabel Claire's hand. He let her hand drop, and they both backed up a few paces. This technology was so new and there were seemingly endless effects that they had not predicted. Would taking a few steps back make any difference? Should they have separated themselves by miles, or was there any safe distance to do what they were about to do? That was the problem—no one knew. At least they would have the answer to one question after the harvester was turned off.

As Ed stood there thinking of everything that could happen, he felt different. Looking down, he saw his fingernails reflect the glow of the incandescent woman not three feet from him. Or was it a reflection? The light seemed to come from within, rather than without. Ridiculous, he thought, and shoved his hands into his pockets. Then he heard it. A few bars of some strange song echoed through his head in the very brief moments before Barry finally did it—something about an egg hatching.

When the harvester turned off, so did Mabel Claire Mabrey, and so did every firefly for miles. The old woman simply went dark and fell over. Hundreds of lightning bugs likewise went dark and fell from the sky, and all of this happened in a split second. The meadow that had been brimming with swirling lights abruptly plunged into a deep and quiet darkness.

"Good God, she just fell over." Barry was in a panic. "Where is she? Is she all right? Mabel Claire! Ma'am, Mrs. Mabrey!" He scrambled towards the small, prone figure, stumbling in the blackness.

Ed and Patrick were kneeling by the still woman's side, feeling for a pulse, but there wasn't one. "She's gone, Barry."

"Wait! If I turn it back on, maybe she'll be all right," Barry pleaded.

"It's worth a try." The other two voices drifted through the darkness on a cloud of fear.

Barry quickly found his way back to the harvester. He punched in his code again and hit enter. "Anything?" he called out.

"Nothing. Even the damn bugs aren't moving," Patrick called back. He turned to Ed. "I'll call 911."

"I'll take her inside while you call, but then we have to leave." This was a hard decision for Ed to make. "If we try to explain what happened, people will panic. Not that it won't be obvious soon enough, but most people haven't started putting it all together."

"Or, they won't believe us at all," said Patrick. "Think about it. We only know what we know because of our call line and the digging that Ray has done. To anyone else, this might look like a homicide. Do the three of us look like we belong here?" Patrick gestured to their surroundings.

Barry gently transported Mabel Claire's head and torso. Ed carried her feet while Patrick called it in. Ed reasoned that they would have at least thirty minutes before any emergency vehicles would arrive this far out in the country. He knew calling 911 would do Mabel Claire no good. They had called to make themselves feel better about what had happened. Ed knew the human brain could not survive longer than a few minutes without oxygen.

"Does anyone know CPR?" asked Barry. "We should try to revive her."

"I agree," said Patrick, entering the living room.

The deeply shaken men carefully lowered the old woman onto her worn couch.

"Let's try," said Ed, feeling a considerable amount of guilt. "Compressions and breaths, right?" He began pushing on her chest while Barry pinched her nose and administered the breaths.

They worked on her for a solid fifteen minutes, to no avail. Then, they really had to go.

"Thank you, Mabel Claire, and I'm sorry," Barry whispered as they left.

Driving on the mountain roads was harder at night. There were no street lights. "It's like I was saying at Mabel Claire's," said Patrick. "We only know the extent of the statistics ourselves because of our tip line information, but I'll guarantee you that most people would still rather believe their problem is something they ate, or a new prescription playing with their mind. They only call us as a last resort, and their problems aren't things they want to share with someone else just yet."

Ed thought about the files he had read from the call-ins that Patrick was describing. "I know it's dark, but it's not that late. As long as we're out here and before law enforcement connects our passcode to the harvester near Mabel Claire, we should go to the Freeman Farm."

"I don't know if I can do that tonight, Ed," said Barry, his voice shaking. "I just killed an innocent woman. Let's just pick up our stuff and go home."

"We all knew the possibilities," said Ed, "and death was one of them. Even Mabel Claire understood that. Besides, we needed to find out how a power outage would affect people, not just cornfields."

The lesser evil for the greater good? Ed was disgusted with himself. It certainly wasn't the kind of slogan he'd ever lived by, but everything was changing these days, and fast.

"Do you think that local law enforcement will even connect the harvester to her death?" asked Patrick with his eyes on the road. "I think it's highly unlikely. There are no physical wounds to suggest any assault, and the woman was in her eighties. I don't think that a small town has the means or the want to investigate this situation too deeply."

"Let's hope you're right," said Ed, staring out of the passenger side window into the dark woods flying by. "We'll find out when we arrive back in Washington."

"What kind of person do you think she was?" asked Barry.

Ed could tell that this was going to be an ongoing issue with Barry. It was sad—tragic, but there was a lot more at stake than just one old woman. He didn't know how much more there would be or how it would ultimately present, but he could feel in his gut that this might just be the beginning. Suffocating in the cramped rental car, they drove back to the motel, packed up, and checked out. Afterwards, the three drove through the night like the devil was chasing them, hitting Washington shortly before daybreak.

CHAPTER 12

Life's spark is elusive, its essence is not.

The number of incidents has been grossly underestimated. Does anyone have any explanations?" Ed looked to the room, not really expecting an answer.

No one around the conference table made a sound. What should they say? What could anyone possibly say to make it better? Something had gone wrong with the harvesters.

Hard as it was, now was the time for the truth, and Ed was prepared to be direct. This conference room held the best of the best. That's why he'd summoned them to the meeting. He had run everything by the President, who had approached him about Barry's passcode having been entered into the relay harvester in North Carolina. Miraculously, he had not been fired. President Morgan agreed with him about the gravity of the situation and Ed was now charged with damage control for the project he had spearheaded.

"We were wrong, very wrong," Ed continued. "I was wrong. The statistics are too overwhelming to be coincidence any longer."

He tried to make eye contact with every person at the table. "There is a correlation between the harvesters and the strange things happening to more and more people."

If some of the reports were correct, and Ed now knew they were, he had the feeling that what they'd already seen was only the beginning. "If each of you would please open the folder in front of you, we'll get started."

In the eerily quiet room, Ed watched with grim fascination as eleven rapidly paling men and women read through their reports from beginning to end. Even after they were through, no one said a word. Not a throat was cleared, not even the occasional nervous laugh. Instead, one by one, they looked up and focused on the face of the Secretary of Energy, Ed Marker.

Troy Phillips from PR was the first to speak. "She really died?"

Ed solemnly nodded his head.

"But, Ed, things can only get worse if we don't get the harvesters' influence out of the picture. So, what if we can't shut down those big relay models? Couldn't we..." Troy's voice trailed off into thin air.

"Couldn't we substitute less damaging smaller models and replace the relay station?" It was Barry who finished Troy's statement for him. "We thought of that too, but we don't know whether the accumulated damage from smaller ones will eventually be the same. Maybe it will just take a longer time to have the same effect. It *could* buy us some time, but how much? Would it be any longer than the time it takes to build the smaller harvesters and replace the relays?"

Ed looked at Troy and could tell he was out of ideas. Give Troy a toxic waste dump or a radiation leak and he was one of the best in the business, but even he couldn't fight the unknown.

"There are factors at play here other than the harvester," said Ed. There was no way to soften any of the blows he had to deliver today. It would take too much time, and they had little enough of that as it was. "There has to be something else involved, because not everyone living or working near a relay harvester is affected—or at least not yet."

"Granted," Ed continued, "the harvester is the non-negotiable factor. It absolutely cannot be manipulated without terrible danger, and that leaves us only the human factors to deal with. What we need to do," encouraged Ed, "is to find the key variable, the one influencing susceptibility to the harvesters." Looking around the highly polished table, Ed could see his colleagues begin to process this new task.

"How can we determine what comes into play and what doesn't count? Is there a set of rules or an algorithm that can help to guide us?" asked Evelyn from the Public Health Department.

"The only thing we have at our disposal, unfortunately, is the process of elimination. Today, I'm going to make 'starting point' assignments. They're the most obvious places to begin, but if your research leads you down a different path—feel free to redirect. Let me know for sure, but go with it. Hopefully, our instincts are going to take us in the right direction."

Ed had never held such undivided attention in his life, but he was too preoccupied to appreciate it. "I've got at least one assignment here for everyone. Remember, the priority is to find out which group of people is being affected and, more importantly, why." Ed paused and sent an e-mail with the breakdown of job assignments to everyone in the room.

"Oh, and I don't think I need to stress the importance of the security around this issue. To let any of this out now would be needlessly cruel. At this point, we can't help anyone, and a leak might start a panic that would make it impossible to study the actual demographics involved in our problem. If people break from their normal routines in a panic situation, what parameters will we have left?"

Patrick discreetly cleared his throat and eyed his boss meaningfully. Realizing that Patrick wanted to address the group, Ed was more than relieved to hand the discussion over to anyone who could offer something constructive to the meeting.

"Ed, you forgot to mention the public service announcements," Patrick reminded gently.

"Oh, you're right." As it was, Ed felt lucky to have remembered as much as he had. "Go ahead and fill everyone in." Ed sat down and gave Patrick his full attention.

Patrick was well prepared, as usual. "We'll have to issue something like a product warning. Not that many people would have a reason to turn off their harvesters, any more than they would have turned off the electricity going into their homes."

"But once people start to connect their strange happenings with the harvesters, there *will* most likely be a number of people trying to turn them off," said Evelyn. "What type of announcement specifically could we issue to deter *this*?"

Patrick acknowledged Evelyn's question with a nod and continued. "The power system is password protected." He paused and took a sip from his full bottle of water. "But, in this information age, everyone has access to ever-evolving technology which could potentially pinpoint passwords. This announcement would have to detail possible physical harm to those who might power off a harvester. It would have to be severe enough to dissuade any rogue hackers with this agenda."

"Also," Evelyn continued, "we cannot discount any foul play from those of us within secure organizations, or those organizations that we assume are secure." She leaned back in her conference chair, waiting for another one of her colleagues to weigh in on her point.

"Exactly," said Patrick. "We have elevated the government clearance level necessary to qualify for a power shut down passcode. We have also implemented a system where the passcodes are changed every twenty-four hours."

From halfway down the table, Henry, their chief statistical analyst, cleared his throat and tentatively spoke up. "The beauty of the harvester was its simplicity, remember? Clean, safe, and limitless energy."

"We all have to let that line of thinking go." Ed took the reins again. "I know what I'm about to say is abrupt and may be unfair, but it's very necessary. I am asking anyone still in denial to please get up and leave. No hard feelings, but we don't have time to convince any of you of the truths that we have just discussed. You're either in or you're out. There's no in-between. There can only be definitive action from this point on, because none of us knows exactly what might happen next or how long we may have to solve this problem." Ed glanced around the table and no one moved to get up.

"Fine then," said Ed. "You all have ten minutes to put together the warning. It will have to be carefully worded, possibly involving a discovered mechanical problem or something similar. As we have discussed, they won't be the actual dangers, but must be convincing and potentially life-threatening. The alternative is unacceptable."

Ed slowly looked up and down the conference table. "I can't tell America what I've told you today. We have to know more. We have to buy ourselves some time. The cumulative effects of the small harvesters may surface soon. In that case, the problems will begin in North Carolina. We'll need to be looking there first."

"What kind of window are we expecting?" It was Henry again.

"We," Ed spread his arms wide, "have no expectations whatsoever. Things could begin to crop up this afternoon, or maybe nothing concrete will surface for months. If we're lucky, we will learn enough from those already affected to help those who aren't, at least temporarily."

Ed clutched the brief notations he'd made on torn sheets of paper just before the meeting as though they were life preservers. "I want you all to live and breathe possible commonalities until we find them. Any help you need—you've got it. Any clearances you need—you've got them, too. The only thing you haven't got is time. We meet again in person in three days, and I'd rather have some answers even before then."

"We'll start with the census database," said Patrick, "the largest collection of demographic information in the country." Patrick brought up the census site and typed in his passcode. "With a new layout of the site, I can filter and manipulate the data to compare any of the measured traits against geographic locations."

"Great! Now, Troy," Ed directed again. "You check all the environmentally hazardous locations near the relay harvesters and run an analysis to see if there is any connection between known, or little known, or even previously unknown sites. I've sent you case files as encrypted e-mail attachments. Dig, Troy, really dig."

"Right, Ed," Troy looked up. "The only thing is, the huge relay harvesters sit nowhere near any questionably hazardous locations. Our office had been under strict orders, scouting and assigning locations for them. We didn't want any bad publicity linking environmental damage to the harvesters. Even if it was pre-existing environmental damage, the press would still have found some way to blame it on the new technology."

"Check anyway," asserted Ed. "We're in the situation we're in right now because mistakes were made, even though the plan was considered flawless at its inception. Mistakes happen. Run the analysis."

Troy nodded in agreement, saying nothing else.

"Fine then." Ed needed no more push back. Now was not the time to argue, but the time for action. He redirected his attention down the table. "Evelyn, I'd like to put you at the National Institutes of Health until further notice. We're pulling in as many affected people as possible for extensive testing."

"Not a problem," said Evelyn, packing her computer up in the case as she spoke. "I'd like to suggest that all of us and our immediate family members have basic physicals and labs run as a baseline because of our anticipated exposure to whatever we end up finding."

"Great idea," Ed agreed, "and please remember that your resources are unlimited. If there is any equipment you need that you don't have, call me. There won't be any forms to fill out or red tape to navigate. Whatever you need will be bought and shipped immediately."

"I'll remember that, Ed," she said, turning to walk out of the conference room. "I'll be in touch if I even think there might be something."

Since Ed was moving around the table one seat at a time, Barry was next.

"Barry. Barry!" Ed was calling the man back from somewhere else, and could only hope Barry was bringing some answers back with him.

"Sorry, Ed. You were saying?"

"I just wanted to let everyone here know that you'll be running experiments from every angle you can think of. Any thoughts yet?" He scanned Barry's face.

"Not yet. I really haven't gotten it all up and rolling. If I could find a new slant, some way I haven't looked at it before, it would help." He looked up and down the table. "Also, I'm sorry. It wasn't supposed to turn out like this."

No one spoke, and Ed did not respond verbally to Barry's apology. There was no time for sentiment or for looking back. Continuing right on around the table, Ed doled out an assignment at the Bureau of Environmental Control to the next two candidates. "Who knows, maybe the deciding factors are environmental in origin," he encouraged.

Ed next addressed the men in uniform from the Department of Defense. They had been sitting in silence for the duration of the meeting, having been briefed on the situation already before driving up from the Pentagon. "I know that you've received instructions on how to proceed already, and I won't even pretend to know how to direct you on military strategy. I only wanted to have the military presence here so that in case it's needed, you will have been fully informed from day one. We must all be as prepared as possible for whatever comes next."

"We're already prepared for anything, Secretary Marker," said the Commandant of the Marine Corps.

Ed waited for more from the Defense representatives, but that was all he got. "Well then, I guess that's it for right now. Don't forget, today is Monday. I want us all back here at eight Thursday morning." Ed reminded the group. "Keep in touch. Check in with me every day, even if you think you have nothing to report. It could tie in with someone else's information. Good luck."

Ed was pretty well wiped out, considering that he'd gone without any sleep for more than twenty-four hours. What could be happening with the harvesters? His mind kept running round and round the question. Was it meteorites? Could it be gas escaping from geologic faults? God only knew, because he certainly didn't, and there were so many directions to exhaust.

Friday morning, Ed sat at his desk scanning the list of reports which had continually come in. Nothing, nothing, NOTHING!! he thought dismally. They'd all reported back all right, just as he'd asked, but no one had anything much to report. No breakthroughs or brainstorms, only the fading hope that someone had been luckier than themselves. Today would no doubt be more of the same. Ed fumbled with a small package of liquid Coffee-mate and spilled it on his shirt. The pressure was mounting everywhere, even his fingertips.

• • •

The ancient probe was buried and unearthed many times over. The ground beneath its ever unmarked hull buckled and dropped, only to be elevated again and again as surface tectonic pressures were released. At last, the planet's mantle stabilized, and this exorbitantly expensive probe found a final resting place hidden beneath sand and clay, later shaded by lengthening shadows from distant buttes and cactus sentinels.

Its tanks were empty after the successful dispersion of its long-ago cargo. The ship itself remained in pristine and perfect working condition, even after millennia. The alien matter introduced so long ago was in place, tiny intruders poised for their chance to shape and surprise, mold and manipulate, still waiting.

Then one day, a new frequency band was carried on soft warm breezes, a frequency created by the planet's newly discovered energy source. This new energy modulation awakened the sleepers, and they flexed their pre-programmed, primordial powers. This world, however, was no longer primordial, and they had not yet been a part of its powerful creative forces as planned. Instead, they were now part of a mutational process. So strong was their inherent persistence that the very stability of the planet's substance and life forms were gradually compromised, changing until they began to resemble that which had been intended from the very beginning, that which had been demanded of them from their inception, entertainment and the unexpected.

CHAPTER 13

FRANK DODD
Atlanta, Georgia

Wearing an out-of-date linen suit, Frank Dodd pored over the figures before him. Hunched, squat, and unimposing, he knew others disregarded him completely. Who cared? He was a numbers man, and rightfully proud of his twenty years at the Census Bureau. He had been promoted to the Atlanta Regional office two years ago. With a quickness born out of fanaticism, Frank evenly buffed all the exposed parts of his desk.

Damn, it had happened again! Frank broke from his reverie to stare in horror at a familiar scrawl, the words screaming up at him from the top sheet of paper on his desk. THE EGG IS HATCHING, FRANK! WHAT DO YOU REALLY SEE?

What did he see? Nothing! Hell, he didn't even remember writing it. But Frank *had* written those same words repeatedly, and he knew it, whether he could remember doing it or not. There was no mistaking such precisely correct penmanship. Day after day, he'd been finding these sentences staring up at him, but even more disquieting was the gift that seemed to have come with them. What was happening to him, he agonized quietly.

Carol, from the cubicle beyond his, was coming his way. Shit! Frank quickly covered his mystery phrases with a nearby Kleenex box. If she had any idea of the man Frank was becoming, the snooty bitch would never snub him as she did. She passed him without saying a word and made no attempt at friendly eye contact.

I'm becoming a mathematician!!, Frank screamed silently after the departing shapely figure. "Ah, forget it," he mumbled, and began to re-stack an already organized pile of papers. No, he was no longer a mere statistician. Most people couldn't appreciate the difference between the two, but he knew *one* discovered new worlds, and *the other* moved in later to take inventory. He took one last look at Carol. Damn, she was good-looking.

Adjusting the glasses on his nose helped to restore Frank's composure. He smoothed the rapidly multiplying wrinkles in his linen pants and redirected his thoughts back to work. His work, though, was not what it used to be. The speed and accuracy with which he made calculations could now rival a computer.

Frank quickly lifted the offensive paper from his desktop and placed it into his bottom drawer with the rest of them. Put it out of your mind, he told himself while placing several crisp, clean sheets of paper perpendicular to each other. Here it comes again. I can feel it happening, he thought in amazement as his right hand flashily transcribed amazing mathematical discoveries. New and unknown theorems, principals, and calculations poured from the tip of his favorite pen. He could see the interwoven patterns of black holes and wormholes. Time and space were to be manipulated, folded, and shaped like slick origami figures. After a solid hour, Frank's right hand was severely cramped. He rubbed the clenched muscles in his fingers until they began to unfold.

He'd show them all, those smug know-it-alls, if he could even believe it himself. What's the point, he thought sadly while packing up his notes. He was sick and tired of wasting time on things he couldn't show anyone else. He continued in his efforts to flatten the wrinkles in his pants as he rose to leave for the day. Finally, Frank cleared off his desk as he did at the end of every workday—everything in its place.

I'm either a genius or an idiot, he thought. If anyone else knew about his new capabilities, they'd either promote or fire him. Unfortunately, Frank had to admit he was ill-prepared for either.

He arrived home and microwaved his dinner before settling comfortably into his favorite seat in front of the TV. It was such a relief to block out everything but Jeopardy, except the noise from the relay harvester in the field next to his apartment building. Rubbing his ears until they were hot, he attempted to keep out the noise, that wretched noise nobody else could hear but him. Between his numbers and that damn noise, his head was so full that an explosion couldn't be far off, or more likely, a migraine. He spread a stained napkin on his lap and continued to eat his TV dinner in exquisite personal agony.

At work the next morning, a surprising request from the DOE and its accompanying files were sitting alone on his otherwise impeccably clean desktop. Knowing that he'd cleared his desk before leaving last night, as always, meant that whomever had left the paper on his desk must have been working late. "I didn't leave until seven-thirty," he mumbled, while picking up the note to read his assignment.

Odd, he thought, after re-reading the standard yellow Post-it note again. The bureau got requests for statistical information all the time, but this was not an everyday request.

> *Frank,*
> *Please study files for commonalities: jobs, locations, military service, health, etc. Gather data and report to me ASAP. Check your e-mail for your passcode.*
> *-Don*

Intrigued, Frank immediately logged onto his computer and scanned for the desired information. At first glance, the people in these files were just a random group. But they can't fool me, he thought with confidence, requesting access to the more personalized files for each.

I shouldn't be allowed access to information this confidential, he thought, as the true importance of this task became more and more apparent. A coded password? What was going on? Maybe someone had gotten wind of his new talents. No, he decided, he'd been too careful.

What a chase this was! Frank was invigorated as numbers, facts, and figures flew through his mind at a dangerous speed. Carol made her first pass by his workstation for the day, but he didn't even notice, and as always, she tried not to.

Frank was only supposed to be compiling the requested information, but it had gone past that now. I can't stop it, Frank thought in a panic, as he easily accessed his expanding computational skills.

Glowing numbers flew by on the computer screen, but Frank was way ahead of them. He sat in front of the console with his eyes closed to eliminate the distraction, and felt information sorting and falling like coins through a machine into millions of personalized informational slots.

So much for the false commonalties, thought Frank triumphantly, sweeping them aside with a mental wave of the hand. Any one of them could have kept investigators following false leads and blind alleys for weeks, but not him. Frank easily cut through the surface similarities, convincingly documented though they were, and saw beyond.

So, there's genealogy involved. He was fascinated by his discovery. The anomaly perpetuated genetically through these genealogies was so prevalent in the study population that Frank couldn't imagine what type of factor he could be tracing. Was it a disease, a sexual preference, or a predisposition to violence? He wondered curiously, knowing all the time that it was none of the above. Nothing that commonplace would interest the high levels of government involved in this request.

What to do? Frank sat back and wondered how he could make this work to his advantage. *No way I'm going to let this slip away into the usual paper trail,* of that much, he was certain.

In the end, it was fairly simple, "love me, love my dog," he concluded out loud. If they wanted his information, they'd get him too, and somehow he had the feeling they'd take it any way they could get it.

CHAPTER 14

When the enemy is both within and without, we are surrounded.

Frank was easily able to trace the request back to Ed Marker. He arrived at the DOE to hand-deliver the findings. Frank never even reported back to Don, his immediate supervisor, who'd made the request. There was a sense of urgency to all of this, like a sound so highly pitched only dogs could hear it.

"Good morning," said Shane brightly. "Do you have an appointment with Secretary Marker?" Shane eyed the newcomer, noting his wrinkled suit.

"I'm Frank Dodd, and no, I don't have an appointment, but I know that Secretary Marker will want to see me right away," he said, adjusting his stance to accommodate his armful of files and the computer bag slung over his shoulder.

"I'm sorry, but Secretary Marker has nothing available for the next two weeks," Shane stood there politely, waiting for Frank to accept this and schedule an appointment.

"I have to see him today," said Frank.

"Look," said Shane. "The best I can offer you is to send Secretary Marker a message. What would you like me to say?" Shane sat down in his office chair again, poised to type up a message on his computer for Ed.

Just as Frank drew in a breath to make his next plea for an immediate meeting, the outer office door opened, and a harried Ed Marker walked through.

Ed had barely entered the room when Shane jumped from his chair like a wound spring, trying to shield his boss from the unexpected visitor.

"Secretary Marker," said Frank, meeting Ed at the door. "There's something important you need to see. Is there somewhere we can talk?" Frank glanced over at Ed's assistant.

"And you are?" asked Ed. He wasn't sure if he was a new hire or someone off the street bypassing the whole call-in reporting system.

"Apologies," said Frank, setting down his files on Shane's desk and extending his hand. "I'm Frank Dodd from the Census Bureau." He immediately snapped up the files from the desk. "We need to talk."

Oh Lord, thought Ed. *Could this be a break?* "Please, come in." Ed opened his office door and swept his arm in an open invitation. "I'll be just a moment."

Ed shut the door and walked over to Shane, who was rearranging the items on his desk that had been disturbed by Frank's files. "Shane, call Barry and Patrick and get them over here yesterday."

"I'll do it right away. Do you want any coffee or water?"

"Coffee would be great," said Ed. He appreciated Shane's attention to detail and needed that coffee.

•   •   •

Joint Genome Institute
Berkeley, California

Their problem was all grounded in coded genetics, but who could understand all this stuff? Not Ed; but there wasn't a choice. Surrounded by the top geneticists in the country, he felt like an idiot. His physics degree could have been made from construction paper and crayons for all the good it was doing him now.

Ed had sought out and personally overseen the formation of this assembled group of geneticists once Frank Dodd, the walking computer, had shown him empirically that the root of their problem was genetically based. He vividly remembered how difficult it had been trying to keep up with the precisely intense little man.

Ed knew he was now literally holding the answer in his hand. Swirling in a small corked test tube were the strange genetic spores, or whatever. Too small to be seen individually, they merely clouded the liquid. Somehow, these scientists had isolated them by putting genetic material from both those affected and unaffected through the necessary testing. Finally, they'd come up with these extra tiny bits of flotsam.

"Don't give me the details. It would waste both of our time. Just hit the highlights." There was no time to spare, and Ed was trying to stay on top of the crashing wave as it broke on the rocks. "What is this stuff?"

Dr. Mann spoke for the assembled group of scientists. "We don't know exactly what it is, but we know what it's not. It isn't and never has been a part of any natural human genetic evolutionary process."

"So, what does that mean, Doctor?"

"Simply, it means that this 'stuff' isn't human genetic material. We've never seen anything quite like it before. The material seems to have been engineered to act as a kind of hitchhiker. It binds to human DNA but doesn't affect it at all, or at least it hasn't in the past."

"So, not everyone has this hitchhiker?" These guys were a lot easier for Ed to follow than that overly detailed Dodd.

"Not exactly," Dr. Mann hedged. "It seems to have more to do with each individual's personal time frame. Theoretically, its initial function could have been merely survival, but in people who have become overtly affected by the harvesters, the non-human material has become more than a non-functional appendage. The very structure of the DNA has been violated in those experiencing the difficulties."

"Let me make sure I understand you correctly, Dr. Mann. We've somehow been sabotaged genetically?" It sounded more ominous by the minute, and Ed was already thinking ahead to possible damage control. Pay attention, he reminded himself, quickly refocusing.

"Not exactly, but possibly. However, if you're looking for a powerful foreign source here on Earth for this, I can guarantee there isn't one. The science of genetics anywhere in the world is completely incapable of engineering something of this complexity yet, and I stress yet."

"When, Doctor? How far advanced exactly is this material?"

"Secretary Marker, if our suspicions are correct, this hitchhiker is like a seed that has been planted in fertile soil."

It was an analogy for the layperson. Ed knew the scientist was dumbing it down, but was grateful because he needed to understand this.

"Our guess," Dr. Mann continued, "would be that this happened long ago when the population was very new and small or even non-existent, and has been passed on genetically as the population of the Earth has slowly been breeding itself into its present-day billions. The fact that virtually everyone seems to carry the seed indicates that originally, the entire population was involved in the planting." Dr. Mann paused.

Ed could tell the doctor was waiting for him to catch up.

"Naturally, genetic tampering on such a large scale nowadays would be completely impossible to keep secret, even if we had the technology, which we don't. So now, years after the original event during which the seeds were put into place, some people carry more of it than others because of the random breeding since then."

"The ones carrying the most sensitivity to this genetic material are the ones in my files, right?" Ed concluded with satisfaction, not even waiting for the doctor to agree. "Why is this 'seed' being triggered now? Are the harvesters doing it, and if so, can we turn the seed off by finding a way to turn the harvesters off safely?"

"We don't know ourselves." One of the other scientists was speaking. Ed looked at her nametag: Dr. Lucy Chen. "This material has been around for millennia, unchanged and unseen. Suddenly, it's triggered, invades the country's DNA, and is no longer passive. Instead, it seems to be actively asserting whatever strange components and characteristics it brings upon its hosts."

Dr. Mann jumped into the conversation again, "Secretary Marker, genetic material has never changed like this to our knowledge. Yes, cell chemistry alters and genetic damage occurs in exposure to radioactivity or toxins, and this, in turn, affects the host. To affect the host on a more than cellular level, however, is unheard of."

Ed was getting ready to challenge him, but it wouldn't do any good. No amount of arguing could change the facts.

"We don't know what triggered the seed. Was it like a timed-release cold capsule planted for a timely harvest? Did it need certain optimal germination conditions, which have recently been realized by the harvesters perhaps, or by the ozone layer's depletion, or any number of other possibilities? It's all pure speculation, at this point."

"Be assured that we're working on it," said Dr. Mann. "As awful as this situation is, it's like giving chemists several unknown elements for their periodic table or handing biologists a whole new phylum of animals to study. This is something the world of genetics has never seen. You can be sure that we will have every geneticist in the world clamoring to join this project and an endless supply of free labor from graduate programs."

"Can we turn it off, or get rid of it with a vaccine?" His mind had jumped beyond this branch of science to the medical front. There was a cure for everything. You just had to find it. "A foreign body shouldn't be too hard to get rid of. The body's natural defenses can just be pointed in the direction of the invader." Ed saw Dr. Mann smile at him as if he were a toddler, but then went on to explain.

"The problem, Secretary Marker, is that the body does not identify the seed as an invader. That is only one of the situational marvels which we are beginning to appreciate at this moment. If this ability alone could be replicated at will by the medical community, it would have tremendous medical applications. Our bodies have not only accepted its presence unchallenged for so long, they are now willingly co-mingling genetic material. Once this is done, there is no longer an outside invader, so to speak, only a very human by-product.

"*Can we turn it off?*" Dr. Mann repeated Ed's original question. "Who knows. Ask yourself this, Secretary Marker. Once it's in our systems and functioning as an integral part of these people, would it endanger them to turn off part of who they had become from the cellular level up?"

"Generally," interjected Dr. Chen, "a genetic change does not affect the living generation, only the as yet unborn, or next generation. This is why we fail to see the error of our ways until it is too late so much of the time. What's happening is completely against the natural order of things, as we know it."

Ed was having visions of Mabel Claire Mabrey's swift death in a far-away field. "You mentioned radioactivity and environmental toxins. Could they possibly be the cause for this extra genetic material? Could people have developed this mutation themselves?" There was still hope, and if the ball could be thrown back into the familiar court of environmental issues, Ed could resume play. "If that were the case, this could already be the next generation."

"Unfortunately, that isn't the case." Dr. Mann said with a sympathizing half-smile. "We've walked through that scenario as well. In the first place, adaptive genetic mutations take more than the mere hundred years in which pollution has become such a health hazard. Second, many of those affected live in what are nearly pollution-free areas, or at least as pollution-free as you can find nowadays. Third, by gathering and testing genetic material from all living and some nonliving blood relatives of those involved, we can track the seed back through the generations before environmental hazards became a factor."

So much for that possibility, thought Ed, but there were still others. "Doctor, could it have been a mutation whenever it first appeared rather than some sort of seed that was 'planted?'"

"It could have been, except for one thing." Now, more of the scientists gathered around, leaving their stations and joining Drs. Mann and Chen.

"What one thing?" asked Ed. What was halting production in the lab and drawing everyone into earshot? More bad news—just what he needed to hear.

The serious Dr. Mann interrupted Ed's thoughts. "That one thing, Secretary Marker, is a substance we cannot identify. It has no counterpart on Earth."

"What are you saying?" It was less of a question and more of a statement. He needed to hear them say it, even though this would be impossible, something out of a movie, something that could never truly happen.

Dr. Chen interrupted Ed's thoughts. "It is extraterrestrial genetic material."

Okay, then. She'd said it. The problem has been isolated and identified. Now, what were they going to do?

• • •

Department of Energy
Washington, D.C.

Ed moved a pile of clutter from a chair in Barry's office at the DOE and sat down next to the window. It was overcast again, for the third day in a row.

"So, what did you learn out in California?" asked Patrick, not taking a seat and skipping right to the point of the meeting.

Barry just stared from behind his desk, covered in peanut shells from edge to edge. Ed knew Barry had been having a hard time with this, but waved his hand to get the inventor's attention.

"Whatever it is, just say it," said Barry, without making eye contact.

Instead, he was looking off to the side. Ed knew by that glazed sideways stare that Barry *was* thinking, veering away from his fixation on regret. He was working on the solution, as they all were. Good. Regret was a waste of time.

"What exactly does that mean, *no counterpart on Earth*?" Patrick asked.

"It's not derived from this planet," said Ed, "and doesn't respond to earthly physiological constraints. We couldn't have possibly anticipated any of this. We took all the standard precautions and conducted all the necessary testing before letting harvesters go on-line in North Carolina. Who knew it would take a cumulative effect to surface."

"I guess," Barry grudgingly agreed. "But then, where did this hitchhiker come from, and how did it find its way into our gene pool?"

"I still think," asserted Patrick only half-heartedly, "that some kind of biological warfare is more likely than extraterrestrial sabotage."

"Well, forget it. The report's right here." Ed held up a thumb drive. "Also, the stuff has been around too long for biological warfare. Would you like to go through it again?"

"No, thanks," declined Patrick. "Certainly they ran some astronomical number of tests on the stuff, and they're right, okay? I just don't like it. I'm with Barry. How did this happen? Things like this aren't supposed to happen in real life. Aliens don't just come by sprinkling their genetic fairy dust into the atmosphere."

"Do you think I didn't ask?" Ed stared him down while thinking of how he'd questioned Dr. Andrew Mann for hours. The services of the eminent Dr. Mann were the best that money could buy.

"Normally," Ed explained patiently as both other men strained to understand, "it requires genetic co-mingling, you know, birds and bees kind of stuff. So maybe you weren't too far off with that alien/caveman love nest theory, Patrick. On the other hand, we know absolutely nothing about this substance. It could have fallen in with a meteorite, or rained down as cosmic dust to find its way into our system."

"Okay, so let me get this straight," insisted Barry. "We don't know where it came from, or exactly what it is, or its purpose, either. We only know what happens when it mixes with human DNA as a result of being exposed to harvester frequencies."

"You're forgetting the cornfield, Barry." Ed reminded him. "This stuff's potential victims go beyond just human DNA. The parameters seem to require merely an organic substance."

"Not much to go on." Patrick was disappointed. "Somehow, I thought they'd have more answers." He gave an involuntary shudder. "I don't like the thought of that stuff inside of me. It's like having cancer and waiting to see where the tumors grow or having some parasitic worm in your gut."

"Well, back to our original hope; can they do anything constructive, like finding a vaccine or something?" voiced Barry, unconsciously tapping an empty coffee cup.

"Nope." Ed's certainty was disappointing. "Not any more than they could cure any other genetically based disease or condition once it was in place."

"But," interjected Patrick, "if it doesn't show the same constraints as our own genetic material, maybe they'll find it responds differently than ours does to vaccines and such."

"I suggested as much to Dr. Mann toward the end of our long conversation," Ed responded. "He essentially assured me they intended to follow up completely, while at the same time blowing me off like a piece of lint. I think all my questioning was getting him a little upset. Too many of his answers were simply, 'We don't know.'"

"So, what do we do now?" The pitch of Barry's voice had risen.

Ed tried to bring down the level of negative energy in the room by offering the only available solution. "We just keep doing more of the same, tracking down anything and everything. We're going to find out more than ever because we've taken off the blinders." He rose out of his chair and turned to look out of the window. The muted gray clouds, out of place in the August sky, had a calming effect on him.

"Can't argue that," Patrick had to agree.

Even though Ed had offered nothing new in the way of a plan, Barry seemed semi-encouraged.

"Don't worry about me," Barry forced a grin. "I haven't given up." He stood and headed for the lab he'd set up down the hall.

Patrick worked into a visible agitation after the door shut. "Puts a new perspective on UFOs, doesn't it? Like maybe they're keeping an eye on their lab mice or something."

"It gives me the creeps too," Ed had to admit.

"Ed, I didn't want to hype Barry up any more than he was already, but this takes everything way out of our areas of expertise."

"This report takes our problem right out of this world, Patrick." Ed paused for a moment. The pun had been unintentional. "Let's get out of here. I love Barry's office, but lately he's had something in here I'm allergic to. Can't figure out what it is." Ed scanned the room on their way out.

As Ed's hand flipped off the wall switch, his shirt cuff brushed against a stack of documents piled precariously next to the small prototype of the harvester that had previously been Barry's pride and joy. This formerly prized possession had fallen from the grace of its lighted alcove into a very appropriate spot on a table right beside the door, looking as though it were very literally on its way out.

By the time Patrick and Ed reached the elevator, the stack of documents had shifted against the harvester model, knocking the switch firmly onto the highest setting. Barry had never used any but the lowest. It had never been necessary when demonstrating its capabilities in such a small space.

After several minutes, the darkened office filled with odd sounds coming from various surfaces. There were shifting and cracking sounds coming from the rock specimens and geodes Barry collected and displayed. On dark, shiny desktops, they moved and shook, reshaping themselves.

CHAPTER 15

RENE
University of New Mexico

With her petite form settled nicely into a comfortable position, Rene scanned the sky with her telescope. Her dark skin, hair, and clothing blended completely with the balmy, black night. The only sign of her presence was an occasional glint of light reflected from the few shiny metal parts of her telescope.

She knew astronomy was an odd hobby for someone her age. Still, sitting under the stars like this, it was all she'd ever really wanted. Dew carpeted the field, and Rene stood to refold her blanket into a dryer seat. Sitting down gracefully, she marveled over her acceptance to the state university. She had gotten a full scholarship, too. Staring into the telescope's eyepiece, Rene looked into the future. Oh, she'd never live long enough to see it, but it was the future.

She had begun her education by signing up for a summer class. At the university, Rene had seen what she'd been missing. Thanks to a generous endowment, the school had acquired an extremely high-powered telescope, and Rene had been completely captivated.

Were it not for building maintenance, she would be at the lab with the school's high-powered telescope now, instead of using her own out on the University's damp soccer field.

"Mama, you should see it," Rene's calls home were peppered with talk about the telescope.

She never spoke of friends, or boys, or parties, only that telescope, and since you couldn't marry a telescope, Rene knew her mother wasn't holding out any hope of her meeting someone at school anytime soon.

Determined to take full advantage of her opportunity, Rene approached all schedules with total disregard; trading, wheedling, and bartering for as many time slots as possible with the high-powered window to the stars.

"Please, can you come back in the morning?" she attempted to persuade the electricians who were threatening to shut down the lab during her time slot. Her pleas were fruitless. The workmen had their orders, and were determined to turn off the electricity despite her complaints.

"Why don't you go watch them installing that relay harvester across the street for a while," suggested one of the men, rolling his eyes. "Everything will be up and running again within about three hours."

"Three hours?!" Rene was horrified by this waste of time, but there wasn't anything she could do about it. Downtime was wasted time. She was losing a scheduled two-hour slot, with only a week left before the fall semester. It would soon be impossible to get so much time with the telescope as a freshman on a full campus. Oh well, you can only do so much. Rene attempted to calm herself, knowing that she was already spending as much of her remaining time as possible with the coveted equipment. During the month of August, she only had to contend with a handful of other die-hard summer term students.

Ahh, she thought happily later that evening in the dark, having been able to return to the quiet lab after the electricians had departed. She had the rest of the night to herself. "Guess I'll start over there," Rene mumbled to herself, pointing the machine toward a familiar sector. Relaxed and at peace with old friends, the hum of a nearby exit sign was the only sound in the lab, until her startled gasp. Rene looked away, rubbed her eyes gently to clear them, then looked back. It was still there.

She was in disbelief. "I can't be seeing this," she insisted emphatically to the empty room. "There are physical properties saying so." She wanted to run and find someone, wanted to pull their arms, drag them back to the lab with her, and make them look. "Damn it, there's no one but me." Her voice trailed off as she was drawn up into the inky blackness and the field of vision began to broaden and deepen.

Looking through the eyepiece, the stars began to move toward her. They passed by slowly on either side, getting faster until they were streaks of light streaming by. It was like watching the Starship Enterprise go into warp speed!

She should have timed it. Her mind danced around the realization, but what relevance could it have had without all the other information necessary to calculate a position? Eventually, the star streaks slowed, finally stopping in place all around her. *I don't recognize one single star pattern*, she thought, looking into the unfamiliar sky.

Then, near the corner of her eye, she saw movement. Something was coming towards her rapidly. It was a ship of some sort; huge, with a burnished metallic sheen set against the blackness of the void. Colored lights set into the hull shone like jewels, backlit by a bright inner source. The front part was triangular, like the head of a snake, or the prow of a ship slicing straight towards her. It was hard to see what shape the vessel took as it spread and grew behind its cutting edge because it filled her entire field of vision within seconds.

My God, it was like standing on a railroad track watching a train speed towards her. As hypnotic as it was, her every instinct screamed, "Back up. Run!" Instead, she froze in place as the ship flew just inches above her, blocking out the blackened sky completely. It was immense, and she watched as it passed over her, spreading from horizon to horizon.

She noted unfamiliar markings, outlines of doorways, lighted semi-transparent windows, and the smooth beautiful gloss of the thing. Rene saw it all, and then it was gone, behind her somewhere, and she couldn't turn to follow.

The surrounding stars shimmered, as though it was all a mirage seen over the edge of a hot horizon. Then the shimmer cleared from bottom to top, exactly as though someone was pulling up a zipper to shut their jacket, and poof—the sky was back. Scanning the sky through the university's glass dome ceiling, she was both disappointed and relieved to see the same old stars in the same old places.

·   ·   ·

She'd been right about the fall semester. It was nearly impossible to secure a block of time with the telescope. However, what she had not anticipated was the fact that she might no longer need it.

For the last few nights, her little sister, Evette, had been keeping her company on Facetime in the early darkness before bed. "Watcha doing, Rene?" she asked contentedly, snuggling her stuffed bunny and trying not to miss her big sister.

"Looking at a spaceship, Evie." Who was going to believe her besides a ten-year-old?

Evie giggled. "Tell me more, Rene. Who's on the spaceship?"

"I really don't know."

"But, Rene, it's your story. You have to know."

"You're right, I'll finish it tomorrow. Now, time for you to go to sleep."

After blowing her sister a kiss and ending the session, Rene looked up into the dark, and the curtain opened. She quickly passed through what she knew into what she didn't, but the unknown was becoming more recognizable with each episode. Rene was wildly constructing star maps in every spare minute she could find.

"Rene, you need more sleep, girl. You've got circles under those eyes," she recalled her mother saying, but her mother was always worrying about something.

I do have circles though, Rene acknowledged as she studied her reflection in the mirror. Staring nightly up into the heavens, on top of her daily responsibilities, was taking a toll on her appearance. "But I'm not tired," she would argue to her mother. "I know I look kind of worn out, but just the same, I'm not tired, Mama." No one was winning, and it was becoming a tensely running commentary.

Rene continued to see the ship and knew from her maps that it was on a straight course. Straight for where, she asked herself uneasily, knowing she had a better idea all the time. The real question was why. Why was she seeing this, and what did it all mean?

As she continued her mapping efforts, Rene was certain that she would find the edge where the known and the unknown met. Then, she thought, she would show the right people what she'd seen, what they would have to see, too.

Meanwhile, and most importantly, the egg was hatching, and she was a part of it. She wasn't sure what it all meant, only that it was coming closer every day. Sometimes, she could almost grasp it before the whole thing skittered away into the stars like a bag of fallen marbles.

Oh well, maybe tomorrow, she half promised herself philosophically. Tonight had to be enough for now, she thought, continuing to look up into the sky beside her beloved, personal, but now completely unnecessary telescope.

CHAPTER 16

When the pupil is ready, the mentor will appear.
—Buddhist Proverb

Ed looked up as the door to his office opened to admit a flushed and shaking Barry. The distraught man hadn't bothered to knock, or even to shut the door behind him.

Striding to stand before Ed's desk, Barry dropped a pile of rocks onto its surface as though they were burning his hands. "They're not the same." He watched his boss expectantly.

"The same as what?" Ed picked up the stone closest to him and briefly examined it.

"These were some of my geodes. Now look at them."

"What are you talking about? These aren't geodes, Barry."

"Not anymore, they're not. Come with me." Barry hurriedly gathered up the rocks and turned to exit through the still-open door to the outer office. "Follow me! I've got something to show you."

"Secretary Marker?" called Shane as Ed walked briskly past his assistant.

He turned around at the door. "Yes, Shane?"

"Lunch. What would you like for lunch?" Shane stood up expectantly, waiting for Ed's order.

Lunch. It seemed so trivial these days, but seeing as how he was not extraterrestrial, or at least not yet, Ed knew he still had to eat. "I'll take a turkey club with avocado."

"Anything to drink?" asked Shane, writing Ed's lunch order on a Post-it.

"Iced tea... unsweet."

Ed turned and quickly caught up to Barry, picking up stray rocks that had fallen from the inventor's grasp either on his way into or out of Ed's office.

Barry held the elevator until Ed stepped on.

"What the hell is going on, Barry?" Ed grabbed his friend's arm. "Where are we going?"

"My office."

"Oh my God, why didn't you just call me on the phone?" As if Ed didn't have enough to do already.

Barry looked dumbstruck at the simplicity of the thought, then shuddered. "I didn't want to be in there by myself."

By this time, they were striding down the hallway and approaching the door to Barry's office. "But why?" Ed was exasperated.

"You'll see. Open it." Barry pushed Ed towards the knob and waited.

Ed opened the door and stepped into the office, deliberately avoiding the pile of papers in his path. He looked up after negotiating his way through the mess at the doorway, then stopped and stared unbelievingly around the room.

"See," Barry said from the doorway. "See what I mean?"

Ed saw all right. He remembered Barry's geode collection, the one he'd used as paperweights, sitting heavily scattered on piles of paperwork throughout the office. Barry was right, they weren't geodes anymore.

They were still rocks, or at least Ed thought they were. Some looked like a congealed mass of molten ore, others had a lacy honeycombed appearance. The ones that most closely resembled the geodes from which they'd formed had huge, pointy, elongated crystals jutting from the curved inside surface of the formerly symmetrical bowl-shaped geodes. There were others with such smoothly planed surfaces they seemed to be manufactured rather than naturally formed from rock.

"Yeah, I see, all right. When did all this happen?" Ed quickly dropped the rocks he was holding as they began to tremble and crackle in his hands. "What the hell?" He took a step back from the fallen pile of stones and realized that each rock in the room was heaving, or breaking, or something! Ed turned to leave. He didn't want to be in there, either. Then, Barry stepped into the room and shut the door behind him.

"Watch this," he reached beside him and switched off the small, model relay harvester. Immediately, the noisy movement ceased, and his office became as quiet as a tomb.

"Shit." Ed collapsed into the nearest chair, crushing the boxes and folders beneath him.

"Exactly," Barry agreed.

"How is this happening?" asked Ed. "We know about the alien hitchhiker commingling with our DNA, but these are inanimate objects. Rocks are not alive, or at least they have never *been* alive. They're not *supposed* to be alive, Barry!"

"Ed?"

"Go ahead, I'm just thinking out loud." Ed waved for Barry to continue.

"That's the scary part. Animals, people, and even plants have always had the ability to grow and change over their lifecycle, but never rocks. Their textures and structures were formed under certain environmental conditions throughout Earth's history, never to change. Rocks are constants."

"Nothing is constant anymore," responded Ed, rubbing one eye. It just kept coming.

"I know this is a lot to take in, but this small model emits the same frequency patterns that the larger ones do. As far as I know, my office is the only one experiencing these changes at the moment, but these harvesters are all across the country." Barry looked over at the small model. "If this small model can produce this much change, imagine what a relay harvester could be doing."

This is exactly what Ed was thinking as he continued to rub his left eye.

"Barry, I'm sorry, but I've got to get out of here. I can feel a migraine coming on and my pills are at home."

"Yeah, okay. I mean, I'll see if I can find out any more about what's going on here. You go home."

"Thanks. I'll have to."

Ed arrived in his three-bedroom apartment and headed straight back to the master bath. After locating his sumatriptan tablets and swallowing one with a cool glass of water, he sat on the edge of his bed and hoped that he had taken it in time to stave off the worst of the migraine.

He just needed a moment, an hour maybe, to let the medication circulate and take effect. He was already getting the pulsing, blurred vision in his periphery. Grateful for his blackout curtains, Ed removed his shoes and lay back on his bed. Just an hour.

The vibrations of his phone drew him out of the blackness. Ed held up the device and saw an unknown caller displayed. A wave of nausea hit him and he sent the caller directly to voicemail. Then he turned the phone off altogether. He would not be any good to anybody if he could not shake this migraine by the next morning. Comforter pulled up over his work clothes, Ed turned on his side and hoped he could fall asleep.

It was still dark when he woke up during the night. The bedside clock read three a.m. It wasn't just the curtains; it was still night. He felt sticky and sweaty under the comforter, and made a cautious move to get up—no pain. The migraine was gone. If only all problems were this easy to solve. One pill and a long nap seemed pretty simple compared to everything he had been dealing with lately.

He made his way to the dresser and got out a pair of plaid pajama pants, then rinsed his mouth out with water. Food. He hadn't eaten since yesterday morning. He recalled his lunch order from yesterday and wished the turkey club was in his fridge. Ed lived alone and didn't do much cooking, never having seen any benefit in the time it took to prepare a meal for one. So, his options were rock-hard, week-old pork fried rice or dry cereal. Definitely pork fried rice. He sat down on the couch and ate the microwaved Chinese food with a spoon in front of the news.

"An increasing number of doctors are reporting strange cases showing up in their emergency rooms," said the newscaster, standing outside of George Washington University Hospital.

Ed didn't recognize the young reporter.

"Just today we received an anonymous call from one of the hospital employees, detailing the spike in unusual health issues." The reporter held her microphone out to a woman wearing a gray pantsuit.

"The arm was completely blue," said the hospital's PR representative. "We ran all the vascular testing available, but there seemed to be no cause for this."

"Was this person in any pain?"

"The color change was not painful or bothersome for the patient."

"Is it true that by the time this patient was discharged, the blue coloring had spread over their whole torso?"

"That is all the information I can give," said the hospital representative.

"So, there is no medical explanation for this...change in skin color?" the reporter prodded.

"None that we could find."

"And this patient was released?"

"That's all we have," said the woman.

"Well, that's certainly enough," said the reporter. "You heard it here first on WDTV 6." She smiled into the camera.

Ed flicked off the TV. They'd have a lot more to cover before this was all over. He pulled out his phone and turned it back on. Three messages. Two were from Barry and he listened to those first. Nothing important. He had just been checking up on Ed and his migraine, wanting to know if he would be at work the next day.

Next, he listened to the message from the unknown caller. Great, Ed had sent the Secretary of State to voicemail.

Hi Ed, this is Secretary Al Hammond. I just wanted to give you an update on foreign relations in association with the strange goings-on. Other countries are experiencing some of the same glitches. Call me in the morning and we can talk.

Glitches? Way to downplay the situation. Ed walked over to the sink and filled a glass with tap water. He took one more sumatriptan as a precaution and went back to take a shower. There was no point in going back to sleep now. If he did, he would wake just in time for rush hour traffic. If he left by four-thirty, he would get there in twenty minutes.

• • •

Despite being worn out and tired, Ed was planted at his desk, scanning the top news stories online. *Baptists See the End of the World, Catholics Can't Be Sure.*

His office had been "encouraging" journalists not to incite the population, whatever the hell that meant, he groused.

His phone rang, and Ed debated whether to answer it. Shane would not be in for at least an hour, but anyone who was working at this ungodly hour couldn't be all bad, he reasoned, picking up the receiver.

"Hold for the President, please," came the official request.

The President came on the line and began his line of questioning.

"No, sir. We feel the situation is becoming far too big to control." Admitting this was a relief.

"No, sir, we won't do anything without your say so," Ed assured President Morgan. "Goodbye then, sir."

The phone rang again. Since when was everyone calling his office at six a.m.? Ed answered it again.

"It's Ray," the investigator announced himself, with no preliminaries. "Why haven't you been answering your phone?"

Ed looked down to see that his phone was still on silent—with fourteen missed calls!

"Hey," continued Ray. "I've got an interesting one for you. It's being carried by the midwestern papers. A Mary Beth Hatcher, alias *Madame Olga*, claims to smell water coming and has dry-docked a boat in her backyard waiting for it."

"Like Noah's Ark? Is this more religious fanaticism? Or something real?" Ed wanted to hear everything. Things were changing so fast, it was getting harder to separate facts from imagination. People needed their world to make sense. They were twisting facts and rationalizing situations to make the unknown seem more familiar.

"Yeah, maybe," Ray's voice cut into Ed's thoughts. "Anyway, could be that you'll want to get a flight out there right away. Patrick's been following this one and says it's for real. He'll be calling you later, wants to go with you. That's if you decide to follow it up."

Ed scrolled through his missed calls and saw that three of them had been from Patrick. "If it's worth a call from you, it's worth a trip to me. I trust your instincts, Ray." Over the past few weeks, Ed had developed a sincere respect for Ray.

"Well, I'll be in touch with anything new." Then Ray was gone.

He and Patrick were heading to Thorpestown, Iowa. By Ed's estimation, there was a rapidly narrowing window before everything went to hell, but at the moment plans were still to give the geneticists a week or so to see whether they could come up with some kind of vitamin or reverse mutation that could clear everything up.

Meanwhile, Ed was sure that things had gone far beyond damage control. So, picking up his lucky pen, he worked on a speech he hoped would not incite widespread panic. All the vaccines and vitamins in the world wouldn't be able to help the rocks he'd seen in Barry's office. What had happened with the rocks? They were supposed to be inanimate. This took things to a whole new level. It wasn't merely living organisms that were being affected by the alien DNA, but objects. It was something Ed didn't even want to think about unless it became necessary, but in the back of his mind, he knew more trouble was coming.

CHAPTER 17

Saguaro Rock, Arizona, 2008

D r. Gregory Ross had resolved to move onto the Saguaro military base after yet another failed relationship. He had kept a small apartment on the outskirts of Yuma for years, often wondering why he did this. Most of his waking hours had always been spent in the Saguaro compound.

Online dating sites had given him the tools to find a partner, but even with the aid of advanced algorithms, it was still necessary to be present in a relationship. He was almost sure this was why his two years with Lisa hadn't worked out. The only lady in his life to whom he had ever given proper attention was Addie. The longer he worked at the Rock, the less he left the compound. It had taken him two weeks to even notice that Lisa had moved out.

Ross had been recruited directly from the biophysics lab at UCLA for his research on the effects of quantum physics on the physiology of multicellular organisms. It was only fitting that the love of his life would be a purple, gelatinous collection of cells at the center of a burgeoning career in biophysics.

He had now accepted that he was a man in his fifties who would most likely never start a family. *Where would he find the time?* he asked himself as he sat in the lab watching the numbers play across the screen, sipping coffee from a cardboard cup.

The red light above the security door flashed, indicating that he had a visitor.

"Dr. Ross," Admiral Price stepped into the room and greeted his old acquaintance. "It's been a long time."

Dr. Ross stood to greet the Admiral. "Yes, it has. How long, would you guess? About fifteen years?"

"Ever since Addie's oversight became the responsibility of the Secretary of Defense," Admiral Price responded, smiling. "It makes sense. A Naval officer should never oversee a landlocked project."

Both men laughed and Ross offered the Admiral a cup of coffee. The men had kept in touch even without in-person visits.

"Thanks, but I'm fine." Without being invited, Price took a seat on one of the lab stools.

"Are you here to sign up for the trial? We're still looking for test subjects," asked Dr. Ross, knowing that the Admiral would once again refuse.

"Test subjects?!" The Admiral's gaze flitted nervously to the door behind which he assumed Addie was being housed.

Ross responded to the question in his eyes. "She's still there. I can enroll you in the study today," he continued with good humor.

"Why would I want to stop time now, with two bad knees and a face full of wrinkles?"

"Your choice." Dr. Ross walked over to the computer screen.

The research relating to Addie now consumed four floors at Saguaro Rock, but the original lab containing the control tank only admitted those with the highest clearance, and always included a military security presence.

"Take a look at this," urged the doctor, gesturing to the computer screen, "twenty years of data." He scrolled through some files and pulled up one in particular labeled "Animal Trials."

Ross opened two photos for comparison rather than bringing up the replication speed spreadsheets. They wouldn't mean much to the decorated war hero and soon-to-be-retired Navy SEAL.

"Thanks for skipping the spreadsheets," said Price. "All soldiers aren't necessarily digital warriors." The Admiral shifted his weight on the stool.

"I know," Dr. Ross smiled. "Look at that." He pointed to side-by-side photos of mice.

"I see two mice," stated Price.

"Look closer. It's the same mouse." Dr. Ross pointed to the pink patch of skin on its nose. "We identify Stewart by that mark."

Dr. Ross could sense that the Admiral was losing interest, so he got right to it. "Stewart hasn't aged, either. These photos were taken seven years apart!"

"How can you tell whether he's aged? He's covered in fur." The Admiral rolled his eyes and let out a small chuckle. "It's amazing how funny things become when you're retiring. It feels good. I've always been too serious."

"Just hear me out," Ross pressed on. He had a captive audience, for now. There were so few people with his level of clearance. He had to share his finding or he would burst.

"All right, I'm listening." The Admiral leaned in.

"The life span of a mouse is one to two years. This is why they're used so often in trials. A shorter lifespan allows us to see how these animals are affected across generations when exposed to a carcinogen or fed a certain diet—whatever you want to test. In this situation, we have not observed change over generations because the mice simply do not die!"

"Could you imagine if this type of thing fell into the wrong hands?" The Admiral paused in thought. "Just think of a wartime situation where your enemy couldn't die."

Ross redirected his visitor's train of thought when he clicked on another file. "Look at this wave. Well, you can't really call it a wave."

The Admiral looked at the wave. "And?"

"No, really look." Dr. Ross was unamused. "Waves are uniform. They're graphed using the function y=sin(x). This creates a smooth, arcing, uniform wave with amplitudes and wavelengths unique to each type of frequency. This is a normal wave, or rather a commonly known wave. Now," the doctor overlaid Addie's frequency on the wave model, "this is Addie's. Do you see it?"

"That tiny blip in each wave?"

"Exactly! We've finally been able to measure and graph the frequency. It took us over twenty-five years to develop the technology to identify this *blip*."

The Admiral continued to give Dr. Ross his respectful attention.

"It's this blip that we can't recreate. If we could... it could change the world."

"Don't you have a whole compound of scientists to go over all of this? I have my final briefing with the Secretary of Defense in a little over an hour. I just came down here to see if you wanted to grab some lunch beforehand."

"That's the thing," said Dr. Ross. "The team of researchers knows all the physics involved. They have a mathematical model and graphical representation of the new wave, but they don't know where it came from. They have the science and the tools to measure, but no knowledge of Addie. There's no one I can talk to outside of the Secretary of Defense, the President, Colonel Walker, and you, now that Josh is gone."

Ross held out his hands and sighed. "We're on the verge of the biggest scientific finding in human history and there isn't anyone for me to talk to, save the briefings I give to the Secretary."

"There aren't many of us," the Admiral agreed, nodding his head, "but you knew the job when you took it."

"Never a truer statement." Ross conceded. In actuality, he was just as happy not to have company. People annoyed him. The exciting work he was doing was more than enough reward for anything he had to endure.

"Why don't we take the cart to the café and bring our lunch back here?"

The Admiral had shifted the conversation back to lunch, again. He really was leaving the game. Ross had lost his audience, but he'd become used to the solitude that came with his position. He allowed himself to stand down for a moment and enjoy the Admiral's last visit.

"Fine. Let's get lunch, but we can't eat in here." The two men exited the lab together. "So tell me, how does it feel to be retiring?"

"Pretty darned good, to be honest. I can say whatever I want now as long as I don't mention Addie." Admiral Price smiled.

"Well, congratulations to you." Ross knew it was well deserved.

"Take another left here. We'll use the service elevator," suggested the Admiral. "Do you think they'll have their creamy potato soup today?"

Dr. Ross laughed out loud. Potato soup was the furthest thing from *his* mind. "I don't know. I guess we'll find out."

CHAPTER 18

MARY BETH HATCHER
Thorpestown, Iowa

Standing in front of the run-down storefront, Mary Beth Hatcher eyed the rusty sign hanging at an odd angle. *Madame Olga's Psychic Readings*, it said, or at least it used to. Now it read *P--chic Readi--*, but people still knew what it meant. It didn't matter, though; she admitted sadly, with tears forming. They still weren't coming. Ever since she'd started warning about the coming water, business had all but died out, and all the weird headlines had clinched it.

Brushing the tears away fiercely, Mary Beth walked past the hand-painted lettering on the front window. She'd painted it herself in better days, she remembered proudly. A countrywoman with mousy blonde hair, Mary Beth certainly didn't look the part of her alter ego, the exotic *Madame Olga*.

Strolling with resignation through the empty waiting room and into her "reading" room beyond, Mary Beth easily saw it for the sham it was. Sunny and bright, with an old linoleum-topped table surrounded by four chrome chairs upholstered in the same shiny plastic pattern; there was nothing either dark or mysterious about the place, she admitted with disappointment.

The only thing even hinting at her profession was the large, clear glass globe centered on the table. What a joke, she thought, perilously close to more tears. She'd never really been able to afford a real crystal one. Oh well, Mary Beth sighed, lovingly lifting the heavy ball and packing it into the handled bag at her feet. It had all been good while it lasted.

Stepping back into the afternoon sunshine and locking the door behind her, Mary Beth decided to walk home. She left her car parked in the rear of the building and began strolling down the main street and out into farm country. Each farm she passed on her way held some memory or other.

After going about a quarter of the way home, she heard a vehicle coming up the road behind her.

"Hey, Olga, need a ride?" The driver of the pickup truck reached over to open the door for her.

"Thanks anyway, Hardy, but I'm just getting some exercise. Say hi to Sandy for me, all right?"

"Sure thing." Hardy drove on.

Funny how everyone thought of her as Olga now, Mary Beth smiled sadly to herself. It had been years since anyone had called her by her given name. "Why should they?" she asked the nearest stalk of corn. In her capacity as *Madame Olga*, she'd become the county's equivalent of a psychiatrist. Not that anyone would admit it. Even Mary Beth realized vets were far more important in these parts.

She continued down the road, swinging the bag holding her "crystal ball." It was a leisurely trip, and the walk left her with plenty of time to remember. She thought back on how her high school class had graduated. Some classmates headed off for bigger cities, while she'd stayed because her parents couldn't afford college. Being stuck in Thorpestown hadn't meant that Mary Beth had no ambitions.

The smell of the water drew her out of the past. It's going to rain, she'd told herself when the smell began to follow her. Or maybe after such a wet, early summer, the water table could just be up, but that wasn't it at all. Mary Beth kicked up an angry cloud of dust with her shoe. She was more sure of it than ever. Two weeks ago, she'd gotten up one morning and put on her rain boots instead of shoes, and there hadn't been a cloud in the sky. From that moment on, things had gotten worse, and now, she had taken a second mortgage out on her house and parked a boat in her backyard. She hadn't even bought a trailer for it. Why bother, Mary Beth asked herself. She just hoped it was a big enough boat.

Mary Beth had always had a talent for divining water. She'd been able to smell it ever since she could remember, always right, too. Well, she was still right. There was water somewhere close by, and lots of it! Suddenly, her nose was overcome by the smell, and it made her sick. The scent was so strong she felt as though she was drowning.

What is wrong with me? Mary Beth had no idea. Maybe I don't want to know anyway, she admitted weakly.

So much for the relaxing walk home. It was giving her way too much time to think about things like the fact that her story had gone from the local to the state news. Then, it was finally picked up nationally for a laugh. THIRTY-FIVE-YEAR-OLD WOMAN WITH DIVINING TALENT DRY-DOCKS BOAT IN BACKYARD. It made for big news. Great, just great, she thought, wishing she'd taken her car after all, but it was too late for almost everything, nowadays.

Mary Beth arrived home, exhausted and grumpy, only to find two men waiting for the infamous *Madame Olga*.

"Ms. Hatcher, we're from the Department of Energy, and we've heard about your boat."

"I don't know why you'd come all the way out here to laugh. Usually, people can do that just sitting at home." Mary Beth plunged shakily ahead. "I'm not crazy. There is water here. If people around these parts would stop cackling long enough, they'd see the low spots are already getting muddy like they do after a rain, only it hasn't rained in two weeks. The streams are running faster and the wells are higher, but no one wants to see it." Her voice faded with exasperation. "What else do you want to know? Maybe you'd like a tour of the *Ark*," she offered sarcastically.

Ed was fascinated. Here was a woman who'd been ridiculed and made into a national joke. She was showing signs of strain, for sure, but Mary Beth Hatcher wasn't backing down.

"Ms. Hatcher, we're here because we believe you, not to laugh at you." Ed was trying hard to convey his sincerity. "I'm Ed Marker and this is Patrick Hagen, and we'd like for you to tell us what's happening here."

"I'd like to see some identification, if you don't mind." Mary Beth requested. "I've had too many kooks coming around lately."

"No problem." The two men each extended their government security cards to the stubborn woman in front of them, who looked both items over carefully before returning them.

"I know our visit is unexpected. Maybe if we came back after dinner, you'd be willing to sit and talk with us about your predictions." Ed was prepared to depart, giving her time to compose herself. He and Patrick had to catch a bite, anyway.

"Maybe you two would like to come in and have some supper with me. It's just leftover night, but there'll be something for everyone," she offered.

Ed and Patrick nodded in acceptance and Mary Beth ushered them inside, leading them back to the kitchen. "Why would a government bureau be interested in what I have to say?" she asked.

Patrick and Ed seated themselves on the dated dining chairs. "We're checking into a possible connection between your problem and the harvesters," said Ed, folding his hands on the tabletop.

"Would you mind explaining to us how this whole thing started?" Patrick requested while adjusting himself on his plastic seat.

Mary Beth popped the first Tupperware of leftover spaghetti in the microwave.

"Sure," she said and went on to explain her history of divining and the story of the storefront where she did her *psychic readings*, eventually ending up with her latest prediction. "I told myself it meant rain, but the only water I've ever smelled was always underground, and so is this, but not for long."

"Why do you say that?" Ed waited patiently for her answer as she lay the assorted leftovers on the table, along with three tall glasses of water and some plastic-ware.

"Same reason I bought the boat," she said, sitting and joining them at the table. "The water's coming. It's so close now that I can hardly breathe. I'm figuring that within the week, people will be laughing out of the other side of their faces, but it won't make me any happier."

She had tears in her eyes, and her voice was cracking. Then, she changed the subject.

"Nobody came by today, not one single soul. Funny how things work out sometimes."

She lifted the handled bag from its place on the floor beside her chair.

"I've spent years knowing that I couldn't really see into the future. On the other hand, what I did wasn't harming anyone." Lifting the glass sphere out of the soft bag, she set it gently before her on the table. "Closed up the shop today. There's no point in my sitting there by myself."

Ed could see that the little glass ball meant a lot to *Madame Olga*, but it was equally easy to see that she was almost afraid of it.

"Never have seen anything through it except the tabletop in all these years, even if I let on otherwise." Mary Beth smiled a sweet, remembering smile. "At least I never had until a couple of weeks ago. Now, I only wish I could see the table again."

"Is that why you bought the boat?" Fortified with a full stomach, Patrick was eager to bypass this sentiment, but Ed gave him a quieting nudge under the table. This woman didn't need any more pressure than she already had.

"No sir, it's not." The spirit returned to her voice. "I bought the boat because I can smell the water coming. I'm awfully glad to have it parked out back because now I can see the water, too."

"In the crystal ball?" Ed questioned gently.

"Yes, and it will not be like the flash floods that have swept through this part of the country from time to time over the years. This water is just going to rise out of the ground—simple as that. Nobody will drown. They'll all have time to save themselves, but not all of their things. It'll come too fast for that. Of course, even if I could get people to believe me, I'm not sure where I'd tell them to go."

"Why?" Patrick was not at all sure he wanted to know the answer.

"Because it's going to flood the entire county, at least. There's water everywhere I look, and it's not going to go away like those other floodwaters, either. This will be permanent, like a lake or an ocean or something."

"Ed, we ought to look into the status of any local emergency evacuation programs. Sounds like we may need them," Patrick suggested.

Ed did not answer Patrick, but took note of Madame Olga, who was looking even paler as she continued to stare into the glass sphere.

"Don't worry," Ed reached out and took her small, chilly hands in his. "We'll make sure people listen."

With desperation, Mary Beth locked eyes with Ed and begged, "Why? Why do you believe me? What's really going on here? Why send two government officials to see a flaky woman with a weird vision and a boat in her backyard?"

Ed could hear the fear in her voice.

"Why take me seriously at all?!"

"Because you live not fifty feet from that relay harvester." Ed pointed out the darkened kitchen window. All he saw was his reflection, but he knew it was out there. "Because everything is changing." He retracted his hands from hers and rubbed his face in exhaustion. Ed's eyes burned. He had started the day early with limited sleep and there was no rest in sight. It was most likely the fatigue and stress that caused Ed to do what people have been doing to *Madame Olga* for years—he told her everything.

"Now I *know* I'm not crazy, but I don't think I like the alternative, either," said Mary Beth, trying to wrap her mind around what Ed had just explained to her. "This may not be the best time to tell you, but the water is only the part I've told people about. There's a lot more."

There was no way they were leaving her behind. Mary Beth only took thirty minutes to pack and close up the house. It would all be gone by the time she returned. It was pointless to lock the door. Anything of real importance to her, and there wasn't much; she locked away carefully on the boat. Finally, she let out the long, extra heavy anchor, which had cost an additional five hundred dollars, and the three drove off into the evening.

•　　•　　•

As harvester frequency modulations built to increasingly higher concentrations, so did their stimulating effect on the unearthly material. Now, these tiny alien seeds bored more deeply into their targets and became powerful enough to send out a signal of their own.

As designed, their specifically tuned vibrational signals triggered the probe's long-unused computers to activate its homing beacon. Mission accomplished, it flashed across the galaxy. Come see. Come play.

This message was sent again and again, in repetitive bursts. Once activated, the directional beacon had been designed to signal a welcome to its financial backers until they arrived in an anxiously excited vanguard, prepared to assess the lucrative possibilities of their endeavors.

The intervening years had been harsh ones for the probe's planet of origin. Such an undertaking for purposes of entertainment would no longer have been possible or even desirable. It had been such a long time since the probe's departure amid the carnival atmosphere of a perfectly non-productive upper-class lifestyle, but the situation had changed drastically. There were no longer those who served, and those who waited expectantly. There were only survivors. To them, the newly arriving signal was completely unexpected. The probe's extravagant investment scheme had been considered a failure many phase periods in the past. They'd been wrong. It was their last chance, and they eagerly prepared to take it.

CHAPTER 19

COLLEEN
Cay Islands- off the Southern Florida Coast

Athletically built and wearing her usual khaki shorts and T-shirt, Dr. Colleen Maxwell stood knee-high, feeling the gentle pull and tug of the surf as she contemplated what seemed to be the same water that had been there two weeks ago, but it wasn't. Twisting a strand of long, sun-streaked hair around a finger, she had to admit it wasn't even close. The water's chemistry was now so strange that she didn't know what to make of it at all.

She shook her hands dry, and admired the beautiful island where she and her research partner, Tony, had been working for eighteen months on one government-sponsored program or another. They were researchers first, friends second, and lovers incidentally, and Colleen missed him in his absence. Tony's mother was in a deep depression, and he'd been pulling her out inch by inch for the past month back in Baton Rouge.

"It'll still be a few more weeks," he'd disappointedly informed her during their last phone conversation.

"Could I ever use some of your wild ideas *now*, Tony!" Colleen wistfully twirled the strange water sample around and around in its glass tube. Watching the liquid form a small whirlpool, Colleen stood musing about her recent tendency towards procrastination. It was completely uncharacteristic, and she knew it masked both curiosity and unease.

After three weeks of testing, she'd be damned if she was any closer to knowing what was happening to the seawater. Tests for salinity showed a drastic drop, but this decrease didn't begin to account for the other strange properties of the water.

Colleen dipped her finger into the test tube and placed a drop of the water onto her tongue; yup, it was salty, but not *as* salty. The fact that the ocean was less salty would have been unbelievable, but the fact that it was only less salty within five hundred yards of the island was truly puzzling to her.

She dumped out the tube. It was time for some action, and a determined Colleen returned to the lab. Turning on the computer, she sent her query by e-mail up through the ranks. *Had this phenomenon ever been noted before?* she asked. *Was there a harvester close to the island?* they replied.

Stupid question! thought Colleen angrily. Wasn't there a harvester close to everything, nowadays? If they couldn't do any better than a question for a question, she seethed, what was the point? She decided to get in touch with Tony.

"Are you okay, Colleen?" He finally asked with concern as their conversation neared its end. "You sound preoccupied." He could tell something was wrong, but it couldn't be helped. Tony wasn't able to leave his mother yet, not until they had her anti-depressants adjusted properly; the doctors were adamant.

"I'm fine, Tony, just... busy."

"Well, don't go making any discoveries without me," he laughed into the phone.

Too late for that, she thought. "See you in two weeks." Then she hung up.

The whole chemistry of the water was changing. "Damn this equipment," she boiled, angry with the old, inadequate instruments at her disposal. I need the capability to do actual chemical analysis, she complained bitterly. But would it do any good anyway, she asked herself with resignation

The water from the lagoon didn't even smell right anymore. It still had a clean, fresh scent, not like stagnant water, but without the biting tang of salt she remembered so well. Something strange was going on. She was more certain with each passing day. Colleen knew there was a substance displacing the salt. Constantly licking her lips and even her arms in confirmation, she unsuccessfully tried to pinpoint the new taste: spicy, tangy, and elusive, but not salty.

To her complete consternation, the color was changing as well. It was difficult to tell in the deeper parts, but she could see the turquoise shallows taking on a pink tinge. Each day Colleen watched the lagoon get redder and redder, and less and less blue.

But there was more, and she faithfully documented each discovery, typing away daily in the lab journals. Sea life was changing right before her eyes. Each day she watched as former inhabitants of the lagoon followed the saltwater further out into the sea, leaving behind nothing but sparkling pink waters, which Colleen tested regularly for signs of life. At first, there had been none, but now things were different. Now, there was life again! I've got to figure this out, she demanded of herself, captured by the novelty of her subjects.

Were there thermal vents changing the salinity and killing off previous life, only to usurp their place with mutated bacterial growth? Colleen didn't think so. This was certainly no red tide. Unlike a red tide, the affected area remained the same for days, never growing or dwindling.

Each day Colleen watched the newly emerging pink, snowflake-like organisms swim, trapped between two glass slides on the microscope. She did this until some of the "critters" got too big to fit. "Moving day, guys," she announced happily, forced to move her specimens into glass containers. There they sat, silhouetted against the screenless windows with light shining through the swirling, rosy water. Less than one week later, Colleen spent another afternoon finding, filling, and relocating even larger jars. She continued to watch these creatures grow just as she'd watched the sea monkeys when she was smaller, until the tiny "snowflakes" gradually outgrew their jars, as well.

If Tony could only see this. It was exciting, but hard not to have anyone to share in the findings. This is incredible, observed Colleen with a great sense of accomplishment, while building small holding areas in the shallows. She pulled a sharp splinter from her finger, and wondered just how big her new charges would get. Forced to construct larger and larger pens further out into deeper water as they got bigger, there seemed to be no end in sight.

I know better than this, she told herself forcefully. These things should be reported to those funding her research, but she just couldn't bring herself to do it. After all, wouldn't it just bring hoards of people, and possibly disturb the natural order of what was happening?

She'd been watching for weeks, and now the lagoon itself was the holding area for the largest animals. Its waters went from light pink near the beach to ruby red in the deeper waters, and the life developing within these waters seemed as bound to them as the normal sea life was to theirs.

Colleen was fascinated as she snorkeled along the dividing line between the red and bluish-green waters. Both the new and the old sea life would swim briefly in the purple waters where the colors mingled, but then they each scurried back to the safety of their respective sides. Slathered in sunscreen, Colleen hovered between these two worlds for hours at a time, watching and recording observations.

But now, the red waters were moving further from shore. It was no longer a contained phenomenon, and Colleen was finally forced to go public. Her superiors would arrive any time. Actually, it would be kind of a relief. She hadn't been feeling much like herself over the last few days, anyway.

CHAPTER 20

Ladybug, ladybug, fly away home.
Your house is on fire, your children are gone.

E d had wanted Mary Beth to be comfortable. He was mostly sure that her gift was real. These days, how could anyone be sure of anything? They were still *following every lead*. This was the mantra he clung to for security and for confirmation that he was doing the right thing as they pushed forward through this ever-evolving crisis. Looking admirably around the apartment Ed had procured for Mary Beth, he realized it might be too modern-minimalist for her comfort. Chrome and glass throughout, far from homey. Then, he turned to the glass-topped dining table with the huge, real crystal globe the DOE had secured for her use. Ed never thought he would see the day when a crystal ball was a legitimate business expense. He rolled his eyes inwardly and snorted a small laugh, even though he truly did not find it funny at all.

Mary Beth emerged from the restroom down the hall. "It's nice," she said, her eyes scanning the apartment.

"Have you seen the dining area?" asked Ed, expectantly. As much as Mary Beth reminded him of the chaos that was his everyday life these days, she also brought him away from it, out of his head.

It was strange. He honestly could not place his feelings for her. At any rate, he wanted her to be happy with the impressive orb on the table.

"What's this?" she asked, walking up to the crystal sphere.

"It's yours," Ed responded, shoving his hands in his pockets. He just didn't know how to stand around her. "I hope you like it. Well, more than that, I hope it works."

"I do, and I don't," said Mary Beth, taking a seat at the end of the table furthest from the crystal. Would she see the same vision that had overtaken her well-used glass ball a mere thirty minutes ago?

"You don't like it." This was a question as much as it was a statement.

"It's not that," she insisted. "It's just that... well, I've always wanted to leave the small-town life behind and live somewhere like Washington D.C., but this isn't how I imagined it would happen. I know it probably sounds selfish, but I just want to be normal, even for one day."

Ed felt for Mary Beth, but he was first and foremost the lead on this project. He had to keep his focus. There was simply no time for feelings, but he needed Mary Beth and her abilities. "How about a normal slice of pizza on the way to the meeting downtown?"

She sat there for a moment, eyeing the crystal ball at the other end of the table. Did she see something? Ed wondered. "We could get Gyros instead."

"No," said Mary Beth, rising from the table. She grabbed her purse and headed for the door. "Pizza is fine."

She and Ed took their seats in the conference room at the DOE. "It's not what I expected," Mary Beth admitted with sadness.

"What do you mean, not what you expected?" Patrick prodded.

"The waters are going to shift globally. This isn't a local phenomenon."

"What do you mean *shift*?" asked Ed. They hadn't talked about what she had seen in the apartment. He had given her some room to breathe at lunch instead, relaying some childhood anecdotes over their slices of mushroom pizza.

"I'm not exactly sure, but I'd like some maps, please."

"We've got a computer program for that," Patrick explained, flipping up the laptop in front of her. "This program is designed for work with topographical models. I'll teach you how to use it."

"Okay," she said, following the mouse clicks on the laptop.

"The system was initially created to model the rising sea levels in association with global warming," said Ed. He looked down at his buzzing cellphone. "I have to take this."

Ed walked out of the conference room with the phone to his ear.

Patrick took over, sliding the bars on the adjustable parameters and familiarizing Mary Beth with the program. After this brief tutorial, she got to work trying to recreate what she had seen in the crystal ball back at the apartment.

"I don't want to keep you from anything," she said to Patrick. "I think I've got the hang of it now. It's just going to take some time."

"I get it," said Patrick. "It's hard to concentrate with someone breathing down your neck, literally. That's fine. I'll give you some space. I have to call Ray, anyway."

Patrick rose and made his way to the door, leaving Mary Beth by herself, as desired. "If you need anything, you can buzz Shane, at least until five. He's at extension 215." Patrick didn't wait for a response and promptly left Mary Beth to her project.

She manipulated the maps for hours, trying to match the physical world to her vision. The first time she stopped to check the time, it was four fifty-five. She pressed Shane's extension.

"Yes," Shane said brightly. "Is there anything I can get for you?"

"Yes, well maybe. I know you're leaving in a few minutes, but I could really use a coffee."

"Not to worry," said Shane with inflection. "The DOE has authorized overtime, and I'm at your disposal until at least eight.

I'm saving up for a Mediterranean cruise." He paused for effect. "Anyway, would you like a latte, frappe, straight coffee, espresso? What's your deal?"

"A latte would be nice, mocha flavor?"

"Perfect. Anything to eat—pastry, sandwich, Chinese takeout?"

"Doughnuts?"

"Done," said Shane. "It shouldn't be too long. I'm rolling my extension over to my cell phone if you need me while I'm out."

"Thanks."

Half an hour later, it was Ed who walked in with a dozen doughnuts and two lattes. "How's everything going?"

"Shane, you've changed."

Ed gave her joke a sympathy laugh as he opened the box and set it on the conference table. He took out an apple fritter and sat down opposite Mary Beth, chewing and waiting for her to fill him in on any progress.

"So, I know exactly what I'm doing in the program now. It's very user-friendly. That's not the issue," she began, then paused for a sip of her mocha latte wrapped in a cardboard sleeve to hold in the heat. "The problem is that I've been creating these maps with the new bodies of water I see rising out of the ground, but nothing is fitting together."

"What do you mean by that?" Ed tried not to put too much pressure on Mary Beth by asking too many questions or being too forceful. He could see her eyes were not focused on him even as she spoke directly to him. She was still thinking, puzzling it out behind the glassy expression she gave him.

"Look," she took the mouse in her hand and Ed slid his conference chair around the table until he had a good view of her computer screen.

She manipulated the map of North America. "This is what I see." She adjusted the bars for water area and depth, and the low-lying portions of North America disappeared under water.

"Wow," Ed looked on as Florida was completely submerged. "How long is this going to take? I mean, how long do we have to warn people?" As he asked these questions, it occurred to him he would have thought Mary Beth to be a crazy doomsdayer only months ago; mentally ill, perhaps, but things had changed. Was it the end of days? No. They would make sure of it. He tried not to let his mind go there.

"You haven't seen what I need to show you yet," she said, continuing to make changes to the maps. "Here, look at this map of Asia." This time there were land masses where none had been before, in addition to the new bodies of water.

Ed looked on as new mountains grew out of the North China Plain. *The rocks!* It occurred to him. He thought about the rocks that had cracked and grown and changed in Barry's office. It wasn't just the low-lying areas that were in trouble. "Have you seen all parts of the Earth, or just these two continents?"

"I've worked on the maps from all different angles, but the hard part has been putting it all together. I only get glimpses of the changes from select vantage points. I just can't find a way to make it cohesive." She rubbed her eyes and her forehead.

Ed could see the frustration building up. "Do you need an Advil or something?"

"No. I don't have a headache. It's just, have you ever been so close to knowing something and still cannot grasp the entire concept? You know you're almost there, but still can't understand it fully?"

"Look, maybe you should be done for the day," said Ed. "Go home, get some sleep and attack this with a clear head in the morning."

"Would you follow that advice?" she asked him with one eyebrow raised. "I don't think there's going to be a lot of relaxing from this point on. The only way I can clear my head completely is to allow myself to slip into the visions, but even then, my head is filled with what they're showing me."

"Who?" asked Ed.

"What do you mean *who*?"

"You said that *they* were showing you," Ed explained.

"That's not what I meant," she assured him. "I can't focus here."

Mary Beth stood and closed her laptop. "Do you have a bag for my computer and a charger?"

"Shane knows where they are." Ed stood and grabbed the doughnuts from the table.

They both walked out of the conference room and down the hall, finding Shane at his desk scrolling through pictures of the Mediterranean. *If he only knew*, thought Ed.

"Secretary Marker," said Shane as he minimized his screen. "Is there something I can get you?"

"We need a computer bag and a charger."

"Absolutely!" He sprung up from his chair and opened a cabinet, extracting the needed supplies. "Working late, again?"

"Yes, and no. We'll keep at it, but we're leaving for the day," said Ed. "You can take off if you'd like, unless there's something you need to finish up."

"No, sir," said Shane, shutting down his computer and grabbing his jacket. "I'll see you in the morning."

Shane always had something going on in his personal life. Ed sometimes wondered what it would be like to have so many friends, but he was more of an introvert, so he would probably never know.

"Do you want any company?" asked Ed. He thought about going home to his empty apartment.

"I'm okay," said Mary Beth.

Ed noted that she still had that glazed look in her eyes. "*So close to knowing something and still unable to grasp the entire concept.*" He thought twice before he spoke again, not wanting to interrupt her thought process.

"You're new to the city. I'll make sure you get home."

She didn't respond to him.

There was a different feel on the city streets as they walked toward the metro station. People were going about their normal business, yet they seemed more hurried or rushed than usual. As much as the DOE had tried to keep the strange happenings out of the news, it was becoming nearly impossible. There were so many changes taking place. If a person hadn't experienced something themselves, they knew second or third hand of someone who had. Passersby were speaking in hushed tones on their phones or softly to their companions.

As they continued down Independence Avenue, Ed observed the shelves inside small convenience stores lining the sidewalks. Shelves that were usually brimming with products were noticeably less full. Nothing alarming, but noticeable. He did not mention this to Mary Beth, as she had made no attempts at conversation.

She abruptly stopped outside of a three-story gym, where business people went to work out and wait for traffic to die down before making the commute back to the suburbs. She looked in through the window.

"Do you want to go in?" He wondered if she had been thinking that a workout might do her some good or help her relax.

"No. Look!" she said, pointing through the glass. One woman on a treadmill pretended not to notice them and Mary Beth continued to point. She was looking past the woman at the TV screen behind her. She walked briskly to the glass doors that read American Fitness Club and pulled the right-sided door open forcefully. Mary Beth made her way past rows of ellipticals and treadmills to a giant flat-screen hanging on the wall.

The gym attendant approached her and asked her if she was considering becoming a member, but she didn't respond. Ed caught up to her and answered for her. "We're just looking. Sorry. We'll leave."

Ed put his arm around Mary Beth and she melted onto the floor, sitting cross-legged next to a stair climber grinding under the weight of a sweaty patron.

The attendant noticed her seated position and pressed on. "We also have yoga classes," he continued, gesturing to a class that had just begun in the back of the gym.

Motioning everyone away, Ed kneeled beside Mary Beth. Her eyes were still locked on the large TV screen displaying a gigantic spherical sculpture hanging from the ceiling in the lobby of the Intel building in Santa Clara, California.

Crowd control wasn't hard. The gym members ignored them, not wanting to interrupt their routines. The attendant went back to his podium near the entrance to scan membership cards as others entered.

"What is it?" asked Ed in a whisper barely audible over the hum of the cardio equipment.

Mary Beth didn't respond. She was in a vision, her eyes locked on the TV screen.

"Here, we need to move," insisted Ed. "We can't stay here on the floor." He tugged her under the arm.

"What are you doing?" she asked, standing up with the force of his tug.

"Good, you're back," responded Ed.

"Get the computer out," she said breathlessly, looking pale. "I have the answer."

"What do you mean?"

"That's it. That's the answer!" She pointed toward the TV. By now, the screen had changed, displaying some type of pillow advertisement, but she knew what she had seen. "It's not a sculpture. It's a globe!"

"Let's go next door," insisted Ed. "There's a coffee shop where we can plug in the laptop. Let's get another coffee or whatever you want and you can explain it to me."

Once situated in a remote corner of the coffee shop, Mary Beth explained herself. "Ed, I didn't black out, I zeroed in. I saw it—not the sculpture, the planet. The only thing I'm not sure of is whether it was the future Earth I saw, or somewhere else. Let me pull up a picture of the sculpture on a split-screen." She took a sip of black coffee and waited for the picture to load. "Yes, here it is. The sculptor is Frieda Hinkle from California. How can we get in touch with her?"

"I'm on it." Ed sent Patrick a text, asking him to track down this Frieda Hinkle. He knew Shane was probably already two drinks into happy hour with his friends.

"Good. Now, watch me overlay my maps with this model of the globe."

Ed took note of how tech-savvy she was for a girl from the middle of nowhere. "Would you look at that?" Ed breathed. "They match. At least they match where you've been able to construct your model."

A text from Patrick knocked Ed from his reverie. *Frieda Hinkle 669-555-2058.*

"Did he find her already?" asked Mary Beth.

"I've got her number right here." Ed turned his phone toward her, displaying the text.

"How did she know about this?"

Ed took that as more of a statement than a question. "I'm going to call her. I hope she'll talk to me. My number comes up as a private caller, so she may not answer."

"Here," said Mary Beth, "just call her from the computer. You can use the earbuds and I'll put on the talk to text so I can follow along."

"How did you learn all of this?" Ed smiled at her.

"I'm from Iowa, not Mars. We have the internet." She rolled her eyes and continued to pull up the program.

Thirty minutes later, they were back to square one. "Okay, so it turns out that Ms. Hinkle hasn't the foggiest." Ed was frustrated with their blind alley. "Just another harvester anomaly."

"Be fair, Ed. She told us what she could. Without her sculpture, I'd still be putting the jigsaw puzzle together." Mary Beth reached for Ed's hand in a comforting gesture that became slightly awkward. She withdrew her hand.

"You're right, it did save time. I'm just not sure what to do with that time." Ed was at a loss for his next step. He had to inform Barry and Patrick. Maybe they would have a suggestion or more information, or something. Ed needed to keep pushing forward. He wasn't sure he would be able to stand the pressure if he were to stop. Just keep moving.

"Thank you for everything that you've done," said Ed.

"Are you breaking up with me now that you have what you want?" Mary Beth said jokingly.

"What? No. Oh, I get it." Ed laughed. "No, I appreciate what you've done. We have a visual of what we're up against globally now. That's huge!"

"You know I'm just kidding," she assured him. "I have to tell you, though, that I'm kind of worn out. The visions that I get with altered states of consciousness drain me." She looked at her half-empty cup of coffee.

Ed could see the circles under her eyes. "Why don't you go home?"

"I'll take you up on that offer this time."

"Do you mind if I take the computer back to the office? Unless you need it for something else?" Ed inquired.

"No." She permitted him to take the device. "I'll be asleep as soon as my head hits the pillow. I'm feeling slightly lightheaded."

"Will you be okay to make it back to the apartment?"

"Absolutely," Mary Beth assured him. "Go back and fill everyone in. I would feel better resting if I knew that progress was still being made."

Ed didn't need much convincing. "Okay then, I'll see you tomorrow?"

"You will."

Ed heard the door to the coffee shop open and close as he packed up the computer and wound up the cord.

Barry and Patrick weren't hard to find. Both were closeted in Patrick's office, working with some of the department's more useful reports. Within minutes, both were standing beside the computer monitor in Ed's office, thoroughly briefed and suitably amazed.

"This model could save lives," said Patrick. "That is, if anyone believes all of this. At least Mary Beth thinks it will happen gradually."

"That *is* the consensus," Ed agreed, darkly sarcastic. "The slow but steady progression is also probably the thing that will help sway public opinion before it's completely too late. When the waters begin to rise, they'll continue, and the public won't be able to deny it even if they want to."

Barry ran his fingers through his hair. This had become a nervous habit of his as of late. "But is that supposed to help the Iowa family, whose farmhouse will become a lakeside cabin or the people along the East Coast who will have to watch whole states sink into the ocean—slowly, of course?"

"It can't be stopped, Barry. At this point, we've got to at least be thankful that whatever is happening isn't a faster process—so far, anyway," said Ed, knowing that he was not in-fact offering Barry any reassurance.

Ed relayed what Mary Beth had told him about a drastic increase in coming earthquakes, not immediately, but coming. Along with the gradually escalating earthquakes, there would be shape-shifting rocks, and increasingly aberrant mutational anomalies. "Her visions have become broader, more than just seeing the rising water."

Ed looked at the faces of his friends. Things had changed, in the world obviously, but also in how the three of them perceived this problem. Was being forewarned the same as being forearmed? God, he hoped so, because Ed was expecting a final report on feasible solutions from Dr. Mann in exactly twenty-four hours. If there weren't any magic bullets, and at this point, Ed knew better than to expect the impossible, it was time to go public with everything. He and President Morgan had been gauging when it would be best to inform the American public.

• • •

The next day, Patrick called his boss with the latest disturbing news. "Ed, we've gotten a report of a red tide off the Florida Keys."

"How large an area are we talking about, Patrick?"

"Large enough. There's a research station on the island that seems to be in the middle of it all."

"And?" Ed knew there would be more; there always was, nowadays.

"A huge relay harvester happens to be located on the island. Dr. Colleen Maxwell is in charge of the research facility. It seems her partner has been away on personal leave and she's made several strange inquiries of her superiors recently. Sounds like trouble. Want me to go?"

"No, I'd better field this one. I'll take Mary Beth, too." Ed decided as he spoke into the phone, staring hard at the table-top globe sitting in front of him on his desk. It had been painted to be the exact duplicate of a certain sculpture in Santa Clara. At the moment, all he could think about were the oceans of ruby red water surrounding the landmasses on his new toy.

Like hell it was a red tide, thought Ed. They didn't have a clue as to what they were reporting. "Maybe Mary Beth can tune in on something helpful while we're there. After all, water seems to be her specialty," Ed speculated.

"I sure hope so," said Patrick. "By the way, has she come any closer on her estimate for the timetable of the rising water levels?"

"Yes. We've got about two weeks, give or take a little." Mary Beth had been definite in her schedule of events, and right on all counts so far. "That's the good news and the bad news. Anyway, gotta go. I have a conference call scheduled with Dr. Mann."

"I hope he has something for us," Patrick said and hung up.

Before Ed joined the conference call, he issued some instructions to Shane to get in touch with Mary Beth and secure two tickets on a flight to the Keys.

"Hello, Dr. Mann. Sorry to keep you waiting so long." Ed was formal and polite.

"Yes, Secretary Marker," Dr. Mann hesitated. "I'm sorry to say that I have some terrible news. I've, ah, underestimated the potential mutational factor in the newly formed genetic material. It's much more common than predicted." Dr. Mann wasn't used to making apologies.

"By exactly how much did you 'underestimate,' Dr. Mann, and what kind of mutations are you anticipating?"

After a long pause and a deep breath, Dr. Andrew Mann began speaking. "I wasn't even close. Some of the genetic material resulting from the combination seems to remain stable, but a steady percentage mutates radically. You see," he hurried on, "normally genetic replication is exact. It allows for differences in personal appearance, intelligence factors, and things like that, but remains within normal physical and functional levels, except for the wild cards which produce birth defects and similar variations." These were the facts.

"Once the gene pool for an individual is in place, however," the doctor continued, "a person doesn't wake up with a genetic physical abnormality like Spina Bifida one morning out of the blue. This is because the mutation of a gene sequence has to happen during a one time conception and creation process within the womb. After that, it remains steady.

"Even most diseases appearing later in life have been linked to a genetic predisposition. So, although it seems these illnesses pop up from nowhere, they've actually just been waiting in the wings, so to speak. We were under the mistaken impression that the one time initial combination of the two different genetic materials would also result in a new, but likewise stable, set of genetic parameters."

"It doesn't?" asked Ed somewhat sarcastically.

"Sometimes yes, sometimes no. It's not anything we feel confident in predicting any longer. The ratio of the radically mutated genes seems to be holding steady at around twenty percent, but presently, anything is possible. Maybe those whose material hasn't gone into a continuing second divisional shift will do so in a month, or a week, or three years. Without predictability, genetics is nothing."

"So, what exactly are you trying to say?" asked Ed.

"Essentially, what I'm telling you is that I've become useless to you except for being a sideline commentator who calls the plays as they happen. My apologies, Secretary Marker."

"Ed, please." Not that it made any difference how he was addressed. "I might have known the problem was too big for your people to get their arms around. What we'd been assuming was that what we have been seeing would continue. You're saying it's not so. Correct?"

"I don't know, Secretary Marker. The changes we see now could be all of it, or only a portion of what will finally happen. As I said, nothing may happen to someone now, but in eighteen months, they could mutate. Or, consider someone who has changed dramatically already; they could mutate again or have, as we call it, a second divisional shift. All we know for sure is that we know nothing for sure."

"I'd like to send someone over to work on this with you," said Ed. "You've heard of Barry Davis?"

"Yes, the inventor of the harvester," Dr. Mann voiced curtly.

Ed picked up where the awkward silence left off. He knew that Dr. Mann was leaving his opinions of Barry unsaid.

"Yes. Contrary to what you may believe, Barry is brilliant and needs to be working on something that hits on frequency modulations, genetics, and cell structures with the very best, and in my estimation, that's still you."

"I am not above working with anyone who may be able to offer new information in dealing with this crisis," said Dr. Mann practically.

"Barry's come up with a few new angles. Combining genetics with physics may yield new possibilities."

Dr. Mann agreed that there was no harm in combining their skill sets.

Ed thanked the doctor and hung up. He would head back to his house and pack for the Keys.

CHAPTER 21

Baltimore, Maryland, 2022

Your grandpa is ninety years old today, kids." Silence. "Are you guys listening?" Rebecca adjusted the rearview mirror to see both of her teenagers looking at their phones, AirPods plugged into their ears.

"Hey!" She waved her hand around from the driver's seat. "Listen up, you guys."

"What?" asked Chris, taking out one of his AirPods.

"I'm watching a TikTok," said Emma. "What is it?"

"You guys can't be on your phones when we get there."

"Why not?" said Chris. "Grandpa can never hear anything we say. I don't even think he knows who we are anymore."

"I think old people are creepy." Emma rolled her eyes and went back to another short video.

"That's enough. I don't want to hear anything like that once we get there. Does everyone understand?"

"I don't understand why I couldn't drive," Chris exhaled louder than necessary. "I mean, I have places to go after this. Mom, I'm graduating this year."

"We're visiting your grandfather as a family."

"How come Dad doesn't have to come this time?" asked Emma.

"Your father is mowing the lawn."

"I would have mowed the lawn," Chris chimed in.

"Just promise me you'll both smile when you see him. He gets confused. Whatever he says, just play along. Okay?"

"That's so weird, Mom. Why are we lying to him?" asked Emma from the back seat.

"We're not lying," said Rebecca, exiting the Beltway. "We just don't want to agitate him, sweetie."

"Whatever. We'll smile." Emma agreed. "Are we going to have lunch there?"

"Yeah, their hamburgers are pretty good." Chris looked interested. "Kind of strange though, because no one there can chew anymore."

Emma laughed at her brother's joke.

Rebecca didn't know whether to scold, laugh along, or just ignore them. She opted for choice number three. *Whatever*, as the kids would say.

They pulled up to the retirement village. The grounds were immense and well-manicured. A rainbow of flowers spilled from every bed and it smelled of new mulch. Bright green grass cut in a crosshatch pattern carpeted the rolling acreage. Admiral Price, now ninety, had lived on this campus for ten years, but he didn't enjoy the gardens much anymore and had spent most of his time napping over this past year.

"Maybe today will be one of his good days," said Rebecca as she put the van in park. More silence. She rolled her eyes and turned around. "Everybody out."

Inside the facility, it was clean and upscale. The common rooms had high ceilings and decorative stained glass with intricate crown molding. You could choose anything from formal dining to a quick burger from any of the many restaurants available for lunch. The wheelchairs and canes looked sterile and out of place in such a polished setting.

The three of them walked up to the check-in counter. Rebecca felt good when they greeted her by name. She was visiting enough.

"You're here for the Admiral?" Rose smiled from behind the counter. She was slightly bent with a puff of white stiff curls and a smile circled by a starburst of wrinkles.

Rebecca couldn't help but think that she looked more like a resident than an employee. "Yes, we are. How's he doing today?"

"Well, the girls parked him next to the birds in the main hallway this morning. He seems to like them—when he's awake." Rose smiled at them again.

"Thanks." Rebecca surveyed her teens, making sure that they had their AirPods out. "Come on, you two."

Flat commercial carpet absorbed the noise as they walked down the long corridor. He was sleeping, sitting up in his wheelchair next to a sizable cage holding four parakeets chirping away.

"Hi, Dad," said Rebecca loudly.

The long-retired Admiral did not move.

Rebecca inspected him closely, noting the rise and fall of his chest. He was still alive, and she placed her hand on his shoulder. "Dad?" Rebecca said again, even louder.

"What?" said the Admiral.

"Happy Birthday, Dad."

"Rebecca."

"Yes, Dad. It's me, Rebecca. Emma and Chris are here, too."

"What's McClain doing here?"

"Who's McClain, Dad?" asked Rebecca. Even though she was shouting, no one turned. Shouting was a common form of communication with the residents whose hearing was not the best.

"What are you doing here, McClain?" Admiral Price looked at his grandson.

"Um... they stationed me here?" Chris responded, looking over at his mom.

Rebecca gave him a nod and a thumbs-up.

"You're supposed to be in Bermuda, McClain."

"Um... I'm on leave?" Chris looked at his mom again and received another thumbs-up.

"Rebecca, this is Seaman McClain. Is this your wife, McClain?" The Admiral looked at Emma.

"Uh, yes?" said Emma, taking a step closer to her brother and forcing a smile.

"Beautiful. Nice to meet you," said Admiral Price.

"Nice to meet you," said his granddaughter.

"Now, McClain, we need to talk." The sleepy Admiral suddenly had a burst of energy. "Rebecca, would you and Mrs. McClain like to get some lunch while the men talk?"

Rebecca looked over at Chris and gave him a look that said *would that be okay with you?*

Now, it was Chris who gave the thumbs-up sign.

There was a good kid under all of that teenage snark. "Sure. We'll grab a burger at the café and let you guys talk."

"Thank you, dear. You're such a good girl."

Rebecca gave Chris one last look of gratitude. She would make sure to get a bacon cheeseburger for him. She and Emma headed back the way they had come, toward the café.

"McClain?"

"Yes."

"We have to move Addie."

"Who's Addie?" asked Chris.

"Exactly. You've always been able to hold on to sensitive information."

"Right."

"It's all over the news. All of it."

"What's been on the news?" Chris asked.

"Enough. I get it. You're free to speak, McClain. You know what I'm talking about."

"Oh, right." Chris kept his answers brief. Short answers were safer with Grandpa.

"Those deformed reptile people. You know. The ones with all the scales in North Carolina?" said the Admiral.

"I've seen the stories," said Chris, *really* trying to play along. "I saw it on the news in Bermuda."

"Are you okay, McClain? I know you're stationed in Bermuda. I was there with you last week. Have you fixed the damned air conditioning yet? Never mind. Listen up. We have to move Addie. Do you understand how important this is to the President?"

"Absolutely. I mean...yes." Chris looked around, but there was no one to rescue him from the conversation.

"All of it," said the Admiral. "I hear all of it. They think I'm sleeping, but I'm listening."

Chris just looked at his grandpa.

"I hear all of these girls talking about what they see on their phones. It's happening, McClain. We have to make sure that Addie is safe."

"Sure. No problem," said Chris.

"Here she comes," said the Admiral.

"Who?" asked Chris.

"I told you that was enough of that, Seaman."

"Hi. I'm CNA Tracey. It's time for the Admiral to rest." She smiled kindly at Chris.

"I understand," Chris said, grateful to be rescued. "I'll see you soon, Grandpa. Happy Birthday." He walked quickly down the hall, headed for the café, and didn't turn back.

"I don't need to rest," asserted the Admiral. "CNA Tracey, more like CIA Tracey."

"That's enough of that now, Admiral. We don't want you to get too upset." Tracey pushed Admiral Price in his wheelchair down to his room.

The walls were tastefully decorated with framed mementos of his many successes, testaments to a long and honorable naval career. He had achieved the distinguished rank of Admiral before retiring in his seventies. There were medals and awards from his service, but also family photos, most of which were of his wife, Amy. She was a strikingly beautiful woman who had stolen his heart almost a lifetime ago. Tragically, Amy's passing several years prior had left him alone to wither away parked next to a birdcage.

The Admiral looked from his favorite picture of Amy over to CNA Tracey. "Could you turn on the news?"

"Sure, but if you start getting upset, I'm going to have to turn it off. We don't want you having flashbacks again." Tracey wheeled him in front of the TV and turned it on, placing the remote on the small coffee table next to his chair.

"Look at that!" shouted the Admiral. Again, no one came rushing over or even poked their head into the room. Shouting was background noise at the home.

"Look at that," agreed Tracey as she drew up a syringe full of Vecuronium. She injected the lethal drug into the Admiral's wasted muscle tissue, her assignment complete.

CHAPTER 22

To care is a blessing, to care too much is a burden.

The small, chartered plane was a necessity, but Ed wished it wasn't. He held both hands firmly over his queasy stomach, stifling small belches from escaping his mouth. Flying as often as he had in the past weeks, Ed's stomach had gotten somewhat used to the feeling, but this puddle jumper was a different story. Every time the seaplane went one way, his stomach went another. He certainly hadn't been much company to Mary Beth, who was watching him sympathetically in a distracted sort of way he'd come to recognize. He turned his attention to the window, hoping for some relief.

"Look at that, the water is changing!" Ed pointed below at the spreading red stain.

"It's so beautiful," Mary Beth said, surprised by her own response, "but look at all the movement below the surface in the red area." She leaned closer to the window. "To be seen from a distance like this, those things must be enormous."

"If the reports are correct, it's spreading at an incredible rate in all directions." Just once, Ed wished, it would be nice if the reports were wrong.

"It's all happened so fast," Ed continued queasily. "As Dr. Mann said, there's no way to predict when, how, or how many times these mutations will occur, or to what extent. The tremors have just made the news. Look." Ed held up his phone, showing Mary Beth a recent news feed out of Maryland, *Deep Creek Lake Doubles in Size after 6.0 Quake this Afternoon.*

"It's all over social media," Mary Beth agreed. "It's been mostly religious posts this morning. People are trying to explain the inexplicable, trying to assign reason and purpose to the random mutations."

"That's the problem," said Ed. "None of this is predictable, and when people are left without an explanation, God's will can be used to explain away just about anything."

"So you're not religious?" she asked.

"And you are?" Ed deflected, answering a question with a question.

It's not that he wasn't religious. He just couldn't blindly accept these global changes as God's will. To believe this, he would have to relinquish trying to help and reassign responsibility to God.

"I'm just not ready to give up. Are you?" he added.

"Who's giving up?" she responded, scrolling through the news feeds. "I'm here, aren't I?" She glanced up at Ed, who looked particularly gray as she continued to read the posts and comments.

"Look, Ed, I know you're waiting for society to collapse under the strain of all of this, but believe it or not, as *Madame Olga*, I was a student of human nature for too long to believe it's going to happen the way you think. People may surprise you."

"Maybe," but as another student of human nature, Ed wasn't very hopeful.

They would inform the public tomorrow. The President of the United States was scheduled to speak at six p.m. The President's words had been carefully crafted to offer information and hope, to bolster the feeling of a country united, but no solutions would be offered. There weren't any to give.

Predicting the rioting and the end of the world mentality from a fraction of the population, his speech would detail military imprisonment for any citizen who broke from their normal routine. They could not have a breakdown in the food supply, availability of heat, transportation, all the necessities. People would be expected to continue with their normal jobs and routines indefinitely or be detained and imprisoned by the US military.

"Are they really going to have troops in tanks and humvees patrolling civilians?" asked Mary Beth, placing her phone face down on her lap.

"Is that any more surprising than what we've already seen with this?"

"I guess not," said Mary Beth. "I just never thought I would see anything like this."

"No one did," said Ed. "But with the patrolling also comes the evacuation and relocation programs the military has set into place. Sometimes, sacrifices to personal freedoms have to be made to maintain order and safety in a crisis situation."

This flight needs to be over soon. Ed's stomach caught his attention again. He had taken no motion sickness medication because he could not afford to feel drowsy. "As soon as we land, we need to be on our way to the lagoon to find Dr. Maxwell. Okay?"

"Fine by me, but tell me, do you think these sea creatures are dangerous?" she asked as the seaplane carrying them so roughly landed on the pastel pink reef water.

"I know only as much as you do." *Thank God*, Ed thought as the engine stopped and he unbuckled his seat belt.

The beach was deserted. This was odd, he thought, rallying quickly now that he was no longer hovering, buffeted in mid-air. They waded to shore, holding their waterproof bags over their heads, all the while looking out for the monsters they had seen from the plane. Thankfully, it looked like those were sticking to deeper water. When they got to shore, Dr. Colleen Maxwell was nowhere to be found. She should have been there to meet them.

Wind from the propellers gusted as the plane slowly backed further out to sea and then turned into its long ascent from the surface up into the sky. It would return in the afternoon to retrieve them. Where the hell was she?

"Let's check inside," Mary Beth suggested practically. She started toward the research facility down the beach.

• • •

DR. COLLEEN MAXWELL

Colleen saw the plane pass overhead at the same time that Mary Beth noticed Colleen and her companions below, but the distance from the island was too great for her to arrive before the DOE agents. Colleen was newly streamlined and slipped easily through the ruby red waters, but her size was now considerable, and her sheer bulk made for lumbering, though graceful, progress.

She was literally as big as a house and loving every minute of it. No longer human, Colleen was not bound by all the rules and regulations which had hounded her research. No more paperwork, she reveled. There were no more hands to hold the pen.

She knew so much more now and could feel the strange chemical brew making up her bodily cells. Colleen was perfectly balanced and adapted to this new environment, and this was a new environment. The earth as they'd known it was going the way of the dinosaurs, shaping itself into something unrecognizable, yet familiar on a gut level, and she was a part of it!

How would the agents react to a new and improved Colleen, she wondered, while slowly nearing the lagoon? It was here that yesterday she'd witnessed the beginning of her transformation.

Not feeling herself, a short catnap on the beach had seemed in order. More tired than she'd realized, Colleen hadn't awakened until the tide had come in and washed gently against her. At that point, it was obvious that something was drastically wrong.

With legs stuck together, she'd been unable to push up onto elbows receding into a rapidly growing body. There were appendages, yes, but nothing which would support her new bulk.

Colleen panicked and was terribly uncomfortable in the bargain, thrashing like the fish out of water she'd become. Gratefully, she'd surrendered herself to the incoming tide. Her awkward movements on the beach were soon forgotten as the weightless buoyancy of the lovely pink lagoon waters carried her far from shore.

Mary Beth headed into the building so quickly that she didn't take time to look around, but Ed slowed and stopped as he looked from one plant mutation to another. If he wasn't mistaken, some of them looked like those giant alien trees Patrick had photographed in the cornfield. Maybe this was a link to follow. He sure hoped Dr. Maxwell had plenty of canned food to offer for lunch because Ed wasn't about to eat the fruit off of anything growing on this island. He heard Mary Beth calling to him. Maybe she'd found Dr. Maxwell.

"Ed, look at this." She motioned from the doorway. Mary Beth was studying the rows upon rows of jars lining the walls of the small research building. "If I were back home and saw all of this, I'd think someone had gone berserk with their yearly canning. These are canning jars, you know, but whatever's in them is alive."

She was holding one of the smaller jars up to the light of the window. This jar held deep, blood-red water and two tadpole-like creatures, each with four pairs of trailing appendages and three brightly glowing eyes.

"Look at the color differences. Some jars are pink, some are dark like this one, and there must be a jar for every shade in between," she said.

"Do any of these animals, or fish, or whatever, look familiar to you at all?" Ed asked, wrinkling up his nose and sniffing the air loudly.

"No, not really, but what's that smell?" Mary Beth didn't find it offensive, just different and overpowering.

"It must be the water. I noticed it outside, but it wasn't as strong as it is in here. Let's get out of here and see if we can find that researcher."

"Not yet," said Mary Beth. "It's not so bad when you breathe through your mouth. We need to check around here first. Colleen must have notes, somewhere."

"You're right," Ed agreed.

Mary Beth opened the jar in her hand and sniffed. It was the water all right. Without thinking, she stuck her finger into the murky red and swirled it around gently. She suddenly came to her senses as the two small creatures in the liquid stopped swimming and quietly observed the finger disturbing their home.

"Wow," she breathed. "This is weird."

The two animals looked from the stationary finger into her eyes, as Mary Beth stared hugely through the thick canning jar glass.

"Careful. They could bite and what if they're poisonous?" said Ed, eyeing Mary Beth as she continued her uneasy stand-off with the creatures.

"Ed, I can't explain it, but I know they wouldn't hurt me." She kept her finger still in the water. "I think they like me. Look."

They both watched as the creatures inched slowly nearer to Mary Beth's dangling digit until they were rubbing against it like aquatic cats.

"Sorry, guys. We have work to do," Mary Beth informed them, as she withdrew her finger. After putting their discoveries back into proper order on the shelf, Mary Beth and Ed searched through desk drawers and file cabinets slowly and thoroughly, collecting a mountain of research notes. They could not log onto the computer.

Colleen had done a very careful job of documenting the strange phenomena she'd been studying. Ed was impressed by the sheer volume of notes and was sure that all of this would put them closer to some kind of understanding. They would have to box all of this up when the plane returned later in the afternoon.

He and Mary Beth were on their way out the door when a sudden thought made him turn and walk to the small cot in the corner of the room. Looking under the pillow, Ed came up with a personal diary. "Now, this will tell us more than all the rest put together," he said, holding the diary up and handing it to Mary Beth. "But let's take it outside to read it. I'm tired of breathing through my mouth."

Mary Beth agreed and followed him out of the research facility, onto the sun-baked sand of the lagoon.

It took their eyes a moment to adjust to the bright sunlight after having been in the dim lab for upwards of an hour. After he had regained his sight fully, Ed noticed some screen contraptions set up in the lagoon and decided to see what they were or what they might be holding.

As he approached the waterline, he saw it was a pen of some sort. Dr. Colleen Maxwell had been studying the captives in their stages of growth on a much larger scale out here in the lagoon. "Mary Beth," he called out to his partner. "Come and look at this."

She approached Ed at the waterline; the journal tucked under her arm. He was scanning the surface for any signs of life.

"Look!" said Ed, pointing out into deeper water.

"I *am* looking," Mary Beth shot back, eyes still on the waters contained within the screen.

"No! Look out there!" Ed insisted.

Mary Beth gave Ed her attention and shifted her gaze to where he was pointing out in the deeper water just beyond the screen. "What is that?"

Ed kept the creature in his sights, not wanting to take his eyes off of it for a moment for fear of losing it in the waters. It was a humanoid whale thing—huge. "I'm going out to take a closer look."

"No, you're not!" said Mary Beth.

"I've got to," said Ed. "We've come all this way, and I'll be separated from it by the screen."

"That flimsy screen isn't going to do you any good," said Mary Beth, annoyed at his poor judgment.

"I really can't explain it," said Ed, "but I feel drawn to this creature. It's like you said; I know it isn't going to harm me."

"Ed, it's one thing to swirl fingers in a jar with tadpoles, and quite another to stand within chomping distance of a possibly carnivorous mutant creature thirty times your size."

Ed had not waited for Mary Beth to finish her plea, wading into the pink waters of the screened-in area. Larger tadpole-like creatures brushed against his legs affectionately as he made his way to the outer limits of the pen.

Mary Beth turned around and looked at the research facility. "They have to have some kind of watercraft here," she mumbled to no one in particular. She ran around the back of the building, dropping the journal in the sand, and found a one-person kayak propped up on the stucco wall in the shade of the building. Mary Beth dragged the small boat down to the water's edge only to find that Ed had crossed over the screen and was treading water right next to the big whale thing.

The kayak slid soundlessly into the water and she dipped her ore into the lagoon to her right, then to her left, cutting through the water on her way out to meet Ed and whatever that was out there. The tadpole-like creatures stared through the blood-colored translucent waters of the lagoon. She finally reached the outskirts of the pen and called out to Ed, who had been creeping slowly out to sea with this creature, completely mesmerized.

"Ed," she shouted. "Come back! You're out too far."

Ed waved at Mary Beth, unable to hear what she was saying over the natural sounds of the ocean waves pushing him up and down as he floated with his new companion.

Mary Beth waved him in like a lifeguard with one hand, holding onto the ore with the other.

Ed could not ignore this sign. He started back to Mary Beth, flanked by the bulk of the creature he had swum out to meet.

Mary Beth held the kayak steady in one place on the opposite side of the screen as they approached.

Ed had drawn close enough to Mary Beth to speak. "Mary Beth, meet Dr. Colleen Maxwell." He held his arm out in an introduction like she was some kind of giant school project. "Colleen, this is Mary Beth Hatcher."

The whole thing was such a weird experience that for a moment Ed had forgotten about the harvester's part in all of this, merely reveling in the extraordinary moment. "Come on, get in." Ed coaxed Mary Beth.

"I'm fine here," said Mary Beth. "I'm not sure I understand what you're telling me, though."

"Believe me, you're no more surprised than I was." The voice coming from Colleen's new form was deep and booming, sounding neither male nor female.

"You can't be serious?" exhaled Mary Beth. "When did this happen to you? How fast was the process? Oh, and what about all those jars in the lab?"

Colleen interrupted Mary Beth loudly. "I'm so glad you mentioned them. Would you please bring the jars out and dump the small ones into the lagoon and then release all the penned animals. I was trying to keep them safe and study them, but there is no danger out here for them." The resonant voice was very commanding and her speech pattern had a spellbinding sing-song quality.

The sun shone on pink sparkling water as Ed and Mary Beth listened harder than they'd ever done in their lives; and the former Colleen Maxwell explained about her nap and subsequent changing form. "Since then, I've gotten stronger and larger by the hour, but now I feel the transformation slowing, or possibly shifting. Who knows?" With no shoulders to shrug, her bodily gesture was useless. "Could you possibly do me another favor?"

Both Ed and Mary Beth agreed to this.

"Would you please bring out the mirror from the lab so I can see some of what I've become, and then could you use the boat so we could speak further out in the deeper water? These shallows are uncomfortably warm, and my body can't be out of the cooler water and exposed for that long."

"No problem, we'll meet you as far out as you need." Ed rolled over the screen, poised to swim to shore.

A tear slid down Mary Beth's cheek. "Sure thing." She responded absentmindedly. She looked into the researcher's eyes. "Colleen, I'm so sorry," she whispered.

"Don't be; it's just hard getting used to all of this so fast. Honestly, I wasn't much of a success at anything but research. Now, I'll certainly have my fill of it with all these new experiences and phenomena to study.

"To be honest, I don't even know if I'll be able to speak or think in the same way once the change is complete. I've already faced that fact. So it's a good thing you've come now. Please, just get me the mirror."

Mary Beth nodded her head and pointed the kayak toward the shore to go; then turned back around. "We found your diary, you know. It may be important, but if you'd like, I'll burn it."

"No, read it. I have no secrets, but I do have to go further out now. I'll wait for both of you."

Mary Beth acknowledged Colleen's statement with a nod and passed Ed on her way to the beach in the kayak.

"I'll get the boat if you get the mirror," Ed called after Mary Beth from the wake of her watercraft. There was a moderately sized fishing boat docked at the far end of the beach they would use.

The novelty of the situation was wearing thin, and horror was settling over Ed as he tromped out of the sea, his shorts dripping with what looked like red tie-dye. He wasn't sure whether the mirror was a good idea. Poor Dr. Maxwell wasn't a pretty sight.

Her new appearance wasn't much of a surprise. Large, lavender, and streamlined; she had the same four sets of dangling flipper-like appendages as many of the creatures Ed and Mary Beth had released into the lagoon. Her face was still semi-humanoid, but the features were huge and spread over a large frontal head area. Her eyes had taken on the inner glow which had characterized most of the strange creatures they'd seen, but there were still only two of them. Colleen's mouth was a giant slit in her face, and with not too much more of a change, it would become impossible for her to mouth the words which were giving her some difficulty already.

After sailing the larger boat into deeper water, Mary Beth held up the small available mirror to Colleen's best advantage.

Although only able to see a small portion of herself, it was enough. "This is about what I expected to become, but I want to know why this is happening," said Dr. Maxwell.

That the harvester had triggered genetic mutations and chemical changes didn't seem good enough, but it was all they had to offer her. Turning to look behind them, all three saw the island looking like an eerie movie set with unnatural vegetation silhouetted against the sky, set in a pink, watery plain; and above it all, the huge relay harvester swaying in the island breezes.

"The whole process is documented in my lab reports and notes. In the beginning, it was a slow thing, but now it's picked up speed."

"I saw some of your work," said Mary Beth. "It was very impressive and thorough."

Colleen was thoughtful. "I think there are brand new substances here. Not new combinations, but new elements themselves. None of the marine species in the red zone are like any in the blue. I've checked and re-checked. They're all brand new!"

Even without the traditional inflection of her old voice, it was impossible not to sense her excitement, Ed noted.

Suddenly, one of Colleen's larger companions rubbed her hindquarters in a slippery and sensual display of affection, and Colleen tried to push it away so she could concentrate. "It's beautiful out there, and you should see some of the adaptations. They're ingenious."

Ed knew that Colleen's research partner, Tony, was scheduled to return on the same hopper which would pick them up within hours. "Will that pose a problem?" he asked sensitively.

Momentarily Colleen froze, and slowly Ed could see her mentally overcoming the hurdle. "We always made a good team. I guess we still could." Colleen directed her request to Mary Beth. "Would you please warn him?"

Ed assumed they had been lovers after Colleen had directed this personal favor toward Mary Beth. He would let her handle that one.

The rest of the afternoon passed quickly with the exchange of information and frustrations. "Don't worry," Colleen told Mary Beth as quietly as was possible during their goodbyes. "I think I'm going to be very good at this." With that, she dove from sight to swim with the new creature, who had once again come to tickle her flank.

Ed could sense her ties to land and her old life fading from what she had considered important only half an hour earlier. They would make sure and explain everything to Tony when the plane arrived.

• • •

The Oval Office
Five-thirty p.m., Washington D.C.

Yesterday's trip back had been a silent one, with both Ed and Mary Beth too affected to even want to discuss Colleen's transformation. After a partial night's sleep, Ed and President Morgan were going to hold their news conference.

Both looked like hell. "Let's try to put a positive spin on it," the President suggested in the anteroom just before in his own annoyingly, politically conscious manner.

"A positive spin?" Ed was almost struck speechless. "You've got to be joking. People are watching their friends and family change before their eyes, and we're supposed to tell them it's okay? What about the coming floods we're anticipating?" Ed almost bit his tongue in half, attempting to swallow further sarcasm.

"I'm not suggesting that we tell them it's not a problematic situation, Secretary Marker, but what good will it do to scare the American public?"

"They're already scared to death, Mr. President," Ed was taken aback. "Most probably because they don't know what's happening. Everyone realizes that there are an unusual number of physical changes occurring in the population, but they don't know what's behind them. Just think how frightening that's got to be to the average citizen. Our news isn't good," Ed continued, "and we can't pretend that it is. Waters are just beginning to rise, and the expected geological shifting hasn't even begun yet. Combined with the disclosure of an alien mutational seed, I think we'd better go on as rehearsed, don't you?"

"I suppose we'd better," conceded the President.

Ed thought about how much time he'd had to digest all of this information, piece by piece. Now, they were just going to lay everything on the shoulders of the men and women in America all at once.

He *had* thought ahead enough to stock up on general household items and non-perishables, anticipating the worst from at least a small sector of the population, especially in the cities. There had been some rioting over the past week. People were burning businesses, looting, and crowding into the streets to protest. What they were protesting, Ed had no idea. One man's sign on the news had read just "Stop the Changes!" Who did that man think was behind all of this? Well, he and the rest of the country were about to find out.

"Five minutes to air," said the President's media liaison.

The cameras were in position and the lighting was set. The President and Ed sat in strategically placed chairs in front of the presidential desk. A water pitcher and two filled glasses sat on a table between them.

"Okay, are you ready, Mr. President?"

"Yes." He said this with confidence.

"Just stick to the speech," said Ed. "The people deserve the truth."

"We're live." The cameraman pointed to the President.

Good evening, America,

This isn't at all what I had expected to address in my second term as President, but we find ourselves in an unprecedented situation as a nation. Undoubtedly, every citizen is aware of the strange mutations that are occurring across the country and the globe. The goal of addressing the nation this evening is to provide the American people with as much information as we have uncovered. We want to keep everyone as safe as possible and to preserve as many of our daily activities as we can.

This being said, please pay attention, and do not think this is misinformation. We have had the finest scientific minds working to uncover a cause for the changes that have been happening to our environment and our bodies. What they have isolated is non-human genetic material."

Ed could feel the President veering toward a "positive spin" with the words "non-human genetic material" and broke in. "By non-human, we mean not from this planet." There, Ed thought that was very clear.

The President did not falter and continued, righted by Ed's comment.

"Yes. Secretary Marker is correct, and this genetic material is within all of us and everything around us. This material has been a hitchhiker in our bodies for a long time, though the exact length of time cannot be determined precisely. We do know that the frequencies emitted by the harvesters have activated the genetic code. This has caused it to commingle with our DNA, producing all the changes that we have either witnessed or experienced.

Now, I need everyone to listen. We will not turn off the harvesters. No American citizen will attempt to turn off a harvester. This has already been attempted by more than one group of people in more than one country. I refer you to the last incident in Sweden two days ago. We've learned that turning off the harvesters is fatal for everyone carrying this genetic code. Those who have mutated more than others are the first to die, but the others who have been less affected are not long to follow. Anyone attempting to turn off a harvester will be arrested and charged with treason. Their families will also be imprisoned.

We have the combined forces of the United States military patrolling our cities, neighborhoods, and rural areas. They are fully armed and ready to imprison any citizen who does not follow this next set of rules. Because so little is known about what or when things will change, we need to continue our activities of daily life. This will help us sustain the goods and services that we need for survival. We will not pick and choose who is to continue with their jobs and societal functions. So, every American will continue to work in their same jobs, at their same capacities, throughout this global crisis.

The threat of military force and action is only to keep society functioning safely, as we hopefully learn more about how to reverse these changes and return to normal. Every American needs to do their part by continuing with their daily lives, activities, and jobs.

One thing we know with certainty is that the waters and landmasses of our planet will be changing. Our team has determined what our planet will ultimately look like after these transformations are complete. Because we have been able to gain this knowledge so quickly, millions of lives will be saved through our relocation programs. Extensive areas will be flooded and some will be permanently underwater. There will also be new mountain chains and landmasses rising from the sea. I am going to ask that every American check the relocation website. You must type in your address. If your home is not in a safe zone, you will be assigned to a relocation camp. The military will provide transportation to your destination. There is also a link that will take you to a list of everything that you will need to bring with you to these camps.

In addition to rising water levels, we anticipate frequent and severe earthquakes in the coming weeks. Please stay tuned to your local news stations. We will be making safety calls throughout the earthquakes. If it is not safe to leave our homes for a period of time during the worst of the quakes, we will issue warnings. If you are in a shelter-in-place zone, you will not be apprehended for breaking from your daily routines.

I wish I had more answers for you, but we have the world's leading experts in every field researching this crisis from every angle. It is not a question of if we will find the solution, it's a question of when. I urge you to do your part by continuing to take care of yourselves, your families, and your neighbors. You can do this by continuing to live normal lives and performing your normal activities while we get this unprecedented global crisis under control.

Thank you and God bless."

"We're off," said the cameraman.

President Morgan let out a sigh and turned to Ed. "How did I do?"

Ed could see that he was genuinely insecure about how it had gone. "You did fine. You got the message across."

"The last thing we need while we try to figure everything out is lawless chaos in the streets," said the President. He took his first sip from the glass of water sitting beside him.

Ed agreed with this, but he wasn't sure whether the President's hope for peace in the streets of America was for the benefit of civilian safety or for the benefit of his image. "Let's hope we have enough servicemen stationed in the cities tonight."

"Mr. President," interrupted his media liaison, "the first polls are in—only forty percent positive, sir. People want to know more about the alien DNA. They want to know if the planet will be invaded, sir."

We already have been, thought Ed, *from the inside out.* He walked out of the White House unnoticed as the media analysts and PR team got to work after the presidential address. Ed got into his car and said, "Call Patrick."

"Hey, Ed," came Patrick's familiar voice through the car speakers. "I saw the whole thing. I noticed what you did with that redirect and our college selves would have been proud."

Ed laughed a little. "The whole thing went much better than I'd hoped," he stated, driving from the White House back to the DOE, and the motion of the car was soothing to his jangled nerves. So far, there was no panic in the streets, but it was still early.

"Have you heard anything from Barry?" Ed asked.

"Actually, yes. It was a good move to pair him up with that geneticist. They seem to work well together. Barry rattled off all kinds of ideas he'd been having when I spoke to him this morning."

"What kind of ideas?" Ed was tired of dead ends and interested in anything that held possibility.

"Oh. Listen to this. Barry says that he's turned into some kind of human magnet. They've got him working in a shielded lab so he doesn't screw up the other equipment."

This wasn't what Ed meant. It took a lot more to shock him after having seen Dr. Colleen Maxwell morph into a new species of marine creature. "If they come up with any solid ideas, let me know."

"I will," Patrick assured him. "When does Mary Beth say the rock shifting will start?"

"Her best guess is within two to three weeks. People will barely have time to begin recovering from the flooding waters before the geologic shifts begin." Ed's face mirrored his misery.

"It's going to be a real mess after the quakes and shape-shifting start." He was mentally picturing the misshapen geodes from Barry's office. "Listen, I don't think I'll be back in tonight."

"Good plan. Go home, Ed. There's nothing else to be done at this point."

Unfortunately, that was Ed's problem. There was nothing they could really do, but it would not stop him from trying. He headed home to look for something appetizing enough in his pile of canned goods.

Ed surveyed his pantry. He could make anything from spaghetti to beef stir-fry, having stocked up on meat in his freezer as well. At least there was no danger of losing power with the harvesters.

A cool puff of air hit his face when he opened the freezer, but even though he had all of this food, he wasn't in the mood to cook. He was tired, but also restless. Relaxation and sleep were not in his immediate future. Pacing around his apartment and lying awake all night was much more plausible. He needed a distraction, some company. The clock on the microwave read seven forty-five. Maybe Mary Beth would be free, since she was new to the area with no family or friends around. It wasn't too late to call her. Maybe she hadn't had dinner yet. Some company would be nice. Any distraction would be nice.

It was decided. "Hello, Mary Beth?"

"Hi, Ed. What's going on?"

Something was always going on these days. He heard the alarm in her voice, as if she was bracing for new information. "I don't need anything," he began. "There's nothing new happening. I'm just wondering if you would like to get some Chinese with me."

"Sure," she said without hesitation.

Her immediate positive response surprised him a little. In a matter of minutes, he was in his car, headed to Mary Beth's to pick her up for dinner. The city streets were far less crowded than usual, and Ed was sure it had everything to do with the humvees and armored military vehicles patrolling the area. Nothing says a night on the town like a marine with an M27 in hand staring you down.

Two knocks. She opened the door right away. "You ready to go?" she asked Ed, not inviting him in first.

"Absolutely," he said. "Things are a little weird out there, but honestly, I've never felt safer on the streets of D.C." A small joke.

"I know, right?" she said, eyeing the uniformed serviceman in front of her building. "This is all so crazy. Everything, I mean, but I find my thoughts always returning to Colleen. I don't know why that particular incident hit me so hard."

"Who's to say?" said Ed. "I think everyone is just trying to stay as level as possible, but we're all bound to have moments of extreme compassion for humanity in this crisis. Moments where we can see some of ourselves in others and it scares us." Ed pulled the car out from the curb.

"Yeah, I guess." She stared out of the passenger window.

"So," Ed broke the silence, "on that level, the level where we're all just people and not those charged with saving society, I know where we can get the best Chinese in the city. Welcome, by the way."

"What do you mean by that?" She took her eyes from the window and looked at Ed.

"We swoop into Thorpestown, introduce ourselves, take you back to D.C., immediately put you to work," Ed paused. "You're new to the city. So, welcome."

"Thanks," she said sincerely, letting out a breath that she must have been holding in for days and smiled.

"What do you say we take a small time out, just long enough to eat dinner and have a drink? Who knows how much longer we'll have an opportunity to do something like this?"

"That sounds good to me," said Mary Beth. "Two hours couldn't hurt."

The Chinese cartons double-bagged in plastic over paper must have weighed ten pounds. They had almost ordered one of everything. On the way back to Ed's apartment, they stopped for some wine. He had neglected to stock up on bottles of wine, but the rest of society had not. The only wine available was in a box, but they took it.

Comfortably seated on Ed's couch in front of the television, they spread out a Chinese feast on the coffee table and filled their wine glasses from the box, which dispensed the red liquid like water from a cooler.

"To the end of the world," said Mary Beth, holding her glass up to Ed.

That wasn't funny at all, but sometimes if you couldn't laugh about things, you might just unravel completely. Ed held his glass up to hers and nodded before taking a long sip and setting back on the sofa. He relaxed his shoulders for the first time in weeks. He would give himself a few hours off and be better for it.

CHAPTER 23

Saguaro Rock, Arizona, 2022

President Morgan, sir," one of the uniformed military guards stationed outside the elevator on S32 of the Rock blurted out in shock as the President of the United States stepped off the elevator, flanked by a pair of secret service agents.

"What's your name, soldier?" asked the President.

"Caruso, Mr. President, sir."

"Corporal Caruso, I need to see Dr. Ross."

"Yes, sir. I'll call for transport." The soldier touched a device in his ear and made the request. Within minutes, a small electric cart was driving away with the President, followed closely by a second cart packed with presidential security.

"I understand you want to go to Dr. Ross's lab. I've just radioed the research department and they've advised me that the doctor is in sector seven," explained Caruso as they drove. "I can take you there."

President Morgan rode with the enlisted man and dismissed him outside of sector seven. Then, he turned to the security agents and instructed them to stay outside.

Caruso parked his vehicle and prepared to wait as long as necessary while the President stood patiently in front of a facial scanner, waiting for the metal door to admit him. He stepped into sector seven, knowing that Addie was just one door away. "Dr. Ross."

The doctor stood up. "I was expecting the Secretary, sir."

"In light of what's happening out there," President Morgan scanned the lab and saw that it was in disarray. "I wanted to make this trip myself."

"I know it's a bit messy, but they won't give anyone clearance to help in this sector. It's just me in this space, has been for years."

The President had his eyes locked on Addie's door.

"I heard they're shutting down the program. Mr. President, is that true?" asked Dr. Ross, genuine desperation in his voice. He had devoted the prime years of his life to his work here. "We're so close. So close to isolating..."

The President cut him off. "If Addie were no longer of any use, you would be the first to know, Doctor. You shouldn't believe everything you hear. Right now, I need to see her." President Morgan walked to the second facial scanner and a second metal lock slid open. He pressed through the doorway and there she was— Addie, a constant enigma, never having changed in all these years.

"I have your monthly package, sir," said Dr. Ross, coming up behind him with a cooler. Inside the box were several vials of deep red fluid kept cool by plasma pouches.

"I won't be needing those anymore, Doctor."

"Oh?" Dr. Ross braced himself on the wall with one hand while holding the heavy package with the other. Now in his sixties, his bursitis was acting up. All those years of sitting at that computer screen, no doubt. He had spent his entire career at the Rock with Addie.

"Why not, sir? Exactly what is going on out there?"

"It's the harvesters, Doctor. As you know, those frequencies they're emitting have activated a genetic hitchhiker woven into the genetic fabric of the entire human race. Hundreds of millions of years of evolution, or possibly genetic sabotage, are happening within weeks, sometimes within hours."

"I've heard everything, but I had assumed it was also being embellished." Dr. Ross was pragmatic and had not left the compound in years. The rocky roads leading to Yuma were more than his aging joints could absorb. "I've experienced no such changes. Very few here at the Rock have, as far as I know."

"There's more," said the President.

Dr. Ross looked at him expectantly.

"The Rock is not just a research facility and classified military base. It has become an underground community. Though you would understand it to be more of a bunker, it's the size of a small US state, completely underground. The Saguaro Rock facility you've always known is only a small portion of what we really have here."

Dr. Ross furrowed his eyebrows. There wasn't a part of the facility with which Ross wasn't familiar. This place was his home.

"Part of why I'm here today is to ask you to be a part of this secure community moving forward." The President paused and studied the doctor's expression. "You know more about Addie than anyone else living today, and we need your knowledge."

"Where is this community?"

"Like I said," the President repeated, "this is just a small section of the Rock."

"A small section big enough to house multiple military divisions," stated Dr. Ross, hand still on the wall, steadying himself.

"Correct," agreed President Morgan. "This subterranean community has been under construction far longer than the Saguaro you know."

"Why would you choose me to be a part of this community? I'm so old." Always thinking logically, Dr. Ross continued. "All of my research has been documented. Why waste any resources on an old man?"

"There are no wasted resources," said the President. "All of the resources are renewable. This community can sustain itself completely. Forever, if that's what's needed."

Dr. Ross took a moment to formulate his next question. The President's visit was unexpected, and the conversation was moving quickly. "So everything we've been hearing has been true?"

"Yes. And there'll be much more to come. Things are changing faster and much more dramatically as time goes on."

"So, we're hiding, not fighting?"

"Just think of the Rock as a last resort. If all else fails, a small portion of us can go on, hopefully."

"Indefinitely?" Dr. Ross sought reassurance. He was still trying to catch up to what the President was saying. Underground at Saguaro, things had been more even and predictable than they had been on the surface.

"Yes. Indefinitely."

"What do you want me to do?" asked the doctor.

"Nothing yet," said President Morgan. "We're about to go through some serious geologic shifting. I sincerely hope that this doesn't destroy the Rock. Parts of it are very close to the Earth's core. If too much seismic activity takes place near those sections, we'll have to close them off and our plans for heating the community will need to be rethought."

"Rethought?" asked Ross.

"These are uncertain times, Doctor. We don't know everything. We can only do our best with all the information we have at any given time. Let's just hope that the core stays intact over the next few weeks."

For maybe the first time in his scientific career, Dr. Ross was at a loss for questions, but this did not last long. Why had they never told him about this community? How had he not noticed its existence? All this time he'd thought that he had top clearance. This new information gave him pause. His concern was not what he now knew, but the rest of what he didn't.

"I can't stay long," said the President. "I've got business in other areas of the compound to attend to. As I've just said, things are spiraling out of control on a global scale." He continued to stand, showing no indication of entertaining a long conversation. "I'll send you the file on New Saguaro Nation. My meeting you here today was only to soften the surprise of what you'll be reading in the file and to let you know that it's all true. Please consider New Saguaro's offer. If you accept, there *is* a place for you."

The President spoke through his earpiece to the agents stationed outside of the door to sector seven. "Get the council ready."

"Where is this New Saguaro Nation? The entrance? Who else has been selected?"

"It's all in the file. I haven't got the time to go over these details one by one with every recruit, but this is a time-sensitive situation. Read the file. I'll need your answer soon."

After the President had left the sector, Ross sat back down and placed the rejected cooler on the far corner of his desk. Why were these vials no longer a top priority? The questions just kept coming.

CHAPTER 24

When in doubt, call the wizard.
—Ed Boggs

Thirteen days on the dot, Ed circled the date on his kitchen calendar absentmindedly. Yesterday, the geologic movement had begun.

"Come in," Ed responded to the knock on his front door. He was expecting Mary Beth and had left the door unlocked.

She slipped in quietly, leaving her wheeled suitcase in the foyer. "How are you holding up?" she asked, walking towards the kitchen where Ed stood preparing two peanut butter sandwiches.

"Okay, I guess." They both lived alone and had decided that they would be better off waiting out the earthquakes together. Time passes more quickly in the company of a friend. "I'm glad you're here." Ed was sincere.

"I know," she acknowledged. "Everything has changed so much. On the way over, I saw people wandering around everywhere, just looking and staring."

"Yeah, well, I've been watching the news. It's crazy, all right," Ed said as he steered Mary Beth towards the couch and turned up the television's volume.

The harried newscaster was reading such unbelievable copy that it was hard for the well-coifed woman to keep a slight tremor from her voice. "It seems that our hitchhikers have an equally virulent effect on inorganic matter."

"Exactly," agreed Ed, nodding his head as if the newscaster could see him.

"Actually," the strengthening voice continued, "the phenomenon is quite beautiful, unless it happens to split your house in half, or turn the floor of the marble lobby in your office building into a sea of sharply thrusting crystals, or any number of other inconvenient and dangerous scenarios." As the anchorwoman recited these particular instances, each was flashed one by one on the television.

"Look at that," Mary Beth said, watching the images play across the screen.

There it was, again. Both she and Ed heard the familiar cracking sounds coming through the walls.

"I know the damage is bad," said Mary Beth, "but I hate these noises even more. It sounds like the entire planet is some giant egg that's cracking."

Mary Beth covered her ears to block it all out, and Ed moved closer to comfort her.

"There are enough troubling frequencies circling the globe that no place on the planet seems to be immune," the reporters' voice droned on. "In some places, we've seen a sudden heaving and thrusting. In others, the process is gradual but just as transformational." Ed turned off the TV. Neither he nor Mary Beth needed a running commentary.

They were in a shelter-in-place zone. All of D.C. qualified for this classification. Most of America had qualified for the past three days. The noise came all hours of the day and night. Flights were grounded. Public transportation halted.

He had not needed to throw away any food—his freezer still running on full blast; and the lights in the apartment cast a warm glow. Earthquakes would not interrupt the harvester's frequencies, and so, one thing the world had was unlimited energy, for better or worse.

He and Mary Beth got most of their news from their cell phones, which still had signals. Thankfully, the harvesters also fed cell phones. It was ironic that humanity was tracking the global destruction caused by the harvesters on technology powered by these same machines. If only they could be turned off without deadly ramifications.

Within a week, the process had slowed and regulated, leaving the landscape pretty well unrecognizable in places. They had spent the majority of this time hunkered down in Ed's apartment. His position at the DOE had required no travel of him during the topographical transformation. The President had issued a warning urging citizens "to stay at home until the earthquakes stopped." Not that one place was any safer than another, but at least people would feel the sense of security that came with being in their homes in these times of uncertainty.

"Have you had any more visions?" asked Ed.

"If I had, you would have known," she informed him. They had spent the last week together in the apartment. "I got a call from my old neighbor in Iowa yesterday. Patty used to bring me baked goods every now and again, probably just as an excuse to sit down and talk to someone."

"What did she say?" Ed asked, sitting down on the couch in the living room. It was hard to get used to doing nothing, having been as busy as he had always been. He was genuinely curious to see what Mary Beth's neighbor had to say, because he too was now bored and waiting for an excuse to talk to Mary Beth.

"Well, you saw the boat in my backyard, right?" Mary Beth did not wait for a response. "Yes, you did. Everyone knew about it. That dry-docked boat made me the laughingstock of the entire county. Anyway, it's now floating in deep water, tethered by the anchor. I told her she could move onto the boat," Mary Beth continued, joining Ed on the couch. "She doesn't have any family, and I had stocked it with provisions before I left."

"That was nice of you. How long do you think she'll be able to survive with those provisions?"

"That's the beauty of living on a boat," said Mary Beth. "She is completely mobile, but where she would go is a different story altogether."

"Things are so weird," interjected Ed. "Things we would never have had to consider in the past are now parts of everyday conversation, like navigating the boat. Who knows where there will be a new rock formation under the water's surface that could pierce the hull as your neighbor sails? Also, if she wanted to fish for food, what would she catch? Can people even eat those creatures that we saw in the lagoon?"

Every question led to another question, but that was the new reality. So many questions, and too few answers.

CHAPTER 25

STANLEY
Daly City, California, the San Andreas Fault

Stanley Mason moved towards the nearest seismological monitor, where he recorded the latest measurements. Though this quake phenomenon was worldwide, he was especially concerned with California, and why not? After all, Stanley reasoned, while resetting the machine, he lived only a stone's throw from a major California fault.

When beginning his career as a seismologist years before, Stanley had decided it was important to live near his data. Unfortunately, right now this meant knowing the ground beneath his feet was even less stable than usual, but the possibility had always been there. At least I'll go down with my ship, he thought heroically. Of course, so would the rest of the world.

Stanley took out a yellow bandanna to wipe away his sweat. The total population of Los Angeles was bolted to the ground, getting ready for the "big one," but this time, they weren't alone. Stanley had watched many of his neighbors just up and leave the state. "It's finally going to fall into the ocean, you know," they told him and anyone who would listen long enough.

They might just be right. Stanley tucked the damp cloth back into his pocket and considered the thought seriously. Still, most people couldn't afford to just walk away from their lives any more than he could. They had homes, jobs, families, and now fear. Besides, where would they go? The same thing was happening everywhere. Stanley certainly had no transfer plans himself.

Moving to the next monitor, he observed the latest gyrations of the local tectonic plates. Oddly enough, he knew that the figures he was gathering would match others throughout the world exactly, number for number. It was contrary to everything he'd ever learned about stress relief, but the data didn't lie.

He pushed aside an overgrown thicket to uncover the next monitor. One thing was for sure, Stanley's career had certainly taken off. He was in such demand that he couldn't be in all the places he was needed. There must be a psychological comfort quotient involved in "calling in the expert," he reasoned logically.

Stanley was in semi-hiding this afternoon, assembling the report he was presenting to a DOE big shot who was flying in for a consultation tomorrow. He'd been sitting at the edge of his unmown yard, occasionally slinking in and out of the rosebushes to check on various monitors he'd set up. The cool glass of apple juice he sipped was refreshing after all the stale, lukewarm cups of coffee he'd had lately. Odd how roses and apple juice smelled so much alike. He'd never noticed it before.

Maybe everything was going to settle into the sameness Stanley had noticed in the two smells. The tremors certainly had. At first, the pattern had been random. Where they happened, how long they lasted, and their level on the Richter scale were so different that it merely looked like an increase in world-wide, low-level activity. At that point, it was enough to pique Stanley's interest, but not enough to grab the public.

It was a different story now, he thought, resuming his relaxed position in the lawn chair. Quake locations were no longer isolated, in fact, there were no longer locations at all, per se. Tremors were happening simultaneously in a grid pattern across the globe. It was as though, Stanley thought again for the millionth time, someone had mathematically plotted points and said, "Let her rip."

Location, location, location. It had always been the important factor in both earthquakes and real estate, but not anymore. Stanley finished his juice in one long gulp, thinking of how location had been the first variable to stabilize into a recognizable pattern. It had soon become obvious that there were no longer any "good" locations.

Shortly thereafter, the interval times between quakes equalized, finally steadying out at about three per day regularly. Since then, however, Stanley and the others like him had confirmed that the quakes were shortening in duration, and the severity level was settling into a stable, fractional number on the Richter scale.

Stanley didn't think this pattern could hold; or could it? He was completely baffled. It would be against all the odds and defy everything they'd ever learned if this went on in such a never-ending rumble. Where were the points of stress building and releasing in all this steady movement?

Shutting his eyes in an attempt to block out the questions and maybe even get a little nap, he felt himself drifting off. *Where indeed,* he wondered on his way toward some very heavy delta waves. It would take more than even Stanley's expertise to figure this one out. If his suspicions were correct, this wasn't the big one—it was something much worse.

CHAPTER 26

Knock on the sky, and listen to the sound.
—Zen Saying

After more than a week of staying at home with Mary Beth, the DOE had approved travel again, and people were back at work. Seismic activity had calmed down and become more predictable—at least for the moment. September was half over. Kids were back in school and would hopefully not have any more interruptions.

On his flight back from California, Ed reviewed his visit with Stanley, the latest media sensation and full-time quake expert. It had only gone so-so. At least so far, volcanic activity hadn't increased, Ed thought gratefully. The quakes were enough, anyway. "Stan the Man," as the seismologist had taken to calling himself, could not give either rhyme or reason to the general patterns he was observing, but Ed could tell he was enjoying his expert status immensely.

Ed leaned back in his window seat, taking in the view from above. The landscape had changed. It wasn't the same country he had always seen. He missed the patchwork of fields, cities, and trees that were so familiar. Now, crystalline forms jutted out across the countryside. Ed sighed slightly and closed the window shade. He dialed Patrick and waited.

"Ed?" Patrick's exhausted voiced was very clear in his ear. "How was California?"

"Still there, last time I looked. Sorry, not even funny anymore. Actually, the seismologist had nothing concrete to tell us, but that's not surprising. How's Mary Beth?"

"She's fine, but she asked me when you were getting back."

"Has she come up with anything new at all?" asked Ed.

"No, not really." Patrick barely hesitated, but Ed picked right up on it.

"Give." It was a command, not a request.

"Well, I don't know if it's anything, but she seems kind of antsy, and she has the globe hanging from the ceiling on a piece of string."

"So?"

"With the lights out."

"And?"

"She has a paper clip hanging too, and she doesn't want to talk about it yet, at least not to me."

"Great." Ed was both exasperated and flattered. "Listen, keep a close eye on her. I should touch down in about forty-five minutes, not that I want to touch down at all. No quakes in mid-air, you know." For the first time, Ed's stomach was actually doing better in the air.

"I guess you're right, but Ed, is this a good time for you to hear the geologist's report, or would you rather wait till later? It's not a secure channel."

Ed laughed until tears trickled from the corners of his eyes. Suddenly, the very concept of security was so ludicrous to him.

"You have a report? Hit me," Ed said, shaking his head from side to side, having regained his composure. There was nothing that could surprise him at this point.

An exasperated Patrick complied. "I hope you're in such good spirits when I'm done. I had my meeting with the geologist, Trevor

Matthews, yesterday. We met in his lab." Patrick recounted his meeting to Ed.

• • •

Geology Lab
University of Maryland College Park

"Explain it again." Patrick remained semi-confused. "If rocks don't have genetic material, how can they be changed by our hitchhiker?"

"They're not growing, Mr. Hagen. It's an impossibility, hence the popularity of pet rocks." Dr. Matthews didn't venture a smile. His voice was severely hoarse thanks to several days of non-stop explanations. "They're changing and shifting, but not growing. Something, presumably the same thing that's switched on the genetic soup, is changing their underlying crystalline structure."

"What would do that?" Patrick asked. Time was running short. "Forget it, Dr. Matthews. We both know I'm asking whether the harvester is the cause."

"Yes, we both know it, and we can both almost say for certain that it is. Frequency manipulation can affect crystalline structure, but to have the massive changes now occurring would be unbelievable if it weren't actually happening."

Patrick continued with the questions. "So far, so good, but the fact remains, rocks are inorganic. I know it's a redundant statement, but how do you explain this?" Patrick was visibly frustrated. The human race was being stalked on their own turf and the predators were gaining rapidly.

"Your genetic catalyst must have been incorporated into the very structure of the rocks on an elemental level, but I can't tell you how. According to my education, it's all impossible, anyway; but then I trip over boulders in the parking lot, or have to worry about crystal stalagmites in the lobby." Dr. Matthews stopped to cough hoarsely and took a drink. He was unsure of how to continue.

"Yeah. And?" Patrick prodded.

"I'd like to explain this before I show it to you. Come over here." Dr. Matthews walked over to a counter across the room on which sat a microscope surrounded by a pile of crushed rocks and sandy grit. "Take a look."

To Patrick, it was far from impressive. "So? I see some sparkly rocks." He sat down on the metal stool in front of the microscope and looked again. Patrick was about to turn away, but stopped when Dr. Matthews encouraged him to keep looking.

It took a full minute for him to see the phenomenon. It wasn't reflected light shining from the rock faces. The rocks themselves were generating tiny pinpoints of light. It was something rocks didn't normally do. "What's happening? Why are they blinking like that?"

"You've got me. You know about as much as I do. We're in trouble, Mr. Hagen. Sell your condo if you have one, and buy a mobile home like everyone else if you can still find one," advised the eminent geologist, Dr. Trevor Matthews.

•   •   •

"So, there's nothing new," Ed mused in mid-air. "How reassuring."

"True," Patrick agreed, "except for the fact that his rocks generate light, and so far, others don't."

"So, what else did he say?" Ed urged. "What do the lights mean?"

"He didn't know, Ed, but it was creepy. Guess *none* of the experts are doing us any good, are they?"

"No, they're not... I'll see you soon, Patrick."

Ed called Mary Beth next to see what exactly was going on with the mobile she had created in his office.

"Hi, Ed. Did you find out anything new from the seismologist?" she asked from his dark office.

"I just had this conversation with Patrick," he responded. "Nothing new, well everything is new, but no explanations."

Mary Beth eyed the paperclip dangling from the ceiling.

"Any recent developments?"

"Actually yes," said Mary Beth. "I spoke with a young astronomy major from the University of New Mexico, Rene Lawson. She had phoned the tip line, and they transferred her to me on your office line. Your phone must have been turned off for take-off."

"What did she have to say?"

"Well, we ended up doing a virtual meeting so that she could show me the maps she's created."

Ed accepted a small bag of pretzels from the flight attendant and asked for a Sprite. "What kind of maps?"

"This is so crazy," Mary Beth began. "Maps of star systems beyond ours. She also gave details of a spaceship approaching, on a straight course to Earth, through these other star systems." Mary Beth paused for a breath.

Ed was silent, waiting for more details.

"Basically, she was just warning that this ship is on its way."

"Do you believe her?" asked Ed. He had only known Mary Beth for a short while, but they had been through so much together, and he trusted her judgment. She *was* a student of human nature.

"I do." Mary Beth responded.

"So you saw the planet, and she sees the ship," Ed stated. "The hitchhiker had to come from somewhere."

The docked ship was, at last, loaded and ready for release. Nothing the likes of this fine craft had been seen in thousands of years. The conveyance was immense, because it had to be. Their final exodus was beginning. There would be no goodbyes because there would be no one left behind. Every last one would be leaving this time, along with all of their accumulated possessions. They fled so they would not perish. There was little enough margin for safety as it was.

What would they find? Who could know, and what did it matter, anyway? Any available information on the long-ago probe's original genetic materials and mission had been shrouded in secrecy, and had remained so ever since. Competitive espionage had been avoided at all costs, so very little was known about what this wandering tribe could expect at their eventual destination.

Brief explanations available at the time of the probe's launch touted its future genetically manipulated creation as "a world of new wonders," the ultimate excitement, awaiting those whose long-ago tedium had become overwhelming. It was to have been a place for adventure, one combining the familiarity of their home environment and yet incorporating the new and unexpected. Their ancient ruling class was said to have been willing to pay exorbitant amounts for the opportunity to visit this new and exhilarating "play world."

Were they now prepared to colonize the intended playground of their hedonistic forefathers? What did it matter? There was no choice. At least they were sure of one thing—there would be no competition for this new world. The one fact which had remained consistent throughout all the documentation was that it would be an uninhabited planet.

Naturally, it would be incalculably far away. After all, it had taken dozens of phase shifts for the signal to return home with its beckoning calls. Sodok, the leader of his people, such as they were, was prepared to live out his life on the journey. After he passed beyond his duty, his children would follow him as guardians of their living heritage. The proud, desperate people huddled in the hibernation chambers below would see the new world, but he never would. No matter, it was time. After releasing their gravitational tether, he watched his homeworld recede quickly, and then explode in a blinding flash as the lumbering craft shifted into a higher speed.

CHAPTER 27

Saguaro Rock, Arizona, 2022

Earth's core has remained intact," said President Morgan as he and Dr. Ross rode the elevator down to S32. "The quakes didn't release any magma."

"So, what exactly would you have me do in this New Saguaro Nation?" Dr. Ross had read the entire file, cover to cover, no less than a dozen times. Presently, he braced himself on the wall of the elevator. His hip was acting up again.

"Exactly what you've always done in the lab."

"Speaking of the lab," began the doctor, "the earthquakes have wreaked havoc on all of our equipment. None of the systems are down, but the programs are running slower and glitching. Is there any money to replace hardware?"

"I wouldn't worry about that," assured the President. "We've taken care of everything."

"How so?"

"Just wait," said the President. "We've been working on this place a long time. You're not the only one heading up research on an Addie."

Ross's jaw dropped. "What do you mean *an Addie*? Is there more than one?!"

"Two, to be exact... that we know about," explained the President matter-of-factly.

President Morgan had admitted this freely, and Ross was offended. He'd spent his life in pursuit of gathering all the knowledge there was to collect surrounding Addie. Now, he was finding out that he'd been working with only half the facts.

"Why hasn't anybody told me?" boiled Dr. Ross. "I've devoted my career to studying her. If others were studying another Addie, our knowledge could have been combined, and so much more could have been accomplished!"

"We couldn't keep them together," said the President gravely. "They're far too valuable. We have only just brought Zoe here to the Rock. She or he has been housed elsewhere until two days ago. Now, they'll remain here together. No one could have predicted the catastrophic state of the world. This is the safest place for both of them, while everything is sorted out on the surface."

Ross was genuinely enraged. "But what if it isn't sorted out? Since we last spoke, the Rock has lost a large number of soldiers to the changes."

"I'm sorry. I don't have all the answers. Please hold on to your questions for a bit longer, while I tell you what information I do have." The President led Dr. Ross out of the elevator to the waiting cart and security entourage.

Dr. Ross eased himself into the passenger's seat. "How many people can this place support?"

"We have over fifteen hundred home pods." President Morgan drove the cart down a long corridor with security close behind. He drove slower than he would have ordinarily driven, avoiding fissures in the floor and new rock formations encroaching on their route.

"The quakes have done some damage down here." Dr. Ross held onto the cart with both hands. It was another bumpy ride, as they all had been since the quakes.

"It's time you saw the lab."

The President drove the cart down a new corridor Ross had never seen before. "When was this made?"

"Just recently," Morgan responded. "We needed another entrance." He manipulated the steering wheel, quickly dodging yet another crystal invading their path.

"Did it have anything to do with this Zoe? How long ago was she discovered, and by whom? Is she the same as my Addie?"

"Similar," said the President.

"How is she different?" So many questions.

"I'll put you in touch with Dr. Wagner. I can answer general questions, but he'll be the one to get into the science with you. He's in the lab."

President Morgan put the cart in park and gestured for Dr. Ross to follow. He positioned his face in front of a scanner identical to the one outside his own lab and they were admitted onto a new elevator, which took them and a number of suitably observant security personnel an additional forty-seven floors down.

"I had no idea New Saguaro would be this far down." Ross was amazed.

"This isn't New Saguaro," Morgan smiled slightly. "New Saguaro is an additional ninety-eight kilometers down. The Earth's Core sits 2,900 kilometers from the surface. Ninety-eight kilometers was found to be the most sustainable depth for the nation regarding its proximity to the Earth's core."

There was another elevator change. Once they started moving, a screen built into the wall began playing a welcome video.

"We had this made for our new arrivals," said President Morgan. "Let me know what you think."

The video touched on most things Dr. Ross had questioned: lighting, food and water sources, heating and cooling, energy, waste treatment, everything—except for the Addies, that is. Those questions, he was told, would have to be answered by Dr. Wagner. The video confirmed all that the President had said and the contents of the file. Production and waste feeding into one another to create a perfectly sustainable existence for the Rock's population. All resources were renewable. As long as the sun continued to shine, the Rock could continue indefinitely.

• • •

"President Morgan." Dr. Wagner had been waiting, and approached the two with his right hand outstretched toward the President. After shaking hands, Dr. Wagner turned his attention to Dr. Ross.

"So, you're on board, then? It's wonderful to meet you. We have so much to do."

"Do I really have a choice?" Ross knew that even if this would not be the safest place on the planet, it would still be a dream come true. He had a second opportunity of a lifetime with Zoe, and finally someone with whom to share research. Seeing Dr. Wagner's enthusiasm helped him fully process the reality of Zoe. He felt younger and more excited than he had in years.

"You've timed your visit perfectly, Mr. President." Dr. Wagner reached into the insulated shoulder bag he wore, removed a sealed cup filled with a deep red liquid, and handed it to the President, who drank it all.

"Thank you, Dr. Wagner. It's nothing like Shultz's, but it will certainly do the job."

"I've made a spot for Seaman Shultz," Wagner reported. "They can move him any time."

Dr. Ross stood staring at the two men with his mouth open, frozen and unable to speak after what he may have just seen. He had been requested to send away vials of Shultz's blood ever since the President had taken office. Ross had assumed they were being sent to another research facility. Had the President of the United States been drinking Shultz's blood?! Why?

CHAPTER 28

HERB

Greenbelt, Maryland
NASA Goddard Space Flight Center

Herb McElvy, of NASA Goddard Space Flight Center, was performing a job he considered way ahead of its time. With precision in his bearing, indicative of prior military service and a haircut to match, Herb was monitoring for signs of active communication in space. High frequencies, low frequencies, radio waves, radar, sonar, lasers, phasers, etc., well, not exactly all *that* inclusive, he admitted. Still, he liked to believe that an ant couldn't take a crap on Mars and scream home to its mother without his knowing about it. Looking around the state-of-the-art electronic monitoring station, Herb felt the assumption was pretty right on.

With the news full of such odd things lately, Herb was happier than usual to shut out the real world and enter his quietly mechanized corner. NASA had its ears on both the near and the far, and there was always something to hear. Through careful filtering, he easily adjusted the equipment to avoid "junk waves."

Sometimes, Herb actually put on the earphones and listened, but mostly, he'd given it up years ago. Today, as usual, he was letting the computer listen for him. He opened his bag lunch, and contentedly watched the instruments scratch away, recording random sounds.

Crunching thin carrot sticks, Herb wondered about the sounds as he always did. Naturally, NASA's primary interest lay in the signals coming *towards* Earth, not leaving. However, Herb was well aware that both were monitored. Global political ramifications being what they were, any defensive posture was a good one, and he considered himself one damn fine watchdog.

He dug into his cottage cheese, and continued to eye the mechanical arms graphing unheard transmissions. For him, there was always anticipation as he scanned these recorded emissions from deep space. Someday, it would happen. There would be contact. Why not on his shift? He fingered the five-dollar lottery ticket in his pocket. Hadn't he bought it for the same reason?

The routinely graphed sound waves might seem hopelessly complicated to some, but to Herb, they were as familiar as his own face. Noticing an interesting flutter in the delicate tracings, he tore off the particular section of the paper, stood, and hurried down the hall.

"Here you go, Dave. Happy hunting." Herb handed the slip of paper to the nearest astronomer.

"Same to you, Herb." Distractedly, Dave waved his colleague towards the door.

"Easy for you to say," Herb retorted with good humor. "All you guys need to get your juices going is a star imploding or a galaxy expanding. I want someone to talk back!"

"Yeah, life sucks, doesn't it?" Dave was enjoying their familiar running dialog. "Hey, and enjoy your lunch." He'd noticed Herb's unfinished carrots lined up with the pens in his shirt pocket.

"Yeah, right," Herb headed back down the hall towards what was left of his lunch. Dave had a quick wit, but despite the humor in their recent exchange, Herb felt the astronomers had a boring job. Oh well, back to work.

Herb settled in comfortably in front of the console. Dessert was a granola bar. Then, a new squiggle on the paper caught his eye. This squiggle was coming from Earth, not space, and was in a previously unused and always unmarked portion of the graph paper. Obviously manufactured, it had established a pattern, repeating itself endlessly, and he'd never seen anything like it.

Leaning forward with eager interest, for the first time in over four years, Herb put on the headset and tuned into an Earth-originated signal. *What would it sound like?* he wondered. After much adjustment, he tuned in on the correct frequency. It was strong, steady, and well-received. The result, however, was not the well-modulated voice of a disc jockey or anchorman. Instead, it sounded like a cross between something human and something computer-generated, in screechy staccato bursts and long wailing highs and lows. Occasionally, it would settle into a recognizable word-sound pattern, but then the sequence would begin again. Herb quickly yanked the headphones off. "Shit, my poor ears!" he groaned. It was like listening to fingernails on a blackboard, but much worse.

If the pattern was decipherable, and they all were, Herb knew that the GSFC computer at his disposal would crack it at the push of his button. Odd, he thought, after five minutes had passed with no results. Later in the afternoon, Herb was finally forced to admit that the sounds were not to be identified as any foreign language or dialect, neither were they some difficult code. What were they?

After pinpointing the precise time, the questionable transmission began. Herb took some notes before making several inconspicuous phone calls. This could be interesting, he thought, not ready to let go of it yet. At least he should be able to get to the bottom of this without too much red tape. After all, according to his information, the signal was coming out of rural Arizona, and what could be of interest to anyone in Arizona?

CHAPTER 29

If you want to drown, don't tease yourself with shallow waters.
—Bulgarian Proverb

An uncomfortable Dr. Michael Holbein was sitting solidly at his desk with a humidifier blasting clouds of moisture into the air when Ed, Mary Beth, and Rene let themselves into his office. Average in height and frail-looking, the Director of the NASA Goddard Space Flight Center stood awkwardly. "Ah, Ms. Rene Lawson."

"You remember me?" Rene said with surprise in her voice. Dr. Holbein was astronomical royalty. She had attended one of his virtual classes last semester.

"I remember all of my students, even the virtual ones. At least, I try to."

"At the risk of sounding cliché, I'll have to cut this reunion short," Ed interrupted. Ever since his experience in the lagoon, Ed had gotten a lot more straightforward. The world was changing by the hour. He thought back to the moment Dr. Colleen Maxwell lost her ability to speak, then redirected his attention back to the present. "Please, sit down, Dr. Holbein, and clear your desk."

Holbein obliged, sitting behind his desk and moving various trinkets to the floor. "What's this all about?"

"Rene," Ed held his arm out, ushering Rene to Dr. Holbein's desk. Rene unrolled the star charts she had drawn on paper the size of construction blueprints. "Dr. Holbein, could we use a couple of your paperweights to anchor the maps?"

"Absolutely." Holbein placed some of his Star Wars memorabilia on the edges of the large sheets and began analyzing the star charts.

After a short while, Dr. Holbein looked at Rene and weighed in. "What you're proposing isn't so hard to believe. In this line of work, we've all been debating the UFO issue for decades and living the consequences for months. However, the data upon which you're basing your suppositions is not just faulty, it's simply impossible. There's no way you could have generated star charts like these." He pointed to the maps.

Mary Beth spoke up for Rene. "Most people have removed the word 'impossible' from their vocabularies by now, Dr. Holbein."

"Most people are gullible." Dr. Holbein folded his hands in his lap and leaned back in his well-worn desk chair. "In my position, I have to be practical above all else. We're in a precise business here at NASA. Our space program is based on mathematical fact, physics, chemistry..."

"Dr. Holbein," Ed interrupted the man's dissertation on academic integrity. "You're fired." They couldn't waste any more time with someone who was in denial. Anyone who wasn't willing to accept the changes occurring every day and adapt to them had nothing to offer their cause. Ed knew it was hasty, but he was in touch with the President every day. He had been given top clearance and permission for any sweeping action necessary in their pursuit of a solution to this worldwide phenomenon.

"Wow, Ed," said Mary Beth. She glared at him with narrow eyes.

Since they had become roommates, he could count on Mary Beth for even more honesty than usual. "Dr. Holbein," Ed walked over and opened the door, encouraging Holbein to exit. He felt a slight regret, but the time for social pleasantries had come and gone. When people were turning into whales, abandoning decorum along the way paled in comparison.

"This is out of your jurisdiction," insisted Holbein feebly.

"I'm sorry, but it's not," denied Ed. "Please take a moment and gather any of your personal items."

Dr. Holbein blinked at a strangely rapid rate. As he glanced around the room, no one spoke out in his favor, not even his former student.

"In a way, this comes as a relief to me," said Dr. Holbein. "I'd been considering retirement for quite some time, and given the current state of everything, I had finally made my decision to leave. Then, the presidential order was issued, and I was forced to stay on."

Holbein didn't explain any further. The only thing he took was his industrial humidifier. What stood out to Ed as the doctor passed by on his way out the door was the milky second eyelid, which would occasionally move smoothly across the surface of the man's eyes. Ed also took note of a scaly tail hanging from his lower back, rendering Dr. Holbein unable to tuck in his shirt. This must have been why he required the humidifier.

Dr. Holbein turned around in the hallway outside of the office to address the group one last time. "It's not much of a big deal, anyway. Nobody's going to even live long enough for retirement, so why hang around?" The aging doctor adjusted the heavy humidifier in his thin arms and walked down the hall to the elevators.

As the three of them had watched Dr. Holbein's exit speech, they'd been uncomfortably aware of the fork forming in his tongue. Then, he was gone.

Mary Beth's shaking voice was the first to be heard. "Poor man."

"Yeah." Rene's sympathy filled the room. "Poor guy."

"I need to find someone else that can help us here," said Ed. "Rene, do you know who would be in line to take Dr. Holbein's place here?"

She pulled out her phone and after a quick search of the Internet, "Sherry Williams," she said, "but she quit last week. It doesn't say why. She wouldn't talk to the media."

"Well, she's either in jail for breaking from her daily routine, or has changed to the point where she could no longer perform her duties here at NASA," offered Mary Beth, sitting on the edge of the desk.

"I'll just have to see who I can find," said Ed, following Dr. Holbein's path out of the office.

"Ever since the earthquakes, things have accelerated," said Rene. "We'll be running out of people soon. Just look at Dr. Holbein."

"I know, it's not very encouraging," said Mary Beth, "but don't give up. There are a lot of good people involved, and we're all in touch daily. We've lost a few who've changed beyond usefulness, but mostly the adaptations are just inconvenient. Ed gets his hair cut twice a day, you know."

"That's a pain, but not anywhere near what some people are experiencing," Rene agreed. "Why doesn't he just pull it back in a ponytail?"

"I think he just wants to appear untouched," Mary Beth offered. "Looking at someone who has remained unchanged offers hope and encourages cooperation."

"I suppose so. Who do you think he'll find to take Dr. Holbein's place?"

Mary Beth giggled to herself at the thought of Ed's probable recruitment techniques.

"What's he going to do? Walk down the hall and pick someone at random?"

"I never thought I would see anything like this," said Mary Beth. "But anyone who already works in this building or is *still* working in this building is as fine a choice as you could get these days. At least they will have some rudimentary knowledge of what NASA is doing and hopefully know who to go to with any questions." Mary Beth found the pot of coffee Holbein had set up in the corner. "Want some? It could be awhile."

"Yeah, thanks."

"In the meantime, tell me about the ship again. Can you ever see who's inside?" Mary Beth handed over the cup.

"Not really." Rene tried to warm her hands against the Styrofoam. "I see shapes silhouetted against the lighted interior, but it happens so fast, and my angle has been very awkward each time. I seem to find the ship just as it's passing over, never arriving in time to see its actual approach."

"Do you get a feel for their size, at least?"

"Not really, although if I were pushed for an answer on that point, I'd say they're rather small."

"Small as in a little person or a Volkswagen?"

"Good question." Rene smiled crookedly. "I don't know, but I'll keep on trying. One of these times, if I catch it head-on and have more time, maybe, well, who knows."

"Maybe," Mary Beth encouraged. "I'm sure..."

The door swung open, interrupting their conversation, and the newly appointed Director of the NASA Goddard Space Flight Center preceded Ed into the room. Funny thing, though, the new recruit was not smiling.

"This is Herb McElvy, the sound analyst." Ed introduced the newcomer. "Please meet my coworkers: Rene, astronomy student; and Mary Beth, hydrologist."

Herb smiled blandly. "Look, Secretary Marker, I've been trying to explain to you, I'm not qualified to step into Dr. Holbein's position. We're in completely different departments. I wouldn't know where to begin."

"Look, Herb," Ed said sincerely. "I know this is not ideal, but we don't have many people to choose from and we don't have much time. Actually, we don't know how much time we have or don't have, but we're trying to find a solution before there's nothing left to solve."

Herb continued to look reluctant until he spotted the materials on the desk. He rounded the desk and stood, paging through the star charts. "Where did these come from?" he demanded, his voice a far cry from the meek man Ed had herded down the hall. Herb looked up expectantly. "Were they here? Have they been holding out on me?"

"No, sir," Rene interjected. "I brought them. I made them. They're accurate."

"You look pretty young to work here," said Herb. "I haven't seen you around before."

Rene once again launched into both the explanation for her star maps and her certainty that a ship was coming straight towards Earth.

Herb paled and seated himself halfway through the explanations. When she finished, he was only briefly silent. "When did you first see this ship, Miss?"

"Right from the beginning, it was in August."

"And you believe it's coming straight here, as though homing in on a signal?" Herb's voice was low as his brain placed what he thought just might be the missing piece into their puzzle.

"Straight as an arrow, Mr. McElvy."

He looked at her silently for a moment. "My God, they're really coming, unless we can stop them, or even want to," he trailed off. "I don't know how you did it, Secretary Marker, but I believe I'm the right man for this job, after all. If you'd all follow me, please."

They had no way of knowing what it was they were seeing, but still, Herb asked, "Do you see this?" He pointed to his mystery frequency band. "After what you've shown me, I think it might be a homing signal."

"What makes you say that?" asked Mary Beth with much trepidation.

"Because it also began this summer, and I've yet to determine exactly what it is. I have, on the other hand, determined all the things it is *not*. It isn't radio, TV, electromagnetic, or microwaves, or anything else known to modern science."

"So, this is your little side project?" Ed traced the peaks and valleys of the questionable transmissions with a steady finger.

Herb was uncomfortable with the connotations of Ed's question and hurried to explain further. "Yes, and no. I've been discretely in touch with the military, the State Department, and local Arizona officials. My clearance is complete and has allowed me access to answers to any questions I posed. A visit to the site turned up nothing but a barren patch of desert.

"In the end, I concluded it was merely an anomaly created by natural forces, possibly a signature for some kind of tectonic release mechanism, but now I'm not sure. The signal is strong and regular, never deviating. Having determined what I thought it was, I put it out of my mind, but in retrospect, it's always been too regular for a natural phenomenon."

"Who else knows about this?" Ed was trying to stay one step ahead of the game, but it was getting harder by the minute. This could be a break. Maybe whatever was serving as the beacon had been the contaminating factor. Maybe if they could find whatever it was and get rid of it, things would go back to normal. It wasn't even a logical train of thought at this juncture and he knew it, but bubbles were all nice before they burst.

"No one else knows," admitted Herb. "Well, at least no one knows that I ever questioned its source at all. By the time I made the report, its origin was not a cause for concern either in my mind or on paper."

"Where in Arizona?" Ed demanded.

"Nowhere, Arizona, Secretary Marker, Cactus Corner. It's not near anything. The park service is the agency that did the on-site inspection. There wasn't even a local government office close enough to utilize."

Ed was on his phone as Herb finished, while his mind swirled ahead. He was planning more than a small field trip.

"I need to touch base with my contacts at the Department of Defense first," Ed said, "and let the military put their precautions in place. An unknown situation could turn out to be nothing or everything. Regardless, I've got an appointment with some *world-renowned* botanist working in D.C. tomorrow morning. He's got a collection of weird botanical adaptions from around the world we are going to check out. According to him, extraordinary things are cropping up. Of course, we all know 'unearthly' is the proper terminology. Anyway, after that, we'll be leaving for Arizona as soon as we are given the go-ahead."

Herb looked practically transfixed with joy. "Wouldn't miss it for the world, but I could still kick myself for not checking this out more thoroughly."

• • •

Ed waited curbside for Patrick to show up. Barry was keeping Ed company in front of the towering building.

"I have to say, I'm enjoying the feel of actual sunlight," said Barry. "All I've seen for the last few weeks has been the inside of the lab, even when all the earthquakes were happening." Barry held his arms out and pointed his face toward the sky.

"I'm just grateful for the military presence," Ed said as they both watched a humvee full of Marines ride down the road, prepared to detain and shoot anyone causing civil unrest. "I never thought I would be grateful for something like that, but it's better than the country going to hell."

"I know," agreed Barry. "Could you imagine the looting and the riots? No one would be safe anywhere. We would also be completely cut off from goods and services, because I can guarantee you no one would be going to work."

"No kidding," said Ed. "I mean, I know there are shortages of everything right now, but we still have the essential items and most of our creature comforts."

"Speaking of creature comforts," said Barry. "I'm going to grab a coffee next door. You want one?"

"Yeah, sure. It's kinda cold out here." Ed put his hands in his pockets. It was an unusually cool September morning in Washington. His hair was its afternoon length, and keeping his ears warm. Shane had canceled Ed's morning haircut because of the meeting with the botanist.

Ed thought about Shane as he waited for Barry to return with the coffee. He hadn't been his normal chipper self lately, but who was? All the shortages had come about not because of the mass exodus from the workforce. The military had seen to that. It was because people were not working at full capacity. They were warm bodies doing the bare minimum, scared, not knowing what the next hour would bring. This global crisis had become the ultimate socioeconomic equalizer. Everyone had more in common than ever before. The differences that used to divide populations so dramatically didn't seem like tremendous differences anymore. They would all wait and watch together as the people of Earth. Ed laughed under his breath at his own thoughts. They reminded him of some cheesy sci-fi movie from the 1960s.

Patrick pulled up to the curb, and this brought Ed out of his wandering thoughts. Where was Barry with that coffee? Ed opened the passenger door.

"Hey, can you wait a minute?"

"Sure," said Patrick, "but we're supposed to be there in twenty minutes and we're thirty minutes away. We have to take an alternate route because of the crystalline structure that has 395 shut down."

"I'll be quick." Being late didn't mean what it used to mean. Ed had always been punctual, but he was becoming less exact with each passing week. Even he was not immune to the cloud of mild depression that had come along with the global crisis.

He walked up to the coffee shop and opened the door, just as Barry was walking out.

"Thanks, Ed," said Barry, with a coffee cup in each hand. "Here." Barry handed him the coffee.

"Thanks. I gotta go. Patrick's here." Ed hopped into the car and left an indifferent Barry standing on the street sipping his coffee and tilting his face up to the sun.

"Just one coffee?" asked Patrick.

"Sorry."

CHAPTER 30

ART

Washington, D.C.
The National Arboretum

Well, that was it! There was absolutely no room for more specimens, decided Dr. Art Bowler, strolling through stack upon row of fresh, dried, and drying plants. Fingering a bizarre flower, Art had to admit that he had no preconceived notions left.

Overcome by a fascination with these mutations, Art had pretty much moved in with his work. He glanced over at "home sweet home," which was now a cot in the corner next to a jumbled heap of both clean and dirty clothes, although he hadn't slept there in days.

Done with his inventory of sorts, Art contentedly returned to the spot on the floor, where he'd spent the majority of his time for the last three days. I must look like an overgrown hamster, he thought with concern. Hoping that nobody would catch him sitting on the ground, in his circular nest hollowed into the sawdust floor, Art's eyes scanned the room self-consciously.

Ever since Monday, he'd been craving contact with the ground. I can't even find my shoes anymore, he realized with alarm. Contact with Mother Earth was now so important that he no longer wore them.

Perhaps it was just a reaction to being shut up with all these crazy plants. Then, catching himself fluffing up the nearby pile of sawdust, Art concluded that he desperately needed some fresh air. This need for fresh air and sunlight overtook his attraction to the ground, and he headed determinedly out the side door to check on his new monster seedlings.

Interesting, Art thought, as he noticed having difficulty in grasping the doorknob. His coordination was going, too—how depressing. Or was it that his fingers had seemed to be just a little too long? No, Art shrugged off the thought and kept going, his mind filled with other things. This afternoon, he'd have to get his information in order. Tomorrow, some DOE reps were coming for it.

Passing the fertilizer bin in a shady corner of the lush courtyard, Art stopped and planted his feet firmly as a tremor passed through, shaking the ground beneath him. Afterward, he assumed his feet had just sunken into a misplaced pile of manure. Yuck. He glanced down to investigate the reason for his difficult attempts to walk.

No pile there, but oh, how Art wished there was! At least the sight of himself sunken ankle deep in shit would've just made him mad. Instead, his blood turned to ice as his heart raced.

I've grown goddamned roots! Art was horrified as he saw his toes were a green and brown mottled color and had elongated so much that they crept down into the ground. How deep were they? Who could tell? He panicked, bending down to claw frantically at the dirt, attempting to rescue himself. Shockingly, his fingers were likewise engaged in the same transformation. They'd grown so long in their efforts to reach the nourishing earth that he watched horrified as they swung like viny ropes in the breeze, growing visibly longer and longer by the minute.

Art tried to gather up his trailing fingers. Maybe if he could just knot them together, but it wasn't working. Two had already snaked their way into the ground, even during his frantic efforts to contain them. His panic was paralyzing. "NOOOOoooooo!" Art opened his mouth and screamed, realizing as he did so, that there was no one to hear him.

This has to be a dream, thought Art, as he tried to pull his arms up. But no, it wasn't a dream, it was a nightmare, and it was real! He was like Gulliver among the Lilliputians, tethered to the ground by countless root-like filaments protruding from his own body. His panic level was rising, but the scientist within him pushed it away. "Keep calm, and maybe the solution will come to you," he told himself again and again until finally, his heart rate slowed and his breath came more easily.

He scoured the recesses of his mind. All of his years of botany should prove very useful in his immediate situation. What should he do? He tried to think, but all that kept coming to mind was how good it felt to be attached to the warm, sunny ground. He pulled his mind back from this comfortable place and tried to think.

At least there was no pain, no hunger or thirst, either. In fact, there was no discomfort whatsoever. The sun was lulling him into a state of complete relaxation. Attempting to focus, Art noticed new sensations. His whole body was turning a greenish lavender, and he could *feel* himself responding to the sunlight.

Well, I'll be damned, Art marveled. *I'm opening up like a solar collector.* He was expanding with a sense of robust good health and well-being. How wonderful! No, this was not wonderful, but he couldn't fight it. His body was absorbing from the earth and the sunlight, nourishing itself like any plant would do, but he wasn't a plant. *I'm a person, a scientist, and...* but it all felt so good.

Then he heard the noise, and all of his good feelings were quickly flushed down the toilet. He knew that sound. How many nights had it kept him awake until finally becoming part of the background? The easily recognizable noises meant his charges were alive and well, because it was the particular cracking noise they made while growing at a tremendous rate.

But these sounds weren't coming from other plants. They were coming from *him*. They were internal, horribly loud, deafening even, because they were from his own body.

Good God, my expansion isn't just warm fuzzy thoughts. It's legitimate physical enlargement, Art realized belatedly. *I'm growing, and growing, and growing!* It still didn't hurt, but it was scaring the hell out of him. Art estimated that his new self was about eight feet high by the time the sun set and his photosynthetic growth stopped. Then, the moon rose in the sky, and his relief soon gave way to the worst fears yet as he recalled the strange, alien growth patterns which the moonlight elicited from his test subjects. Once again, Art's body crackled.

CHAPTER 31

The past is too late to revisit, but too close to resist.

It was wrong, all wrong! The signal was getting much stronger each day. According to his calculations, the continuing message should have shown no marked strengthening until at least his children's children's watch. Yet, it was getting stronger day by day. Had he miscalculated, or was there another explanation? How could they be getting closer to the correct destination? After all, the probe had been gone too long for them to have come this close so quickly; or had it? Perhaps they had flown through a wrinkle in time. Was such a thing even possible, Sodok wondered, feeling woefully inadequate.

The ship on which they traveled had been manufactured in ancient times and had been no more than a mammoth museum artifact until the truth about their future had been uncovered. Oh, the scramble for knowledge, so long disregarded. How well he remembered it, and how close they had all come to destruction.

• • •

The door was unlocked, but nobody seemed to be around as Ed and Patrick let themselves into the quiet arboretum.

"Dr. Bowler? Art Bowler? Are you here?"

"Save your voice, Patrick. No one's home."

"Well, let's go, then. Maybe we can leave for Arizona a little early."

"Maybe." Ed was wandering around, studying the weird assortment of plants spilling from every corner of the vast building. "I don't know much about botany, but I know that I never saw anything like this in my biology classes." He held up an exceptionally odd, yellowish specimen.

"Put it down, would you?"

"Wonder where our host could be." Ed wasn't ready to give up so easily. They had their departure time set for that evening, and the others were busy spending the day trying to figure out an ETA for the possible UFO.

Patrick and Ed's meandering progress took them by a partially opened door leading to an outer yard. "Let's check out here, Patrick. He could be taking a break."

Leaving the building, they entered a walled garden which was wildly overgrown with plants looking like they'd come straight out of the Little Shop of Horrors. Both men pressed through the overgrown area, calling out for their missing scientist as they went.

"Over here." It was faint but repeated over and over until Ed and Patrick broke into a cleared area next to the facility's fertilizer bin. There, taking up a good portion of what used to be the only cleared ground in sight, was what was left of the elusive Art Bowler.

"You must be from the DOE."

"Holy shit!" said Ed. He thought he was immune to the shock that came with witnessing new mutations, but this one hit him like Colleen Maxwell. Like hers, Dr. Art Bowler's transformation was radical and comprehensive. He had changed completely, beyond recognition, and Ed could hear the difficulty in his speech, just like Dr. Maxwell's. They didn't have long to communicate with Art Bowler before he would be forever silenced.

"Hello?" Art's face was still recognizable as human, but its flexibility was severely limited as it hardened slowly into a bark-like substance.

"How long have you been like this?" Ed was always trying to pinpoint something, even when he hadn't the vaguest notion of what.

"What time is it?" asked Art foggily.

"About ten thirty in the morning."

"Well, I've been stuck here since about four o'clock yesterday afternoon. So, I guess that makes it about eighteen hours now?"

Just then, the sun emerged from behind some passing clouds, sending warm rays over the building and onto all three of them. The loud noises began immediately, startling both Patrick and Ed and sending Art into an intermittent moaning wail.

Patrick was poised to run, with nowhere to go.

Ed looked hard to make sure his feet weren't growing roots, too.

"It's the plants. This is the sound they make as they grow, the sound I make now." Art's voice was becoming a hollow whistle as his words passed through rigidly pursed lips.

"How about I cut you loose and we all go inside?" Ed wanted to keep moving.

"No use."

"How do you know? We haven't even tried."

"No, but other people have. Did either of you look around inside at all before you came out here?"

"Yes, we did, and to be honest, some of what's in there is pretty creepy and not particularly plant-like." Ed remembered the gory specimens.

"You're right. I've spent months trying to catalog what I assumed to be new phyla of plants, and some of them represented just that. But then there were the ones like me, the ones who became more than plants, but less than human, only I didn't recognize them at the time." Art's eyes were becoming no more than round knotholes far above his visitor's heads, but they cried bitter tears as his trunk shook with grief and fright at what he was becoming.

Patrick and Ed were too horrified by what Art might say next to offer comfort.

"They were people until they just *weren't* anymore, until they got sucked into the ground like me, and later were cut down and sent here for study."

It was like Colleen all over again, except Art couldn't swim away.

"I don have much tib lef. Ples don cut me dowd, let me becom, let be lib!" Art's growth noises came to a crescendo as he tried to continue, but his tongue was too thick, swelling to fill the empty and now useless mouth cavity.

"You won't be cut down." Ed guaranteed gently. "Studied probably, but then I'm sure you'll understand, and guarded most definitely."

Art's roughly textured head nodded in the higher breezes.

"Do you think he understands?" asked Patrick.

"I hope not. It would be a blessing."

Ed stepped to one side as a tendril dropped from one of Art's overhead arms to bury itself in the rich black dirt like a quick earthworm. They both watched uneasily as an orifice opened in the side of Art's trunk, and Patrick quickly stepped back from the widening hole.

As they turned to leave, the shade beneath Art became tinged with lavender. By the time the two men were inside, there was a very fine purple mist issuing from each of the many new openings in Art.

Back in the car, Ed vented loudly. "We need to get to Arizona as soon as possible and take as much back-up as we can. I don't care who gets spooked! Oh yeah, and we'll have to run another public service announcement requesting that people please not pick any flowers, and stop mowing their lawns, and stop trimming their hedges!" He shivered despite the heat blasting in the car. "Don't forget to remind me. That Art guy needs to be placed under twenty-four-hour watch. For all we know, this is just the beginning."

"Yeah," Patrick cringed. Ed had his hair, and Barry was weirdly magnetic off and on, but Patrick remained unaffected. At least he was presently still unaffected. The folks at NIH regularly examined Patrick and the smaller and smaller number of others like him to see if they couldn't come up with some kind of cure.

Their small plane carried only the pilot, Patrick, Ed, Mary Beth, Barry, Rene, and Herb. Ed had been unable to reach the President prior to take off, so he had to put certain key emergency contingency plans into standby mode himself. Their homing signal wouldn't necessarily be unmanned.

Ed had not hidden the fact that this problem was too big for their small task force and their world-renown experts. He had collaborated with the Secretary of Defense and a military transport plane followed theirs. The military would provide protection in the event it was necessary.

The Secretary of Defense had wasted no time. He had been preparing for everything since this crisis was originally identified during their conference at the DOE. Now, waiting on the ground in Arizona, were divisions of both the Army and Marine Corps, armed with heavy artillery and three tank regiments each. The aviation combat element of the Marine Corps was on standby across the border in New Mexico.

Ed thought about the seriousness of what they were about to find. The military was already stretched paper-thin, patrolling the streets to squelch any civil unrest before it could progress to any organized or large-scale violent protests. For the military to spare these resources was a testament to the gravity of the situation they were about to enter.

After the news of the other-worldly origin of the hitchhikers had been released, many citizens had turned to sky-watching as a nightly pastime. Half watched in fear, and the other half with hope. Ed felt both afraid and hopeful as they approached their destination.

"Down in back, Davis," yelled the pilot from the nearby cockpit. "You're screwing up my equipment." This wasn't the first time he'd had problems with Barry Davis on this flight. The magnetic fields he emitted wreaked havoc on the lab equipment as well.

"Gotcha, Pete." Barry moved to the rear seat furthest away from the pilot's end of the plane. "How about someone throwing me a sandwich?"

Barry always ate when he was nervous, and Ed knew it. He'd put on quite a lot of weight in the past months. "Here, have mine, too." Ed handed him two subs across the cabin.

Mary Beth turned in her seat to face Barry. "I know I should probably be more apprehensive, but after the floods, quakes, and personal transformations, how much worse can it get? What can these aliens do in person that they haven't already done indirectly? Enslave us? Kill us? Are any of these things worse than being driven from your home or watching your loved ones change beyond recognition?"

"Maybe the whole thing was just a mistake, and they're coming to fix it." Barry offered between bites.

"Or to finish the job," Rene added quietly.

"The signal's getting stronger as we get closer." Herb was monitoring the table full of shielded equipment he'd set up on the plane.

"Let's stop avoiding the real question," Ed suggested. "If we find out that this is a homing signal, then what? How much time have we got, and should we attempt to turn it off? Do we want them to come or not, and would turning off the beacon make any difference at this point?"

"We've got two months, give or take a few weeks." This time, Herb was the man with figures at his fingertips, as he dropped his time bomb.

The cabin was as silent as a courtroom after sentencing.

"Hell, by that time, there might not be anyone left," said Patrick, nervously cracking his knuckles.

Rene quickly brought the conversation back to ground zero. "Mr. McElvy's figures only hold up if we've been able to set the scales correctly on all of my maps. We've assigned the same scale to all of them, and it's based on one in which the unknown intersects the outer reaches of what we know to exist. Naturally, it's a very bold assumption, but there's no need to bring in experts to help document our figures. Without a positive frame of reference, there can be no certainties, anyway. Two weeks, two months, or two centuries; this time frame is only our best guess."

The thought was sobering.

Herb took up where Rene had left off. "By plotting the course using Rene's periodic sightings and the scale system we've just explained, both Rene and I feel the ship isn't traveling terribly fast."

"Let's say," Rene added, "not nearly as fast as we'd expect from a civilization able to manufacture and manipulate a factor such as the hitchhiker."

Another thoughtful silence was interrupted by Mary Beth. "Maybe it's not the same civilization. Maybe they intercepted the signal but aren't responsible for its transmission."

"Our thoughts exactly," Herb admitted uncomfortably.

"Or maybe they're just not in a hurry." Barry had stopped chewing long enough to say.

"And," Herb raised his hand to interject, "maybe it is only a physical anomaly, as I assumed at first."

Ed looked away. "I'm going to touch bases with the transport. They've got to be brought up to speed."

For the next hour, the cabin was fairly quiet, as the sky surrounding the plane darkened. All the while Ed kibitzed with the transport, the White House, the landing field, and God. At a certain point, his voice got even lower.

Suddenly, the silence was broken as Barry's voice carried breathlessly while he pointed out the window towards the ground beneath them. "My God, look!"

Everyone else scrambled to look out their closest window into the darkness surrounding the plane. Below, it was like a Fourth of July display, but this display wasn't airborne.

"Just like the rocks in the lab." Patrick recalled the softly winking crystals.

"It's happening worldwide as dusk approaches." Ed had been briefed on the progress of the lighted rock formations just a half-hour ago. "They hum, too—not right away, but after a few hours of being lit or whatever, it begins."

"It's breathtaking." Mary Beth stared raptly at the twinkling light show beneath them. "But what do you suppose it means?"

"Same thing it meant even when the lights were too faint to see," said Patrick derisively. "We didn't know then, and we haven't got a clue now."

At that moment, they all heard the landing gear descend.

"Hey, Ed," Pete called from the cockpit. "You wanna come up here, please? I've got a couple of questions for you." He was spooked.

"At least he won't need any landing lights tonight," said Barry.

Ed made his way to the front of the plane to see what Pete needed.

CHAPTER 32

FORREST
Yuma County, Arizona
Sonoran Desert

Forrest and Sheila Carbury had been working together for six years, married for three, and digging at their desert location for two days. Despite distinctly opposite appearances, they were equally miserable working in the broiling early August sun.

There's not an important archeological dig anywhere near our camp, thought Forrest nastily as the sweat ran in tiny, meandering rivulets down his body. How had Sheila ever come up with this site, and how had he let her? After all, with an archeologist and an anthropologist in the same family, at least one of them should have known better. Digging more forcefully than he should have, Forrest vented his anger. This getaway was supposed to have been relaxing!

Sheila had been having a problem recently with bad dreams. He had thought this would be a nice getaway for the two of them, but it had turned into this. He thought about their conversation leading up to the trip.

"You talk in your sleep all night long, Sheil—something about eggs hatching." Forrest hadn't been complaining, but he wasn't getting much sleep, either. "How about a camping trip to take your mind off everything?"

"That sounds amazing, and thanks!" She'd hugged her husband.

"You pack and I'll shop for provisions." They'd both known she was thinking of campfire food, but now all of that seemed like another lifetime.

Look at her over there, Forrest thought, watching his wife work herself into a frenzy, searching for something that wasn't there. *I should have taken the damn tools out of the trunk before we left,* but it was too late for that now. The idea of a camping trip had been good, so where had it all gone wrong, Forrest kept asking himself.

Everything about this damned trip had been bizarre right from the get-go. A mere forty-eight hours ago, they'd been driving through the desert, when suddenly, Sheila had insisted he turn into no-man's-land.

"I don't know why, Forrest," she'd practically been in tears, "but can we camp over there somewhere?"

"It's okay, honey. Sure, we can set up camp anywhere you want." He'd hurried to soothe his upset wife. "You point, I'll drive." Their four-wheel-drive vehicle was a must for any archeologist.

"Go north," Sheila had smiled through her tears as he'd maneuvered them off the road and wound his way around boulders and cacti.

Oh well, Forrest consoled himself silently, forcing his shovel down further into the drying clay. At least he could use the huge relay harvester they'd passed as some kind of directional marker later.

Forrest was tired of replaying how they had ended up there in his mind. He was tired of digging. They were supposed to be on vacation. At the risk of upsetting his wife, he dropped the shovel and looked up at her. "Should we quit and go camping like we had planned? It's not too late."

"Logically, I know what you're saying, Forrest, but we can't stop digging. I can't explain it, but I can't stop digging. It's a need, something I feel, like needing to quench a thirst."

He didn't respond to this, and Sheila said nothing further. In his cloud of pessimism, Forrest felt like he was melting. They'd been at the dig all morning, and he was long past wilted. The sun was searing, and he wiped his brow with an already stained bandana. Everything was orange, the stain, the dirty sand, even the heat felt orange to him.

If only he could stay mad, but how? She's so happy, Forrest told himself hesitantly. At least she seems to be happy, he second-guessed, knowing that in reality, his wife's body was as tight as a guitar string ready to snap. He could feel the tension every time he touched her and see it from across the thirty feet separating them. They'd been up at the crack of dawn and working till dark for two days. Some vacation!

But I'd call it quits if I really wanted to, Forrest admitted to himself. Strangely enough, deep down inside, *he* was becoming convinced there was something here. At any rate, it was just too damn hot to go on.

"Hey, Forrest, look at this!" Sheila's voice urgently called to him.

He immediately lifted himself from his crouched position and hurried over, knowing his wife's voice well enough to recognize the excitement. She must've found something. "What is it, Sheila?"

She was staring intently ahead, gently dusting the dirt and clay from a two by three foot scored surface embedded in the mammoth, recently displaced cliff of shifted strata in front of her. Glyphs became more prominent with each swipe of the large, soft-bristled brush. "It's not like anything else I've seen from this general area. Actually, it's not like anything I've ever seen from *anywhere*, Forrest. The representations are all different."

"It looks like a doorway." He was becoming just as excited as his wife. "My God, Sheila, this could be a burial chamber. I know it's not in character with any of the ancient local civilizations, but this could be big." Forrest pulled the brush from his back pocket and helped uncover their newfound treasure.

As they worked, the dirt fell away more and more readily. "Forrest, it's metal," she admitted uneasily. Both of them knew that metal this finely crafted was an impossibility in the time period encompassed by this rock strata. "Look. There seems to be some kind of entrance mechanism." This thing had never belonged to the Anasazi.

Forrest's impatience with the heat was gone. It had vanished quickly, the professional investigator taking its place. This could be what they'd always dreamed of, a previously undiscovered culture. He marveled while continuing to dig—a culture capable of exceptionally advanced metallurgy skills. It would be something they could work on together, each using their own expertise to assemble the missing pieces of the puzzle. Forrest's thoughts were way ahead of him, as he pictured an exciting future stretching ahead. So what, he told himself defensively. Dreaming never hurt anyone, and right now it was helping him to pass the time while they continued to uncover their find. Besides, both he and Sheila were too excited for words.

"Just dust the edges," said Sheila. "Then, we'll see if either of us can figure out how to get it open."

Sheila seemed unnaturally calm, especially compared to her erratic and agitated moods of the last two days. Now, she was single-mindedly fixated on their discovery. Finally, the large, slightly curved surface in the cliff was cleared of its dusty covering.

"Ready, Forrest?"

"Yup, here goes." Bracing his feet to strengthen his stance, Forrest pulled at the door forcefully, but it didn't budge.

"Here, let me try." Sheila stepped forward and ran her hand around what appeared to be the edge of the opening. Her sweat dripped steadily despite a tightly secured headband. "Ouch." She'd been cut by a slightly jagged edge. The cut was not dangerous, but it was deep enough to draw blood.

"Are you okay?" Forrest leaned forward solicitously.

"It's only a scratch," Sheila insisted with preoccupation. She instinctually sucked on her injured finger. "But what's this?"

There was a small lavender stain on the hull near where Sheila's blood was quickly drying in the blistering sun. Forrest watched as she took the injured finger out of her mouth and ran it over the interesting discoloration that trailed down into the barely perceptible seam of the doorway. He then saw the questionable marking disappear beneath her touch—or was it absorbed?

"It's nothing," Sheila informed her husband.

"Let me see," said Forrest, taking Sheila's hand and turning it palm side up, expecting dusty purple residue, but there was nothing, at least not that he could see.

"See, it's nothing," she insisted.

"You're probably right," Forrest agreed. They'd been out in the heat all day and the shadowy colors of the desert were brilliant and beautiful, but also played tricks on the eyes.

"Oh," Sheila said, taking her hand from his and shaking it out as if relieving a cramp.

"What is it?"

"I don't know," she said. "It feels tingly."

"We're both up to date on our tetanus shots, at least," offered Forrest. "I'll get the first aid kit. A Band-Aid and some antibiotic ointment should be enough."

"Wait. Don't leave. I'm feeling kind of strange."

"Strange like how? Are you dizzy? Do you think you might be dehydrated? Let me get you some water." Forrest had some in a Yeti container attached to his belt. He opened the lid and offered the cool liquid to his wife. "Here, drink this."

"No. I can't." Sheila stepped forward to fiddle with the door mechanism again.

She sounded far away, like she hadn't heard a thing he had said. "Sheila, you should drink something."

"Yeah," she said without really paying him any attention. She continued to work at the door mechanism until the door slid aside, silently revealing a pitch-black interior.

"Step down Forrest. It will activate the lights." She moved aside for him.

"What lights? How would you know there are lights?"

"I...I just know things about this place," she said.

"Like what?" Forrest was getting concerned.

A lot was going on in the world these days, and Forrest was sure that they didn't even know the half of it. This vacation was supposed to be a break from all the bizarre breaking news and all the tragic physical ailments that were popping up with increasing frequency. It hit very close to home when Sheila's sister, Linda, suddenly lost her sight. That had put Sheila very close to the edge. It had not been Forrest's intention for their vacation to push her all the way over.

Sheila had not responded to his question, so he repeated. "What things do you know about this place?"

"It smells like home," was all she said.

Forrest stepped closer to the entrance. Home smelled like pizza, cats, and Pine-Sol. This place smelled like the spicy tang of metal.

"Sheila, let's pack up for the day. We've done enough, and we can start exploring the interior tomorrow morning."

"We can't stop now," she insisted. "I'll keep going. If you want to go back to camp, you can."

There was no way he was going to leave her alone in this state, though he wasn't even sure what "this state" was. He was an anthropologist, not a psychologist, but right now he was a husband who loved his wife and she needed him here. "Okay, I'll go first." He stepped over the threshold and lights came on.

"Look, Sheila. My God, look at all of this." His voice carried up loudly from below. He was turning in circles, slowly taking in the impossible. Beginning with the precise planes and angles of the descending ramp, everything got increasingly more unbelievable. What could explain the metallic sheen of the walls, or the illumination, seemingly without source, which had activated as his foot had first touched the ramp?

"Someone must be playing a joke on us, honey. This isn't three or four hundred years old. There's metal and what looks like plastic, there's even ventilation!" Forrest felt a whoosh of freshly cooled air brush against his sweaty neck as he spoke, the feeling raising more goose flesh than he already had. He'd been calling up to his wife as she stood casting a long shadow from the opening.

"No, Forrest, it's real."

"It can't be. There wasn't the technology for any of this back then. Maybe it's a government project or something."

"Silence." Her word was a command rather than a request as she held up her hand to ward off any argument.

Forrest watched Sheila slowly walk down the ramp and step to the middle of the room. She spun slowly on her heels and moved towards a side wall. Her hands extended confidently, and she touched a lighted panel, tapping the "dots," tracing the "lines." Most spaces on the walls were covered by flush, softly glowing symbols, gauges, and glyphs. Sheila seemed to be familiar with all of it.

"THEG SA HA CHING." Sheila repeated this six times. Then she stood there, hands at her sides, watching the wall begin to glow. A diamond formed on her forehead, glowing softly and steadily.

What was wrong? Forrest wanted to shake his wife back to her senses, but it might not be such a good idea. You weren't supposed to wake sleepwalkers, and Sheila sure looked like she was in some sort of trance. "The egg is hatching, the egg is hatching." Who cared, and why was she repeating it? This was too weird, just like her dream.

I'll carry her out of here if I have to, thought Forrest as he prepared for a quick exit. First, she'd started with all the mumbo jumbo, but now she must have touched an activating sequence of buttons. The walls were changing fast, progressively becoming murals, huge, moving, living, and breathing murals. It was like an

IMAX theater. By now, Forrest was long past scared and closing in on "scared out of your ever-lovin' mind," and on top of everything else, Sheila was crying.

"What's wrong with me, Forrest?" she wailed into their climate-controlled cocoon.

Thank God. She'd finally snapped out of the trance or whatever, and the weird glowing thing on her forehead was gone, too.

"That's it," he said, hoisting her over his shoulder and trudging quickly back up the smooth ramp, past the flickering images. Enough was enough, but he knew it would not be that simple.

Later that evening, Forrest and Sheila sat around the campfire, but not too close. Even though the sun had set, it was still August and the nighttime desert temperatures stayed around eighty degrees.

Forrest was not sure what to say and what not to say to Sheila. She had once been so easy to read, predictable, and fun. Now it was like camping with an IED. She appeared calm at the moment, but that could change. The President was supposed to address the nation that evening, and he wanted to hear what the President had to say, but wasn't too sure what it might trigger for Sheila.

"More corn and black beans?" Forrest extended the pan with the camping fare to Sheila.

"No thanks," she said. "I'm sorry."

"You don't have to apologize."

"But I do," said normal Sheila. "I honestly felt like someone or something had control of my body and my mind back there." She looked down at the dusty ground.

"Look," said Forrest, trying to make eye contact unsuccessfully. "I know you and your sister are close, and I know that it's been hard for you to watch her struggle."

"That's the thing, babe. So many people are struggling right now. Where is all of this coming from? So many strange things are happening to so many people. Doctors have no idea what's going on? What *is* going on?"

She was getting worked up again. Forrest decided at that moment that he would not put his curiosity over his wife. They would not watch the presidential address.

"Look, Sheil, we have over a month left on our sabbaticals. Why don't we plan on staying here, taking our time documenting and cataloging our find? We'll let our families know that we're okay, but we won't watch any news. We'll try to keep our minds off of things for a while, just enjoying the excitement of this unusual find and our time together."

Sheila let out a long sigh. "That sounds good to me."

"Come over here," said Forrest. "I'm done with dinner." He gave her an enticing look.

Her eyes met his and their plan was set into motion. Just the two of them. No strange happenings or tense situations, and definitely no doom and gloom newscasts. Just the two of them in a lightweight sleeping bag under a sky full of desert stars.

CHAPTER 33

GARY
Manhattan, New York

Gary Zuplo, small, pinched, and perpetually stooped, was used to being the bearer of bad news. To be honest, he even thought of himself as a herald of doom, atmospherically speaking. Gary had the ugly job of testing and charting the city's air, which got dirtier, filthier, and less breathable by the day.

The first time he'd seen a harvester staring out from the nineteen-inch screen in his living room, Gary had been speechless with joy. From then on, he'd rejoiced. There would be no more acid rain, the skies would clear, his hated air quality index would become obsolete, and Gary Zuplo would be out of a job—hallelujah! He still celebrated daily.

Climbing the steps to the rooftop collection station on this sunny, cloudless day, Gary looked forward, as always, to watching his beloved birds circle overhead. They caught flight on the cool late September breeze that rushed past the city's skyscrapers. Okay, so maybe he was a little preoccupied with these aviary companions. What was the big deal, anyway? Some people loved dogs. He happened to love birds.

At least, he thought thankfully, opening the door and walking out onto the roof, no one in the office had any idea that mild-mannered Gary was a closet skydiver. Wouldn't they get a laugh out of that. He could just hear them now.

God, he loved the time spent in free fall, not that it was terribly often. After all, skydiving wasn't a cheap hobby. No, definitely not cheap, thought Gary, but worth every penny. His skydiving was fast becoming an obsession. He'd been disturbed to find himself longing to jump from the rooftop on more than one occasion lately. It wasn't a suicidal urge, and for that he was grateful, but more of an obsessive compulsion.

The breeze felt good. The downy growth that now covered much of his body was making his shirt most uncomfortable. No problem; off it came. At least he could cover his particular physical oddity with clothing when necessary. So many people didn't have that luxury.

Lunch was a pleasure, and he shared it eagerly with the birds who swooped through the air to catch the morsels he threw aloft. Sooner than he would have liked, it was time to dress and return to his post. Maybe just a little longer; he bargained with himself, making no move to leave the rooftop. Instead, he was unwillingly compelled to walk over and stand on the small, knee-high ledge outlining the edges of the building.

Here it comes again, Gary worried as he felt the impending urge to jump. This time it was so strong. *Oh God, what have I done?!* Gary panicked, realizing belatedly that he'd taken a step into thin air, and it was too late to correct the movement. His balance was already shifting forward too much to allow for any compensation. If this was truly to be his last moment, Gary decided he was prepared to lean into his destiny. Having made the decision, he extended his arms upwards as the wind whipped around his body and waited for death.

What the? He felt a slowing in his speed, a jolting, stationary moment he recognized as a parachute opening. Gary's eyes popped open immediately, knowing that he wasn't wearing one. In his moment of shock, he veered dangerously, gliding towards the looming side of his building. Luckily, instinct kicked in. Newly aerodynamic, Gary took stock of his fledgling wings and easily glided higher into the city sky, buoyed on the warmer currents stirred up by sun-baked streets and rooftops.

The tiny, individual downy filaments covering the underside of his arms and the sides of his body had grown longer and longer, while weaving themselves into quite a well-anchored, yet gossamer-like, set of wings. The rest of his questionable covering was morphing into an insulating and protective layer, much akin to feathers, although sharp and stubby.

Gary felt the flex and pull of skin and muscles working to accommodate his gusty progress higher into the sky. My God, he was flying! His wildest dreams had come true, and Gary wheeled and dived, glided, and climbed higher. Where would he go? He thought about his itinerary while climbing still higher into increasingly thinner air.

In the end, he had no more choice in his destination than he'd had in whether to jump. Keep climbing, he urged himself, aware only of the need to go higher and faster. In time, the sky changed slowly from sunny cerulean to a deeper and darker vacuum. It was lonely but exhilarating. There was no more oxygen, but his body had no further need of it. Gary, who had always been so trapped in a concern for the breathability of Earth's atmosphere, had been set free. He looked disbelievingly down at the planet, then shrugged his now muscular shoulders and turned in the correct direction. After all, the call was quite clear.

CHAPTER 34

Birds of prey do not sing.
—German Folk Proverb

According to the legends, there would be greeters to accompany them on the last leg of their journey. If these rumors were correct, the creatures would merely whet their appetite for the coming attractions, but it was only hearsay. Of course, there was always that place where fact met fiction.

Now, with the signal getting stronger daily, Sodok scanned the inky blackness for signs of a sentinel. After all, if this part of the legend were true, perhaps the others were, as well. Considering the scope of their legends, it was a very disconcerting thought. Somewhere between their doubts and hopes would be the truth.

As it had been prophesied, their ship was to be escorted on the final leg of its journey. The creatures were oddly colorful and fanciful, familiar and yet alien. Would everything, he wondered, be as unsettling in the new destination?

Each greeter was a combination of frail delicacy and muscular power, but there were so many of them. A great swarm surrounded the ship and performed, Sodok assumed, for their benefit. On wings that billowed like outsized cloth sails, they moved easily through the outer weightless vacuum, alternately cavorting and careening playfully, or traveling in formation with military precision. It was their eyes, however, rather than their antics, which held Sodok spellbound. One minute they held madness and the next mischief, but through it all, they led on, never ceasing. What sustained and directed them, and was he wise to follow this welcoming horde, after all? In the end, there was no choice. Where else were they to go?

• • •

As the small plane unloaded, its passengers stepped into a lighted fairyland. The ground sparkled beneath their feet as tiny crystals of sand and dirt blinked rapidly on and off. Even more spectacular were the buttes seen from this distance, mammoth and shining like children's glow sticks half-buried in the sand on a beach.

"After all the bizarre and twisted things the hitchhikers have caused, I can't believe my eyes." Mary Beth turned in circles, mesmerized. "It's gorgeous."

"It's these glowing rocks that are preventing the military from visualizing the satellite images to survey the area," said Ed. "We're effectively blind because of this recent phenomenon!"

She said no more.

Their small group would soon be swallowed by the size of the military forces on the ground, like a fly in the mouth of a large bass. With no advanced imaging or surveillance, they had only sheer numbers on their side, hopefully. Ed had his earpiece fitted and would be in constant communication with the Major Generals of both military branches. He was the one person who knew the most about all anomalies created by the extraterrestrial biologic material. He would be on standby to answer any questions, if he happened to know the answer.

Three M109782 armored troop carriers rolled quickly from the transport plane. It was impossible to speak above the rumble without an earpiece. These carriers would transport Ed's team and the other new arrivals from Washington across the desert.

Originally, Ed and the other department leaders had thought that darkness would help maintain at least a small level of surprise should they come upon an alien signaling post. But tonight, there would be no true darkness. Instead, their procession would be well lit and easily seen. That was what was truly surprising about the sudden presence of military vehicles crunching their way across the sand and rocks to meet them at their landing site. Where had they come from? Ed could not recall having seen them from the air, but two divisions of the military and all the heavy transport and firepower that went with them should have been almost visible from space.

The President had deployed both the Marine Corps and the Army. Major General Pearson commanded the Army division comprised of three brigades, each brigade with three thousand troops. The Marine air-ground task force had brought with them a war time Marine expeditionary force of fifteen thousand men, commanded by Major General Sanchez. The ACE, aviation combat element, of the Marines was off site in New Mexico on standby. The six tank regiments between the two branches of the military covered the area of half a city block. This magnificent show of force took Ed's breath away. He had gotten a hold of President Morgan before landing, but no words could have prepared him for this display.

"Welcome," boomed Major General Sanchez through Ed's earpiece. "Thought you'd never get here."

"Where did you all come from?" asked Ed. "We didn't see anyone when we flew in just fifteen minutes ago."

"That's military intel," said the Major General.

"Fine." Ed could sense his status as an outsider in this combat environment and didn't press the issue. He climbed into the armored troop carrier and sat down in front of Barry. Within thirty minutes of landing at White's Field, the convoy was underway.

"Well, this is it," said Barry, not looking at anyone in particular.

"Yup." Patrick was staring from windows that were getting dustier by the minute. "This is it."

"This is what?" said Rene, wringing her hands.

Herb reached out in a fatherly gesture to take her cold, fidgety hands in his.

Mary Beth and Ed sat side by side directly behind the driver. "So, from what you've heard, how pervasive is this illumination anomaly?" she questioned quietly.

"It's happening everywhere. The whole thing isn't right, but people are captivated by the sight of them. Glowing rocks seem so innocuous when you consider how they've long since shaken themselves into every conceivable shape and texture."

"Ed," she started.

"Yes?" He turned and looked Mary Beth in the eyes. They were tired with worry.

"I can feel the ship coming closer."

"How? What else can you tell us?" Ed probed. "Any advanced information would help to give us an advantage."

"I wish I could escape into a vision right now, but all I have is an unsettled feeling in my stomach."

"Are you going to be okay?"

She nodded.

"People are calling them landing lights," Ed offered.

"Maybe they're right."

"Maybe they are. What do you think?" he asked.

Mary Beth answered too sharply. "Who wants to think?"

Ed could sympathize with her agitation. "Do you feel anything else as we get closer?"

"Apprehension, like everyone else, but do I feel any aliens? No. Not around here, at least."

Ed pulled out a tablet from the compartment on the back of the seat in front of him. It was hooked up to a video feed from the vehicle leading the military procession. Multiple feeds came from the lead Marine Raiders' helmet cams. Ed watched the grid of video feed and waited.

"I know how this goes against your grain, Ed, but I'm still glad to have them here with us."

"If it weren't necessary, I wouldn't have involved the President and all the firepower that comes with him. Everything we have uncovered so far, tracking down every lead with every expert, it all points to Arizona. I'd rather have this be the overkill of a lifetime than be under-prepared for what we may find." His voice was heavy with resignation.

Mary Beth leaned back in her seat and stared hard at the darkened window while her reflection stared right back. The window clouded over and became black. Then slowly, as she continued to watch, lights reappeared. These were no longer the warm desert lights. Instead, they were cold, faint, and spread over vast distances. It was a view far beyond this world.

Ed continued to watch the video feed. He didn't notice Mary Beth sinking into another vision.

"Ed? Ed!" Mary Beth poked him hard. "I'm seeing something." Her voice was strained with urgency. When he didn't respond, she tried again without turning her head, lest she lose the vision. "Ed! Wake up!"

"I'm not sleeping." His tone belied his captivation. "I see it too, but I can hardly believe it!"

Her head snapped around momentarily to face Ed. Yet when she turned back, her vision remained.

"Rene, Patrick, everyone, get over here quick!" Ed's command was loud and abrupt.

They all moved through the vehicle, cramming themselves around the small window to watch Mary Beth's vision unfold.

"Look, there's a bird." Barry couldn't believe his eyes.

Veering through the darkness of space, the creature came at them quickly. "No, it's definitely not a bird." Patrick could see its humanoid form despite all the feathers and alien features.

"I think it can see us, too," Rene gasped and leaned backwards.

The thing flew closer, glided up to the window and kept pace with them. Its cavernous mouth, with no lips to soften its movements, broke into a crookedly obscene and toothless grin. As the creature turned and flew quickly from their view, they saw dozens of others like it approaching, and behind them, a spaceship.

Rene leaned forward again to crowd the window. "That's it!" Her finger glided along the glass surface, pacing itself to the ship's progress. "It's the one I've been seeing all along. But what are those things? I've never seen them before."

"Maybe they're what's inside?" Barry's guess was as good as anybody's.

The armored vehicle slowed, and the window cleared.

"How did you do that?" Barry asked. "How did you share your vision?"

"I don't know. I mean, I didn't try to do it." Mary Beth hit the seat in front of her as they came to a sudden stop.

Ed turned up the volume on his earpiece and waited for direction from the Major General.

"We're here."

Obviously, thought Ed as he awaited further instruction.

The rest of the group moved back to their seats, nervously preparing to debark.

"No one's getting out." Ed motioned for everyone to take their seats. "We're here as consultants and aren't to be placed in any dangerous combat situations." At the direction of Major General Sanchez, Ed flipped on the screen that would broadcast the feed from his tablet to the rest of the passengers.

"Like one side of this hill is any less dangerous than the other," said Patrick, pointing to the glowing, gravely mound behind which their vehicles had parked.

One of the empty rectangles on the screen came alive as the lead's helmet video camera was turned on.

"Well, this is it." Ed picked up the radio handset and made contact. "You're coming in perfectly, but turn up the sound." Immediately, the volume increased, and those viewing heard the crunch of feet against the ground as the line of protectively suited and heavily armed men made their way across the desert toward their homing signal. It wouldn't be long now.

"Do you think those bird things were them?" Barry watched the screen, half expecting something to swoop down and carry the soldiers away like large alien vultures.

"Definitely not." Patrick sounded sure. He shifted uncomfortably in his seat, staring straight ahead.

"How much further, Colonel?" Ed asked.

"Only a few hundred yards to go, sir," the Colonel whispered into his helmet's mic. It seemed deafeningly loud in the silent metal vehicle.

"Did anyone else get a look at the last birdman before everything went poof?" Patrick couldn't have been the only one to see it.

Silence.

"Well, I did." Patrick continued. "And whatever flew by at the last minute was wearing what was left of a UPS uniform."

"Let's go, men." They heard the Colonel give the order and watched as the camera crested the last hill even before the soldier wearing it.

What was next? Every one of them was braced for whatever would come into view, everything except for what they saw.

"It's just a campsite." Mary Beth was the first to react.

It certainly looked as simple as that, Ed had to agree. There was a closed tent and a canvas shade shelter held up by four poles. The standard campfire burned low as music from the tent blared out classic R and B.

"And here comes the military." Barry was spellbound watching the advancing soldiers rush in with weapons leveled, surprising the two campers, who were locked in an embarrassingly nude embrace.

With all the earthquakes that had plagued the world as of late, it was no wonder that the campers had paid their thunderous approach no attention. They had caught them completely unawares.

Undaunted, the soldiers spread out into a search formation and swept the area while the couple was allowed to dress. "We've found something over here, Colonel," a faceless voice announced. With those words, their first line of defense swept into the questionable area, leaving the surprised couple guarded nearby.

The jostled vid cam followed a heavily armed line of men and panned the indicated cliff side. It showed a hole or tunnel entrance.

"The signal's coming from in there." One soldier held an instrument above the dark hidey-hole.

From over by the fire, the woman camper yelled. "It's a spaceship, but for God's sake, don't damage it. There's no one inside." She was crying hysterically and being held motionless at gun point.

"My wife's right. This is a rare find. There's never been another archeological discovery like it. Any destruction of this site would be unforgivable." His voice continued while at the same time he tried to calm his extremely distraught wife.

"What the hell are you doing here anyway, and get those guns out of our faces! We have rights too, you know," he growled menacingly at his captors, not knowing about the vast military assemblage just over the hill. "Has anyone here got the slightest clue as to the value of our discovery?" The man ranted on while the woman continued to weep.

At that point, the Colonel walked to stand in front of the cameras. "Secretary Marker," he addressed Ed directly. "I think we could use some help here." He then went to inform the tank regiment it could stand down and directed his men away from the hole.

Ed had heard enough and switched off the volume. He exhaled in relief and frustration. It had been overkill. Military resources squandered on a campsite, *a campsite*, but there was still the signal coming from the spacecraft. Even though there were no extraterrestrials at present, they were on their way, and this time, everyone knew they were coming.

CHAPTER 35

CLARENCE
Laurel, Maryland

Clarence Walburn scanned the complicated crossword puzzle with a practiced eye. His intense fascination with words demanded constant daily challenges. Looking more like a squared-off, monosyllabic longshoreman, Clarence's ruggedly defined features and low center of gravity would never have suggested his preoccupation with such things.

"Too bad I can't talk anyone into a rousing game of Scrabble," he baited his family as they played video games. Although they rarely shared his passion, he had a live one tonight. All right! Clarence rubbed his hands together in anticipation and then happily set up the game at the kitchen table.

He was contentedly keeping score, and they were having some nice father-daughter fun, until he began setting out particularly unusual combinations of letters and claiming they were words.

"In what lifetime, Dad?" Trina asked her father.

He didn't know what to tell her.

"Stop cheating, or I'll quit," she demanded.

Out came the foreign language dictionaries, and although they had a million of them, no luck, so no points.

"Cheating," scoffed Clarence each time it happened. "I'm not cheating," he insisted to his offended daughter. "They are too words, Trina," he was certain of it. The game was called a draw, and his questionable words were not totaled with the rest. As always, Clarence realized with resignation, his family was making a point of keeping him honest within his passion.

Later that week, Clarence took time to wonder about his preoccupation with this unknown language. He sat perched on a worn stool in his basement shop, making little blank wooden squares into which he burned one odd sign after another. This is nuts, he admitted. Still, he felt compelled to continue his folly. He could no longer talk anyone into Scrabble. So what? Who needed them, anyway? Certainly not him, and truly he didn't. What he needed to do was better done alone.

Ah yes, perfect. Clarence held up his latest square. The squiggles, dots, and angles were all in the correct sequence, and he carefully laid it aside. He knew each one was gibberish, or at least that's how they seemed. Such exotic combinations were unprecedented, unpronounceable, and impossible. But they're real, screamed another level of his brain, and he knew it was true. He knew that each phantom word had a rich tapestry of history behind it.

Tonight, while his family streamed the latest season of their favorite show, Clarence sat arranging the odd Scrabble tiles into new word combinations. Later, when everyone was in bed, he knew that he'd creep down the stairs to sit for hours making up crossword puzzles, ones using the symbols. The thought bothered Clarence, but not enough to make him quit.

"What's this?" Judy questioned her husband as she logged onto the computer several days later, noticing a new file.

"Oh, nothing; I've just been cataloging some of my new symbols." His words were casual, but they belied an increasing obsession. Please don't go into the file, Clarence prayed silently. If she were to see the detailed alphabetical listings for his non-existent language, he wasn't sure who would be more embarrassed, he or Judy.

Was he cracking up? Clarence had to agree that maybe his family was right. But, if he could just keep it confined to the study, nobody else needed to know. With so many crazy things going on these days, who'd even notice? Clarence watched with relief as Judy bypassed his files without a second thought.

Noting his wife's complete indifference to the new files, Clarence finally felt secure enough to consider beginning his pronunciation guide. "Come on, honey," he offered. "Meet me in the kitchen, and I'll get you a cup of coffee."

"Maybe later, Clarence. I've got some things I want to finish up first," a preoccupied Judy replied without even looking up from the screen.

"Okay, I'll start the pot." Clarence turned to go, already mentally picturing the tonalities he intended to capture. Not surprising to him was the fact that he could not verbalize most of the needed sounds. Clarence knew what they were. He just couldn't reproduce them. It didn't matter, though. Someone would be able to do it, of that he was sure, and so the work continued.

CHAPTER 36

Must we always pay the piper to dance to the music?

The military personnel sitting just beyond a limited circle of light from the campfire were divided into two groups. One group remained in their anti-contamination gear, but the other had compromised the integrity of their suits and now sat beside removed helmets. Those without headgear couldn't have cared less about further alien contamination. "How much more contaminated can we get?" they goaded their more cautious companions. "Our genes are part alien already!" The entire highly trained group sat expectantly, watching the dark hole in the displaced hill, ready to jump to the assistance of those on guard around its perimeter.

Closer to the fire sat the shaken couple. Amazingly enough, they'd turned out to be social scientists, Forrest and Sheila Carbury. Both campers were busily discussing their findings with a spellbound audience.

"We'll be happy to show you all of it," Sheila offered unnecessarily, given there was no choice in the matter.

Listening closely while simultaneously panning the horizon, Ed considered the fact that their surroundings already looked like an alien landscape, with towering rock intrusions glowing unnaturally. In the distance, he saw a lake which had recently formed beyond cacti left from the area's many years as a desert.

"How fast is that water rising?" Barry asked, as if reading Ed's mind.

"It's not," Forrest assured him. "Hasn't risen in over three weeks now. We figure the level has basically stabilized."

"Right," Patrick commented sourly. "Things are stabilizing. This light show is just our imagination."

"Patrick," Ed cautioned.

"Do you have any idea how long this thing's been buried here?" Rene's scientific juices were running. "I mean, it's obviously been pushed upwards by the quakes. You can see the strata lines are all shifted."

"We're talking bottom layers, meaning that I couldn't even begin to guess how old it truly is." Sheila's voice was disbelieving, even though she knew it all to be true.

"This is it then? This is where our hitchhiker came from?" Mary Beth was uncharacteristically eager to nail Sheila down to a definite answer.

Forrest jumped up in her defense, startling those guarding the ship's hatch. He paced while explaining. "If this ship crashed carrying alien matter, and it was spread by whatever means during Earth's primordial-soup days, yes, this site could very well be ground zero for the hitchhiker. However, from what we've been able to observe, the ship did not crash. Sheila and I haven't been able to find any damage."

The group was restless with this verbal report, and so was Ed. "I think it's time for a tour," he stood, and the rest followed suit. "You mentioned lights before?" He looked at Sheila, suggesting she lead the way.

"Yes, there are lights which activate upon entry." Their group slowly approached the guarded area. "We're not sure whether they're sensitive to motion, or heat, or life forces in general."

They stopped directly before the hole in the recently displaced strata, which they all knew to be the doorway to the actual alien ship.

"Sheila and I will go first." Forrest advanced quickly, casting disparaging looks at the wary military presence.

Despite repeated assurances from the scientists, the soldiers raised their weapons as Forrest and Sheila disappeared into what immediately became a lighted passageway with a ramp leading downward at a slight decline.

"Come on. There's nothing to worry about." Sheila waved them inside.

Mary Beth was one of the last ones in line. She called Ed over and whispered to him. "I feel as though we're close to something, close enough to put our hands around the answer. It's there, and then it's gone."

Ed acknowledged her with a singular nod and followed inside. His attention was diverted from Mary Beth as he took in the construction of the alien craft. The edges were rounded, smooth, and continual. How beautiful, he marveled, and so obviously advanced, although somewhat antiseptic in his opinion.

"Ed," Mary Beth whispered, again. "It's like I can smell them, the ones who were here before, the ones who sent this ship on its way. Who are they, and where are they now?" she mused. "I have no answers, but I can still smell them."

"We all wish we had more answers," Ed responded, still caught up in his own thoughts. He also wondered about who they might be. Were they birdmen capable of free flight through space, or so fragile that they had buried themselves in the ground all those millions of years ago? Or, after all that time, had they merely become us? Were there to be no aliens, after all?

Sheila was busily pointing to cryptic glyphs covering the walls. "At first, we attempted to translate them, or at the very least, to find a correlation between these markings and the earliest known written languages. There's no doubt that this ship has been here since long before recorded time. Naturally, if whatever species manned it was particularly long-lived, they would've had a tremendous influence on any newly forming societies." Her listeners were easily following her step-by-step logic, and so she continued.

"We tried for weeks to find some kind of trail leading from these glyphs to any known language at all, but that led us nowhere. So, rather than look for languages possibly having formed from these glyphs, we looked at various languages and civilizations as possibly having a common alien core, tracing them back. It's the same idea, but approached from two opposite directions. At any rate, we've had no success, so far." She shrugged off their failure.

Ed eyed the glyphs and couldn't make out anything, either. Not that it would make sense for him to try if two seasoned professionals were at a loss.

"Luckily, our lack of success doesn't apply to everything." Sheila walked over to an elaborate panel. "I'm certain that this must somehow be responsible for your signal's transmission. Unfortunately, we've been able to learn very little about the way these controls work, so I couldn't tell you how to stop it, but look!" She smiled mysteriously and touched a series of colorful designs carefully. "It's all right," she assured her audience as the lights dimmed and the walls were immediately covered by several large, moving pictures.

One showed a forest that Patrick thought looked uncomfortably like a certain cornfield in North Carolina. It was lavender beneath the canopy, and from holes evenly spaced in their trunks, bled a lacey mist floating gently to the ground.

Ed poked Patrick's ribs. They both exchanged a look in recollection of Art, the botanist they had seen transform only hours ago.

The bizarre movies continued, but one image held his attention. It was huge, centered on the largest wall, and featured a beautiful planet set against a jet-black sky sprinkled with clusters of stars.

The sphere was vividly alien and beautiful, with its ruby red seas and irregular landmasses.

"That's it," Rene pointed excitedly. "That's the model you showed me. It looks exactly like that," she sucked in her breath with a large gasp and nearly jumped out of her skin as the planet exploded before their eyes.

"My God," Sheila ran to stand with her face inches from the wall. "My God," she repeated. "It's gone, Forrest, it's gone!"

"This hasn't happened before?" Ed asked as Herb McElvy stepped up beside Sheila.

"Never! It's always just been spinning slowly on its axis. One of the first things we did was to map its surface areas, and now it's just gone!" Sheila was close to tears.

"Gone." Herb repeated, studying the emptied screen closely. He held his hand up to where the planet had been. "Look, here and here are large chunks of debris, possibly here, and look at the starlight shifting in its intensity as the energy wave from the explosion passes."

"Have any of the other movies changed?" Barry grilled a dazed Forrest. "Do you suppose this means that the actual planet is gone, too?" The last question was addressed to no one in particular.

"None of the others have changed as far as I can tell. They're all still just the same," Forrest said honestly. "Look, Sheil, everything else is still the same. Sheil? Sheil!"

Ed focused his attention back on Sheila. She had a vacant expression on her face, having been animatedly explaining her findings to the group only moments earlier.

"They're gone, Forrest. They're all gone." Briefly, she seemed close to collapse, but then as they watched, a glowing diamond took shape on Sheila's forehead.

"Who is responsible for this?" her commanding voice was thick with accusation and boomed loudly before falling once again into tones of despair. "We can never go home now," she whispered.

With those words, the Colonel, who'd been hovering on the edges, jumped to attention. "Keep those two in your sights," he barked, and the soldiers trained their weapons on the distraught couple.

"Don't shoot, for God's sake. She's pregnant." Forrest jumped to stand in front of his wife. "You don't understand. Sheila doesn't know what she's saying. She was just like this when we found the door and opened it. We worked for weeks to find out how to start all this," he pointed to the movies flickering beyond them. "Sheila just knew which buttons to press, like she was in a trance or something. Damn it, since she's come out of it, we haven't been able to figure out how to work anything else."

"That's certainly not the picture you both presented when we spoke before." Ed asked for the Colonel's men to stand down.

The well-trained officer had his men maintain their positions. "Get the man with the vid cam up here in front with us," barked the Colonel.

Forrest looked sheepish as the soldier stepped forward. "Get everything that woman does on film, and don't miss anything!"

The commotion within the ship was heightened as Sheila began issuing orders, accompanied by sweeping gestures. The tone in her voice demanded obedience, and the diamond beneath her bangs continued to glow vividly. Occasionally, she seemed to revert to her old self but continued to repeat odd phrases while performing what appeared to be some ceremonial ritual involving many hand movements and a lot of bowing.

Those gathered in the flickering lights watched, spellbound, but Ed was nervous about the woman's well-being. She was mentally unstable, perhaps even schizophrenic, moving easily from an acquired commanding presence to her own personality. Perhaps he should stop her; unless she knew the answer, the magic button on the panel to press that would make it all go away. Before he'd even had time to make a conscious choice, a report came through his earpiece from one of the men outside.

"There has been a data breach, Secretary Marker."

"What do you mean?"

"Someone has tapped into the video feeds."

"Can you block them?" Ed was tech-savvy, but no IT specialist.

"I can take the system down and reboot with extra data protection software and..."

Ed cut the soldier off in mid-explanation. "How long is that going to take?"

"At least thirty minutes, but we won't have any video feed during that time and none of the cameras will be able to record."

"That's too long. Whoever is looking in, let them look. We need this footage, and we need our communication systems up and running."

The Colonel, unaffected by technical issues and trained in the art of combat, gestured for his men to close in on Sheila.

"You stay away from my wife." Forrest moved quickly to intercept the uniformed officers even as the rest of the soldiers moved in behind the Colonel. The resulting confusion allowed Sheila enough time to reach the panel.

Instinctively, she manipulated the familiar controls. Her movements were swift and direct, and there was nothing tentative about either her intent or delivery. Within moments, the movies disappeared, and the room was plunged into darkness, momentarily stopping everyone in their tracks.

"Sheila? Sheil, where are you?" Forrest called into the dark room.

Seconds later, battery-operated lights, which had been brought in quickly by those on guard, were trained in Sheila's direction. They lit up the area just in time to see a section of the wall sliding closed as Sheila disappeared into it. She was muttering the same foreign intonations under her breath as she vanished from sight.

"Sheila!" Forrest yelled, horrified, as he ran to the wall, attempting to pry it open. There wasn't even a seam to indicate an opening had ever existed.

"Mark that spot," the Colonel shouted over the confusion. "Everyone out!"

"Shit, now what do we do?" Ed's question was rhetorical and not meant to be overheard, so he was surprised to hear it answered through his helmet mic.

"No need to worry about it now," said the voice. "Thanks to the United States Army and an infrared vid cam, we at KTCM got the whole thing on film—LIVE!"

It took a moment to sink in. "Live?" Ed questioned softly at first. "You mean truly LIVE?!" his voice screamed through the microphones. "You mean that you assholes broadcast this LIVE!"

"Yes, sir, that's exactly what I mean," said Joe Kacer, the KTCM announcer. "It's been quite a night. First the rocks light up, and now this."

"Have you any idea what you've done?" Ed spoke loudly as he moved away from those being herded from the ship and tried to avoid the soldiers stationed on guard beside him. "Allowing this to be broadcast is unconscionable. My God, have you stopped to think about what this might do to people, the panic you may have started?"

"Now, hold on," the disembodied voice turned deadly serious. "We've gone that route for years—UFO cover-ups, sightings, abductions, and who knows what else. But that was then, and it was kid's stuff! Think about it. Some people are such mutants already that they could hop in there with you and fly away. Now there's a fact for you. Scare the people? We barely have any *people* left!"

The military IT unit blocked the media station from the communication system easily, now knowing exactly who was behind the breach, but it was too late.

By now, every station in the world would be running this video, Ed thought. As detestable as Joe Kacer was, he had a point. People couldn't be any more panicked than they already were. He only hoped that they didn't get any footage of the magnitude of the military forces that had gathered at the site. Ed knew from talking to the President earlier that they had had to pull a lot of military presence from the streets to put together such large units for this mission. The military men were not immune to the mutations that everyone else was experiencing and their numbers were declining rapidly. Hopefully, the civilians would not put two and two together and realize that the ratio of military to civilians in the cities was drastically down. Then they really *would* have a problem on their hands.

CHAPTER 37

Killing the messenger doesn't change the message.

Clarence sat in his living room, streaming the news segment repeatedly.

"What does it say?" his wife, Judy, asked for what seemed like the fiftieth time.

"I'm not sure yet," he replied impatiently. "The lighting is so dim, and some images are too fuzzy to make out at all."

Clarence could feel his wife's tension and reached out to comfort her. As he gently pulled her to lean against him, Clarence took a break to explain. "There are so many types of sentence structures. Each language has its own way of building with words. In English, we say 'the red ball,' but the Spanish equivalent translates to 'the ball red.' I'm not sure exactly what it is I'm seeing, at this point."

"I understand you can't be certain, but at least tell me what you think those markings mean," she pleaded. "They look just like all that stuff you've been working on for months, Clarence. You're sitting there translating as you watch. How in the world did you ever come up with all of this on your own, anyway?"

"I don't know," and he didn't. All Clarence knew was that he wanted to be left alone to work his word wizardry. For months, his family had pooh-poohed his efforts. Now that his "Scrabble talk," as they'd called it, was turning out to be an alien language, he was suddenly terribly interesting to one and all. In fact, the kids were asleep on the floor where they'd curled up with couch pillows while watching breathlessly as he'd scribbled notes.

"Look, Judy, I'll tell you what I think I've made out so far. It makes no sense, which is why I'd rather not."

"That's all I wanted to begin with."

"See that top row of writing?" Clarence locked eyes with the television screen. "Well, I think it says WELCOME TO something or other. I can't quite get the third word."

"Welcome to blank?" Judy mused, softly repeating the phrase over and over. "What else, Clarence?"

"Well," he forwarded the recording ahead some more. "See there; that row of glyphs going off the screen says something equivalent to COMING ATTRACTIONS."

"What about the other markings, the ones beside those mosaic designs?"

"Oh, those aren't sentences. They're much simpler and more direct, things like flight controls—you know, altimeters, temperature gauges, and things like that. There are a few odd ones, like the one I read to say PHASE SHIFT PERIOD right there." He pointed to the lower portion of their screen. "Right next to it, the one that says..." Suddenly, Clarence looked hard at the TV and forwarded the video slowly, his previous thought forgotten.

"What is it?" Judy asked hesitantly.

Something was making Clarence's normally ruddy complexion turn deathly pale. It was obvious even in the room's low light.

"I just finally made out the label beside one of the gauges, that one in the middle and towards the top. It says something like GENETICALLY ALTERED FREQUENCY MODULATION LEVEL." He dropped the remote like it was on fire.

"You don't think it's measuring the hitchhiker somehow, do you?"

"Could be." Judy retrieved the remote. "Look," she went backwards through the film. "There," she paused the machine. "Look at the row of buttons beside that gauge you think measures the genetic frequencies. Keep your eyes on it." Judy moved slowly forward through the frames of film. "There! Did you see it change?"

It had changed, all right. Clarence had seen the subtle shift in the colors as a new gradient appeared gradually on the control panel.

"It's increasing, Clarence. The level is going up."

The two sat quietly, holding hands, and Clarence could feel his wife's nails hard against his palms. After five minutes, Clarence turned on the live news.

According to their noisy and persistent anchorman, "the footage has captured imaginations worldwide. In the polls, very few are frightened, most are relieved, and some are expectant," blah, blah, blah.

"How can they possibly have taken a poll already, and at this time of night?" Judy was incredulous.

"Stranger things have happened." Both laughed uncomfortably.

"They haven't got a clue, have they?" Judy asked.

The news report had said that linguists everywhere were baffled, but working hard to decode the strange markings within the alien ship. They'd also admitted that no investigational work on the craft could begin until Sheila Carbury was rescued.

"What about that woman? Do you think they'll be able to get her out, Clarence?"

"I'm sure they've already re-enacted her manipulation of the panel's controls, and the door has most likely opened for them, too."

"But?" Judy knew there was one coming.

"But I'm not sure if she'll be there anymore. According to my translations, the markings on the wall beside the disappearing doorway say, TRANSFER MODULE."

Judy registered no surprise. "I suppose we should call the local station first. They'll probably be able to put us in touch with the right people."

"Probably," Clarence agreed and went back to scanning the same video as his wife dialed beside him.

• • •

The following afternoon, their meeting was taking place in a standard army-issue tent, which was Ed's new base of operations. "I'm sorry for what seem to be such intense efforts to keep you to ourselves, but as you can see, beyond our perimeters it's a perpetual field day."

"Yeah, it looked like a whole town had sprung up from what I could see from the air." Clarence was not surprised by anything he'd seen so far.

"People have come from all over the country after having seen the video footage. We've asked everyone to return to their homes, but it's hard to convince people of anything when they have nothing left to lose," Ed smiled. "You wouldn't believe the number of calls we've been receiving from people claiming to be able to translate the new language. So, Mr. Clarence Walburn, let's see what you can tell us."

Those gathered in the too-small tent murmured in agreement.

"Yes, Mr. Walburn," a general in the back row was outspokenly eager to have the translations continue. "*Coming attraction!* What's that supposed to mean? The partial translations we've received have been insufficient, not satisfactory at all." The uniformed man adjusted his glasses while he waited for Clarence to respond.

God save him from the military, many of whom, in Ed's opinion, were showing far too many signs of wear. "Easy now," he attempted to project a calm appearance.

"Look, I only translate." Clarence shrugged his shoulders while Ed attempted to soothe the beribboned officer. Clarence's button-up short-sleeved shirt ballooned out as he stood in front of the AC units brought in to cool the crowded tent. He'd been rushed there straight from the helicopter, and since then, each person in attendance had been hanging on his every word. After a solid hour, he'd had just about enough.

"Look, hard as all this is to take, it beats the hell out of not having a clue," Ed attempted to mollify the group, and everyone else grudgingly had to agree.

"Welcome to *blank*? Have you been able to narrow that one down any further, Mr. Walburn?" Ed renewed the interrogation.

"I've done my best to answer your questions, but we're beginning to criss-cross the same ground," Clarence reasoned. "Maybe, if I could *see* the ship...? The light level in the news video made it difficult to make out too much more than I've already told you."

"Of course, you're right. Lead the way, gentlemen," Ed deferred to the ever-present guards, who led them towards the ship. Ed and Clarence walked slowly together, deep in conversation, and were followed by the standard assortment of political and military hangers-on. The background hum of the military camp and the shantytown around its borders made the air feel thick.

"As you can see for yourself, we've uncovered most of the thing." Ed and Clarence were heading directly for the enormous ship, which still sat amid heavy machinery loading a steady stream of dump trucks with dirt and debris. "There's still a small section of the tail left to free."

"It's amazing." Walking closer, Clarence stared awestricken at the impeccably preserved ship. "It looked big from the helicopter, but the soldiers whizzed me into that tent so fast I didn't even have a chance to turn around once I was on the ground." Though they were still a fair distance from the ship, Clarence felt himself walking into the cool of its shadow.

"Luckily, the ship settled itself into a sandy stratum which we've been removing with relative ease," Ed explained. "We're still working on the end portion, which landed in different material and is lodged tightly in rock."

"Well, what do you think of her?" asked one of the assembled generals.

"Very impressive, sir. May I?" Clarence stepped up to the hull of the ship and traced the markings beneath his fingers. The metal was smooth, with no grooves or raised markings to highlight the glyphs.

"Does it help to be near the craft?" Ed asked. The soldiers had given them some space to talk and stood a few paces back, guns held to their chests.

"This is truly bizarre," said Clarence. "The physical contact has brought on a flood of tactile and mental sensations. I can *feel* their meaning." He paused in awe of the novel sensation, then continued. "DIVERSION, that's the name of the ship, or at least it's the closest equivalent I can think of, although the meaning also seems to imply a great deal of capital investment. It's hard to explain how many different concepts they've incorporated into just a name."

Ed listened to Clarence. He would let him talk it out to himself out loud, whatever would help him decipher the meanings of the glyphs.

"Maybe," Clarence said absentmindedly. He walked to the doorway where he paused briefly, then entered. As Clarence walked, he maintained physical contact with the ship, trailing his hand along the wall beside him. "As my hand passes over these glyphs," Clarence explained, his concentration intense, "I'm receiving very concrete, definite images of their meanings." In response to the anticipation of those filing in behind him, Clarence began a verbal recitation. "COMFORT CONTROL; IDENTIFICATION SCOPE PARAMETER; PURELY ORNAMENTATION, CREATED BY THE SECOND PHASE SHIFT CLAN."

"What's a second phase shift clan?" Ed broke through the man's intense concentration.

"Not sure yet."

Ed had pulled Clarence back from a great distance with his question. Now, they were passing the famous sliding door section of the wall.

"How's that woman doing?" Clarence asked. "My wife was wondering what had happened to her."

He meant Sheila Carbury, of course. So, there was no need for Ed to ask.

"There wasn't much information in the news, only that she'd been found safe and unharmed," Clarence prodded Ed for further information.

"That's exactly what happened, Mr. Walburn," Ed was candid, with a few notable omissions. "She was found three hundred miles away, where she claims to have just appeared. Additionally, Mrs. Carbury was approximately one month into a pregnancy when she disappeared, and just days from delivery at the time of her reappearance."

Ed knew he had shared a lot of Sheila's personal information, but Clarence was their main line to translation and he wanted Clarence to feel as though they were not holding anything back from him. Ed needed his confidence, but also had to respect Sheila's privacy, and did not discuss her unstable mental state. What was the point, anyway? After all, according to her husband, she'd begun to have her episodes well before using the alien transport mechanism, and a glowing forehead was hardly worth mentioning nowadays.

Although Ed left it unsaid, Mary Beth had flown out to be with Sheila. Some kind of time shift had occurred, so the unusual birth was going to be another media event worthy of suppression. According to Mary Beth, the woman wouldn't even allow a sonogram, so there was nothing to do but wait.

"Judy, that's my wife; she'll be glad the woman's okay, so far, at least."

"Mr. Walburn," Ed tried to redirect the conversation back to the translations. "My report stated that you translated the markings beside this door to be TRANSFER MODULE."

Clarence ran his hands slowly over the writing as the crowd filled the hushed entrance area.

"TRANSFER MODULE, yes, that's it. I was correct, but there's so much more. Transfer is used in a sense beyond that of just moving from one geographical point to another. It's more like beginning an adventure or a new level of experience."

Clarence turned to Ed. "I know my translations are generating a lot of interest, but would it be possible for me to work with the least amount of interference? Truth is, all these people make me a little nervous."

Ed looked questioningly towards the generals who nodded. It was as good as done.

"Lunch in forty-five minutes okay with you?" asked Ed.

"That would be great. Thanks."

Ed conferred briefly with the military personnel and reported to Clarence. "Listen, we're posting a guard both inside and outside." The entourage began filing out of the spacecraft. "It's just standard procedure, and there'll also be someone with a camera documenting your work. Sorry, but it's the best I can do."

"That's fine, thanks. Oh," Clarence reached into his pocket. In all the excitement, he'd almost forgotten. "Here's a copy of all the translation files I've been working on for the past few months." He handed over a thumb drive.

"I'm sure you'll want to have your experts check it out. The language seems to have an interesting and logical progression to it. It's deceptively simple. I've been amazed at the complex variety of concepts incorporated into even the simplest of symbols."

Ed pocketed the thumb drive. "Thank you." With a wave, Ed was gone. He was sure the military linguists had hacked into Clarence's computer and were analyzing this same data already, but it was nice to know that Clarence was so forthcoming with any information he had.

Clarence was left with only the posted guards and his shadow wielding the camera. Though the ceiling was quite high and the room spacious, the controls were meant to be manipulated by a shorter being. Clarence, at six feet tall, had to stoop slightly to study them. He headed directly towards the control panel on the end wall and reached out, covering it completely with his left palm.

"I wonder why he started there?" Ed was watching along with the rest from the tent as the camera picked up Clarence Walburn's every move. One place was as good as another, but somehow he knew it hadn't been a random choice. "Listen," Ed ordered, "take Clarence a chair and some paper and pen, and don't forget his lunch."

They watched Clarence for hours. Ed ate his Italian sub with kettle chips while he watched Clarence eat his lunch. After Clarence had crumpled his sandwich wrap paper into a ball, he went around the cabin, laying his hands upon every control panel and marking on the pad of paper the soldier had given him. Ed reached for a giant deli chocolate chip cookie as he continued to watch the live feed. He shouldn't have been hungry at a tense time like this, but when was it *not* tense? Watching his waistline was trivial compared to what was going on. He shrugged to himself and also took a giant sugar cookie from the catering table in the tent, cooled by the steady flow of the portable AC.

"Let's zoom in on his paper," said Ed into the air. The IT specialist connected to Ed's earpiece followed his direction silently, and the camera zoomed in for a close-up of Clarence's translation of WELCOME TO blank. It was no longer WELCOME TO blank. Instead, Clarence had written WELCOME TO DISNEY WORLD or WELCOME TO ADVENTURE WORLD or SOMETHING THE EQUIVALENT OF THESE TWO.

What a weird thing to feature so prominently, Ed speculated uneasily. "Show us what is written above this," Ed directed the cameraman.

THEG SA HA CHING

"Mr. Walburn?" Ed didn't want to disturb him, but it was time to check in. He spoke to Clarence through his earpiece. "What does THEG SA HA CHING mean?"

Clarence adjusted his earpiece before answering. "Ed, this is the actual phonetic translation of the alien symbols being sent again and again into space." Clarence carefully reached out and adjusted the signal's interference sensitivity button.

"The signal has changed," a corpsman reported to the group, still observing Clarence hard at work. "Listen!" The amazed technician routed the sound through speakers rather than his headset, and "the egg is hatching, the egg is hatching" sailed through the air monotonously.

A deafening roar came from the crowd of civilians around the military base.

"Did you do that?" Ed asked, and Clarence nodded.

"What does it mean?"

Clarence looked into the camera. "Maybe you'd better come back over here and take another look so I can explain it all in person."

Ed had a foreboding feeling about what Clarence had to tell him. He suddenly felt very alone, even in the crowd of military officials. His mind wandered to the people who had been his constant companions throughout this end of the world scenario. Mary Beth was with the very pregnant Sheila Carbury. He wished he could be with her, or back at NASA with Rene and Herb, working day and night to pinpoint an actual date of arrival. He'd even rather be at NIH with Patrick, studying the new rash all over his friend's body. Patrick already had Barry for a babysitter, though, and certainly didn't need him. Ed needed to hold himself together. This was the first time he had felt this emotionally out of control, but how much could one person take? He took some deep breaths and tried to prepare himself for answers. Finally, there would be answers.

• • •

With so much solitary time on his hands, Sodok researched the history of this project carefully and discovered many helpful details. He found that there had been a second attempt at another exciting new world after this first had failed.

The riches available to their ancestors must have been staggering. To throw such excessive wealth into a project which had already failed once was beyond belief. Yet this project was far from a failure seen from his vantage point, merely happily delayed.

What, he wondered, had ever happened to the second ship and its genetically manipulated destination? Had there truly even been such a mammoth second undertaking? Excess bravado and boasting had been such a large part of those long-ago times, and what did it matter, anyway?

His job was to become as knowledgeable about their destination as possible. Besides, if there had been such a successful diversionary project, it would have been common knowledge for countless phase shifts. After all, modesty had never been practiced by the leisure class.

In the meantime, Sodok studied the more pertinent and less obscure records. There was no need to delve further than necessary, since it now seemed that time was of the essence as they approached their destination far faster than expected.

CHAPTER 38

It is a bold mouse who nestles in the cat's ear.
-English Folk Proverb

E d waited nervously in the ship's control room for Clarence to disclose his revelations.

"We'll start at the beginning and work our way through to the logical conclusion." Clarence was stationed beside the controls with which he'd chosen to begin his presentation. "First, let me say that I don't believe this ship has ever held alien space travelers. All indications point to it being some type of unmanned probe."

"Which indications are those?" asked someone from the back of the assembled group.

Clarence passed his open palm over a lighted area in the panel. A map appeared on the console. "This is the entire ship." His audience was suitably impressed, everyone still watching the video footage from the tent.

"Well, the ship is larger than just this one room," Ed moved closer to the map, "but there have been no further attempts to gain access to the other areas since Sheila Carbury's rescue attempt, especially with the promise of your translations in the wings."

"As you can see," Clarence was continuing, "several huge storage and dispersal tanks seem to comprise the majority of the ship, and if I'm reading everything correctly, they're registering empty."

"Was the cargo our hitchhiker?" asked Ed.

"Very likely," Clarence answered, "considering our present predicament and some of my other findings. For instance, over here is a mutational frequency modulation gauge, which is working capably as we speak." Ed and Clarence walked over to the gauge.

"Since the night of the ship's discovery, this row of lights has become more vivid and registers to a higher mark on the console."

"Then it could be measuring the hitchhiker," Ed studied the gauge closely.

"I believe you're correct," Clarence agreed, "and I also believe that though the tanks register as empty, there could be some small bit of residue clinging to the inner surface of these huge, hollow tanks."

"If only we could access the rest of the ship safely." Ed's thoughts were moving quickly with each piece of new information.

"Oh, but we can, or at least as safely as possible, with the control panel readable and at my fingertips, but..."

"But?" Ed asked. The eyes of all the virtual onlookers locked onto Clarence's fingertips.

"The tanks aren't what I called you to see, any more than the debatable safety of this ship's exploration. I'm increasingly uncomfortable with some things I've discovered."

"Such as?"

"Such as," Clarence took a steadying breath before continuing, "this." He pressed another button, and a beautifully modulated yet computer-generated voice seemed to come from every direction at once. Clarence almost jumped out of his skin. "I thought it was just going to be another movie." He was able to catch some of the tonalities detailed in his pronunciation guide.

Ed wasn't ready to have his guided tour end yet, so stepping forward, he quickly touched the same area Clarence had just activated. Luckily, the voice was silenced immediately.

"The panel implied an overview would be displayed. I'm sorry to have startled you like that, Ed. That questionable label intimated more than a simple overview. It was more like WELCOME TO THE ULTIMATE EXPERIENCE."

"Do your concerns primarily center around this ambiguous welcome?" asked Ed.

"No, sir, not exactly. I guess I should just say it. I think Earth is a stop on some kind of galactic fun tour."

Ed glanced around the control room and shifted his stance uncomfortably, processing this information. It was not the fabled "we come in peace" scenario.

"This cabin seems to be a control tower, so to speak, for directing the construction, maintenance, and visitation details involved in some kind of giant theme park." Clarence stopped briefly, eyeing his audience's reaction before beginning again.

"Remember the movies the Carburys turned on? Well, the panel refers to them as coming attractions. There's an extensive bank of controls here that seem to involve reservations for short and long-term accommodations, travel arrangements, and experiential preferences."

Ed requested Clarence activate the movies for himself and the virtual spectators. Clarence obliged.

Leaves rustled in a purple forest as a scene moved silently. Then, Ed moved down the line, recognizing the lighted mountains of rock in another. He continued down the row of advertisements, gazing at pictures of a world that was looking almost identical to their own. "Well, the coming attractions aren't coming anymore. They're here," Ed grimly voiced what everyone already knew.

Writing appeared beneath each of the moving squares on the wall's surface, and Ed pulled Clarence aside to ask, "What about the big empty one over there? What does it say beneath that one?"

Clarence took a moment to formulate his answer. "Well, the glyphs beneath each scene seem to describe the wonders of each displayed sensory stimuli."

"I figured out that much even without a translation, but there are not any sensory stimuli in the blank one. What does it say, Clarence?"

"That one is the most prominent, the largest."

"And?" Ed was edgy and did not need a recap.

"It seems to hold a great deal of significance, because it's supposed to show," Clarence lowered his voice even further, "their home planet. It further seems to require some serious acknowledgment, like our pledge of allegiance, or a prayer, or something. So much of this stuff combines elements of pure sensory pleasure with religious overtones."

"What about this hatching egg, Mr. Walburn? What does that mean?" asked Major General Sanchez over the speakers. "It sounds like that could be something we need to be prepared for."

"Ah, yes. Sorry I didn't bring it up sooner. The meaning of the phrase fits in perfectly with the explanation I've just offered." Clarence quickly continued. "It means, COME AND SEE. COME AND PLAY. OPEN FOR BUSINESS. STEP RIGHT UP?"

Ed was speechless, but it wasn't because he hadn't gotten the drift. On the contrary, he was snowbound. This was the last thing he would have expected of alien interactions with Earth and its population. Dominance, control, curiosity, partnership even, but never a carnival, where a once-thriving planet and well-developed civilization would be made into a simple amusement. His mind wandered to how much cognitive presence Colleen Maxwell still possessed. Then, his thoughts migrated to Art Bowler, cemented to the ground with thick roots. Were their minds locked in a prison or had the essence of who they were disappeared? He pulled his hair back in a ponytail, hoping he would not be the next to find these answers for himself.

The baby was coming.

"It hurts," Sheila moaned loudly, at first. "Oh God, it hurts!"

"It's okay, I'm here." Forrest was trying his best to be supportive, but there had been no time for birthing classes. There had been no time for anything. He rang for the nurse on duty.

Mary Beth was a calming presence as she presided over the unusual birth. Sheila had begged Mary Beth to stay after she'd hesitantly admitted to delivering livestock back on her parents' farm. Mary Beth did not tell Sheila that it sometimes took a winch and chain to produce a calf.

On a high-security ward, in an even higher-security military hospital, Sheila wailed loudly. "I should have had a sonogram. What if it's a freak?" She cried but had to stop as another contraction gripped her.

"It's time to push, Sheila," encouraged the masked doctor who had accompanied the nurse.

"Shut up, and don't tell me what to do." The mother-to-be bore down with sudden and abundant self-reliance.

Those surrounding the increasingly belligerent mother were well prepared for Sheila's abuse as they watched the diamond on her forehead become visible. Since her reappearance, these combative episodes were becoming more and more frequent.

Luckily, by the fourth push, there was a delivery. "You've got a daughter," the doctor announced with pleasure despite his difficult patient, "with a high Apgar score at that." The tiny bundle was whisked away, tested completely, and finally pronounced normal, except for the tiny diamond mark on her forehead glowing brightly in her fury over the trauma of birth.

Sheila was resting when her baby girl was brought back into her room. Mary Beth lifted the infant from the clear plastic cradle and held her close. "Even in the midst of an apocalypse, there is new life," she whispered.

Mary Beth rocked the newborn. "You give me hope, little one."

⬩   ⬩   ⬩

"Hey, Judy," Clarence began. "Yes, it's me. Yes, they let me out for lunch."

"They're working you too hard, love."

"I mean, I get it, but I'm completely drained. I've been working around the clock for days. I'm not saying that my personal comfort is more important than the work we're doing here, but I'm still human, at least for the time being, and that means I require a certain amount of sleep."

"Everyone is so proud of you, Clarence," said Judy. "The kids keep the TV on the news to track your progress. Our kids have never watched the news." Judy laughed at her own joke, but Clarence did not. "Honey, are you all right?"

"I'm just not sure," he answered. "But I have to get back to it. I love you, Judy. Tell the kids I love them, too."

"Would you like us to come out there with you?"

"It's better if you all stay home. Believe me, the kids would be bored in a matter of hours. Let them stay in their own environment with all of their friends."

"Okay, then. We'll talk later. Love you."

"Love you, too."

⬩   ⬩   ⬩

The cameraman, Trip Shullar, was Clarence's constant companion and almost as wrung out as Clarence.

"So, how come they won't let you stand down, either?" asked Clarence.

"I'm the best, just like you, not to mention all the clearances involved. The pond gets smaller every day, and we fish who are left just keep getting bigger and bigger."

"Good point," Clarence agreed readily. "But does it ever give you the creeps that the balance is shifting so steadily? Consider the fact that as our pool grows smaller, the other enlarges. As humanity disappears trait by trait, what is going to take its place?" Clarence walked towards the camera, gesturing and questioning deliberately, much like a talk show host would do. "Who is coming, and why? Should we set up concession stands and sell T-shirts as suggested by what we have learned so far, or just pray that this is all a communal nightmare and we'll wake up in time?"

"I wonder," Trip mused from his position behind the camera. "I've heard that when you die in a dream, you actually die. What do you think?"

"Right now, I'm more concerned about what happens when you die, but your body still slinks, or swims, or flies around anyway."

"Yeah, I guess so."

Both men were quiet as Clarence turned back towards the far panel.

"I've given them all the information there is to be had," Clarence confided to the cameraman, knowing that this meant confiding in the entire military base and possibly the world on camera. "Unless they can find some other mutant who is even better than me, we've hit a brick wall."

"You're doing all you can," said Trip. "Let's get out of this ship for a bit, take a walk, get a drink."

"Thanks, Trip, but I can't." Clarence deliberately stepped in front of the portion of the panel he was manipulating.

"Hey, you're blocking the view." Trip reminded.

"Oh yeah, sorry." Clarence stepped away. After all, they both knew the rules, all actions visible at all times.

Slowly working his way around the wall, Clarence pretended to be notating and studying, as always. Only the sweat forming on his forehead indicated otherwise, and he wiped it away inconspicuously. The proper gauges had been set for the transfer module to follow the homing signal, or at least hopefully they had.

"Hey, Clarence, you really must be punchy. Move away from the door. You know it's off-limits."

As Trip said this, Clarence quickly stepped in front of the same panel that had swallowed Sheila Carbury and touched several places on the wall, blocking the view with his body. He then promptly disappeared behind the closing door of the transfer module.

Trip just missed grabbing him and instead was left holding only a corner of Clarence's shirt.

"Shit." Trip threw down the small piece of cloth. "What the hell did he do that for?" By this time, the highly cleared CIA cameraman could hear the commotion as other observers hurried into the room. "Damn it," muttered Trip under his breath. "Why didn't he just tell me? I would've gone with him."

. . .

"The choice to reveal or conceal has pretty effectively been taken out of our hands, Mr. President. After all, we need to know when and where the guy turns up," Ed said. "There's nothing to be gained in holding out, anymore. There hasn't been since the beginning of this thing."

Ed pleaded his case for collaboration among countries, but didn't get too far. After he hung up with the President, his phone rang. He looked at the screen and saw Patrick. Good.

"It's good to hear from you. How are you?"

"Better now," said his long-time friend. "Look, Ed, I'm sorry for freaking out about the rash. It was just nervous hives, but with everything going on, I was afraid it could have been anything. The beginning of scales covering my whole body, anything. I panicked."

"No judgment," Ed said simply. "Good to know you're okay. Tell me, when are you coming out here?"

"I'm actually on my way to Venezuela. They hauled in something off the coast that looks like one of those bird people from Mary Beth's vision. He can't speak anymore, just squawks through his beak, or whatever."

"Well, unless he knows where Clarence is, they can keep him."

"Any word on our man Clarence?" Patrick already knew the answer, but couldn't help asking, anyway. "Never mind; how's the family taking it?"

"They're holding out hope that he's alive somewhere, sometime," said Ed. "Just like Sheila, they're expecting him to turn up somewhere. But listen, Patrick, Sheila lost eight months of her life through the door. Clarence could be an eighty-year-old man for all we know, or an eight-year-old boy for that matter."

"Have you explained this to his wife?"

"No," said Ed. "Not yet, but we've moved forward with our search. We've altered some photos of Clarence using age-progression technology and have been circulating those."

"Estimated arrival is still the same?" asked Patrick.

"Yeah, three weeks. That's what Herb and Rene have currently estimated. Herb seems to be the only guy I know who's actually happy about all of this," Ed mused. "Well, Herb and the thousands of people living in the pop-up shanty town of tents and RVs surrounding the military camp."

"Isn't the military concerned about civilian safety at the crash site? Or the landing site?" Patrick corrected himself.

"They've been talking about removing the civilians, but didn't want any unnecessary human casualties. Every person we have left still intact is valuable. There are fewer with each passing day.

"Also, think about it. People with nothing to lose are dangerous and unpredictable. Most of these people have lost their homes to flooding, or their loved ones to mutations or the quakes. Then there are the religious fanatics, who seem to be the most volatile. It's a very unstable situation."

"I know what I've seen on the news, but what did the President say last about other countries? How does China feel? Russia? What do these other countries plan to do when faced with the extraterrestrial beings?" Patrick probed Ed for the most up-to-date information, after having been out of communication for over a week.

"Other countries really aren't thinking firepower," said Ed. "They're experiencing the same mutations and land transformations we are, as you already know. This is a global issue."

"Look at what it's taken to bring the world together," said Patrick.

"I know. It's taken facing the *end* for people to *begin* to come together."

"So, if not firepower, then what?" asked Patrick.

"Then what." Ed posed this as more of a statement. "I guess everyone is hoping for a peaceful interaction."

"What about Clarence's Disneyland?" Patrick prodded.

"I know, it's unsettling," said Ed. "The hope is that they might be able to turn it all off and make it all go away."

"Do you think they can? Did Clarence ever say anything about a control that could reverse the mutations?"

"No," Ed said simply. "He didn't."

Clarence said nothing about a control like that, but he never said anything about going through the door, either. He didn't have a glowing diamond on his forehead, but maybe he'd been affected in some way that they didn't know about. He might not be interested in their goal of reversing the mutations any longer. The only way to find out more was to find Clarence. Ed wasn't ready to give up yet.

CHAPTER 39

Trust in Allah, but tie your camel first.
-Mohammed

Twenty-five miles off the coast of Venezuela

Gary Zuplo was back, but how? He couldn't remember. Something about a message flashed across his mind. Yes, that was it. He was supposed to deliver a message, but how, he asked himself? He could no longer speak. Verbalize? Yes. Understandably? No. Not to mention the fact that he hadn't even landed close to his destination.

"Es un hombre de pájaro," the sailors were saying as they fished him out of the water where he floated, too exhausted to move. "¿Hablas Español?"

"Squawk," Gary replied. Then, clearing his throat, he began an eloquent appeal, asking to be taken to certain coordinates. If this was the best he could do, it was all over, he realized sadly. His vocalizations were so irritating that the sailors were forced to cover their ears.

"¿Hablas Español?" It was a logical question, being off the coast of South America as they were.

Try, try again, Gary told himself, but he found that his "voice" was still offensive to his rescuers. If they would only give him some paper and a pen, he was sure that his talons could manage enough coordination to write it all down.

Gary felt a salty wind brush past, ruffling his downy covering, and he could smell the world blowing by. I'm losing it, he thought, as the slippery edges of his humanity became fuzzier, and he attempted to fly into the wind. Oh, no, he realized belatedly that he'd completely forgotten about those holding him loosely in their rescue efforts. Consequently, he accidentally injured some of them quite badly with his razor-sharp talons in the muddled attempt. Even without understanding Spanish, there was no way he could mistake the cage into which they threw him angrily.

The message, the message; his thoughts skirted the important task he'd been given, but it was all too much. Caged, miserable, and once again within the range of the harvesters' vibrational triggering frequencies, Gary felt himself continuing to transform, eventually becoming no more than the wild animal the sailors thought they'd caged.

Rene's childhood home
South Valley, New Mexico

Back home in the cramped Lawson dining room, Rene played Chutes and Ladders with Evie, while trying to put the ship out of her mind. For weeks, she'd been drilled for information. She'd drawn, and they'd calculated. She'd detailed, and they'd calibrated. The scientists and mathematicians had guesstimated and then estimated the ship's size, weight, crew, elemental composition, and wallpaper. There was nothing left for Rene to do. Thank God, she thought.

"Pay attention, Rene. You rolled five, not seven." Evie was having a tough time keeping her sister interested in the game.

"Sorry. Go ahead and put me where I should be. Oh no, there I go again." Rene's red board piece slid down a lengthy chute, and she was back to where she'd started. Too bad they all couldn't start back at the beginning, but it was too late for that.

Their visitors had crossed into known space weeks before and were now on the last leg of the journey. Those weird bird people were still flocking around the ship. When she looked outward, she could see them wasting away before her very eyes. Apparently, sustenance was hard to come by in space. Still, she saw that the ones who dropped away were replaced by endless single files of others like themselves, stretching like rubber bands towards Earth. Rene shivered with revulsion.

"C'mon, Rene. It's your turn again."

"Okay, Evie, how about you roll for me?"

"Can I? I'll roll you straight to a ladder. Just see if I don't." Evie blew warmly on the dice cradled in her hands.

"Seems like someone forgot to blow on the biggest dice of all," Rene mumbled, thinking about the potential scenarios ahead of them.

"Huh?"

"Never mind. Hey, that was a good roll." Rene praised Evie generously and moved her piece the required three spaces, no ladder, but no chute, either. She was getting the urge to look at the ship. No, she told herself. She rarely looked outward anymore, unless directed to do so. They'd made her look every day for weeks, and she was just plain sick of it. Still, maybe just a quick peek while Evie took her turn.

Rene had long ago determined that the windows of the craft were covered by some type of regulated film or coating. This protection was likely essential to those on board, but it left her with nothing more than vague silhouettes. Were they short, or was the light behind them intense, she wondered? Were they oddly shaped, or merely carrying things, she debated? The guessing game could have gone on forever, but she was finished. I'm not the only one, she thought with satisfaction. Everyone except essential personnel had left with her. After Clarence had been missing for over a week, everyone's hope had dwindled, and many craved the familiarity of home. They would be home for the final countdown.

Okay, just one peek, she promised herself because, well, there was no good reason. This was stupid, and she was just about to blink back to the board game. Yup, she could zoom out and pretend things weren't so hopeless.

But wait, what was that? Something about the ship held her glance, and she moved in for a closer look. What in the world was that small marking on the window? Rene couldn't recall ever having seen it before, and she'd become a faithfully trained stickler for details. Looking closer still, Rene was so jolted that in her surprise she knocked over the game board.

"What's the matter, Rene? Are you all right?" Evie was startled, but Rene was already on her way to the phone.

She was calling the same person who'd believed her the first time.

"Mama, Daddy, Daniel, come quick. Rene's acting funny. Hurry!" Evie called for the family, as her older sister scrolled through her contacts.

"Mary Beth? It's me, Rene."

The family had gathered, waiting for an update from Rene.

"Hi, honey. You sound upset. What's happened? Something's wrong, isn't it?"

"Exactly. Look, I'm fine, but I just saw something, something as weird as that birdman with the UPS patch."

Rene was spooked. "Okay, settle into it and just spit it out." Mary Beth tried to ease their way into a tough conversation.

"It was just like the school bus when I was little, Mary Beth, like when I'd blow my breath onto the window to steam it up so I could write on it."

"Okay. Go on," urged Mary Beth. "What did you see?"

"I saw, I saw," Rene decided to just go for it. "I saw an etching on the window of the spaceship."

A stunned Mary Beth immediately found herself at a loss for words. "You saw what?"

"I saw what looked like a C with a squiggle drawn into that coating on those windows."

"Is it still there?"

Was it? Rene wondered as she peeked back into the sky. "Yes, it is."

"I believe you, Rene."

"I knew you would."

"But I don't know what I can do. I'll tell Ed, but what can anyone do?"

"You don't have to do anything. I just had to tell someone," said Rene.

"Tell me, how's your family? Everything else going all right?"

"Yeah, so far, so good. My Dad's turned a light shade of green and we're all on the lookout for leaves and vines, but what else is new. Everyone's got something, right? So far, just a change in color."

"Very true," said Mary Beth. "Rene, someone may call you about what you just saw, but then again, maybe not; hard as that is to believe after all the minor details they've harassed out of you. Most people are more interested in sticking close to home with their families. People just can't take any more change, no matter what or how small. No doubt your pantry is full, and the local grocery store is empty, just like everyone else's."

"Yup, we've all quit work, closed down shop, and come home to die if necessary. Either that or prepare for employment in an alien theme park." Rene looked up and her family continued to watch her. "Funny thing though, Mary Beth, it isn't nearly as bad as I thought it would be."

"Listen Rene, I *am* glad you called, but I have to go now. Ed's going nuts because 'Mr. know-it-all' can only hear my end of this conversation, and it's killing him. Besides, if I don't hang up, I'm going to cry. Good luck."

"Same to you both." Rene rang off and turned to face her family. "What was that all about?" her mama wanted to know.

"Who knows anymore, Mama. Let's just try to forget about all of it. Evie and I have a game to finish."

"I'll set the board back up," the small girl was already seated, picking up the game pieces from the floor and looking forward to spending more time with her sister.

Thankfully, they were very close. It was eerie to watch as their winged guides were consumed from the inside and dropped away into a drying and brittle trail behind them. The ship quietly and efficiently flew on, and soon it would be time to awaken those below. What if the world was not as they expected? It mattered little. This craft had been pre-programmed to follow the homing signal, nothing more. Such programming had made the journey possible. There were no longer any among them who had such skills and hadn't been for many phase shift periods.

The screen which had displayed the destruction of their homeworld was now focused ahead rather than behind. Soon, a new planet would come into view and loom larger with their approach.

Sodok seriously considered not waking his charges until landing safely and assessing the situation, but there were no guarantees. Perhaps the ship would crash; he certainly had no knowledge of such matters. Their only hope was that their ancestors had automated the landing sequence as completely as they had the one used in their departure.

Certainly, to wake his passengers for possible sudden death was wrong, but for them to die in their sleep without proper preparation was unacceptable, as well. Sodok wandered the ship watching, always watching. He stood safely pressed against the glass, which screened harmful emissions but never his view, and stared. He stared at the ship's hideous companions and far beyond.

Nearing the end of their journey, he was unsettled for many reasons, one of which was a feeling of being watched. He was seeing shadows, hearing noises, and even sensing warmth, but there was no one there. The rest were all in stasis. Sodok had checked.

It must have been nerves, or possibly the physical effects of space travel. They knew nothing of such things, but had heard small bits and pieces. Hopefully, his phantoms would vanish as soon as he and his companions landed on their new home.

It was logical, but as Sodok approached his favorite vantage point, he knew it was also incorrect. Someone else was indeed on the ship, someone who had scratched an unknown symbol into the delicate protective coating of the window.

In a way, it was a relief. The decision had been taken from his hands, and now there was work to be done. Immediately, Sodok went to wake those sleeping silently below.

CHAPTER 40

One world at a time.
-Thoreau

Clarence had arrived several days ago, and allowing for what presumably was normal disorientation in this unprecedented scenario had come through the ordeal reasonably well. Being an astronaut wasn't as easy as one might think. Clarence was a solid foot off the ground at all times on this new ship. He squirmed, trying to keep himself upright, which was a physical strain, especially with the difficulty breathing that he had experienced since appearing on the ship.

The being he had been observing had to be heavy, anchored to the floor as it was. At only about four and a half feet, the small purple being still managed to have all his feet firmly planted on the deck.

Clarence had been watching the alien for days without detection. He had only come close to being caught once while trying to write his name in the window. If any of his colleagues were still looking out to the ship, this could have let them know where he had ended up after going through the door. He hadn't gotten past the C when he'd heard the being coming.

This one life-form was the only one Clarence had seen on the ship, which had made it relatively easy to familiarize himself covertly with the immense craft. But there was so much to learn, and for that, he was going to need computer access and alien cooperation. The alien's behavior had been innocuous over the past few days, but it might react differently when confronted with an intruder from a completely different planet.

Clarence floated out from his hiding place. He didn't buff out his fingerprints on the smooth metal surface this time. He wanted to be seen, to communicate. He was face to face with the extraterrestrial being, who looked like he had been startled into a temporary physiological lockdown. The being was still upright, but looked unconscious.

Clarence doubled over in a fit of spasmodic coughing. These fits were coming more frequently all the time. "Are you okay?" He hesitantly reached out and touched the frozen alien before him, but nothing happened.

Clarence pushed himself backward as the smallish creature came to life and moved towards him, spinning lazily on some kind of circular propellant system. "Back off!" Clarence said instinctually.

At the sharp sound of Clarence's voice, the alien reversed his direction.

Who are you, loud creature who has appeared on my ship? You resemble those awful winged greeters. Will you transform into one of them? The entity, Sodok, thought at Clarence.

Clarence could not hear Sodok's thoughts. "Don't be scared," Clarence reversed his direction and pushed himself quickly towards the retreating creature to reassure it. Sodok had four eyes equally spaced around an oblong shaped head, and four arms of sorts, also spaced equally around a knobby torso. It was not apparent whether this little being was moving backward or forward.

I am the guardian of my people and I will not fail them, Sodok thought at Clarence, as he moved down the corridor with Clarence now following at a comfortable distance.

Sodok stopped at the window into which Clarence had etched his graffiti. *This is yours?* Sodok thought at Clarence.

This time Clarence knew what the alien meant, but only because it had undulated one of its appendages at the C on the window. Clarence still could not *hear* Sodok's thoughts.

Then, Sodok spoke for the first time, and continued at length. An amazing feeling of well-being spread over Clarence as he listened with amazement to the sound of the alien's speech. It was like water playing over rocks in a brook, gentle, smooth, and pronounced exactly as he'd explained in his translation guide. Clarence had been right about everything! Without the proper physiological structures to form the sounds of Sodok's language, they would need to communicate through writing, or at least *Clarence* would need to write.

"I did that, yes." Clarence's voice sounded harsh and ugly even to himself compared to Sodok's.

Clarence took the notepad and pen from his pocket that he had been using in the ship on Earth. He scrawled a hopefully legible message in the alien's language. Finished, Clarence looked up and held out the notepad just before another coughing fit seized him.

DO NOT BE AFRAID. I COME FROM YOUR DESTINATION PLANET.

Sodok read the words out loud in his hypnotic voice.

"Our destination is uninhabited. You must be mistaken," said Sodok.

Clarence started on a longer written explanation, trying to convince Sodok of this truth. There wasn't much time left.

• • •

"Hello? Hello? Anybody home?" Clarence's voice filled the softly automated room. "Trip, are you still there?"

Patrick was the first to come rushing into the ship's control room. "Clarence, is that really you?"

"It's me all right." Clarence's voice filled the hull, but there was no Clarence.

"Where are you? It's been weeks since you disappeared."

"I was wondering how the time difference thing was going to play out this time. According to my watch, it's only been about four days."

"But where are you?"

Patrick was back and one of the few remaining authorized personnel on the scene. He, Ed, and Mary Beth had all seen it through from the beginning and would ride it out to the end. Barry had gone back to his magnetically impervious lab in Washington, but he and Herb would return soon, wanting to be there for the event. Now, here was the voice of Clarence coming in over the ship's communication system!

"I'm on the ship, and we're about four to five days out, by my calculations."

"Hold on, Clarence, don't move. Just let me call everyone else. Whatever you do, just don't move!" Patrick fumbled with his emergency call button, but the small core group of observational personnel monitoring from tents and boats in the vicinity were already entering the room.

"Get Ed and Mary Beth over here," Patrick instructed. "Clarence, you still there?"

"Sure, but..."

"Okay, keep holding on." Patrick cut him off. "Get McElvy on the line from NASA." They hadn't installed equipment capable of instantaneous, simultaneous communication for nothing.

Ed and Mary Beth practically fell into the room, arriving excitedly.

"Where is he?" Ed couldn't believe they'd finally found Clarence. Although it was the other way around—*he'd* found them.

"Clarence! Are you okay? Where are you? Why did you go through the door?" Ed had so many questions.

"He's on the ship, Ed," Patrick explained.

"Of course he is," said Ed. "What the hell did you pull a stunt like that for? We've been trying to find you for weeks, and how are you doing that? How are you channeling your voice?"

Silence. "Clarence?" He couldn't be missing again, or could he? "Clarence! Shit, someone get him back online."

"I'm still here, Ed." Clarence's voice came through, again. "What I did was very risky, and mildly foolish, but it had to be done. These ships are outfitted with advanced communication systems. I'm able to communicate with any number of ships, according to the control panels on this vessel. I'm not sure, but I might be broadcasting my voice into more than just the ship on Earth." Clarence fell into another coughing fit.

"Clarence? Are you okay? Are you sick?" asked Mary Beth.

"The air in here is breathable, but not what I'm used to, and not without some uncomfortable repercussions."

"Give us your symptoms, and we'll bring in the experts. We've got 'em all standing by," said Ed.

"Thanks, but I don't think that there is anything anyone can do for me from there." Clarence pushed the conversation forward. "Listen, first I want to know if that Carbury woman and her baby are still healthy, considering my present state."

"Physically, they're both just fine." Mary Beth was kind enough to feed Clarence exactly what he needed to hear. There would be plenty of time later for a more detailed report on their overall health, but this poor man was in no condition to absorb that information at the moment.

"That's a relief, and it means that any physical symptoms I may be having are probably attributable to factors on board this ship."

One of the assembled presidential aides moved her way to the front of the group. "Is the ship manned, Mr. Walburn?"

"Enough about me, eh?" quipped Clarence.

"Not at all. Shut her up." Ed directed with an aggravated gesture. "How are you, Clarence? Details, please."

"As I said before, the air is thinner and probably chemically different. Sometimes I feel sick, other times dizzy or dull, but mostly I'm functional on a perfectly acceptable level." Clarence paused to cough.

"Gravity is off," he continued his report. "I'm always a foot off the ground, but can still feel some of my own weight. My companion is amused at my predicament, and sympathetic with my discomfort." Clarence stopped and waited for the reaction. "Hello? Anybody there?" he queried in the silence, concerned that he'd accidentally broken communication.

"Companion? What companion, Clarence?" Mary Beth asked breathlessly.

"His name is Sodok. He, or at least I think it's a he, is a little over four feet high and must weigh a ton because he connects with the deck at all times. He's a pinky lavender color and seemed happy enough to see me, although I gather he was expecting an uninhabited planet." Clarence paused briefly to let them digest his news so far before continuing.

"I don't blame him for being pleased with my company after watching some disturbing birdmen circling the ship like vultures."

"Interestingly enough," Patrick jumped in, "one of those things was captured off the coast of Venezuela a while ago, so we know what you're talking about." There was no need for Patrick to go into the details of their other sighting.

"Is there only the one alien?" Ed was perplexed. "That entire ship is carrying only the two of you?"

"No," Clarence jumped to clarify their assumption, "there are others, but they're in cryogenic sleep. From what I understand, the ship's program is directed to wake them upon landing. Sodok is just the night watchman, you could say."

Mary Beth shivered and moved closer to Ed.

"How many are there?" asked Mary Beth. The room was becoming restless now.

"Two thousand and forty-seven, exactly."

"Have you seen the others?"

"I haven't seen what's down in the hold yet. I haven't felt well enough to get down there," Clarence admitted apologetically. "Presumably, they are all like Sodok, but it's only an assumption at this point. Judging by Sodok, though, these beings haven't got a blind spot. They're very agile and intelligent, but in my opinion, they're also in trouble."

"How do you know?" asked Ed.

"We've been able to communicate on a very limited level," Clarence answered. "It's hard for me to do too much because I'm so short of breath and fatigued. His people in the hold below are what's left of a two-layered society that was functional eons ago. Apparently, the top strata of society was strictly leisure class—callous, demanding, always seeking newer and more exciting diversions. The underclass lived to see that they were provided exactly that. I'm not quite clear on the other details. The upper class has been gone for so long that those left behind can't even remember their being there."

"Interesting history," Ed responded. "Makes you wonder whether there was a revolt, an amalgamation, or a die-off."

"Clarence," Mary Beth called out to the distant man. "What about the homing signal, the galactic Disneyland scenario?"

"Ah, yes. I was correct in that translation, after all. The Earth was indeed intended to be a playground for their ancient leisure class. The project had been given up as a total loss so long ago that it had been completely forgotten, except for the legends."

"Do they have the antidote, or frequency reversal code, or whatever?" one tech asked anxiously.

There was a pause, followed by the sound of violent retching.

"Clarence, is that you? Are you all right?" Mary Beth's concern registered in her voice. "Can you bring yourself back here?"

The sounds of Clarence's discomfort stopped. "I can't. Believe me, I have tried. The transfer module may only go one way. I'm as fine as can be expected, though. Maybe it's the food. Sodok has been kind enough to share what he has to offer. It's extremely generous of him, since there seems to be a limited supply. Unfortunately, I'm beginning to believe that, although it's nourishing, the stuff must be semi-toxic to humans. Even more unfortunate, it's the only sustenance available, and without food and liquids, I won't be much good for anything."

"Could we send provisions to you through the transfer module?" asked Ed.

"Someone would have to perform the correct sequence of strokes. Provisions cannot be sent without bringing someone else through. That person wouldn't be able to get back, either. Also, if it is done incorrectly, who knows where they could end up, or when? That's just not a viable option."

"How often do you get sick like that?" Ed could only hope that it wasn't often.

"Tell you what," said Clarence. "I'll save the medical details for the doctors. Right now, there's too much more I need to say."

"Okay, but sit down or something," Ed instructed, for lack of any better suggestions.

"Easy for you to say," Clarence joked in response. "It's hard to sit when all I can do is hover. Sodok is more surprised by my difficulties than I am." Clarence instinctually lowered his voice for this next piece of information. "I just can't believe how naïve this creature is."

"What do you mean?" Patrick leaned in closer to speak softly. "How can you say that about something in charge of an interstellar spaceship?"

"I guess we don't need to lower our voices," Clarence realized. "He can't understand me anyway, except when I write things down. Even if he did, Sodok is the first to admit his ignorance. The ship is automated with pre-programmed take-off, landing, navigation, life support systems, you name it. Sodok did nothing more than press the GO button and expects to do little more than press STOP to land."

"Clarence," Patrick questioned uneasily, "what about the homing signal? Are there any new implications there?"

"The planet that exploded was theirs. These aliens left because they had no choice, not because they needed a vacation. This ship was a museum piece, but when the signal reached their planet and activated the ship's long-silent sensors, these creatures saw a way out of annihilation and grabbed it. What they managed to do was comparable to kindergartners flying the space shuttle out of the Smithsonian National Air and Space Museum." Clarence painted an unexpected picture.

"The remaining, and from what I can understand, dwindling population of these creatures poured over archives that hadn't been touched in millennia, and found the purpose and history behind this long-ago project. Most of the pertinent information had been shrouded in competitive secrecy at the time. So, we probably know more than they do."

The room was silent as those assembled slowly absorbed the message that there were no answers.

"Okay, so it's not what we'd hoped for," admitted Clarence. "We're still bringing in this ship. God, you should see this thing. It's huge, and talk about technology! There has to be something here we can use."

Hope weakly seized the room once more.

"Don't give up yet, Ed," Clarence encouraged gently. "These aliens packed up anything of even vague historical or technological value, even though it had no bearing on the life they'd come to know. It's all here, crammed into every nook and cranny of this ship. The thing was built to carry an entire population in every conceivable comfort to a genetically engineered play world. The ship is so large and the population so decimated that it all fit."

Even those huddled in the back were silent. Why bother asking questions? They began accepting their fate. Face it, they were doomed. Clarence's coughing focused their attention away from their own situation and back to their emissary's precarious position.

"Clarence?"

"It's okay, Mary Beth. The coughing is better than the throwing up. Speaking of my symptoms, how's that doctor coming, Ed?"

"Got him online as we speak. Larry? Are you there?"

"Clarence, this is Dr. Larry Knowles. Listen, I'm taking notes, and have some pretty good ideas about what could be happening to you."

"Great!" Clarence was relieved. He would finish briefing the group and move on to the medical attention he was needing more urgently by the minute. "Let me get back to you, Doctor. I'm almost done with my report."

"I'll be here."

"Ed, I can pretty much wrap this up by saying that I'm sure these people pose no danger to us, militarily speaking. Maybe they've got alien viruses or something like that, but these guys aren't looking for trouble. They're just boat people, with the biggest boat you've ever seen.

"I'm sifting through all the information I can, when I feel well enough to do it. Listen, could you get my wife on the line? Then, I want to talk with the doctor again. I'm going to be good for maybe another half hour before I have to rest."

"You've got it, Clarence," Ed would have gladly agreed to anything the man wanted.

"Oh yeah, I almost forgot something weird. Those bird things are gone. Sodok says they've been out there for weeks, but about six or seven hours ago they all flew away, not back towards Earth, though. Instead, they headed back the way we've already come." He began to cough and cough.

Clarence sounded awful, and Ed was worried. "Larry, see what you can do. I'll speak with Clarence's wife until he's ready."

"Well, at least we know what to expect, and what not to expect," said the presidential aide, breaking her silence.

"Do we know what to expect?" Mary Beth whispered to Patrick. "Something is wrong. There's a piece that doesn't fit."

CHAPTER 41

The moon swallows the wind.
-Weather Lore

Atlantic Ocean—off the coast of Venezuela

Gary Zuplo, the birdman, was dead, and the sailors were relieved. Since the first attack, at which time they'd placed him into the cage, the aberrant creature's eyes had gone from intelligent regret, to wild and captive sadness, then finally on to relieved departure.

Two indifferent men quickly disposed of the body, and the sea covered it with small, choppy waves. There was nothing left to do but clean the cage. Both brawny men assigned to this duty were surprised to find words scratched into the bottom of the cage, scrawled with sharp talons into the rust preventive coat of paint covering everything on the ship. These words were in English, so neither man could read them. What could such a strangely violent creature possibly have had to say, and who cared now that it was dead, they asked each other without any genuine interest.

After washing out and preparing the cage, the men callously painted over Gary Zuplo's unheeded message. BEWARE THE SECOND SHIP!

•   •   •

"He sounds borderline, Ed," reported Dr. Knowles. "The extreme fatigue, dizziness, and mild mental confusion are caused by a degree of oxygen deprivation."

"What about the vomiting?"

"From what he told me, I've got to believe there's something like food poisoning involved."

"Is he in real danger? Can he hang in there for a few more days?" Ed hated to sound so callous. "Because the more we know, the better, and he's the only one who can tell us anything."

"I've advised him not to eat anything else," the doctor admitted. "Such extreme vomiting could cause even more dehydration and serious complications. He'll continue to take in liquids and we'll hope they're not the source of the difficulties. Honestly, I haven't got a clue without examining him, or knowing more about what he's ingesting. Then again, there's always the possibility that everyone has sidestepped verbally, everyone but the patient himself."

"I know. Maybe it's an alien germ, some equivalent of the measles, which could wipe out the rest of the population."

"He might make it, Ed, but it'll be close, and you can't push him," said Dr. Knowles.

"Thanks, Doctor, and stay available, okay? I'm flying you out here," Ed insisted. "There's no guarantee that this will be where they land, but it's the best bet we have, and Clarence will need immediate attention."

"I'll be there, but listen, in the meantime, if he starts to complain, or if you notice something change, call me right away. I assume you have adequate medical facilities?"

"The best mobile unit available." Ed had made sure of it.

"So, I've got to ask," said Dr. Knowles. "What happened to the finest doctor available? You know, the one who must've gone along with your great mobile equipment?"

"Something, nothing, everything. We found a huge, empty cocoon in his tent this morning. Does that answer your question?"

"Sorry I asked."

"I thought you would be."

"Okay, well, I'll be there soon enough. The choppers are hovering over my house as we speak. Gotta go pack."

$$\bullet \quad \bullet \quad \bullet$$

Clarence had faded into one of his energizing cat naps two hours ago, but should have come back online by now, and Ed was pacing worriedly. Dr. Knowles was at the ready, leaning against the center console of the ship, arms crossed over his lab coat.

"I know we shouldn't do this, but let's try to rouse Clarence," said Ed. "He sounded so vague last time. With the landing less than four days away, we need Clarence up and running."

"Look," the doctor threw aside his bedside manner. "If you don't allow the man the rest he needs, I can't be responsible for what happens."

"Moot point, anyway," the technician reported. "The guy's not answering. I think he may be down for good."

"Impossible!" Ed stepped to the console. "Clarence. Clarence, wake up, big guy. Time to get up." Silence. Nothing.

At that moment, the sound of water rushing down a mountain stream filled the room, accented with clicks and melodic sounds, and peppered with emotional pauses. It was a soothing linguistic pattern and couldn't be mistaken for anyone other than Sodok.

Ed listened intently for any sign of conscious Clarence for another hour, but there was nothing. He looked at Mary Beth and could see she was exhausted. Then, his phone rang.

"Hello? Yes. Oh my God! Are you sure? How far behind?"

Ed was getting paler and paler as Mary Beth watched.

He hung up and stared vacantly at his feet.

"Ed," she prodded, "who was it?"

"Patrick, calling front the tent. He called to say that McElvy just checked in." He stopped and couldn't seem to continue until she questioned him again.

"And? What did he say?"

Ed looked straight into her eyes to keep himself balanced on the edge of the cliff. He could've gone either way. "There's another ship, Mary Beth." It was as simple and as horrible as that.

"What do you mean, another ship?" Her voice crept towards the hysterical. "I thought Clarence said that his ship held the last of the aliens, that everyone had completely evacuated the planet on that ship!"

"That's what he said, all right." Ed got slowly to his feet and shuffled towards the hatch like an old man. "For what it's worth, that's exactly what he said."

"How far behind, Ed?"

"Herb says just a few weeks."

It was the last thing Ed said before Mary Beth saw the determination leave his face.

ALL WAS EXHILARATION AS THEY FOLLOWED THE SHIP IDENTICAL TO THEIR OWN. THE PLANET FROM WHICH THE FIRST SHIP HAD FLED WAS NOW GONE, BUT THAT WAS OF NO CONSEQUENCE TO THEM. THOUGH IT HAD ONCE BEEN THEIR HOME AS WELL, THEY FELT NO PARTICULAR LOSS, MERELY THE EXCITEMENT OF COMPLETE DESTRUCTION.

THE SHIP SO STEADILY PRECEDING THEM, DRAWN BY A LONG-DELAYED SIGNAL, WAS UNAWARE OF THEIR PRESENCE, BUT THE WINGED GREETERS WERE NOT. THEY HAD EASILY LOCATED THE SECOND SHIP AND THEIR NUMBERS HAD CONTINUALLY

INCREASED. THESE SENTINELS WERE A MACABRE SIGHT, WITH THEIR GAUNT BODIES AND BILLOWING WINGS, DYING IN ACTUALITY, BUT QUITE THE UNUSUAL DIVERSION. HOPEFULLY, THE SICK AND DYING WHICH FLOCKED SO STEADILY AROUND THEM, AT TIMES HEAVING THEMSELVES AGAINST THE HULL OF THE SHIP, WOULD NOT GIVE AWAY THEIR PRESENCE PREMATURELY. AFTER ALL, IT HAD ALL BEEN SUCH A LONG TIME IN THE MAKING, AND THE DIAMONDS ON THEIR FOREHEADS GLOWED WITH ANTICIPATION.

ABOUT THE AUTHORS

Diane Lauer grew up in a military family. She earned her BA in History and Political Science from Bridgewater College. She married and had two sons and a daughter (who just happens to be her co-author). Diane was a stay-at-home mom for twenty-six years while writing, painting, and quilting in her free time.

After her children left home, she returned to school and earned a Master's degree in Acupuncture from the Maryland University of Integrated Health. Afterwards, she opened an acupuncture practice from which she has recently retired.

Diane presently enjoys spending quality time with friends, family, her backyard alligator, and her creative pursuits.

Sarah Lauer Nakawatase lives by the beach with her best friend/ husband, Brian, and three super fun kids. She earned her BA in Public Health Studies from Johns Hopkins University. Presently, she is working toward her RN license with plans on branching out into a hospital setting.

In 2019, Red Sage published her first novel, Southern Souls, a paranormal romance novel set on a haunted plantation. In 2021, she and Diane Lauer teamed up to write Dormant Diversion, a contemporary science fiction novel. This mother-daughter-duo signed with Black Rose Writing in 2022 for this otherworldly project.

Some of her favorite activities include spending time with her family, hiking, swimming, reading, and cooking. Her spice rack occupies twelve square feet!

NOTE FROM THE AUTHORS

Word-of-mouth is crucial for any author to succeed. If you enjoyed *Dormant Diversion*, please leave a review online—anywhere you are able. Even if it's just a sentence or two. It would make all the difference and would be very much appreciated.

Thanks!
Sarah Lauer Nakawatase and Diane Lauer

Sarah Lauer Blackwater and Diane Lauer

We hope you enjoyed reading this title from:

BLACK ROSE
writing™

www.blackrosewriting.com

Subscribe to our mailing list – *The Rosevine* – and receive **FREE** books, daily deals, and stay current with news about upcoming releases and our hottest authors.
Scan the QR code below to sign up.

Already a subscriber? Please accept a sincere thank you for being a fan of Black Rose Writing authors.

View other Black Rose Writing titles at www.blackrosewriting.com/books and use promo code **PRINT** to receive a **20% discount** when purchasing.